Woman in Red

WOMAN
in RED

By

EILEEN GOUDGE

A Member of the Perseus Books Group

ISBN-13: 978-1-59315-444-8
ISBN-10: 1-59315-444-5

To Sandy.

All my love always.

All are but parts of one stupendous whole,
Whose body nature is, and God the soul.
From *An Essay on Man,* by Alexander Pope

ACKNOWLEDGMENTS

First and foremost, I would like to thank my publisher, Roger Cooper, at Vanguard Press, for having the vision, not just in striking out into new territory, but in asking me along for the ride. I am forever indebted to you, Roger, for helping me realize my own dream and in encouraging me along the way with your unflagging energy and enthusiasm.

I would also like to thank, as always, my friend and agent, Susan Ginsburg, without whom no book would be possible. Susan, you are the glue that holds it all together.

This book wouldn't have been as authentic without the people who assisted me in researching it. Thanks to Robin Schwartz, for her invaluable help in the legal department. And to Char Bawden, of Judd Cove Oysters, who in addition to giving me the ins and outs of oyster farming took the time to hand deliver three dozen of the most succulent oysters I've ever tasted. Thanks also to Holly King of the public library on Orcas Island, for picking up the slack, thus allowing me unfettered time to devote to my writing. And, last but not least, a special thanks to Bill and Valerie Anders, for giving me my own moon shot.

PROLOGUE

NINE YEARS AGO

"All rise!"

A rustle of movement around her, the scrape of chairs and feet. Alice was slower to react, her senses dulled, as if by blunt instrument, by two days of testimony: dry, reasoned discourses on skid patterns, blood-alcohol levels, and degree of vehicular damage in relation to bodily injury, all of which seemed to have as much to do with her son, with David, as a chalk outline on pavement with the living, breathing person brought to such a cruel end.

With her palms flat against its surface as leverage, she pushed herself up from the table at which she sat. Her lawyer, Warren Brockman, shot her a look, his gray eyes kind and concerned, and she nodded almost imperceptibly to let him know she was okay. In fact, she was anything but. The blood was draining from her head, and she felt unsteady, a faint, persistent buzzing in her ears, the muscles in her legs quivering like after a mile run.

Lies! she had screamed silently as her son's killer sat up there on the stand, visibly remorseful, as only an innocent man would be—or one who was going out of his way to appear so—giving his distorted version of events. She'd listened and she'd screamed in her head, biting down on the inside of her cheek until it bled to keep her mouth from flying open, her outrage from spewing out into the courtroom.

Now the jury was back with a verdict.

She glanced to her right. Owen White's attorney, a boxy, graceless woman in an unflattering chartreuse dress, stood beside her client, a hand resting lightly against the small of his back. Her strategy had been to paint *him* as the victim, an innocent man relentlessly hounded by a mother unhinged by grief. He even looked the part, soft and harmless, with his pale, forgettable face and blameless blue eyes, his thinning hair the same flesh tone as his skin, and off-the-rack suit that belied his wealth. He might have been any of the nameless, faceless, middle-aged men you came into contact with out in the world, in banks and insurance offices and rental agencies, the ones who smiled at you and chatted easily as they pushed a form across their desk for you to sign.

On the witness stand, he'd answered her lawyer's questions in a quiet, respectful tone. She'd detected no gleam of sweat on his brow, and his eyes behind the wire-rim glasses he wore had been clear as a baby's conscience, only turning sorrowful as they'd come to rest briefly on Alice from time to time, as if he weren't unsympathetic to her plight.

But she knew the real story. Which was why she'd spent the past eighteen months and nearly all of her and Randy's savings trying to bring the man responsible for their son's death to justice.

If only Randy were here now! Her husband had scarcely left her side through the dark tunnel of days following David's death. But once the criminal investigation had been put to rest, he'd grown increasingly impatient with her as the months had dragged on and her pursuit of justice showed no sign of flagging. When she'd insisted on filing a wrongful death suit, he'd gone along merely to appease her and had attended the subsequent court proceedings only sporadically, using the excuse of not being able to miss any more days of work.

In a way she didn't blame him. All he had wanted was to mourn their son in peace. Randy wasn't even convinced they had a case. Wasn't it possible she'd been mistaken? he'd challenged her. The light would have been fading at that time of day and David was all the way down the block, a distance of at least a hundred yards. A little boy they both knew had been prone to taking risks, he could easily have darted out into the road on his bike, just the way Owen had told it.

But she knew she wasn't mistaken. And now, suddenly, she found herself despising Randy almost as much as she did the man responsible for all this. Why wasn't he as outraged as she? What kind of a father would allow his son's murderer to walk free? Randy's glaring absence might even have swayed some of the jurors in Owen's favor. How must it look to them? A crazy lady who couldn't convince her own husband.

Do I look crazy? Alice wondered. *No,* she thought, taking a mental inventory of herself. She'd chosen her dark gray suit with the navy piping and a pair of low-heeled navy pumps for today's court appearance. Her brown hair was pulled back, fastened at the neck with a tortoise-shell barrette, her only jewelry a simple pearl necklace and the tiny diamond studs in her ears.

Throughout the proceedings she'd been a model of restraint as well, someone of whom her parents could be proud. She hadn't indulged in any outbursts, and except for the one time she'd wept silently into her hands at the coroner's description of David's injuries, she hadn't given in to tears. It was as if she'd been training all her life for this; it was what she did, what she was good at. Even at the funeral, she had felt it was her job to provide solace to others. Grieving was something you did in private, with a minimum of fuss.

She looked over her shoulder at her parents. Her mother wore a bright, expectant look as she gazed up at the bench, as if confident that the judge, a large, fleshy-faced man now settling into his seat, would make sure the jury did the right thing. Lucy Gordon believed that anything could be overcome with the right attitude. Like when Alice had been little and prone to car sickness; her mother, convinced it was a case of mind over matter, would press her to join in on sing-alongs and play games like I Spy on long trips to distract her until the nausea passed. (Though, if Alice had managed to keep from throwing up those times, it had had less to do with positive thinking than with a deep-seated terror of making a mess.) Now, with her perpetual schoolgirl's face, framed by a ruffle of graying auburn hair, tipped up in a firm, fixed smile, Lucy was once again refusing to let pessimism get the upper hand.

In contrast, Alice's father stood rigidly at Lucy's side, his austere face frozen in a kind of grimace. Was he angry at her, for putting the family through so much grief? Alice wondered. It was hard to know with her dad. He was a man of few words, an architect whose language was that of line and space. The only time she'd ever seen him cry was as his grand-son's coffin was being lowered into the ground, and even then she wouldn't have known if she hadn't seen the tears leaking from under the dark glasses he'd worn.

Denise, six months pregnant with her second child, stood beside them, a hand resting on the dark head of Alice's younger son, Jeremy. There were those who might have questioned Alice's judgment in having her seven-year-old here for the reading of the verdict, she knew, but Alice had felt it was important for Jeremy to be a part of this moment, one that, either way, would define the rest of their lives.

She turned around, focusing now on the ornately framed painting on the wall to the left of the bench to keep her stomach from going into free fall, as the judge banged his gavel and court was called back into ses-sion. Ironically, it was a portrait of Owen's father, Lowell White, who'd donated the land upon which the courthouse sat—a bit of history she hoped hadn't factored into the jurors' decision. A handsome, florid-faced man, with thick black brows and dark, wavy hair gone gray at the tem-ples, he bore little resemblance to his son. His eyes seemed to meet hers, dancing with bemusement as if he knew something Alice didn't, and she was reminded of the unsolved mystery surrounding his disappearance when Owen was a small boy, a mystery, passed from one generation to the next, which had become a part of Grays Island lore.

"Has the jury reached a verdict?" asked the judge.

The foreman, a big man with military-issue hair and a once-muscular physique now going to seed, rose to his feet. "We have, Your Honor."

Like most of the jury, his was a familiar face to Alice, a manager at the bank where she and Randy had an account, someone she might have smiled at pleasantly in passing and never given a second thought to before this.

The judge instructed the bailiff to bring him the verdict. The foreman handed the folded piece of paper on which it was written to the short, heavy-set man in uniform, who carried it over to the judge. The judge glanced at it, his expression unchanging, before reading it aloud. "We, the jury, find in favor of the respondent."

The words fell like a blow to some soft, unprotected part of Alice's body. She felt all the breath go out of her. Black specks swarmed at the periphery of her vision, and for a frightening moment she thought she was going to pass out. Yet she showed no emotion; her face was as smooth as a pane of glass. Her mind, too, was glass, the full impact of those words sliding away like so many raindrops off a windowpane. She thought, *If I stay very, very still, it will be as if none of this ever happened.*

Warren put his arm around her shoulders and said in a low voice, "I'm so sorry, Alice. We did our best." But she was unable to respond. It was like when she'd given birth, a great, heaving pressure beneath the numbness from the epidural.

Then her sister Denise was at her side, a large, moist presence, looking like a very pregnant Holly Hobbie in her smocked maternity dress. Her brown eyes, pooled with tears, seemed to fill up her whole face, a face as incapable of concealing emotion as a child's. Denise only shook her head, wise enough to know that there was nothing she could say or do right now that would help the situation.

It was their mother who rushed in to embrace Alice, while their father hung back, still wearing that stern look, though Alice could see now that his anger wasn't directed at her—he was staring hard at Owen's back as if he'd like to plant a dagger in it. "Oh, honey." Lucy's voice was choked with emotion. "Don't take it too hard. Look at the bright side. Now you and Randy can get on with your lives."

As if such a thing were possible.

It wasn't until Alice's gaze fell on Jeremy, standing next to his grandfather, looking up at her with a pinched, worried expression, that she roused herself and spoke.

"I'm fine," she said in a calm voice that seemed to be coming from outside her, that of a doctor assuring them that the patient was recovering nicely. "I just need to get home."

"Let me drive you," said Denise.

"No, really, I'm fine," she assured her. In Denise's present, distraught state, she appeared more at risk than Alice of getting into an accident.

For a moment Denise looked as if she were about to insist, but she let it go. Younger by four years, she'd always been the one Alice looked out for, from the time they were children. When the other kids in school had made fun of Denise for being fat, Alice had made sure the bullies knew who they were dealing with. And with her sister's first baby, it had been Alice, not Denise's husband, in bed with a herniated disc at the time, who'd seen her through a difficult labor. Now that the roles were reversed, they were both somewhat at a loss as to how to handle it.

Alice managed a small, bitterly resigned smile, as if to say that yes, it was a blow, but not entirely unexpected. And in a way, she wasn't surprised. Owen White was a -respected member of the community, the heir to one of the island's great fortunes, and she . . . well, she'd become the resident crazy lady. Even those of her neighbors who'd gone out of their way to show support in the days after David's death now looked at her askance. Yes, it was tragic, their eyes seemed to say, but she'd gone too far. Was it fair to punish a man whose only crime was that he'd been in the wrong place at the wrong time?

Walking to her car, holding tightly to Jeremy's hand, she thought that if there truly were a hell, she was in it now. The events of that terrible day ran like a film on a continuous loop inside her head, one she always hoped would have a different ending but never did.

It had been early evening and Randy had phoned to say he'd be working late, that they shouldn't wait for him. But when she'd gone outside to call David in to supper, he wasn't in the driveway shooting hoops, where he'd been the last time she'd checked, and there was no sign of him any-where. Darkness had been closing in, the sidewalk in front of their house swallowed up by the shadows of the gingko trees that lined their street. Yet she hadn't felt worried, not then. She remembered being annoyed at him instead. At eight and a half, David was far too independent for his own good. While Jeremy was content to play in his room for hours, David had been on the move ever since he'd learned to walk; it seemed she spent as much time looking for him as looking after him.

She'd walked out onto the sidewalk still calling his name. She was halfway down the block before she spotted him, a small, fair-haired boy in a white T-shirt and jeans pedaling furiously toward her on his bike. He'd lifted a hand to wave to her, and almost at the same instant a car had rounded the corner onto their street, a silver Mercedes moving at a speed well beyond the posted limit. Alice had opened her mouth to shout to the driver to slow down, but the words caught in her throat, swallowed by the shriek of brakes and the sickening thud that followed, one that had slammed through her as if she herself had experienced the impact.

David, she'd thought, breaking into a run.

She'd found him sprawled face-down on the pavement, not moving. His bicycle, an old Raleigh that had belonged to Randy and that David loved above all things, had been flung into the middle of the road by the impact, twisted into something resembling bent coat hangers. Later, Owen would claim the boy had darted out into the middle of the road and that he'd been unable to brake in time. But that wasn't what Alice had witnessed. David had been in the bike lane that she herself, along with those of her neighbors with young children, had campaigned for; she'd had a clear view of him from where she'd stood.

But it had been her word against Owen's; by the time the neighbors had stepped outside to see what the commotion was about, it was all over. When Alice reported that the driver had been drunk, no one be-lieved that, either. Owen White had a reputation as a churchgoing man, nothing like his flamboyant father, who'd been known to tip back a few in his day. Yet Alice had smelled alcohol on him even from where she'd knelt, clutching her son's broken body to her chest. She'd screamed at Owen to get help, but he'd just stood there wearing a stupefied look, as if not quite grasping what any of this had to do with him, before he'd finally stumbled to his car and driven off.

It was several hours before the police finally caught up to him, by which time Owen had sobered up and gotten his story straight. If his behavior had seemed erratic at the time, he'd explained, it was only because he'd been in shock. As to why he'd left the scene of the accident, it was only to find a phone to call for help. After a cursory investigation that was more a formality than anything, the official cause of death was ruled accidental. Another tragic case of a little boy riding his bike where he shouldn't.

"Mommy, why aren't we going?"

Alice roused from her thoughts to find herself sitting behind the wheel of her car, Jeremy buckled in beside her. A solemn-faced little boy with her dark hair and fair complexion, dressed in the suit she'd bought him for his brother's funeral, and which he was already outgrowing. He was eyeing her quizzically, wearing the deeply worried look she'd seen too often of late. Jeremy had always been the more thoughtful and sensitive of her two boys, but since David's death he'd been so withdrawn that at times it was almost as if she'd lost both her sons.

She forced a smile. "We are, honey. I just needed a minute is all."

"Are we going home?" he asked, when she'd started the engine.

"Yes, honey. Straight home." Where else would she go? To the grocery store for a quart of milk? To pick up her mail at the post office? Mundane chores she couldn't imagine ever doing again much less tackling now.

"Will Daddy be there?" There was a querulous note in his voice that sounded almost panicky.

Alice realized now that it had been a mistake bringing him with her today. But she'd wanted so much to believe the jury would see things her way, she hadn't been thinking straight. Now she was a bad mother on top of everything else. The thought pierced her like a shot through the heart.

She did her best to maintain an even tone as she replied, "Daddy's at work, you know that. But we'll call him as soon as we get home." Even as she spoke, anger was rising up in her again. Where had Randy been when she needed him most? Where was he *now*?

Alice backed out of her slot and was heading toward the exit when she saw Owen at the other end of the lot. She slowed at once, braking to a stop. He was walking with his wife, who had accompanied him every day to court. Elizabeth White, a tall, rail-thin woman, reminded Alice of a greyhound, with her narrow face and long, arched neck, her wide-set protruding eyes. They looked relaxed, smiling at their victory as they strolled along, arm in arm. They would go home to a celebratory supper and a good night's rest, while Alice was left to pick up the pieces on her own. She watched Mrs. White step around to the passenger side when they reached their car, the same silver Mercedes that had mowed David down, while Owen paused to reach into his pocket for his keys.

Later, Alice would remember almost nothing of what came next. In that moment, though, every detail was magnified: a puddle of grease gleaming dully on the pavement near where Owen stood; the reflection of trees swimming across the windshield of a Chevy Malibu pulling out behind him; the innocent sounds of children playing in the small park adjacent the courthouse. The last signposts of the known world before it tilted on its axis, sending her spinning off into space.

Alice had no awareness of her foot pressing down on the gas pedal; it was as if the car were being propelled by a force beyond her control. Then there was only the startled face of her son's killer as she closed in on him, and Jeremy's high-pitched scream.

CHAPTER ONE

The dog was waiting on the landing when the ferry pulled into the berth. Black, with white paws and a white blaze on its chest, it made Colin think of an English butler in bib and morning coat, standing in readiness to greet guests arriving at the lord's manor for a weekend of grouse hunting. A Border collie, from the looks of it, a breed more common to sheep farms than the wilds of the Pacific Northwest. Yet it looked perfectly at home, sitting there on its haunches in the late afternoon sunlight that slanted over the sun-bleached asphalt.

"Old McGinty's dog," volunteered the man at Colin's elbow.

Colin turned toward him. The man was no youngster himself, with his rheumy eyes and thin white hair luffing in the stiff breeze. "McGinty, the artist?" he inquired.

The man gave a somber nod. "Sad about his passing. It was all over the news. Around here, though, we knew him just as Old McGinty. Him and his dog, you never saw one without t'other." He shook his head, eyeing the collie. "Poor thing. Ever' day, rain or shine, he's here to meet the four-forty from Anacortes." Colin must have looked puzzled, for he explained, "The old man went to the mainland once a month or so, and he always took the same ferry back. Except this last time. When he didn't show, that's how we knew something must've happened to him. Weren't nothing would've kept him from that dog, not as long as he had breath in him."

Poor Dickie, Colin almost muttered aloud before realizing that it couldn't be the same dog he recalled from childhood. Besides, it would have sparked his fellow passenger's interest, and Colin recognized a town crier when he saw one. He wasn't ready for the whole island to know his business just yet. If people remembered him at all it would be as the boy who used to visit his grandfather every summer. They wouldn't recognize the tall, solemn-faced man, his dark hair prematurely flecked with gray, as that eager, fleet-footed boy all grown up, except perhaps for the faint resemblance he bore to his grandfather—around the eyes and mouth mostly, which carried the same sadness as had the man they'd known as Old McGinty. "So who's looking after him now?"

"Neighbor up the road took him in." The old man wore a prideful look, as if to say, *Around here we look after our own.* "But feedin' an animal and ownin' it ain't the same thing. That there's a one-man dog." He pointed a bent twig of a finger at the Border collie now rising from its haunches, ears pricked and nose held high in anticipation of his master's arrival.

The man said good-bye and joined the flow of passengers making their way toward the exit ramp, but Colin, lost in thought, gave no reply other than to nod. He remained where he was on the upper deck, in no particular hurry to disembark, as the flow slowed to a trickle of stragglers. The chill of autumn was in the air, but it was memories of summers past that crowded his mind as he leaned into the railing, squinting toward shore, the sharp wind off the sound prying at the upturned collar of his jacket.

It had been more than a decade since his last visit, but not much appeared to have changed. Bell Harbor was just as he remembered it, with its picture-postcard marina and quaint, century-old buildings lining the waterfront—shops and eateries, like the Rusty Anchor, with its namesake anchor out front, where his grandfather would take him for fish and chips on Sundays; and the souvenir shop filled with items to fascinate a young boy. Higher up, on the hill, the commercial buildings gave way to houses and farms, then to unbroken tracts of evergreens as the island climbed toward its highest point, Mount Independence. Already, in mid-October, there was a sugar-dusting of snow on its peak. He was reminded of the time his grandfather had driven him up to the summit in his old Willys, the one year Colin had visited at Christmastime, how wondrous those virgin white tracts had seemed to a city boy used to snow plows and dirty slush clumped along the sidewalk.

"I used to take your dad up here," William had remarked. "He ever tell you about it?"

"He doesn't talk about those days too much." Colin had felt keenly the awkwardness of the moment. He'd been fourteen at the time, his voice reedy with all the changes in his body, which had sprouted a foot seemingly overnight.

"I don't suppose he would." William had squinted off into the distance, wearing a look of sad resignation. There had been only the creak of snow settling under their boots and the whiffling of wings as a cardinal swooped from the branches of a nearby hemlock.

His grandfather was often given to such silences; they'd been as much a part of him as his shock of white hair and the old leg injury that had caused him to limp. And yet they were seldom uncomfortable, even when Colin sensed an underlying sorrow; it was like the sound of the wind in the trees on the cold mountaintop, lonely and peaceful at the same time.

The years melted away, Colin's memories of those boyhood summers sharper than of recent events. He pictured his grandfather bent over his easel, Dickie curled asleep at his feet, and saw the boy he'd been racing down to the cove with his binoculars at the sighting of a whale. Another boy might have been homesick or lonely for the company of other kids his age, but for Colin, those summers had been a welcome respite. He'd experienced a kind of freedom he hadn't known before or since. If his grandfather had spent long hours holed up in his studio, leaving Colin to his own devices, it was just what a young boy sprung from the confines of a row house in Queens, where the great outdoors had consisted of a scrubby patch of grass out back, had needed. Grays Island, with all its nooks and crannies to explore, had been like a magic carpet at his feet, and those endless days of summer had rarely seen him indoors.

But that was Before. Before the world, quite literally in his case, had come tumbling down around his ears.

Colin's mind closed like a fist around the thought, the chill in the air seeping into his bones. The hope that he could escape the more recent past by coming here seemed foolish all of a sudden. It would never be any further away than the nearest bottle in which to drown his sorrows.

A final call from the loudspeaker roused him from his reverie, and he made his way back inside and down the stairs. He was among the last to disembark, and as he exited onto the walkway that ran parallel to the loading ramp, where a caravan of vehicles was crawling its way toward the street, his gaze was drawn to the woman just ahead of him. Slim, dark-haired, around his age—late thirties—and wearing an expression of such intense preoccupation as she trudged along pulling her wheeled suitcase, she seemed scarcely aware of her surroundings. She looked vaguely familiar, but he couldn't place her. Someone he'd met on the is-land? Or maybe it was just that she reminded him of someone he knew. These days, every woman who bore even the slightest resemblance to Nadine brought a tug of painful recognition, of yearning.

The thought that earlier had attempted to surface—the part of his past he'd just as soon forget—thrust its way into his consciousness with such startling suddenness he had to pause to catch his breath, reeling with more than the swaying motion of the ramp. He was gripped by a deep terror. What if he were to discover that he'd traveled all this way only to find he couldn't escape his demons?

When he finally caught up to her, the woman appeared to be bracing herself against some unseen force as well. She stood poised on the land-ing, scanning the passenger waiting area, wearing the anxious, hyper-alert look of someone not quite sure of her bearings. Her full-length wool

WOMAN IN RED

coat that might have been purchased at Goodwill and cheap imitation leather suitcase were at odds with her refined, if somewhat worn, appearance. To the eye of an attorney practiced at spotting such telling details, it suggested someone of privilege who'd fallen on hard times.

He paused beside her, inquiring pleasantly, "First visit?" Normally, Colin wasn't in the habit of making conversation with strangers, but something about her drew him to her. Even with her light brown hair pulled back in a ponytail, and no makeup other than a touch of lipstick, he could see that she'd once been beautiful. She still was in a stark kind of way, as if whittled down by hard circumstances, like a granite peak by the elements. Her wide-set eyes, an indeterminate shade that shifted from gray to green, held the shadow of some deep sadness, and her delicate features didn't match the look of determination on her face—not that of some grand ambition, but of a woman reaching into herself for the simple courage to take the next step.

She cast him a startled, almost frightened, glance, then her expression smoothed over. "No. It's just that it's been a while. I can't get over how little it's changed," she replied, gesturing around her. Her tone seemed that of someone whose own life had altered so drastically, it hardly seemed possible that time had more or less stood still here on the island.

That was something he understood all too well. Hers could have been any one of the faces he'd looked upon in countless AA meetings, those for whom despair had become a way of life and the effort it took to simply go through the motions almost more than they could manage. Yet they kept going somehow, just as he had, one day, one step, at a time.

"I used to come here as a kid," he remarked. "It's been a while for me, too."

She glanced up at the sky, where a thick, gray cloud cover had moved in, bringing the threat of rain. "Not exactly tourist season."

As if on cue, a sudden chill blast of wind sent a loosely tied tarpaulin nearby rattling. She pulled up her collar, holding it tightly about her neck as she hunched inside her coat, shivering. "Actually, I'm here on business," he informed her. "Family business."

"That makes two of us." Her lips curled in a smile that didn't reach her eyes. She obviously hadn't had much practice at it lately.

"Colin McGinty." He put out his hand.

She hesitated before taking it. "Alice," she said, not giving her last name. Her hand, narrow and long-fingered, might have seemed elegant, that of a pianist or a ballerina, if not roughened in a way that told of hard manual labor.

"Someone coming to meet you?" If she had family on the island, it was more than likely, he thought.

"No," she said simply, not offering an explanation.

"I'd offer you a ride, but mine doesn't look to be here yet," said Colin, scanning the cars along the curb for the white Chevy Suburban Clark Findlay, his grandfather's lawyer, had told him to look out for.

"Thanks anyway, but I don't have far to go." After a moment, in which she appeared to have forgotten he was there, she straightened her shoulders and tipped her suitcase onto its wheels. "Well, I guess I should be off. It was nice meeting you. Enjoy your stay."

As he watched her walk away, he continued to wonder about her. Had she taken a wrong turn somewhere? Hooked up with the wrong guy? Or merely gotten hooked, like him? Before Colin could ponder it further, she'd turned the corner and was out of sight.

He hoisted his backpack onto his shoulder. That was when he noticed the Border collie he'd spotted earlier. It was standing half a dozen feet away, its intelligent brown eyes fixed on him with a mixture of curiosity and wariness. Colin sank into a crouch and extended a hand. "Here, boy. It's okay. I won't bite."

The collie—a male, he saw—edged closer. Despite looking well-cared for, he was skittish in the way of pets left to fend for themselves. It was a good minute or so before he'd crept close enough to take a tentative sniff. "Good dog," Colin murmured encouragingly. "See? Nothing to be afraid of." He patted Dickie's head—for he couldn't stop thinking of him as Dickie—which was black except the softly folded tips of his ears and the patches of white around his eyes and on either side of his nose. The dog allowed it, but it was clear he was only tolerating it out of politeness. Either that, or he thought Colin might know something about his master's whereabouts. When it became clear that Colin wasn't going to be of much help in that department, he retreated, sinking onto his haunches to regard Colin with a look almost of reproach.

Colin drew himself up. "I'd take you with me, but I'm guessing you know the way." The dog cocked his head, eyes fixed on Colin as if in comprehension. How much longer would he go on waiting for his dead master? The thought wrenched at Colin. But was it any better knowing there was no hope? When he dreamed of Nadine, with her smile as wide as the world in which she'd lived—a world in which everyone had a good side and every bad thing its shades of gray—he would invariably awake with a fresh sense of loss, knowing that was all he would ever have of her from now on: memories.

When several more minutes had passed with no sign of Findlay's SUV, Colin fished from his pocket the scrap of paper with the lawyer's number on it. But he was unable to get a signal on his cell phone, and when he went off in search of a pay phone, there were none to be found. On Grays Island, the lack of modern conveniences seemed a conspiracy of sorts, a gentle reminder to slow down, not be in such a rush. Here, people moved at their own pace, not by your timetable, and if you couldn't reach someone by phone you'd run into him or her eventually.

His grandfather's lawyer proved no exception. Moments later a mud-spattered Suburban that might once have been white pulled up to the curb. The driver, a very un-lawyerly looking man in a fisherman's hat, stuck his head out the window. "You must be Colin," he said, with a grin. "Hop in."

Colin climbed into the passenger seat. "Thanks for coming to meet me." He stuck out his hand, which was seized in a firm, dry grip. Clark Findlay looked to be in his late forties, early fifties, gangly as a late-summer plant that's bolted, and freckled all over.

"No problem. Sorry I'm late." The lawyer spoke casually, as if it were the norm. "I got tied up at the office. Missus Brunelli. Her husband

Frank passed on a few months back. She's lonely and likes to talk. I didn't have the heart to cut her off. How was your trip?"

"Long," Colin replied, with a weary smile. The flight from JFK had been delayed, and he'd had to stay the night in Seattle, followed by the four-hour ferry ride.

"That all you brought?" Findlay jerked a thumb at the backpack Colin was tossing into the backseat.

"I travel light," he said.

"Smart man. Anyway, you won't need much. Couple changes of cloth-ing, warm jacket, boots, that's about it." As if Colin needed to be re-minded of the island's dress code, or lack thereof. "'Course, it depends on how long you plan on sticking around." Findlay darted him a curious look as he edged his way back into traffic.

Colin offered no response. He didn't know any more than Findlay what his plans were.

They turned off Harbor and began the climb up Crestview. At the summit stood the Queen Anne-style mansion that had once been the home of shipping magnate Henry White, since converted into a bed and breakfast. However many times it had exchanged hands throughout the years, it would always be known to the townsfolk as the White House, a place as firmly fixed in the local firmament as the lore surrounding its original owners, Henry's son, Lowell, in particular. Now, seeing its win-dows lit up and its gingerbread strung with fairy lights, casting a wel-coming light in the gathering dusk, Colin wondered briefly if he wouldn't have been better off getting a room there rather than face the cold, shuttered cottage where his grandfather's presence would be so keenly felt.

Findlay turned left at the top of the hill, headed in the direction of Ship's Bay. "I had Edna give the place a thorough cleaning. It's in pretty decent shape, all things considered. There was some damage with the last storm—some off the roof, a couple of trees down—but Orin took care of that." Orin Rayburn and his wife, Edna, Colin recalled, had worked for his grandfather. "That reminds me, he wants to know if you plan on keeping him on once everything's settled." Findlay was referring to the fact that the probate period was almost up. "You didn't say whether or not you were planning to sell."

"I haven't decided yet," Colin replied.

"For whatever it's worth, property values have gone way up in the past few years. Fifteen acres of prime waterfront could set up a man for life," the lawyer went on.

Or save his life, Colin voiced silently.

The idea that had been growing in his mind ever since he'd learned of his inheritance. The bulk of the estate had gone to his father, never mind that Daniel hadn't even attended the funeral. (Nor had Colin, for that matter, but that was a whole other story.) The house and land on which it stood had been left to Colin, with a small bequest for his brother, Patrick. Colin was free to dispose of it however he wished, but he suspected the reason the old man had left it to him was because he, of all the family, would benefit from it the most—in ways that had little to do with financial gain.

Colin might have fallen out of touch these past few years, not just with William but with the world, so lost in the corridors of his despair he'd been a stranger to himself, but it seemed his grandfather had known what he needed. Just as years ago William had understood when Colin, his life consumed at the time by college and girls and the self-centered concerns of young men, had stopped visiting on a regular basis. Not once had William made him feel guilty. Instead, he'd encouraged Colin to go out in the world, to find himself. When Colin had graduated from Haverford, William's gift to him had been a roundtrip ticket to Greece. The note attached had read: *You're only young once. Enjoy it while you can.* Almost as if he'd had a sixth sense of what was to come.

"I wasn't thinking about the money," Colin replied now. Though in all honesty he could use it. He hadn't held a steady job in more than five years. The former rising star of the Manhattan D.A.'s office, frontrunner for the top spot when his boss retired, had exactly three hundred dollars to his name at the moment. *Make that two hundred and fifty,* he amended, subtracting the amount he'd withdrawn from his checking account to pay for the ferry ride and last night's hotel.

Anyway, there was no point in discussing his future when it was all he could do right now to put one foot in front of the other. He gazed out the window at the twilit landscape skimming past. Houses and barns and pastures had given way to the deep, fathomless green of firs and hemlocks, amid which pale-skinned alders glowed ghost-like and the occasional flash of a white tail signaled a deer. Then they rounded a bend, coming suddenly upon the stretch of pebbled shoreline that curved around the bay, where the last fiery rays of the setting sun had broken through the clouds to cast a shimmering path over the water. If this were a movie, Colin thought, he might have dismissed it as cheap theatrics, but now it brought tears to his eyes. He'd forgotten how beautiful it was.

Within minutes they were turning onto a dirt road that led up a steep, wooded incline before dipping down into a clearing, in the middle of which stood his grandfather's house, facing out on the cove below. Colin climbed out of the SUV when it came to a stop and for a long moment just stood there, taking it all in. The shingled Craftsman cottage, with its square porch columns festooned in vines, and quarter-sawn oak door set with a beveled pane, was almost exactly as he remembered, if slightly more weathered. Out back was the artist's studio where his grandfather had spent so many hours at his easel, and the raised beds, fenced in to keep out the deer, where a kitchen garden had once flourished. His grandfather, when he wasn't painting, had enjoyed gardening, he recalled. He smiled, remembering William telling him once that a seed planted was the simplest way to get results in life as well as a reminder that the best things are often the least complicated.

Below, a path sloped downhill through wind-flattened grass and scrub to the cove. Protected by tall bluffs on either side it was inaccessible by any other approach except boat, the only creatures populating its driftwood-strewn beach the seabirds presently foraging for supper.

Colin pointed out the glistening flat where the tide had receded. "When I was a kid, a man from up the road used to farm oysters there," he recalled. His grandfather had leased the use of the land in exchange for a small share of each harvest.

The memory provoked another, sensory one, so keen he could almost see Mr. Deets crouched there on the beach, shucking an oyster still dripping with seawater for Colin to sample. He'd eaten it more out of bravado than anything, thinking it would be something to brag about to Patrick when he got home. But as it slid over his tongue he'd been pleasantly surprised. It was like nothing else he'd ever tasted, the essence of the sea itself.

"That would have been Frank Deets," Findlay commented. "He passed away a few years back. Lung cancer." He tapped his chest. "I handled the estate for his niece."

"I'm sorry to hear that," Colin told him. The few times in recent years that they'd spoken over the phone, his grandfather hadn't mentioned it and now Colin felt a genuine sense of loss. Mr. Deets had been an eccentric old guy, but Colin had liked him.

Now he stood gazing reflectively out at the view, as it dissolved into darkness, until Findlay at last prompted, "Would you like to see the inside?" As if Colin didn't know his own way around.

What he would have liked was to be left alone, but not wanting to appear rude, he shrugged and fell into step with Findlay as he led the way up the path to the house.

Inside, the place was tidy, but a distinct air of disuse hung over it. Wandering from room to room, Colin was struck by the silence; every creak of the floorboards seemed amplified. The hearth where a fire would blaze in the cool of summer evenings was swept clean, newspapers yellow with age stacked on the hearth beside a basket of kindling. The kitchen, too, was bare except for the handful of provisions stocked in anticipation of his arrival.

Elsewhere in the house, bleached oblongs stood out on the walls where paintings had hung. The only one of his grandfather's works that hadn't been sold off was the portrait over the fireplace. *Woman in Red* was perhaps his grandfather's best-known piece and the most sought after,

yet though he'd occasionally loan it out to museums, William had re-
jected all offers that had come his way through the years.

Colin could understand why it had been so difficult to part with. The
nameless woman in the portrait, seated on a sofa wearing a red print
dress, shoeless with her legs tucked under her, was beautiful in a way that
had captured his imagination as a boy and stirred him even now. There
was something both innocent and sensual in those bare feet, that dress
pulled demurely down over her knees; the glossy chestnut hair, rolled up
in back and pinned into loose curls on top of her head, tendrils spilling
down her neck. The light from the window at her back made her flesh
appear to glow and her eyes—deep green and shot full of gold, the color
of turning leaves—translucent in a way that was almost unearthly. Even
her expression, contemplative, with a hint of a smile on her lips, suggested hidden depths.

Once, a long time ago, Colin had asked his grandfather about her. The
old man's gaze had turned inward, and after a long pause he'd answered
cryptically, "That's a story for another day, son. Why don't we save it for
when you're old enough to have me tell it to you over a bottle of that
good cognac your folks send for Christmas every year."

Sadly, that day never came.

He'd have asked his father, but Daniel's mood always darkened whenever the subject of his old man came up, so Colin had learned early on
that it was best not mentioned. He'd never understood why his father
had felt so much animosity toward William, only that it had something
to do with his grandparents' divorce. Colin was nine before he'd even met
the grandfather he'd known until then only from the cards his grandfather sent on his and Patrick's birthdays and at Christmas, always with a
twenty dollar bill tucked inside. His mom, who believed that family was
family no matter what, had finally persuaded Daniel to let Colin and
Patrick fly out for a week-long visit. In the end, though, it had been just
Colin. His brother, who'd been thirteen at the time and the star of his
Little League team, had refused to go. From then on, it became the pat-
tern, Colin going off every summer for longer and longer visits, while

Patrick stayed behind to indulge in his favorite activities: sports, girls, and later on, cars.

Now, as Colin studied the portrait, he thought about the story William had never gotten around to telling him . . . and the one Colin had never gotten around to telling his grandfather: The story of how he'd lost everything and come undone.

His eyes shifted to the mirror on the wall to the right of the fireplace, where a somber face looked back at him—a face that, at first glance, didn't appear much altered from the one in the framed photo on the mantel from his college graduation. The same ink-blue eyes and the Roman nose he'd inherited from his grandfather on his mom's side. It was only upon closer examination that he saw the lines that hadn't been there before. His smile that had once been one of expectation was rueful now. He knew what to expect: Not a life filled with promise, but one in which the only thing standing between him and the proverbial abyss was a folding chair in some church rec room or VA hall filled with other people in similar straits.

He turned to find Findlay eyeing him curiously. In this small community, there had to have been a fair amount of speculation concerning the return of Old McGinty's grandson. Not that Colin cared. It was a welcome change from being talked about for other, less benign reasons, like the gossip that had circulated around the D.A.'s office during his drinking days.

"I've always wondered about her," he said, bringing his gaze back to the portrait. "Was she from around here, do you know?"

Findlay nodded. "Her name was Eleanor Styles."

Colin flicked him a glance. "You knew her?"

"I wouldn't go so far as to say that. I saw her around, sure, but she didn't get out much, not with her husband so sick. And then she got sick herself." He shook his head pityingly, the same look on his face that he'd worn when speaking of Deets' passing. "My dad, though, he remembers when she was a sight to behold—hands down the prettiest girl on the island."

"She *was* beautiful," Colin agreed.

"The way Dad tells it, half the men in San Juan County were in love with her," Findlay went on. "No one could believe it when she married Joe Styles. Not that he wasn't a nice enough fellow, but a little out of her league, if you know what I mean. Then the war broke out . . ." His voice trailed off. "Joe made it home, but he was never the same after that. Some sort of head injury. I'm sure it couldn't have been easy for her, either, but she stuck with him, right up till the end."

"How did she and my grandfather know each other?"

"She bred dogs to bring in extra cash. Border collies. Your grandpa bought one of the puppies. I guess they became friendly after that." Color rose in the lawyer's pale, freckled cheeks. "Not that I'm suggesting there was anything between them," he was quick to add. "It was just . . . you know . . . the war. And people looked out for each other in those days."

From the way Findlay spoke, as if those long ago events had occurred just yesterday, Colin almost expected to see a younger and more vibrant William, from the days when he'd sported a full head of coal-black hair, stride into the room, Dickie at his heels. But, of course, it wouldn't have been Dickie back then. There had been a succession of dogs through the years, all of them Border collies. Each had lived to a ripe old age and was buried out back behind the woodshed.

Colin turned now to Findlay. "I'd offer you a drink, but I'm not sure what's on hand." He eyed the cherry breakfront where William, not a drinking man himself, had kept a small supply of liquor for when company came.

Just as he'd hoped, the lawyer took the offer as his cue to leave. "Thanks, but I should be heading off. My wife'll have supper on the table before too long, and if I let it get cold I'll have some explaining to do. You know how they get." Findlay winked, one husband to another, before he caught himself and his comradely expression gave way to an embarrassed look.

Colin felt stripped of his defenses, his whole, sad history laid bare. But, of course, everyone must know. In the stunned days after 9/11, it was all people had talked about, who among their circle of friends and acquaintances had been touched by the tragedy—a friend of a friend, the cousin of an old college roommate, the uncle of a former employee. On Grays Island, it would have passed from one person to the next like a found penny. *You know Old McGinty? Terrible about his grandson, isn't it? He lost his wife. They're saying she was in the first tower when it was hit. Never had a prayer.*

The old pain stirred to life once more, but he put on a smile, saying, as he saw Findlay out the door, "Thanks again for coming to meet me. I really appreciate all your help."

"My pleasure." At the door, Findlay handed Colin the keys to his grandfather's old Volvo. "It's been mostly sitting in the garage these past few years, what with his eyesight so bad and all. But the engine still runs, and I had Orin gas it up. Anything else you need, just give a shout. I'll have those papers ready for you to sign, if you want to stop by my office later in the week."

When he was gone, Colin breathed a sigh of relief. Not that he wasn't grateful to Findlay, just that the need to be alone had become as persistent as a dog whining at the door to be let out. Which reminded him . . . Had the Border collie at the ferry landing made it home all right? It was a long walk and with night falling he'd have to make his way in the dark over unlit roads where he'd be in danger of being hit by a passing car. But Colin had more pressing problems at the moment than worrying about a dog that had appeared better equipped to care for itself than he was. Like what he was going to do with himself now that he was actually here. Up until this moment, he hadn't dared think that far ahead.

Well, there was one thing he could do. It wouldn't solve everything, but it would be a start. He pulled the phone book from the drawer in the old stereo cabinet, on which the phone sat. It had been a while since he'd seen one this thin—it wouldn't even hold the "A's" in the Manhattan directory—and it reminded him of just how small a place the island was. In the yellow pages, under the listings for health services, he found what he was looking for and dialed the number for Alcoholics Anonymous.

There were two meetings a week, every Tuesday and Thursday evening at seven, he was informed. If he left now, he could grab a bite to eat in town and still make tonight's, at the Lutheran Church. As he hung up, he found himself thinking of the woman he'd met earlier. Alice. Suddenly he remembered where he knew her from. It had been in all the papers, and now he did the mental arithmetic. Yes, the timing would be about right.

God help her, he thought, pausing as he reached for his jacket. She'd have a tough go of it. For if his every movement was going to be scrutinized, he wouldn't be the only one.

CHAPTER TWO

Standing over the sink in the ladies' room of Svenigan's, Alice stared at the faucet. There was no handle. How were you supposed to turn it on? After several frustrating moments, the toilet flushed in the other stall and an older woman emerged, sidling up to the sink. Alice, making a show of touching up her lipstick, watched out of the corner of her eye as the woman waved a hand under the faucet and water came gushing forth. Then she remembered about motion sensors: They'd just been coming into vogue back when she'd been in the habit of frequenting public restrooms.

These days, she felt like a foreigner in her own country, everything rushing at her faster than she could take it all in: billboards displaying unfamiliar brand names, computerized kiosks, where there had once been smiling tellers and ticket takers; the maze of automated messages and prompts that greeted her when she called a place of business. Any little thing might confound her, even something as simple as a faucet.

The woman seemed to shoot her a curious glance, as if trying to place her. Alice wondered if she was being paranoid; even so, she kept her face averted as she washed and dried her hands. She'd arrived a day early in the hope of speaking with Jeremy before the rest of the family descended on her. It would be less awkward this way, without everyone else around. For Jeremy especially. Being a teenager was difficult enough, and she wanted to be a part of her son's life, not just another complication.

Sixteen. He's sixteen. She struggled to absorb that unbelievable fact. She'd kept track of every birthday and watched him grow through the snapshots Randy and her sister had sent—each new spurt in height, each new sign of maturity, both a source of wonder and of pain—but there was nonetheless a sense of unreality to it. She couldn't stop picturing him as the little boy he'd been, frozen in time like in the photo she wore in the locket around her neck. She hadn't seen him since. Randy had stopped bringing him to visit her in prison. He'd written her a letter explaining that it was for the best; Jeremy had grown so withdrawn he barely communicated, and the visits only made it worse. Both he and Dr. Turner, the psychologist Jeremy had been seeing at the time, were concerned about Jeremy's mental state.

It had nearly killed Alice to be cut off from her son, but in the end she'd gone along. What choice had she had? Now she wished she'd fought harder. Her judgment had been clouded by the guilt she'd felt and she hadn't seen that she'd only been making it easier for Randy, who hadn't wanted to face her for reasons of his own, reasons that had soon become apparent when she was served with divorce papers. Now, as a result, she was a virtual stranger to her son. Worse, Jeremy seemed to have no interest in getting to know her. Her letters had for the most part gone unanswered. When he did write, it was only a few cursory lines. *How are you? I'm fine.* He always signed those letters, *Your son, Jeremy.* As if she didn't know her own child. The thought caused something to twist in her gut, and she took a deep breath to quiet her anxiety at seeing him again.

Ain't no sense trying to undo what's done. Might as well try stuffing an egg back into a chicken once it's laid, drawled a voice in her head, that of Calpernia King. Big, black Calpernia, tough as the tire iron she'd used to beat her abusive boyfriend near to death and about the last person Alice, in her old life, would ever have thought to call a friend. Yet in the nine years she'd spent at Pine River, she'd come to know and love Calpernia, who, for all her tough talk, had always had Alice's back. She wished Calpernia were here now. She could use all the reinforcement she could get.

Alice made her way back to the entrance of the cafe, to retrieve the suitcase she'd left behind the coat rack. Thankfully, Svenigan's was nearly deserted at this hour. The dinner crowd wouldn't begin showing up until the shops downtown had closed for the day and thoughts turned to Ina Svenigan's short rib lasagna chased by a slice of her homemade marionberry pie. The plump, middle-aged woman working the register paused to glance at Alice for perhaps a beat too long, and Alice could only hope the years had done their work in making her less recognizable.

As she made her way up Harbor Street tugging her suitcase behind her, her thoughts turned once more to Jeremy. He ought to be home from school by now; she'd call him as soon as she checked in at the bed and breakfast. The thought caused her to quicken her step as she headed up the hill, her heart tumbling over in her chest like an eager child dashing ahead of her. Then she remembered about his after school job—Denise had written to her about it—and her excitement waned. The call would have to wait.

The wind picked up, bringing rain that lashed at her already raw cheeks. She'd booked a room at the Harbor Inn, known locally as the White House—a small act of defiance on her part, though it hadn't been under White family ownership for decades. It stood at the top of the hill, a lit beacon, its round turret and gables making it look like something out of a fairy tale. *One in which a princess gets spirited away, then returns to her kingdom and lives happily ever after,* Alice thought, smiling grimly.

It was where she and Randy had spent their wedding night—a fairy tale gone awry in the end. Not much had changed since then, she saw as soon as she walked in. A spacious entryway wainscoted in oak and lit by antique brass sconces opened onto the reception area in what had once been the parlor, a large cozy room hung with paintings of sailing ships. A log fire burned in the fireplace and a tray of cheese and crackers had been set out along with a decanter of red wine.

No one was about, so Alice rang the brass bell on the desk. Moments later, a smiling white-haired woman in a dark green cardigan embroidered with jack-o-lanterns came bustling through the side entrance. Her smile faded as soon as Alice gave her name.

"Alice Kessler?" She peered at the reservation book, frowning. "I'm afraid there's been some sort of mistake. We don't have a reservation under that name. Are you sure it wasn't one of the other inns?" Even when she looked up, her eyes seemed to avoid Alice.

"Quite sure." Alice put on a perplexed look, though she had a pretty good idea of what was going on here. It was just the first of what would be many such rebuffs, she thought, with a sinking in her gut. "The gentleman I spoke with over the phone said you had plenty of vacancies," she went on, maintaining a bright, pleasant tone. "Is there a problem?"

"I'm afraid so. We're full up at the moment," she was informed.

"I see." Alice spoke quietly but in a way that made her displeasure known. She should have been prepared for this. It was a small community and people had long memories, many of whom had ties to the Whites.

Heat rising in her cheeks, she said in an overly polite voice, "In that case, may I use your phone? If it's not too much to ask."

None too graciously, the woman pushed the phone toward her. Alice punched in Denise's number, which she knew by heart, praying that her sister was home. Otherwise, she'd be out of luck, no money for a taxi—what little she had on her was in traveler's checks—and the nearest accommodations a long walk away. She couldn't call her mother, either; Lucy met with her book club on Thursdays. Besides, Lucy wasn't expecting to hear from her until tomorrow and, knowing her, she'd gone to some lengths to prepare a homecoming that would only be spoiled by Alice's early arrival.

Luckily, Denise picked up on the second ring. "God! Why didn't you tell me you were coming in early?" her sister chided, sounding delighted to hear from her nonetheless.

"I was hoping I'd get a chance to talk with Jeremy, you know, before having to face everyone else," Alice said.

"Well, your timing sucks." Denise gave a good-natured if frustrated laugh. "I've got a houseful of nine-year-olds at the moment—Taylor's Brownie troop, in case you're wondering what all that noise is about," she added, raising her voice to be heard above the shrill chorus in the background. Gary's still at work and Ryan's at football practice, so I have no one to watch them. I hate to make you wait, but. . ."

Alice was quick to assure her, "It's fine. Get here when you can." She'd waited nine years, she could wait another half hour or so.

It was fully dark and raining heavily by the time Denise pulled up in front of the inn in her ancient Honda Prelude. Emerging from the driver's seat with a yellow rain slicker tented over her head, she rushed forward to envelop Alice in a damp embrace that smelled faintly of chocolate-chip cookies, reminding Alice of everything warm and good she'd missed.

"You're cold as ice!" Denise cried. "Why didn't you wait inside?"

"Let's just say the temperature in there wasn't much warmer." Shivering inside her coat, Alice glanced over her shoulder at the inn's brightly glowing windows.

Her sister didn't question her further, but Alice hadn't missed the flicker of uneasiness in her eyes—this was no ordinary homecoming, they both knew. "Well, even blue with cold, you look good," observed Denise, pushing a hand self-consciously through her own unkempt hair.

"You mean, for someone who just got out of prison," Alice said.

"Hush now," Denise scolded, in the same tone their mother would have used. Briskly, she took hold of Alice's suitcase, dragging it over to the Honda and heaving it into the trunk, which was plastered with bumper stickers like the ones that read, *Well-behaved women rarely make history* and *One people, one planet, one future.*

Her sister's constancy was reassuring in this new, jarring world Alice had entered into. Denise was still the same girl who'd cried over every mangled, furry heap by the side of the road and who'd marched in every demonstration, only older now and the mother of two. It had been a bit of a shock, the last time Denise had visited, to see that her baby sister was going prematurely gray.

"Remember that old VW bug you used to drive?" Alice remarked when they were on their way.

"God, yes. Dad used to threaten to dress up Grampa in his old World War II uniform to shame me into getting rid of it." Denise gave a laugh that seemed somehow forced. Hunched over the wheel, she looked as though she were navigating her way through a heavy snowstorm instead of the rain that was a fact of life in this part of the world. "I used to wonder if that's part of why he and Mom fell in love, because they both had fathers who'd been wounded in the war. God knows they didn't have much else in common, unless you count the fact that they were the only two people on the planet who liked rutabaga."

"They had us, too," Alice reminded her. She was thinking about how strange it would be to walk into her parents' house, the house she and her sister had grown up in, and not find her father there. That had been one of her worst moments in prison, when she'd learned of his death. Now she recalled the words he'd murmured in her ear just before they'd taken her away in handcuffs. *Don't worry about Jeremy. We'll look after him.*

She'd clung to him for a long moment, as if she were being sucked out to sea by a strong tide and he a stanchion. *I'm sorry, Daddy,* she'd choked. *I know I let you down.*

He'd pulled back to look at her, the stern lines in his face giving way to an expression of infinite sadness. *You'll always be my girl. Don't ever forget that.*

And she hadn't. But now he was gone and she would never have the chance to make it up to him. Sitting in the car, staring out at the darkness and listening to the hiss of water under the tires, she felt a renewed sense of loss.

After a bit, she ventured, "How's Mom doing?"

"Better. You know her, she never stays down for long. Besides, with all her activities, she barely has a moment to herself. She belongs to so many clubs I can't keep them all straight. Did she tell you she also signed up for a cooking class? Who knows, maybe she'll be the next Julia Child. Oh, that reminds me. She's planning a supper for the whole family. You're not doing anything on Sunday, are you?"

"Gee, I don't know. I'll have to check my calendar," Alice answered dryly.

Denise didn't respond, and a heavy silence fell, weighted with all that was left unsaid. Her sister had to be thinking about the changes that lay ahead, not just the good ones but the fact that the status quo that had existed for the past nine years would be disrupted. For one thing, Denise's husband, Gary, was deputy chief of police; however much he might like Alice, her presence would put him in an awkward position. And the children Denise taught in school all had parents who might take a dim view of her harboring a paroled convict.

"Thank you, by the way. For coming to get me," Alice said at last, in a tone that conveyed gratitude for more than the ride. *Thank you for not abandoning me. For coming to see me all those years. For giving me a reason to live.* "Gary won't mind my staying the night?"

"Please. You're my sister." Denise waved aside any such concerns, but Alice noticed she hadn't given a direct answer. Now, she chattered on, "Wait'll you see how big the kids have gotten. Ryan's as tall as Gary. He just made the varsity team, did I tell you? We're all thrilled about it. Of course, we told him he can't put football over his schoolwork, not if he wants to go to a decent college." With them barely scraping by on her and Gary's combined income, it was a scholarship or community college, Alice knew.

"Speaking of school, is Taylor still planning to boycott fourth grade?" she asked. Her sister had told her that Taylor was getting teased a lot and often came home from school in tears.

"Oh. Well. You know how kids are. She'll get over it," Denise said with a lightness that belied her concern. "Ryan had me for a teacher, too, and it certainly hasn't affected his social life. In fact, if the girls don't stop calling, we'll have to put in another phone line."

Denise herself had been the butt of every fat joke in grade school, the girl who'd sat on the sidelines at dances and gotten picked last for every team. Alice thought that was what made her such a good teacher; she could empathize with the kids who had trouble fitting in.

Alice wondered what it had been like for Jeremy. She'd missed practically his whole childhood. Oh, what she would have given to have been there even for the tough times! The tears and tirades, the awkward prepubescent years. Instead, she'd had only his infrequent letters that she'd scrutinized like tea leaves, struggling to read some meaning in them. Now, she ventured cautiously, "Have you spoken with Jeremy? About me, I mean."

Denise shot her a guarded look. "We don't see him as much as we used to. He's been pretty busy with his after school job."

"How does he seem to you?" All day the question had been beating like a moth's wings against the window in her heart where Alice had kept a light burning all these years.

"Okay. Really, Alice, he's *okay*. He's a great kid. And so smart! I really think he has a shot at the Ivy Leagues."

"I know he's smart," Alice replied sharply. "I'm his mother, remember?"

"I didn't mean . . ." her sister started to say, but it was too late: the old pain surfaced, punching through the wall Alice had carefully constructed around her emotions. Suddenly it was all too much. She felt dizzy and disoriented, like when waking from deep sleep, her head still clouded with fragments of a dream. Only this was no dream.

"I know you didn't mean anything by it," she said, realizing she'd been unfair to take it out on Denise.

Her sister cast her a woeful look. "I'm sorry. I know this is hard for you. And I'm not making it any easier, am I? It's just that I don't know how much to tell."

Alice's response was immediate and unequivocal. "I want to know about my son."

Denise sighed. "Well, as far as I can tell, he's coping pretty well. But it hasn't been easy for him, either. He hears things at school. You know how it is. Kids can be so mean. My advice is to take it slow. He'll need time to get used to you being back in his life."

Denise turned onto Fox Valley Road, which hadn't been resurfaced since Alice had last traveled it, judging from all the potholes. They

splashed through one after another, each new, bone-jarring lurch seeming
to echo Alice's thoughts. The only thing that had gotten her through all
those years in prison was knowing she'd be coming home to Jeremy one
day. Now apparently she was considered an intrusion. How was she supposed to deal with that? How did you take it slow when you only know
one speed? "I'm not here to make things harder for him," she said quietly,
gripping tightly to the door handle as they bounced through yet another
pothole, mud flying up to spatter the windshield.

"I know, hon. And I'm sure it'll all work out. It's just that it's not going to happen overnight." Denise reached over to pat her on the knee.

It was strange seeing Denise cast in the role of big sister. Growing up,
she had been the one who could never get it together. Forever on a diet in
the hope of being able to fit into smaller clothes, and in a perpetual state
of disarray that extended from her flyaway hair to the mess on her side
of the closet they'd shared. Now, glancing down at the trash littering the
floor at her feet—torn receipts and crumpled straw wrappers, an empty
coffee container and something that might have been a Barbie doll poking out from under a T-shirt—Alice saw that not much had changed. Yet
Denise had become the stable one. The one with all the answers. While
she, Alice, had none.

The rain had tapered off by the time they pulled up in front of
Denise's rambling farmhouse. It was a good half-hour's drive from town,
but, as Denise liked to say, where else could they have gotten such a
spread? Ten acres with its own pond and a barn that housed a horse,
chickens, and a pet pig named Mirabelle—a 4-H project that Taylor
hadn't been able to part with.

As she climbed out, Alice took note of Gary's cruiser, parked next
to one of those seventies' gas-guzzlers, full of dents, which had to be
Ryan's. Her anxiety mounted. She and Gary had in the past always gotten along well but she hadn't seen him since she'd last been to this house
and she didn't know quite what to expect. Would he be standoffish or
welcome her with open arms? There was another concern as well: He
wasn't just her brother-in-law; he was the law. And in prison, it was the

law you answered to. Some of the COs had abused that power, seeming
to take pleasure in harassing the inmates: writing up bogus charge sheets,
giving out work orders when they knew you had a class or were expecting
a visitor; making you wait for hours, sometimes days, for your meds.
Even now, the thought of someone in uniform caused Alice to break
into a sweat.

She was climbing the steps to the porch when the front door swung
open and a figure emerged: a big man in jeans and a flannel shirt, square
and solid as an appliance built to last. "Alice. Good to have you back."
Gary stepped forward to give her an awkward hug. He smelled of after-
shave, his close-cropped sandy curls still damp from the shower. The re-
ceding hairline was the only concession to the years. That, and the few
extra inches around his middle.

The wary look in his cop's eyes didn't match his words of welcome.
He obviously had mixed feelings about her reemergence into their lives;
Alice understood, and she didn't blame him. It was awkward, given his
line of work and who he ultimately answered to. "Good to *be* back," she
said, with forced cheer. "How have you been, Gary?"

"Oh, you know me. Just chugging along. Your sister keeps me busy
when I'm not on patrol. If it were up to her, I wouldn't have a moment to
myself," he teased, slinging an arm around Denise's shoulders and grinning as though they were posing for a family photo.

"Listen to you," said Denise, giving him an affectionate jab with her
elbow. Turning to Alice, she explained, "I've been trying to convince him
to run for county commissioner. We'll need him on our side when they
vote on the Spring Hill project."

Alice didn't know much about the project, except that Denise and her
fellow activists had been campaigning against it for weeks. Some big hous-
ing development slated for Spring Hill that they were trying to block. She
was familiar with the area, though; it was the virgin tract that bordered on
their grandmother's old property. Nana used to take her and Denise on
hikes there when they were young, pointing out all the different birds and
flowers and insects along the way. Now it seemed Denise was determined
that it remain untouched for future generations to enjoy.

"I keep telling her if she's so worked up about it, she ought to run for office herself," Gary said.

"She'd have my vote," replied Alice with a laugh, before remembering that as a convicted felon she'd lost that right. Her smile fell away, and she could see from Gary's expression, an odd mixture of pity and disdain, that the same thought had occurred to him.

As she followed them into the house, Alice recalled what a wreck it had been when they'd first bought it. Their every spare hour had been spent scraping and sanding and painting, restoring the old floors and woodwork until they gleamed. They'd made it into a real showpiece, though at the moment it looked like a tornado had hit it: The living room floor was strewn with construction paper cutouts, discarded socks and shoes, and random items of clothing; dirty plates and glasses lined the coffee table, along with an empty milk jug and a half eaten plate of chocolate chip cookies.

"Guys! Look who's here!" Denise called to the two children at the center of the chaos. "Sorry it's such a mess," she apologized, "but you didn't give us much notice." A teenage boy with his father's sandy curls and athletic build looked up from the computer screen that was occupying his attention. On the sofa, a slight, dark-haired girl dressed in a rumpled Brownie uniform looked away from the TV to stare at Alice.

Alice scarcely recognized her niece and nephew. Ryan had been the same age as Jeremy when she'd last seen him—Alice and Denise used to jokingly refer to Ryan and Jeremy as the twins—and Taylor an infant in Denise's arms. It was a shock when Ryan rose to greet her, easily as tall as his father, sporting a small diamond stud in one ear. She remembered him as a sweet-natured little boy, and it was a relief to see that he hadn't changed when he stepped forward to hug her: a fleeting impression of body heat, musky boy's scent, limbs bumping up against hers. His face was red when he stepped back.

"This must seem weird to you," Alice said, to put him at ease.

"Kind of." He shuffled from one foot to the other, smiling shyly.

"Well, it's pretty weird for me, too," she confided. "You probably don't even remember me."

"I remember playing over at your house when I was little," her nephew said.

"You and Jeremy were always building forts." Alice smiled at the memory. Made of cardboard and stuff scavenged from the garage, those forts usually collapsed with the first rainfall or heavy gust of wind.

"I'm still at it," he said, with a grin. "Only now it's called Shop."

"Well," she said. "I see I have some catching up to do."

"It's cool that you're here. You can have my room, if you like," he said, making Alice fall in love with him all over again. Ryan was the kid who made you smile even when he was getting into mischief.

"Thanks, I appreciate the offer, but the sofa will do just fine," she said. She turned to her niece, now peering out from behind her brother. "You must be Taylor. You were just a baby the last time I last saw you. And just look at you now." She was blossoming into a real beauty, with Denise's clear blue eyes and porcelain skin.

Taylor gazed at her with an intentness that bordered on rudeness. Alice could only imagine what she must be thinking. The aunt that she'd heard so much about must seem a legendary figure sprung to life: the incarnation of much dark discussion between adults when it was presumed little ears weren't listening.

"You look just like your mom," Alice continued when she got no response. Except that her niece was slim as an arrow. Taylor lowered her eyes, wearing an embarrassed look. "But you must get that all the time. You're probably sick of hearing it."

Taylor's thin shoulders lifted and fell in an elaborate shrug.

Alice tried a different tack. "Did you know I went to the same school as you?"

"Uh-huh." The girl gave her a long, considering look, as if wondering how anyone who had gone to Woodrow Wilson Elementary could have ended up in prison.

"I didn't have my mother as a teacher, though," Alice forged on. "Which, I'm sure, is kind of weird. But at least you get plenty of help with your homework."

Denise cut in before Taylor's silence became even more uncomfortable. "Speaking of homework, if that TV isn't off in about three seconds, you'll be spending the weekend cracking books, young lady." She swooped in like a commando, seizing the remote control when Taylor didn't act quickly enough and generally creating a distraction that smoothed over the awkwardness of the moment.

At dinner, it was Denise's lively chatter that carried them through. Gary, too, made a game attempt at conversation and Ryan brought Alice up to date on all his activities. It wasn't much different from the family meals Alice had shared with them in the past, if you didn't count the fact that no mention was made of the reason for her long absence—she might have been back from an extended trip, from the way everyone was acting. Listening to Denise jabber on about family doings and the latest gossip from the teacher's lounge at school, Alice had the strangest feeling she was in a play from which lines of dialogue had been deleted.

"I ran into Aileen Findlay today at the market, and she told me that McGinty's grandson's in town," Denise remarked, as she was passing out bowls of ice cream for dessert. "He came in on this afternoon's ferry. Clark took him over to the house."

"I wonder what he's up to," Gary muttered.

"You cops, you're all alike. You think everyone has some hidden agenda," Denise mock-scolded, giving him a swat on the arm. "Who knows? Maybe he's planning to move here, now that he's inherited the old man's place. Apparently, he used to spend summers here as a kid."

"More likely, he's looking to sell," Gary speculated darkly. Like many of the island's long-time residents, he was innately suspicious of mainlanders. "I know the type. Some fancy lawyer from New York thinking he can swoop in and make a quick profit."

"I don't think that's it," said Denise, sitting down to eat her ice cream. "He appears to be at loose ends, from what Clark could see. Apparently he lost his wife on 9/11. God, can you imagine? The poor man, he probably still hasn't recovered." She cast a fond look at Gary, as if, for all his grumbling, she couldn't fathom life without him. "And then to lose his grandfather on top of that . . . "

Alice was thinking that it had to be the grandfather of the man she'd met at the ferry landing. That was why his name had sounded so familiar. "Are we talking about the same McGinty who painted Nana's portrait?" she interjected. No one in the family had seen the actual painting, only reproductions of it, but it was a part of the family lore. There was also a bit of a mystery surrounding it. All Nana would say, if pressed, was that she and Mr. McGinty had been friendly at one time. But from the quickness with which she'd always dismissed the subject, Alice had always suspected there was more to the story.

Denise nodded. "He passed away about six months ago. You should've seen the crowd at the funeral! There were reporters and everything." She paused, frowning in thought. "The odd thing was that none of his family came." She shook her head. "Must have been some bad blood."

"You're right about that," Gary put in, as he spooned ice cream into his mouth. "I remember my dad telling me it was the talk of the town when McGinty's wife divorced him. She took the kid and moved to New York. That was the last anyone ever saw of them."

"That's so sad. Imagine not being able to see your own child!" Denise blurted before catching herself. Her cheeks reddened.

An awkward silence settled over the table, all eyes carefully avoiding Alice's. It was the eight-hundred-pound gorilla in the room, and suddenly Alice had had enough. Putting her spoon down, she turned Ryan, asking in as casual a tone as she could manage, "Do you know when Jeremy gets off work? I thought I'd give him a call after supper."

Ryan shrugged. "He's working for some landscaper, I think. That's all I know."

"You two don't hang out together?" she asked, surprised. There was a time they'd been practically joined at the hip.

"Not really." Her nephew kept his gaze on the pool of melting ice cream he was slowly stirring in his bowl. "I see him around, sure, but the guys he hangs with . . ." He caught himself, as if to keep from saying something that might worry her. "I don't have much in common with them."

"When you do see him, does he . . ." Alice paused, not wanting to appear any more pathetic than she already did; someone who, like Old Man McGinty, didn't know her own child. But in the end, desperation won out over pride. "Does he ever talk about me?"

The silence that ensued burned its way into her flesh. Then Ryan lifted his head and his eyes met hers. In them, she read the answer she'd been both seeking and dreading, one as bleak as the gray walls behind which she'd spent the past nine years.

"What was it like being in jail?" Taylor piped just then, as if she'd read Alice's mind. She'd been mostly silent throughout the meal, as if taking Alice's measure, or perhaps wondering what it would do to her social status having a jailbird for an aunt in addition to having her mother as her teacher. Now, her voicing what had to be on everyone else's mind came as a rude shock, immediately plunging the table into silence.

Denise was the first to speak. She shot Taylor an admonishing look. "Honey, I don't think—"

"It was hard." Alice cut her sister off, meeting her niece's intent, clear-eyed gaze. "The worst part was being away from my family. Jeremy and . . ." Her throat tightened, and she took a small sip of breath. "Your mom and dad, and grandma. And you guys." She darted a glance at Gary, whose lips were pressed together in a disapproving line. "I've missed so much, but I'm hoping you'll give me a chance to make up for it."

"Courtney Quist says you tried to run over Mister White, and that's why he's in a wheelchair." Taylor's big blue eyes were merely curious, not accusatory.

"Taylor! That's enough." Gary spoke sharply. He looked angry, though Alice suspected it was more at her than his daughter.

"No, it's okay," Alice told him. She turned back to her niece. "I didn't mean to hurt anyone, Taylor. I was just . . . after Jeremy's brother died . . ." *Killed . . . he was killed,* corrected an angry voice in her head. "I was so sad. I wasn't in my right mind. Honestly, I don't remember much of what happened. When I think about it now, it's mostly a blur."

Only it did happen. Not just to you. To us, said the ravaged look on her sister's face.

"Taylor, honey, why don't you clear the table while your brother does his homework," Denise said, abruptly pushing her chair back and standing up. "I'll help you with yours after we get this cleaned up, then you can watch TV." Suddenly she was back in action, bustling about the kitchen, dumping leftovers into plastic containers, and running plates under the faucet.

"Let me help with that," said Alice, carrying her bowl over to the sink.

Denise shooed her away. "No, you must be tired from your trip. Go put your feet up. I'll have Gary make up the sofa bed in the den." She shot him a meaningful glance: the age-old language between husband and wife that communicated more than any words. She was asking him to go along with the pretense that Alice was just an ordinary visitor.

"No, please. Let me do it," Alice said, heading for the doorway. "Sheets and blankets still in the hall closet?"

Denise, elbow deep in suds, called over her shoulder, "Laundry room."

Alice came to an abrupt halt. "Since when do you have a laundry room?"

"Since we added on a couple of years ago. Didn't I tell you? I guess I forgot to mention it," Denise said distractedly. "Anyway, no more running up and down the stairs to do the wash. Plus, we doubled the size of our bathroom. Remember how tiny it used to be? You could crack a kneecap just sitting down on the john. Go take a look. Make yourself at home."

Home. Alice wondered where that was. Right now she didn't feel as if she belonged anywhere, least of all in her sister's house, where the strain of keeping up with Denise's efforts to maintain a kind of normalcy was already beginning to show. She felt exhausted, as if she'd traveled, not just halfway across the state, but back in time. Right now, she longed to stretch out someplace quiet where she wouldn't have to put on a brave face. But there was something she needed to do first. Something that couldn't wait until tomorrow.

After she'd made up the sofa bed in the den, she reached for the phone on the desk and punched in her old number, a number she'd dialed so many times while at Pine River, she could almost hear the jingle of change tumbling into the pay phone on her cell block. It rang and rang at the other end, each trilling burst causing an invisible band about her chest to tighten. Finally, just as she was about to hang up, it was picked up.

"Hello?" Jeremy's voice, deep as a man's. The rare occasions he'd deigned to come to the phone when she'd called all those other times, their conversations had been brief and mostly one-sided. It came as a shock now to hear how much older he sounded.

Alice felt herself go perfectly still. It was as if she were encased in a brittle membrane that would shatter if she moved so much as an inch. Her lungs had stopped drawing in air and her blood had ceased to flow. The only part of her still functioning was her heart, its rhythmic beat like a clock keeping time in a house where no one was home. Her voice, when it emerged, was queer and high-pitched. "Jeremy? It's me. Mom."

CHAPTER THREE

"*Dude, you miss the bus* or what?" Rud peered at Jeremy as though he knew the real reason he was still hanging around on campus when school had let out nearly an hour ago.

Rud, of course needed no reason to be kicking around after hours—he and his buddies moved in their own orbit, like planets around a fickle sun. Normally Jeremy would have welcomed the chance to hang with them, but right now all he could think about was getting rid of Rud and Chuckie, so they wouldn't see when his mother pulled up.

He'd asked her to meet him here rather than at the house. He hadn't wanted to get into it with his dad, who'd been acting so weird since she'd come back, all itchy, like when he'd been trying to quit smoking. Now Jeremy wondered what to expect. Whatever she was offering, he wasn't interested. He'd gotten along just fine without her all these years, what did he need her for now? At the same time, he was curious. He wanted to hear it from her own mouth: To have her explain to him *why*.

Only it might be a case of being careful what you ask for. He'd read in one of those how-to-fix-what's-wrong-with-your-life-in-thirty-days-or-less books that the only way to deal with a situation like this was to meet it head on, to dig deep where it hurt the most. What if he dug all the way down and never got to the bottom? All he'd end up with was a giant hole.

And now here was Rud, the coolest guy he knew, grinning at Jeremy like he was a fly whose wings he'd plucked. "Me and Chuckie here," Rud jerked a thumb toward his sidekick, Chuckie Dimmock, a large, pimple-faced boy who never made a move without Rud's approval, "are heading over to Mike's to watch the drag races. Wanna come along?"

"Nah. I got stuff to do," Jeremy said. Any other time he would have leapt at the offer, but not now.

A slow, knowing smile spread across Rud's face. "Oh, I get it. You waiting on some chick."

Jeremy must have looked startled, for Rud let out a hoot, slapping him on the back. Kurt Rudnicki might be the whitest white boy who ever spoke ghetto-speak, with his pale skin and white-blond hair, gelled into spikes that glistened in the late afternoon sun, but he wasn't dumb. He just didn't have all the details straight. "Yeah, that's it," Jeremy said, in a lighthearted tone, hoping to deflect Rud's interest by making a joke of it. "She should be here any minute."

"Anyone we know?" Rud asked.

"Nah. She's no one," Jeremy muttered, wishing desperately that they would just *leave*.

"You doing her?" Chuckie leered at him.

"No!" Heat flared in Jeremy's cheeks.

"Yo, we got to educate this boy." Rud slung his arm around Jeremy's shoulders, leaning in close, his brown eyes dark holes drilled into the pale, sharp ridges of his face. "Now the thing to do is keep her guessing. Have her think you are doing *her* a favor. You listen to your Uncle Rud now, you hear. He knows what he's talking about. It's all about power, my man, and if you ain't got the power, you ain't got shit."

Jeremy's cheeks burned. "Yeah, well, I'll try to remember that." He injected as much sarcasm into his voice as he could without pissing Rud off.

Rud and Chuckie hung around a bit longer, jiving with him, while Jeremy sneaked surreptitious glances at his watch every now and then, growing increasingly desperate. When they finally took off, the relief he felt momentarily took his mind off the business ahead. It wasn't until he was alone again that the anxiety crept in once more.

The only other signs of life on campus were a group of kids in costume chatting animatedly outside the auditorium, where they were rehearsing for a play, and the varsity team on the football field below doing relays. Jeremy, who just minutes before had wanted only to be alone, felt a sudden sense of isolation that deepened with each shrill blast of Coach Sullivan's whistle and chorus of laughter from the drama club. He wasn't on a team and he didn't belong to any clubs. Socially, he wasn't even in the same universe as his cousin Ryan. Ryan charged the ions in the air just walking down the halls, while Jeremy moved about invisible as a mote of dust, torn between praying he wouldn't be noticed and feeling vaguely let down that he'd succeeded so spectacularly on that score.

Now all that was changing. Over the past few days, people had begun to eye him in a new and unwelcome way. Just this afternoon he'd walked into a classroom only to have the conversation abruptly cease. Even his teachers seemed to regard him differently, as if he were a rare specimen that required special handling. And that wasn't all. Everyone knew that Mr. White more or less ran the town. It wasn't just that he was mayor; he had the power that came with money, and according to Uncle Gary he didn't hesitate to use it. Which made Jeremy uneasy about how things would shake down now that his mother was back on the scene. Life, he suspected, was about to get very difficult for all of them.

He was distracted from his thoughts by a car now making its way toward him between the rows of parked cars, an older model Toyota Celica, metallic green, with a cracked windshield and a sticker on the front end that read *Rehab is for Quitters.* He smiled to himself. It was like something you'd expect to see on Rud's bumper.

The Toyota pulled to a stop, and a woman climbed out, dressed in jeans and a blue North Face parka like the one his aunt Denise wore. Lean like a runner, with dark brown hair pulled back in a ponytail and skin so pale he might have been looking at her underwater. She paused, glancing about uncertainly. Jeremy felt a tug of recognition. When her gaze fell on him, he froze.

"Jeremy?" She began walking toward him.

He pushed himself off the chain-link fence he was slouched against. "Hey," he said, lifting his hand in a lackluster wave. His mouth was dry, and his heart was beating high and quick in his chest. Suddenly he didn't know what to do with the muscles in his face.

She stopped a few feet shy of him, as if afraid he might bolt, staring at him as though she could fix him in place with her gaze. "You're taller than in your pictures."

He shrugged. "You look different, too."

"I suppose I must." She brought a hand self-consciously to her cheek. Her gaze was hot and searching; he could feel it on his skin like a sunburn. "Shall we go for a ride? We can talk in the car." She noticed him looking at the Toyota. "I bought it from a friend of your aunt Denise," she explained. "It was her son's. He's in jail on a DUI and she needed the money to bail him out." Her mouth slanted in an ironic little smile. "It was the best I could do on short notice."

He shrugged and started toward the car, glancing about to make sure no one was watching before he climbed in. When they were both buckled in, he waited for her to start the engine, but she just sat there, looking at him, as if he were the one in the driver's seat. Jeremy felt a ripple of unease, remembering what had happened the last time he'd been in a car with her. He didn't think she would do anything like that again, but it was an ugly reminder nonetheless.

"We could go for a bite to eat," she suggested.

"I'm not that hungry," he said. Usually by the time school let out he was starving, but at the moment his stomach was in knots. Besides, in a public place they'd draw too much attention.

"Why don't we take a little drive then." She turned the key in the ignition and shifted into gear, maneuvering the Toyota out of the parking lot as carefully as someone learning to drive. Exiting the school grounds, she sneaked a glance at him as she made a right turn onto Church Street. "It's good to see you. You have no idea how much I've been looking forward to this." Her tone was casual, but he hadn't missed the little catch in her voice.

Jeremy felt the pressure to respond in kind, but he couldn't bring himself to do it. She wanted something—he could feel it radiating off her like heat—something he didn't have to give.

"Where are we going?" he asked after a bit, as he stared out the window, slouched down in his seat.

"I don't know. You tell me."

Jeremy cast about in his mind, trying to think of a place where they were unlikely to be spotted by anyone he knew. "Dad and I saw this bald eagle's nest when we were hiking in the park last summer." He said the first thing that popped into his head. "I could show you, if you like."

"Sounds good." He had the feeling she would've said the same thing had he suggested a trip to the moon. "I've heard that in parts of Alaska bald eagles have made such a comeback, they've actually become pests. I saw a show about it on TV," she remarked, as she made the turn at the intersection.

He wondered if it was a show she'd watched in prison, and that made him realize how little he knew about her life at Pine River. He had only sketchy memories of going to visit her there as a kid—a room with tables bolted to the floor and gray, cinderblock walls; guards in uniform buzzing him through a series of doors. There was so much he was dying to ask, all the things she hadn't told him in her letters. But he didn't dare. She might get the wrong idea, and think he gave a shit, and the last thing Jeremy wanted was for this to turn into some tearful mother and son reunion. The truth was she was a stranger to him.

They drove in near silence until they reached the turnoff for the state park, where they began the steep climb up the hill, through a tunnel of evergreens thick with ferns the size of small trees. The road ended in a parking area near the summit, and they got out and hiked the rest of the way along a marked trail. The eagle's nest was right where he remembered it, at the top of an old-growth Douglas fir that had lost most of its foliage. "Looks like no one's home at the moment," Alice said, shading her eyes as she peered upward.

"They're probably out hunting for food," Jeremy said.

"They?"

"It's a pair. There were babies in the nest the last time I was here."

She gazed out at the sound below, where small islands wreathed in mist were strewn like so many scattered stones, some scarcely more than a knuckle of rock with one or two trees clinging to them. "I haven't been up here in years. I'd forgotten how peaceful it is," she said. She turned to him, her eyes bright with unshed tears. "Thank you. You don't know how much this means to me."

He dropped his gaze, feeling embarrassed, knowing she wasn't talking about the scenery. "Yeah. No problem."

"I hope we can do this again."

Jeremy went on staring at the ground. With the autumn rains had come the moss that blanketed everything around him in a thick green fuzz. Right now he wanted nothing more than to sink down onto all that furry softness and close his eyes. "I don't know," he hedged. "I'm pretty busy these days. You know, what with school and my job."

"I see."

"My boss wasn't too happy when I told him I needed the afternoon off."

"Well, maybe we could have dinner one evening then."

"Maybe." Jeremy spoke dubiously. "But that's usually the only time Dad and I get to hang out."

He glanced up and saw the hurt on her face. But she did her best to cover it, asking, "How is your dad, by the way?"

"Good. They made him district manager."

"I'm not surprised. He's worked hard for it."

"The only bad thing is that it means more time on the road." Randy's territory covered most of western Washington, many of the doctor's offices and clinics he regularly called on separated by hundreds of miles. "What about you? What'll you do?" Jeremy asked.

"For work, you mean?" She smiled. "I don't know yet. First, I have to find a place to live."

"So you, like, plan on sticking around?"

She seemed surprised by the question. "Of course. Why wouldn't I?"

He shrugged. Part of him wanted her here; another part of him wished she'd stayed the hell away. Mostly, he just felt confused.

"The only reason I'm here is because of you. I want us to spend some time together," she went on, the raw need in her voice making him cringe. "You'll be in college before long, and I've missed so much already."

Yeah? Well, whose fault is that? he felt like saying. He frowned, struggling to keep from giving in to the tears pressing behind his eyes. "I don't know about college. I might take a year off, do some traveling."

She gave him a quizzical look. "Aunt Denise tells me you have a shot at the Ivy Leagues."

He snorted in derision, pretending it was no big deal, though he'd sent for all the catalogues and had been thinking of little else for months. "Let's see how I score on the SATs."

"Maybe I could help with that. I was sort of the unofficial tutor at Pine River. They nicknamed me Teach." She smiled, which shocked him a bit— he wouldn't have imagined she'd have any fond memories of that place. "It wouldn't be the same with you, I know. The ladies I worked with were just studying for their GEDs, and you . . ." She paused. "You could probably teach me. But I could quiz you on the stuff you've learned."

"I don't need your help." He spoke more harshly than he'd intended.

Alice fell silent. All around him the woods crackled as if with static in the stiff breeze blowing in off the water. Violent slashes of yellow stood out amid the deep green—the laurels and poplars his boss, Mr. Barbour, called weed trees—marking the passage of Indian summer into autumn. Over-head, bands of cirrus clouds stippled the sky, and on the ground below boulders and fallen tree limbs lay like the ruins of an ancient civilization.

"I'd be doing it as much for me as for you," she said at last, her voice so soft he almost didn't catch the tremor in it.

"Thanks, but I've gotten along just fine without you all these years."

She shook her head, her eyes filling with tears. "I'm still your mother."

"Yeah? I had a mother once," he shot back. "She used to bake me cookies and tuck me in at night. You? I don't even *know* you."

She looked so bereft, Jeremy almost felt sorry for her. "I never stopped loving you, not for one minute," she said.

"All I know is that you weren't around! I used to cry myself to sleep every night, I missed you so much." His own tears came now, hot and fierce, betraying him. He gave his runny nose a furious backhanded swipe. "I was just a kid. Shouldn't you have thought of that before you . . . you . . ." His throat closed up before he could finish the sentence.

Her own face contorted, as if in pain. "I'm sorry, Jeremy. I never meant for it to turn out this way."

"You make it sound like an accident. I was there, remember? You weren't thinking of me when you ran down Mister White. You were thinking of David. You chose *him* over me. A dead boy." The memory he'd done his best to bury reached up now like some hideous, decayed thing rising out the grave.

"It wasn't like that," she said, the tears in her eyes spilling down her cheeks. "I wasn't in my right mind at the time. I know that sounds like an excuse, but it's the truth."

"If you really cared about me, you'd go away and leave me alone!"

"Jeremy, please . . . "

She placed a hand on his arm, and he shook it off, abruptly turning around and stalking back toward the car. He hadn't gone more than a few dozen feet when he slipped on some wet leaves and lost his balance, pitching backward to land on his rear end. Alice cried out in dismay and came rushing over, but Jeremy only glared up at her from his sprawled position on the ground, as if it were her fault that he'd fallen. Ignoring her proffered hand, he scrambled to his feet, slapping at the dirt and leaves that clung to his jeans.

By the time he straightened, his face was wiped clean of any emotion. "Are we done now? I'd like to go home," he said in a queer, dead voice he scarcely recognized as his own.

——

After she'd dropped her son off at his house, Alice drove slowly back toward the motel where she was staying. She replayed the meeting with Jeremy in her mind. Could she have handled it better? Been more up front with him instead of following Denise's advice to take it slowly? Somehow she didn't think it would have made a difference. Jeremy was hurt and angry, and no amount of explaining was going to change that. It would take time for those wounds to heal. Meanwhile, she would just have to be patient, let him know by her mere presence alone that if she hadn't been there for him before, she was now.

Still, the rejection hurt. In a way, Jeremy seemed further away than when she'd been in prison. Back then, she'd at least had the hope of a happy reunion.

He was so different from his brother. David had been a happy-go-lucky kid, hurtling through life as if he'd somehow known he needed to cram everything into those few short years. Jeremy, in contrast, had been watchful and sensitive. She recalled one time, when he was around three, she'd walked into the living room and found him crying as though his heart would break, where moments before he'd been playing happily with his toys.

"Oh, sweetie, what is it? What's the matter?" she'd asked, scooping him into her arms.

"It got hurts," he'd finally managed to choke, pointing a chubby finger at the sliding glass door to the patio, where a sparrow that had flown into the glass lay stunned.

After his brother's death, Jeremy had retreated into his own world, holing up in his room for hours on end with his comic books and action figures. So ghost-like she used to worry that he would one day simply fade away. She hadn't been equipped to deal with it, though. She hadn't realized it at the time, but both her marriage and her sanity had been gradually coming undone. Randy and she, though they were sleeping in the same bed, might have been in separate universes. Even in their shared concern for Jeremy they'd been at odds, disagreeing on everything from which psychologist would be best for him to whether or not Jeremy should be forced to finish what was on his plate when he said he wasn't hungry.

The motel was situated on Whale Watch Lane, a short walk from the outlook known for its frequent whale sightings. It catered mostly to the summer crowd, so it was fairly deserted this late in the season. But Alice didn't mind that her cabin smelled musty or that the wind, when it was blowing in off the bay, filtered in through the cracks around the door and window frame. For the time being it was home. Best of all, the manager, a middle-aged man who'd reeked of nicotine, hadn't looked askance at her when she'd checked in; as long as her money was good, she could be Jack the Ripper for all he cared. The hot shower she yearned for would have to wait, though; there was something she needed to do first.

She turned onto Bellmore Road instead, headed in the direction of the church where she and her family used to attend services when she was growing up. Pulling up in front, she saw that it was exactly as she remembered, a century-old white clapboard structure with a modest spire sitting in the middle of what had once been an apple orchard. Alice recalled wandering through the orchard with her sister after services, hunting for apples amid the stunted trees that remained, while their parents had lingered on the front steps of the church, chatting with fellow congregants. Now she scarcely noticed the trees as she made her way along the narrow path that led to the small churchyard in back. It was where her father and grandparents, Nana and Grandpa Joe, were buried. And her son.

David's grave, tucked all the way in back, under an old maple tree, would have been difficult to locate if she hadn't known the way by heart. There was only a simple bronze marker engraved with his name and the dates of his birth and death. She'd wanted a proper headstone, but Randy had insisted on something simpler.

"You think advertising it to the world is going to change the fact that our son's dead?" he'd shouted at her, when their disagreement had flared into an argument. "I don't need some fancy inscription to remind me. He's *gone*, Alice. That's the only thing that matters."

Looking into his grief-stricken face she had seen that he blamed her. For not being more vigilant, perhaps—if she'd been a better mother, David would still be alive. And she'd given in to Randy then because she'd known he was right: She *was* responsible for their son's death. If not directly, then through her negligence. Reflecting on it now, Alice saw that moment as the turning point. In the immediate aftermath of their son's death, she and Randy had clung to each other like survivors of a shipwreck, but in mourning they'd gone their separate ways. Randy wanting to move on, Alice unable to.

Yet however many times she played it back in her mind, she could never see a different outcome. It was as if she had been heading down a steep slope, picking up speed along the way, until she'd finally lost control.

Luckily, neither she nor Jeremy had been hurt when her car plowed into Owen White. Owen wasn't so fortunate. Emerging from a coma after two days, he'd learned that he would never walk again. Alice had been out on bail when the news reached her, and it had been clear from the cold shoulders and pitiless looks she'd gotten as she'd walked the streets of Bell Harbor that she'd already been tried and found guilty. If it hadn't been for her family, she didn't know how she would have coped. The only one who'd been less than supportive was Randy; he'd seen that final act of insanity as a betrayal of sorts, proof she had already left him, if only in her mind.

Four months later she was led off in handcuffs, bound for the Pine River Correctional Facility in Olympia.

Alice blinked away the tears obscuring her vision as she gazed down at David's grave. It felt as if she'd lost two sons. But how could she expect Jeremy to forgive her when she couldn't forgive herself? She wouldn't shed any tears for Owen White; he'd only gotten what he deserved. But her family had paid a steep price for what she'd done, and for that she was deeply sorry.

She caught a flash of movement out of the corner of her eye and turned to see a dog streaking down the path that led to the outlook: black with a blaze of white on its chest—the Border collie from the ferry landing the other day. Alice briefly considered going after it—maybe it was lost and its owner was looking for it—but the dog quickly vanished from sight. Anyway, didn't she have enough problems of her own? No job, nowhere to live. Without her modest savings—her share of the inheritance when Nana's house was sold—she, too, would be roaming about without a roof over her head.

With a deep sigh, she started back toward her car.

dog was looking past him toward the house, ears pricked and eyes
eyes that seemed to hold an almost human intelligence—as if at
ment he expected to see his master step out the door onto the
"You're welcome to have a look around if you like," Colin told
but I guarantee you won't find what you're looking for. I'm afraid
" He regarded the animal ruefully. "A pretty poor substitute, I
but if you're game, I could use the company."

d forgotten how remote a landscape this was, a place where nature
way and civilization seemed a distant rumor. On the plus side, he
slept this well in years. In the absence of modern-day distractions
V and the computer, he went to bed when it was dark and rose
the sun. He ate when he was hungry, regardless of mealtimes, and
himself perfectly capable of sitting for hours on end doing noth-
ut gazing out at the water or watching the deer graze. His grandfa-
had left a sizeable library, art books mostly as well as biographies of
ble artists, and Colin had been perusing them, regretting that he
't inherited so much as a thimbleful of the old man's talent. If he
an artist, he'd have been able to capture on canvas what remained
ed inside him, just as William had in the portrait over the fireplace.
always heard that great art was born of great suffering, and if that
true, then he would have created a masterpiece.

After a shower and a breakfast of hot cereal and a boiled egg, he
ded back outside. The sun had disappeared behind the storm clouds
had piled up along the ridge and a cutting wind was blowing in off
ocean. In his old life, Colin would have opted for an indoor activity
a day like this. But he'd already adopted the islanders' habit of ignor-
bad weather. A long walk would clear his head, he thought, throwing
his parka and a pair of old Wellingtons that he'd found in the mud
om.

The Border collie was right where he had left it, holding vigil on the
rch. Colin whistled for him, mildly surprised when the dog fell in bend him as he stepped off the porch. He started down the path to the
ve, the dog following at a wary distance. Worn to a groove by decades

The
alert—
any m
porch.
him, "
I'm it
agree,

He
held
hadn'
like
with
foun
ing b
ther
nota
hadi
were
lock
He'
was

hea
tha
the
on
ing
on
ro

p
h
c

CHAPTER FO

———

Colin found the dog curled asleep on the porch. 1
his third day on the island and he'd just poured hin
and stepped outside to enjoy the sunrise. The furry
into a dog on all fours: the Border collie from t
scooted out of reach, then sat back to eye him waril

"Good morning to you, too." Colin placed his mu
ing and squatted down on his haunches so that he w
dog. "Hungry?" he asked. The dog cocked its head, fi
eyes on him with keen interest. "I'll take that as a yes
inside, returning several minutes later with a bow
Krispies mixed with a little bit of hamburger meat 1
night's supper. He set it down, saying, "I'm sorry if it
used to. I wasn't expecting company."

The dog took an exploratory sniff. Apparently it m
faction for he wolfed it down. It wasn't until Colin tried
his collar that he retreated, looking faintly offended tha
sumed he could be bought off so cheaply. "All right, fair
conceded. He backed off, his hand held out in a conc
"You call the shots from now on."

of foot traffic, the path traversed the grassy slope like a frown line in a Brobdingnagian brow before disappearing into the rocks that lined the pebbled beach below. There, driftwood lay piled in heaps, like massive free-form sculptures. Farther out, the tide had retreated to leave a great flat of silt that glistened in the gray light, stubs of rebar bearded with algae protruding here and there like broken teeth: what was left of the old oyster beds. Useless now, growing nothing but barnacles.

Colin remembered when he was a boy looking out his window at night and seeing the distant glow of Mr. Deets's lantern bobbing along the shoreline. Deets always did his harvesting after the tide had gone out, which at certain times of the year meant getting up at an hour when most people were still in bed, often making more than a dozen trips back and forth to his truck before his work was done, work that over the years had left him with calluses on his hands as thick and ridged as the shells of the oysters themselves.

In the daylight hours, Colin would often tag after him, helping to pound in stakes and tighten lines, digging out the oysters that had broken loose and become buried in the silt. Deets, a crusty old loner, hadn't been much of a conversationalist, but Colin had found him oddly companionable. At home in Queens, with his family, there had been nothing but talk, with very little of substance to say. His mom whiling away her free hours gossiping with the neighbors, and his dad and brother endlessly rehashing sports plays. At an age before Patrick could even add and subtract he could recite the batting average of every player on the Yankees team.

Colin lowered himself onto his haunches, scooping up water as clear as gin from one of the tide pools. He recalled Deets's telling him that there was no better place on earth for growing oysters, and now it seemed a shame to see it lying fallow. But Colin had far bigger concerns at the moment. Like deciding what to do with this place. The sensible thing would be to sell it. As Clark Findlay had pointed out, the land alone was worth quite a bit, and Colin could certainly use the money. When the small account he'd inherited along with the house was depleted he'd be broke, with no prospects. Then what? He'd be just another recovering drunk standing amid the smoking ruins of his burned bridges.

Nonetheless, something kept getting in the way of common sense. For one thing, this place was the only thing keeping him anchored. Without it, he'd be truly lost. More so than in the days and weeks after 9/11, when, in a city plastered with grainy Xeroxes of missing loved ones, he'd at least had a role to play: that of Family Member. For in losing his wife on that day he'd been thrust into the ranks of the similarly bereaved, their collective grief a kind of national emblem. Like the war heroes of previous generations, they'd been sought after by the press and trotted out at official ceremonies. Politicians had courted them and charitable institutions had raised money on their behalf. And if the outpouring of public sympathy had seemed overwhelming at times, it had provided him both with a dark purpose and a reason to go on . . . and to drink.

Two years later, he'd come to the realization that the statute of limitations on his mourning had run out. He'd watched the compassion in other people's eyes turn to pity, then disgust. Yes, you lost a loved one, they seemed to say, but so did a lot of other people, and look how they're moving on. His excuses for not showing up for work on time had worn equally thin, and his frequent hangovers hadn't gone unnoticed. His boss had begun assigning him the bottom of the barrel cases: petty offenders and prostitutes, low-level drug dealers and, in one nastily ironic instance, a drunk driver charged with reckless endangerment. Outside of work, friends who'd helped him through the early days of his bereavement had stopped calling. In the end, there had only been his best friend, Billy Munroe, whom he'd known since the second grade, and even Billy had finally checked out on him after one too many drunken late night calls. "Christ, man, get it together!" Billy had exploded before hanging up for the last time. "This is getting old."

But by then Colin had been past the point of being able to pull himself together. He'd realized on that day, to his horror, horror that had gradually hardened into a kind of grim acceptance, that his dead wife was no longer the reason he drank. While the keenness of his loss remained undiminished, except when dulled by booze—a Ground Zero-size hole in his gut that no amount of public sympathy could fill—it wasn't why he'd been pretty much shit-faced all day, every day. Colin had drunk because he couldn't not drink.

It hadn't always been that way. In college, and later on in law school, at Columbia, he'd done his share of partying, sure, but he'd known when to stop after the party had gone on a little too long. And maybe Nadine had had something to do with it as well. He'd met her during his first year of law school. Even after all this time, he could still recall every detail of that meeting. He'd stopped for a bite to eat at his favorite diner, on Broadway and One Hundred and First, where the food was cheap and the portions enormous, enough to last him all day and still leave money for subway fare, when he'd looked up from the menu to find, in place of his regular waitress, a black-haired beauty with buttermilk skin and the most kissable lips he'd ever laid eyes on.

"You're staring at me," she'd said, with a self-conscious laugh, as he'd sat there gaping at her in speechless wonderment. "Do I have something in my teeth?"

"No, I'm sorry . . . I just . . . you're not Sally," he'd stammered in reply.

"No, I'm not Sally." The girl had given him a saucy little smile, as if they were in on some private little joke. "Did you want to order, or would you rather come back when she's here?"

He'd smiled back. "I'll have the BLT, light on the mayo." She was scribbling the order on her pad, when he'd remarked, "I haven't seen you around before. You new here?"

"It's my first day." She'd leaned in to confide, with a whiff of some subtle scent that had gone through him in a heady rush. "Don't tell anyone, but I'm not really a waitress. This is just what I do to pay the rent." She'd explained that she was an actress, injecting a note of irony into her voice, to let him know that she was aware that she was a walking cliché.

"Have you been in any plays I might have seen?" he'd asked.

"Not unless you were one of the six people who caught the off-off-Broadway production of *Cry in the Wilderness*," she'd said, with a twinkle in her eye.

He'd found her attitude refreshing. The other actresses he'd known all took themselves so goddamn seriously. When his sandwich came, he'd found himself eating more slowly than usual, stealing glances at her as she'd bustled about. When she wasn't taking care of other customers, he'd chatted her up over endless refills of coffee.

Her name was Nadine and she'd lived in the city all her life, he'd learned. She was a fan of Woody Allen movies and her favorite music was jazz; until two years ago she'd lived with her parents, in a co-op on the Upper West Side, but now she shared a fifth-floor walkup in Chelsea with three of her friends. When the check came, Colin had asked if they could meet for coffee later on. Nadine had grinned at that—he was already so wired on caffeine it would take him the rest of the day to come down—but she'd taken him up on the offer nonetheless.

Six months later, they were married. He'd been in his second year of law school and she'd still been making the rounds of auditions, waitressing on the side. They were living in an Alphabet City tenement, barely able to make ends meet, yet he had never been happier. With Nadine, every day was an adventure. She had friends from all walks of life, and the parties she was fond of throwing were a mix young professionals and out-of-work actors, hard hats and transvestites, university students and professors. Colin grew used to coming home from a day of classes to find his wife out on the stoop chatting with one of the homeless people from the neighborhood.

Nadine herself had been a study in contrasts. She'd hated to cook but was a connoisseur of every ethnic eatery on the Lower East Side. She was allergic to dogs and cats but loved nothing better than to spend an afternoon at the zoo. Her only real flaw had been that she was maddeningly late for everything. Yet whenever she finally did breeze in, amid a storm of windblown hair and effusive apologies, after having kept him waiting for half an hour or more, it would always be as if his day hadn't truly started until just then.

The irony was that the day she'd died was one of the few he could remember her leaving for work on time. By then, she'd given up acting in

lieu of a fulltime position as assistant manager at Windows on the
World. He remembered her last words to him as she'd been dashing out
the door. She'd paused, turning to him with that grin of hers that could
melt a polar ice cap, "Hey, you, in the white boxers. Anyone ever tell you
how sexy you are?"

Two hours later she was dead.

Now, five years later, Colin stared at his reflection in the shallow water rippling at his feet. He didn't know how long he'd been hunkered
there, caught up in his memories, but it must have been a while for his
muscles registered a complaint as he straightened. I should get to the
gym more often, he thought, wincing. His main focus, in the six months
since he'd gotten out of rehab, had been staying sober. That was where
he'd been, in fact, at a halfway house in Arizona, when he'd learned of
his grandfather's death. The news had devastated him, largely because he
hadn't had a chance to say good-bye; he'd been so caught up in his own
problems, which, fueled by alcohol, had become all-consuming, that
he'd kept in only sporadic touch. He hadn't even been in any kind of
shape to attend the funeral.

Now it was time to figure out what to do with the part of his life that
didn't revolve around AA.

He looked around to find the dog eyeing him as if it were wondering
the same thing. A bleak smile surfaced on Colin's face. "Come on, boy,
let's get you home," he said, starting up the path.

His neighbors up the road turned out to be a couple around his age
named the Henleys. They had two young children, a boy and a girl who
expressed delight at the return of their missing pet. The little boy threw
his arms around the dog's neck, burying his face in its fur, to which it
submitted with a dignified tolerance.

"We were wondering where he'd gotten to this time. Thanks for bringing him back," said Nora Henley, a brisk little woman with thick, red-
dish-blond hair cut in a wedge. She eyed the dog with a mixture of pity
and exasperation. "We took him in because we were afraid he'd be put
down otherwise, but now I'm not so sure we did him any favors. I think

he'd gladly have followed the old man. The poor thing hasn't been the same since he went." She brought her gaze back to Colin. "I'm sorry about your grandfather. We've only been here a year, so we didn't know him all that well. But he was a good neighbor. Tommy"—she glanced toward the little boy now fetching the dog a bowl of water— "really took a shine to him. We all felt he'd have wanted us to look after Shep."

Shep. Colin turned the name over in his mind. Yes, it fit. What was he but a shepherd who'd lost his purpose in life? "I was around your son's age when I first started coming here," he told the Henleys. "My grandfather had a different dog then, a Border collie like Shep. His name was Dickie. I wonder if they're from the same bloodline."

"Mr. Deets would have been the one to ask," said Doug Henley, a rangy, bespectacled man with thinning brown hair, a good foot taller than his diminutive wife. "He lived in this house for over forty years, did you know that? That's what his niece told us."

Colin recalled now the lawyer, Findlay, having mentioned something about a niece. As a kid, Colin hadn't been aware of Deets having any family; a life-long bachelor, he might have sprung from sea, like the creatures from which he'd made his meager living.

"She lives in Seattle," Doug went on. "That's why she sold the place; she didn't want to be bothered with the upkeep. Frankly, I don't blame her. It was pretty rundown when we bought it." He put an arm around Nora's shoulders. "My poor wife got stuck with most of the work. I was busy wrapping up things on the mainland at the time." He explained that he'd sold his partnership in a group dental practice to open a private practice here on the island.

Colin could see all the work that had gone into refurbishing the old fisherman's cottage. Cedar shingles replaced the original batten-board siding, and a new metal roof gleamed where the old moss-grown one had been. The garden, too, had been transformed, flowerbeds and tidy borders reinforced with railroad ties where there'd been only a wild green tangle. There was even a man-made brook that spilled into a pond stocked with koi.

"The only thing we haven't gotten to yet is the shed," said Nora, gesturing toward the ramshackle structure out back. "It's so crammed full of old stuff, I couldn't even tell you what most of it is."

Colin's pulse quickened. "Mind if I take a look?"

"Be our guest," said Doug, looking as if he'd be only too happy to have Colin take any or all of that junk off his hands.

"Thanks." Colin headed around back under the watchful eye of Shep.

As he pushed open the door to the shed, its rusty hinges gave with a loud squeal of protest. Inside, he batted blindly about overhead until his hand met with a pull chain. He yanked on it and the light came on, throwing into shadowy relief a stack of old crates pushed up against one wall. It took his eyes a little while longer to assemble into individual shapes the jumble around him: coiled ropes, a leaning tower of buckets stacked one atop the other, a pile of burlap sacks covered in mold that gave off a dank odor. Inside a box containing various pieces of equipment, he found an assortment of rusted shucking knives and a pair of leather gloves stiff with age. All that was left of a small yet once-thriving oyster farm.

By the time Colin emerged from the shed, streaked with grime, a vague plan had begun taking shape in his mind. Why couldn't he start an oyster farm of his own? He had the land and nothing but time on his hands, and there was enough equipment here to cobble together a basic operation. He could always buy whatever else he needed. A fine plan . . . except it would mean staying on Grays Island, not selling his grandfather's place. Could he afford to do that?

Can you afford not to? countered a voice in his head. What was waiting for him back in New York except more excuses to drink? It wasn't as if he had a job to go back to, or friends urging him to return. And this way he'd at least have a purpose, even if it made sense to no one but him.

He shook off the excitement growing in him. He'd have to do his homework before he made any final decisions. For now, he merely informed the Henleys that he'd be happy to haul off any of the junk they wanted to get rid of. They told him he could have it all, and he jotted down their number, promising to return as soon as he'd lined up a truck.

He was walking away, with a new spring in his step, when he happened to glance back over his shoulder. The dog, Shep, had gone back inside, but Colin could see him in the window, peering out at Colin, ears pricked as if in expectation. It seemed a good omen somehow.

Two hours later, Colin was standing in line at the public library with several books on oyster farming to check out. The librarian, a pretty young woman with long blond hair held back with a headband, was taking her time with the elderly man in front of Colin, suggesting some books he might like in place of the one he had on reserve that wasn't in yet. No one seemed to be in any hurry, even those in line behind Colin. No clearing of throats or rolling of eyes; no one muttering loudly, *Is this going to take all day?* A reminder that he wasn't in New York; that was why people moved here, to get away from just that sort of thing. His impatience must have shown on his face, though, for he caught the eye of a woman walking past, who smiled knowingly. A woman he recognized at once as Alice Kessler.

As soon as he'd gotten his books stamped, he went in search of her. He found her at one of the tables in the periodicals section. "Hello again. Colin McGinty, we met at the ferry landing," he said to refresh her memory.

But it was clear from the way she was looking at him that she'd needed no introduction. "Yes, hi. How are you?" She kept her voice low, as if not wanting to draw attention to herself.

"Not bad." He realized, to his surprise, that he meant it. For the first time in months he didn't feel an oppressive pall hanging over him. He eyed the newspaper spread open in front of her to the real estate section. "Find what you're looking for?"

"Not in my price range. But I'm not exactly in a position to be picky. As long as it's four walls and a roof over my head, it'll do. What about you? Looks like you've decided to stick around awhile." She gestured toward the books under his arm.

"For the time being, at least. Until I get things sorted out." Colin felt reluctant to discuss his plans. They seemed wildly impractical even to him at this point.

"Family business?" She reminded him of his stated reason for being here.

This wasn't the time or place to get into it, so he merely said, "It's complicated."

"With family, it's always complicated." She smiled. "Just when you think it's safe to go back into the water . . . "

"You sound as though you've had some experience with that." She shrugged, as if to say, Who hasn't? "So what are your plans? Beyond finding a place to live, that is," he asked.

Her expression clouded over briefly. "I've been job hunting, but so far no luck. Seems good-paying positions are hard to come by on this island."

"Keep looking. Something will turn up eventually." Easier said than done when you're a convicted felon, he knew.

A flush rose in her cheeks, as if she'd read his mind.

An older woman seated at the other end of the table made a shushing motion, and Colin leaned in to whisper, "What do you say we grab a cup of coffee? I wouldn't want to run afoul of the library police." She hesitated long enough for him to wonder if he'd overstepped the bounds, then she nodded and rose to her feet.

Outside, they strolled along the sidewalk in companionable silence. She was wearing her brown hair loose today; it was blowing around her face in the wind. She looked prettier than he remembered, not so pale and pinched. Only her eyes were the same—those of someone cold and hungry peering in through a window at a happy family seated around the dinner table.

The weather had warmed up a bit, so they got their coffees to go and headed for the town green. Across the street stood the museum, housed in a log cabin from the days when Grays Island was a remote trading post, but with tourist season winding down there was no one else about, except a teenage boy tossing a Frisbee to his dog and a maintenance worker pruning one of the trees. They sat down at a picnic table, steam rising from their cups to mingle with their breath.

"This is nice," she said, looking around her at the grass carpeted in gold and crimson leaves, the sturdy maples, the creek that wound along the north end of the green. "I've been so busy since I got back, I haven't had a chance to sit back and enjoy the scenery."

"Seems like I've been doing nothing but that," replied Colin.

She turned to him. "I heard your grandfather left you his place." At the startled look he gave her, she added, in a rueful tone, perhaps thinking of her own notoriety, "Word travels fast in small towns."

"Well, you heard right."

"There's talk that you're planning to sell."

"That so? Well, they must know something I don't," he said. "Actually, I'm thinking I may hang on to it."

"So you'd live here full-time?"

"Looks that way."

"Don't you have a job to go back to?"

"Let's just say I'm between jobs at the moment."

"I understand you're a lawyer."

"Was," he corrected. "In my previous life, I was a prosecutor for the Manhattan D.A.'s office."

"I see. Well." She blew on her coffee before taking a careful sip. She appeared unsettled by what he'd just told her. It was easy to see why. What must it have been like for her, all those years in prison? Put away by a hard-hitting prosecutor not so different from himself.

"I'm sorry if I've made you uncomfortable," he said, touching her arm.

"Ah, so you've heard. The infamous Alice Kessler." Her mouth twisted in a pained smile.

"Only what I've read in the papers," he said.

"Don't believe everything you read."

"I don't. Anyway, it was a long time ago."

"Not to people around here. To them, it's like it happened yesterday."

"Like you said, it's a small town."

"You're probably wondering why I came back."

"Why did you?" He sipped his coffee, eyeing her thoughtfully over the rim of his cup.

"My son. His name is Jeremy. He's sixteen." He saw something flare in her gray-green eyes. "He's living with his father right now, but I'm hoping . . ." She bit her lip, and fell silent. After a moment, she said, "What about you? There must be a reason for moving here besides the fact that you inherited a house."

"I'm not sure I have one, unless it's that this just happens to be the last stop on the line." Colin zipped up his jacket against a sudden gust of chill, and sat gazing out vacantly over the green. "If you know so much about me, you probably also know that I lost my wife. Things kind of went downhill after that."

"I'm sorry." He could tell from the way she said it that she was no stranger to that kind of loss.

"She died on 9/11. She was in the North tower when it went down," he went on, finding it strangely cathartic to be talking about it with someone who wouldn't wrinkle her brow in an attempt to understand the unfathomable, who wouldn't be looking for a graceful way of segueing to a less painful topic. "After that, I started hitting the bottle, until it dawned on me one day that the problem wasn't what was eating me, it was *me*." He gave in to a bleak smile. "You'd think that's when I would have known it was time to quit, but it actually took a little longer than that before I finally decided to get sober. I had to lose my job first, and pretty much every friend I ever had. That was six months ago. I haven't touched a drop since."

They exchanged a look that communicated more than any words. She wasn't like most people he met outside of AA meetings, those for whom a life crisis meant getting laid off from their jobs or having their mother-in-law move in with them. Alice Kessler knew what real suffering was.

Now her mouth hooked up in a mirthless little smile. "We're a fine pair, aren't we? They say misery loves company, but right now I wouldn't wish either of us on anyone."

"It must be some comfort, at least, to know you're not the only one being talked about," he said, with a laugh.

"Fortunately that's not the only thing we have in common," she replied, her expression sobering. "I don't know if you were aware of this or not, but apparently your grandfather was a friend of grandmother's. In fact, he painted her portrait. The famous one, of the woman in the red dress. I was wondering if you knew what became of it."

Colin jerked upright, nearly spilling his coffee. "You're Eleanor's grand-daughter?" He could see the resemblance now, and he wondered if perhaps that was why he'd been drawn to her from the beginning. Alice's coloring was darker than Eleanor's, her eyes more gray than green, but it was the same face: fine-boned yet strong as tempered steel. The face of someone who didn't tread lightly through life. "What an amazing coincidence. Now I know why you looked familiar. You're the spitting image of her."

Alice looked pleased. "So you're familiar with the portrait."

"I ought to be. I own it."

Now it was her turn to look surprised. "Really? Would you mind . . . I mean, I'd love to see it sometime." She seemed hesitant to impose.

"Anytime you like," he told her. "I'm usually home. Just give me a call whenever you feel like stopping by. Here's my number." He scribbled it on the back of his napkin.

She carefully folded the napkin and tucked it into her pocket. "Are you sure it wouldn't be a bother?"

"Are you kidding? You'd be doing me a favor," he told her. "It's so quiet out there, I can hear myself think. Which in my case tends to be dangerous."

She broke into a smile, a genuine one that for a dazzling instant lit up her whole face, like when the sun made one of its rare appearances from behind the clouds. In the parking area at the other end of the green, music drifted from a car radio, some seventies ballad, and closer by the boy tossing the Frisbee sent it sailing skyward once more, a spinning blue circle that hung aloft for a long moment, seeming to defy gravity. In that brief moment Colin felt his spirits lift as well.

"All right then. I'll take you up on it," she said. "But first I have to find a job and a place to live, in that order."

"What kind of job are you looking for?" he asked.

"You mean what am I good at besides making license plates?" She shook her head. "Not much, I'm afraid. I used to be a pretty good cook, but I'm a little out of practice."

"There are lots of restaurants on the island," he said.

"None that are interested in hiring a convicted felon. Believe me, I know. I've applied to all the ones advertising for help."

"Something will turn up, I'm sure," he said. "In the meantime, don't give up hope. In AA, we have a saying: 'Fake it 'till you make it.' I've been doing a lot of that myself lately."

"Thanks. I'll keep that in mind." This time her smile seemed forced. She stood up, tossing her empty cup into the trash. "Well, I should get going. It was nice talking to you. I'll give you a call when I know what my plans are."

"Good luck with the search," he said, shaking hands with her as they parted.

"Thanks. See you soon, I hope."

He felt a quickening inside at the thought. It wasn't just that he wanted to get to know her better, it was the sense of connection he felt with her. They were kindred spirits, no matter the different circumstances which had landed them both in the same place. Like him, Alice Kessler knew that the world was full of dark corners and jagged edges.

CHAPTER FIVE

MAY 1942

Eleanor Styles awoke to the sound of the dogs barking in the kennel outside. Even in her groggy, half-aware state, she could tell from the high pitch of the barking that it wasn't a deer or raccoon that had gotten them so worked up, more likely a visitor of the two-legged variety. Immediately she was out from under the covers and on her feet. A glance at the clock by the bed told it was half past eight. So late! Usually, she was up while it was still dark, but she'd had trouble sleeping the night before and hadn't dropped off until well after midnight.

She reached for the chenille robe draped over one of the bed's four squat posts. Normally it would have been hanging in the closet, but with her husband Joe off fighting in the Pacific, she'd allowed some things to slide. It was enough just keeping the rest of the house tidy and looking after her daughter—not to mention the dogs and chickens and victory garden to tend to. It was only in the bedroom she'd shared with her husband of over ten years that her presence had gradually begun to assert itself, like the blackberry vines that had swallowed up the fence along the drive in Joe's absence. Shoes were tucked willy-nilly under the bed and her work overalls, still damp from bathing the dogs yesterday, slung over the padded rocker. Various tubes of ointment and bottles of worming tablets littered the dressing table where powder and perfumes had once stood, and on the nightstand, in place of Joe's *Reader's Digest*s, sat a war bond pledge booklet leftover from last week's drive, a book on canine diseases, and an article clipped from the newspaper listing the new blackout rules.

She padded barefoot over to the window, peering out through the fog of her breath on the pane at a car pulling to a stop in the yard, a dark green Packard she didn't recognize. She was unaccustomed to visitors, especially at this hour, and with the new war restrictions, fewer automobiles were out on the road these days. Was it some sort of official business? She grew cold at the thought. But, no, the man getting out of the car—youngish, dark-haired, wearing khakis and a shirt rolled up at the sleeves—didn't look like a messenger. And if it was bad news, he'd have been an odd sort to deliver it, smiling like he was, as if in pleasant thought, his face tilted up to catch the sun. As he made his way up the front path, she noticed that he walked with a limp. From the practised way he hitched the leg along with scarcely a break in stride, it appeared to be an old injury.

She let out the breath she'd been holding and forked a hand through her hair, which only made it crinkle into a halo about her head, hair the reddish brown of the madrona tree under which the man was now pausing to look around. Then a new thought occurred to her: If it wasn't bad news about Joe, it might be official business of a different sort. In a panic, her eyes flew to the barn, which had been converted into a kennel with an outdoor run enclosed in chicken wire, where at the moment all six dogs were barking madly at the stranger's approach. Catching a movement in the window of the small, furnished room off the dogs' quarters, she wondered if her visitor had noticed it, too. Was that why he was taking his sweet time? Her heart lurched at the thought as a knock sounded.

Putting on her slippers and tightening the belt on her robe, she went to answer the door.

"I'm sorry. I hope I didn't wake you," the man apologized, noting her attire. "I saw the smoke from your chimney and thought . . ." He craned his neck to look upward.

"I keep a fire burning at night," she said. With the wartime ban on oil, even coal was scarce, and the old house Joe's father had built was so poorly insulated that even in the spring months she had to maintain the fire 'round the clock.

"William McGinty," he introduced himself, touching his brow in a jaunty two-fingered salute. "And you must be Missus Styles." She nodded, thinking the name sounded familiar—had they met before? No, she would have remembered that face. He was around her age, thirty or so, tall and whippet-lean, with startlingly blue eyes and a shock of black hair that didn't seem to want to stay put. He looked harmless enough, but that did nothing to put her mind at ease. He could be one of Sheriff LaPorte's henchmen, for all she knew. As captain of the home guard, LaPorte had made it his business to mercilessly hound anyone suspected of being an enemy agent. Like poor Otto Haller, the town's elderly German druggist, who'd been forced to sell his pharmacy and move off the island, his life had become so intolerable. *What would La Porte do if he were to ever get his hands on a real fugitive?* she wondered, feeling an icy chill pass over her.

"What can I do for you?" she asked. Her tone was pleasant, but she kept a hand on the doorknob and an eye on the shotgun propped just inside.

"I was driving past and happened to notice your sign. I was wondering if you had any puppies for sale." The man named William gave her a wide smile that engaged his whole face, a face that might otherwise have seemed austere in its stark angularity.

Some of the tension went out of her shoulders. "Not at the moment, but I have a litter due any day. Was it a male or a female you were looking for?"

"Either one will do. I don't really have a preference." He shifted from one foot to the other, favoring his good leg. Glancing past him, she could see the clothesline hung with yesterday's wash, which she hadn't gotten around to taking down: a sheet billowing in the breeze, a red-checked tablecloth with a burn mark where she'd gotten a bit too assiduous with the iron one time, a corduroy pinafore of Lucy's, a flannel nightgown, several slips, a blouse.

And a pair of men's skivvies.

A jolt went through her. Oh God. How could she have been so careless?

Had he noticed it, too? He might not have thought anything of it, but if he were to learn later on that her husband was off fighting overseas, he'd wonder what she'd been doing with men's underthings on the line. And if he should happen to make mention of it, and word got around . . .

Her gut clenched at the thought. In an attempt to keep him from noticing anything was amiss, she asked, "What made you decide on a Border collie?"

"No particular reason." He made a vague gesture with his hand. Like I said, I saw your sign and . . . well . . . I just thought . . ." He seemed suddenly unsure of himself, as if it had only been an impulse.

"They're working dogs," she informed him, speaking more sharply than she'd intended. "If all you want is a pet, I'd suggest another breed." She had no patience for people who acquired puppies the way they did toys, often discarding them when they ceased to be amusing or proved difficult to housebreak.

But he took no offense. His smile only broadened, deepening the creases that bracketed his wide, expressive mouth like parentheses. She was struck once more by how blue his eyes were; a shade so deep it was almost purple, the color of the crocuses that had recently begun pushing their way up out of the spring-thawed ground. "If you don't mind me saying so, Missus Styles, you sure have a funny way of doing business," he said, in that tone of easy familiarity that made it seem as if he were taking liberties somehow. "If you've got something against me buying one of your puppies, just say so, and I'll be on my way."

She relented a bit, saying in a less frosty tone, "My dogs aren't boxes of soap powder for sale. I want to be sure they go to good homes."

"In that case, why don't you come have a look at mine. I'll introduce you to my wife and son. We live out on Cove Road." So he was married, which surprised her for some reason. "Actually, I wanted the puppy for my son. He has a birthday coming up in a few weeks. He'll be nine."

Eleanor gave in to a small smile. "I have a daughter the same age. They must be in the same class at school. I'm surprised we haven't met before."

"Usually it's my wife who picks Danny up from school," he explained. "Most afternoons, I'm holed up in my studio."

She knew then why his name had struck a chord. "Wait. I know you. You're *that* William McGinty. The artist." There was usually a mention of him in travel articles about the island, and recently there had been a show of his paintings at Darvill's bookstore downtown. "I've seen some of your work," she told him.

"What did you think?" he asked, as if honestly interested in her opinion.

She thought back to that day. She'd been out shopping, with a half hour or so to kill before she had to pick up Lucy from school. She'd ducked into Darvill's, where she'd become captivated by the display of paintings on the walls, landscapes mostly, scenes from around the island, rendered in such detail it was almost as though she were looking at them through a window. "There was one in particular, of a deer standing at the edge of a clearing, with snow falling. It was so . . . I can't explain it . . . It made me feel so peaceful." She felt herself warming. "But what do I know about art? I only know what I like."

"When you get right down to it, that's all that really matters," he said.

She sensed he was being sincere. Before she knew it, she was saying, "Would you like to come inside? I was just about to put on some coffee."

"If you're sure it's no trouble," he said.

"No trouble at all." Eleanor had an ulterior motive. She was hoping to distract him long enough for Lucy to wake up. A whispered word to her daughter to take the wash down, and he'd be none the wiser about the skivvies. "You take yours black, I hope," she asked as she ushered inside. "I'm fresh out of milk. It's such a long way into town, I usually wait until I have a whole list of things to get."

"Black is fine," he said. They were passing through the hallway on their way to the kitchen when he paused to take a closer look at one of the family photos lining the wall, of Joe in uniform. "Your husband?"

"Yes." She felt a little flutter of panic. Suppose he put two and two together and realized men's clothing didn't belong on the line with her husband away at war.

"A Navy man, I see. Where's he stationed?"

"Last I heard, the Philippines. It's hard to keep track. Sometimes weeks
go by without a single letter, then we'll get a whole bundle all at once."
Even then, the letters would be riddled with holes where the censors had
snipped out any mention that might be considered classified information.

"He's fighting for his country. I guess that's all anyone needs to know."
William's expression hardened all of a sudden. "I tried to enlist, but they
wouldn't take me on account of this." He rubbed a hand over his bum
leg, grimacing a bit as if it pained him, though she sensed whatever pain
he felt was more mental than physical. With nearly every able-bodied
man his age off fighting in the war, he had to feel the frustration of being sidelined.

"How did you injure it?" she asked, looking down at his leg.

"I broke it skiing when I was in college. Shattered near every bone.
Damn thing never healed right."

"Consider yourself lucky." The words flew out of her mouth, and she
saw a flicker of surprise cross his face. It was an unpopular view in these
times, to say the least, but hadn't there been enough death and destruc-
tion due to war? Myra Brookbank had lost her son Ernest in the battle
of Tobruk, and just last week Nellie Gerard had gotten word that her
husband's plane went down at Bataan. Eleanor herself prayed nightly for
Joe's safe return.

"I'm not sure my wife would agree. These days, having your husband
around can be a bit of a liability." He spoke lightly, but she caught a trace
of bitterness in his voice. Eleanor was appalled. What kind of wife
would prefer a dead hero to a live husband?

They exchanged a meaningful look; then they were in the kitchen and
she was lighting the stove, the moment past. "Have you had breakfast?"
she asked, as she was filling the coffee pot at the sink. "I could fix you
something to eat."

"Thank you kindly, but I've already put you to enough trouble," he replied, looking ill at ease, as if he weren't used to being fussed over. But she didn't miss the look of longing on his face as he eyed the fresh-baked loaf of bread on the counter.

She insisted, "It's no trouble at all. I may be short on supplies, but the one thing I have plenty of is eggs." She explained that she'd invested in laying hens, intending to sell the eggs to earn extra cash, but that due to rationing, she and Lucy ended up eating most of what the chickens laid.

She went to the icebox and took out a bowl of eggs, some still dotted with feathers. At the kitchen counter, with its cracked porcelain tiles that Joe hadn't gotten around to replacing, she took out half a dozen of the largest ones, wrapping each one in newspaper before placing them in a paper sack. She handed the sack to William. "These are for you take home. No charge," she said, when he offered to pay. He started to protest, but she held firm. "It won't do you any good. I always get my way."

"Always?" One of his brows quirked up in bemusement.

"Most of the time, anyway." Eleanor smiled, almost forgetting her purpose in inviting him in. It felt good, having him in her kitchen—another adult, with whom to observe the morning rituals. It made her feel less lonely. "It's easier when the only one around to talk back is less than half your size." Though Lucy could be as stubborn as she at times.

They talked while she sliced bread and set strips of bacon in the pan to fry. William told her a story about his son, when Danny, at age five, had been learning to ride a bike, falling off it more times than he'd stayed on but not quitting until he'd gotten the hang of it. Listening to him speak, the tender look on his face making it appealing in a way that had nothing to do with good looks, Eleanor felt suddenly self-conscious of her own appearance as she moved about the kitchen in her robe and slippers, setting out plates and napkins, pouring coffee.

She was about to go wake Lucy, who was showing no signs of rousing on her own, when the back door swung open unexpectedly. Eleanor froze at the sight of Yoshi. The boy looked equally startled. Seeing the strange man seated at the table, he came to an abrupt halt in the doorway, the

empty bucket he was carrying, to collect the scraps he mixed with the
dogs' food, slipping from his hand and clattering to the floor. Eleanor,
jolted into action, clapped a hand over her mouth, letting out a muffled
cry.

William leapt to his feet, planting himself in front of her, as if to
shield her. But she was quick to clear up any misunderstanding. "It's not
what you think. He's . . . he's a friend. It's all right, Yoshi," she reassured
the boy. "You're safe." She swung around to fix William with a hot gaze,
as if challenging him to dispute it. The moment hung there like something swollen about to burst, William staring at Yoshi as comprehension
slowly sank in, Eleanor praying that he wouldn't do anything rash. At
last, the silence was broken by William.

"What's your name?" he asked the boy, not unkindly.

Yoshi, his head hung low, didn't reply. At eighteen, he was a boy still,
with a boy's slight build and unevenly cut bangs that hung in a ragged
fringe over his forehead.

"His English isn't very good. But he's harmless, I promise," Eleanor
explained, tripping over her words in her haste to get them out. Yoshi
had worked for Joe on his fishing boat before the war, an orphan who'd
become almost like a son to them. After Joe had gone off to battle she'd
allowed Yoshi to continue sleeping on the boat, paying him to do odd
jobs for her. Then, last month, word had come that Japanese Americans
were being shipped off to internment camps, and she'd taken the bold
move of hiding him in her barn. When Sheriff LaPorte had come looking for Yoshi, she concocted a story about his having run off. She knew
the risk she was taking—she could be charged with treason—but she
couldn't bear the idea of Yoshi being locked up when he'd done nothing
wrong.

She cast William a beseeching look. "You won't tell anyone, will you?"

Until now she'd entrusted the secret only to Lucy. Could she honestly
expect this man whom she'd only just met to keep it as well? A man not
fit to wear a uniform who, for all she knew, might wish to snatch some
glory for himself, if only to become a hero to his wife.

Her heart sank as William slowly shook his head, wearing a look of disgust. *We're done for*, she thought. *This is where he'll tell me I'm a disgrace to my husband and my country.* She felt herself growing angry in anticipation of his words. What right did he have to judge her, or Yoshi? He hadn't seen how hard the boy had worked for little pay, hauling in nets that would have bowed the backs of men twice his size. Even now, he remained grateful for every scrap, uncomplaining in the face of what most people in his shoes would consider an outrage. And what was so patriotic, anyway, about locking up innocent people. *American citizens*, for God's sake. Everyone who went along with it ought to be ashamed. And if she were to be punished for it herself, then at least she'd go down with a clear conscience.

When William spoke, it was a moment before his words filtered through the storm of recriminations gathering in her head. "What kind of a person do you take me for?" he asked.

"I wouldn't know," she replied, thrusting her chin out.

"You know I like dogs." He retrieved the bucket Yoshi had dropped and handed it to him. When William straightened, she saw that he was smiling.

Eleanor remained distrustful nonetheless; she wasn't a woman to be won over by a charming Irishman with a quick wit and a ready smile. "So does Hitler, from what I've heard."

"You really think I'd turn him in?" He flicked a glance at Yoshi.

"You might see it as your patriotic duty."

"Patriotic?" He snorted in contempt, and turned to address Yoshi. "You can relax. I won't breathe a word of this to anyone." The boy eyed him in confusion as William went on, more sternly, "But you're going to have to be a lot more careful from now on. If it had been someone else who'd spotted you, it would have been a different story." Yoshi nodded slowly in comprehension, looking very pale. Eleanor could imagine how it must have happened, the boy not quite awake yet, stumbling around back, not paying attention to William's Packard parked in the drive.

He's right, she thought: They'd grown lax, and had nearly paid a steep price for it.

"I . . . am most grateful to you, sir," Yoshi managed in his halting English.

"You can drop the 'sir.' My friends call me William. Or just plain Will. Now," he turned toward Eleanor, his stern look melting, "why don't you set an extra place for Yoshi here? Seems to me we ought to get to know each other if I'm going to be in on this."

"In on what?" she asked warily.

"You don't expect me to just walk away and pretend I never saw anything?" he said in disbelief.

She tensed. "What are you suggesting?"

"Well, for starters, you don't want people asking questions, so I'll be bringing your supplies from now on," William went on, as if he'd had it all figured out in the time it had taken her to catch her breath. "All it would take is one nosy Parker wanting to know why you're buying enough to feed three people for the home guard to come sniffing around."

"Wouldn't they be suspicious of you?" she asked.

He shrugged. "Maybe, but I have nothing to hide."

She tipped her head back to look up at him, this tall, austere-faced man with his great head of black hair in need of combing. She felt a curious mixture of gratitude and lingering mistrust. Why was he doing this? He barely knew her, and Yoshi was a complete stranger.

"Even so, if you were to get caught, you could get into a lot of trouble," she cautioned. "Why stick your neck out?"

"Maybe it's to make sure there's a pup in that litter with my name on it," he said, breaking into a grin. "Or maybe I'm just plain crazy. Who knows? But you're hardly in a position to refuse."

"So much for winning every argument." She threw up her hands in surrender.

Without further ado, William sat down at the table, unfolded his napkin, and smoothed it over his lap. "I take mine over-easy," he said, as she cracked eggs into the skillet.

A minister's daughter, Eleanor had been nineteen and pregnant with another man's child when she married Joe Styles. He was ten years older than her and nobody's idea of a catch. A working man, a fisherman by trade, with hard, callused hands and a face as creased and weather-beaten as an old tarp. But he had one shining attribute: He'd gladly taken her when no one else would. In fact, Joe acted as though she were the one bestowing this great favor on him, not the other way around, never once making her feel dirty or ashamed, as her parents had. And when Lucy was born, he'd loved her, too, as if she were his own. So Eleanor told herself it didn't matter that she felt no passion for him. Passion was what had gotten her into trouble. Joe had given her something far better: unconditional love.

But there was no denying that her life with Joe wasn't what she'd imagined for herself when she'd graduated from secretarial school at the age of eighteen. Her and only first job had been with the firm of White and Conner and though a whiz at typing and shorthand, she'd been utterly ignorant about the ways of the world. Her new boss, on the other hand, was a man of the world. Lowell White was handsome in the louche way girls found so thrilling, with an air of late nights and cocktails and ruby-lipped women that swirled about him like smoke from the cigarettes that were forever dangling from the corner of his mouth. He was also an astute businessman. Most of his family's fortune had been lost in the Great Depression, but Lowell had used that very slump to his advantage, little by little buying up real estate while it was dirt cheap and selling at a profit when prices went up. By the time Eleanor had come to work for him, he already owned vast tracts and was rich beyond imagining, with the grandest house on the island and a fifty-foot yacht.

Lowell may have been known to have a weakness for pretty girls, but he never showed Eleanor any special favoritism. In fact, her first few weeks on the job he seemed oblivious to her charms: the small waist and high, full bosom; the long, shapely legs that had driven the boys in school to distraction. She might have been a filing cabinet or the blotting paper on his desk, for all the attention he paid her. That he found her unattractive didn't bother her at first, but as the weeks wore on, she began taking special care with her appearance, choosing her most flattering outfits, using a shade of lipstick darker than the one she normally wore, and arranging her tumble of russet hair atop her head like Betty Grable's. Male clients began to take notice—a few even asked her out on dates, which she, of course, refused—but her boss remained oblivious.

So when one morning he stopped at her desk and told her he had some business on the mainland and needed her to come along, she thought nothing of it. She was pleasantly surprised when, on the ferry ride, he chatted amiably with her the whole way. He was different away from the office, warm and personable, asking about her family and her interests. Before long he knew her entire history, brief and uninteresting though it was: that she lived with her parents in the rectory behind the Episcopal Church, and that she had an older sister named Lillian, who'd gotten married last year, a wedding at which Eleanor had been maid of honor.

By the time the business was wrapped up, the ferry they'd planned to take back was long gone. With several hours to kill until the next one, Lowell offered to buy Eleanor dinner. She readily accepted, imagining it would be just a quick bite at a local tavern, but the restaurant he took her to was fancy, the kind her parents couldn't have afforded. Seeing the red-jacketed waiters gliding past, the damask tablecloths set with silver and crystal that gleamed in the candlelight, she felt as if she'd walked onto a Hollywood set. If it hadn't been for Lowell, steering her lightly by the elbow as they were escorted to their table by the captain, an intimidating-looking man in a starched shirtfront who'd greeted Lowell by name, she'd have turned right around and left. Instead, she found herself sinking into the chair Lowell pulled out for her and nodding mutely when he asked if she'd like some champagne.

After her second glass, she began to feel more relaxed. Never mind that the other girls in the office might get the wrong idea. She knew this wasn't what it looked like; Lowell was being the perfect gentleman. So it came as a shock when, halfway through the meal, he leaned across the table and said, quite matter-of-factly, "You're very beautiful, you know."

Eleanor was speechless. "Thank you. That's nice of you to say," she replied primly when she'd recovered her wits. She lowered her head so that her hair, worn loose that day, fell forward to cover her cheeks that were flushed with more than the champagne.

"I'm sure you hear it all the time," he went on in the same matter-of-fact tone, "but I have a feeling you don't believe it. I just wanted you to know it's true. You are. Breathtaking, in fact."

She peeked from behind the curtain of hair to find him eyeing her with an almost fatherly bemusement. Usually when men said such things, they wanted something in return. But Lowell White seemed content merely to have her bask in the glow of the compliment.

"I . . . I don't know what to say," she stammered.

He smiled, and lit a cigarette. His eyes that in daylight could sometimes appear world-weary were seductively heavy-lidded in the candlelight. "When you're a little older, my dear, you'll know that it's a beautiful woman's prerogative to say nothing at all."

"I'm eighteen!" she protested, which only made him smile all the more.

"Eighteen," he echoed, as if marveling that he himself had ever been that young, though he couldn't have been more than forty. "Well, that calls for another glass of champagne."

It might have been crushed diamonds he was pouring, the way it sparkled as it swirled up from the bottom of her glass. And why was it she'd never noticed before how perfectly shaped his hands were? Square and manly as his physique, which was muscular from sailing. Not like her father's pale, narrow ones that, splayed against the nubby black cover of his bible, resembled dove's wings. Lowell's thick brown hair, combed back in Brilliantined waves that to a less discerning eye might have given him the appearance of a slick salesman, had sprung several curls that looped down over his forehead. She found herself wanting to brush them back, thread her fingers through his hair. *What's come over me?* she wondered, aghast at the direction her thoughts had taken.

On the ferry ride home, she imagined it was her all her doing when he slipped an arm around her shoulders and, later on, when he gently kissed her good night. She must have led him on in some way, though in her tipsy state she wasn't exactly sure how. At the same time, she felt excited by his attentions, even knowing that her parents would disapprove. She hadn't felt this way with any of the men she'd gone out with before: the deep thrill that had shot down through her belly when Lowell's gaze had lingered a beat too long or his fingers had brushed hers. Each precious moment of the evening she tucked away to be savored later on; she was reluctant even to wash away the smell of cigarette smoke that lingered in her hair when she woke the next morning.

But amazingly, at work, it was as if nothing had happened. Lowell barely glanced at her when he walked in, greeting her only with a curt, "Good morning, Miss Miner," as he breezed past on the way to his office. All morning she was close to tears, wondering what she could have done or said that had put him off. It wasn't until she was leaving work at the end of the day, after having stayed late to type a letter, that everything fell into place.

She was making her way down the stairwell when she looked behind her and saw her boss, hurrying to catch up with her. They were alone, and when he reached her he grabbed her by the shoulders, roughly almost, pushing her back against the wall and kissing her. Not a gentle kiss this time, but a deep and passionate one that involved his tongue.

"God. I've been going out of my mind all day," he breathed. "It's been torture."

Eleanor trembled, wanting for him to go on kissing her and at the same time feeling she was in over her head. He was her boss, after all. And suppose the stories whispered about him were true? "I . . . I thought I'd done something to make you angry," she said in an unsteady voice.

"Angry?" He gave a short, guttural laugh, as if at the absurdity of such an idea. "My God, I could barely concentrate. You've been driving me crazy, looking like that. Even your perfume . . ." He snatched up a handful of her hair, burying his face in it with a groan. "It was all I could do not to walk over there and kiss you in front of everyone." She shivered, both thrilled and scandalized at the thought.

After that, they began slipping away together after hours. She'd lie to her parents about working late or going to the movies with friends and she and Lowell would go on long drives, or he'd take her out on his boat. It was exciting at first, but after a while she began to grow impatient. Why did they have to sneak around? It wasn't as if they had anything to hide. If it became a problem at work, why, she'd just find another job.

But when she timidly broached the subject, he claimed he was only being cautious for her sake. "I could set you up with another job just like that," he said, with a snap of his fingers. "But that wouldn't solve the problem."

"What problem is that?" she asked, half dreading his reply.

"Your parents. Think how it would look to your father, him being a minister and all. His innocent young daughter under the spell of some middle-aged rogue. Believe me, it's best we take it slow."

"Maybe if he got to know you a bit first, it'd be easier when I told him," she suggested.

"What exactly did you have in mind?" asked Lowell, with a sardonic arch of his brow.

"I don't know." Flustered, she cast about in her mind. "You could start attending services on Sunday, for one thing. If they knew you were a churchgoing man. . . "

Lowell cut her off with a laugh. "Darling, you're forgetting one thing. I'm hardly the God-fearing type."

Eleanor kept her mouth shut after that, fooling herself into believing he would eventually do the right thing.

The night she lost her virginity they were out on his yacht, anchored off one of the uninhabited islands that dotted the sound, where there was only the moon to bear witness. He took his time, plucking away at her inhibitions stitch by stitch until at last they came unraveled. He stroked her as she shivered with pleasure, parting her legs as gently as if they were petals on a rose. When he finally entered her, she scarcely felt the pain. Even then he took his time, making love to her the way she'd always dreamed, not giving in to his own pleasure until he'd brought her to climax. As Eleanor fell back against the cushions and tilted her head up to the sky, the stars spilling across it seemingly within reach, she knew at last what it was to desire and be desirable. The fact that she hadn't waited until they were married seemed inconsequential. He would make an honest woman of her before long, as soon he got around to popping the question.

Worry didn't begin to creep in until several more months had gone by without his making a single move in that direction. She began to notice things, too—how he would sometimes seem distracted when they were together, staring off into space while she chattered on. Then there were the personal calls he'd take in his office with the door shut, when she'd steal glimpses through the glass and feel a flutter of uneasiness noting the expression on his face: the same one he'd worn when romancing her. She told herself she was imagining things—he loved *her!*—but it grew harder to dismiss her fears. When her nineteenth birthday came and went without so much as a card from Lowell, she was crushed.

The hurt and worry made her physically ill. She was tired all the time and sick to her stomach. The fact that she'd missed a period didn't overly concern her—she'd always been irregular—but when another month passed with no sign of it, she could no longer deny what she'd known deep down: She was pregnant. A week later, a doctor in Anacortes confirmed it.

It should have put her into a panic, but Eleanor felt a strange sense of peace come over her instead. Now there would be no more putting off the wedding. Her parents would be upset when she told them, of course, but once they calmed down and saw how good it could be, they'd come around. Lowell, too, once he got over the shock, would be happy about the baby. How could he not be? Hadn't he told her a thousand times that he loved her?

And, when she broke the news to him, she thought at first that's how it was going to go. They were at the office after hours. Everyone else had gone home, so they were alone. Lowell took her in his arms, soothing her. "My poor darling. Don't you worry. I know a doctor who'll take care of it, no questions asked."

Horrified, she jerked free of his arms. "You want me *kill* our baby? How could you even suggest such a thing?"

He smiled, as he had countless times before, at her provincial ways, but this time it wasn't out of affection. "That's being overly dramatic, don't you think. Really, Ellie, this sort of thing happens all the time. If every woman felt as you do, there would be far more unwanted children in the world."

"But . . . I . . . I want this baby." She hadn't fully realized it until the words were out, and now she faced him in defiance.

"Unfortunately, it takes two, and I have no intention of becoming a father just yet," he said, lighting a cigarette, and peering at her through the smoke that swirled lazily up around his head.

She began to weep, still believing it was the shock making him act this way. "You can't mean that. I caught you by surprise, is all. But don't you see? Maybe it's all for the best. And it's not as if we weren't going to be married anyway."

"You thought I was going to marry you?" Perched on the edge of his desk, he laughed in disdain, stubbing out his cigarette. "I'm sorry if I ever gave you that impression, but frankly, my dear, it never occurred to me. And if you insist on having this child, I'll deny it's mine."

"But everyone knows—" She caught herself, realizing that no one knew about them, in fact. That had been part of his game plan all along, the reason he'd kept their relationship a secret, in the event of something like this. But if anyone had been in the dark, it was her.

Lowell scribbled a number on a slip of paper and handed it to her. "When you're willing to see reason, call this number. Don't worry about the expense, I'll take care of it."

But she didn't have to think about it, not for one second. Furiously, she crumpled the piece of paper and tossed it onto the floor.

Lowell pushed himself off his desk, saying, "You're a fool then. If you want to do it the hard way, you'll be doing it without me. We're through, Eleanor. Now why don't you pack up your desk and go." Cruel words that pelted her like icy raindrops.

Eleanor couldn't believe the man she loved, whose child she was carrying, was the same one standing before her, eyeing her so coldly. She covered her face with her hands and wept softly into her fingers, blocking out his hurtful presence. At the sound of his footsteps fading into the hallway, she sank slowly onto her knees, as if in prayer. She didn't know how long she knelt there—minutes, hours?

When she finally dragged herself to her feet, she felt stiff and achy all over, as if from a beating. In a kind of trance, she gathered up the personal items off her desk. As she walked out the door for the last time, she felt not only stupid but dirty, knowing *she* would be the one whispered about around the office in the days to come. Lowell's latest conquest. Discarded like all the others when she'd ceased to amuse him.

Her parents, when she told them, were more devastated than angry. Her father became an old man overnight, stooped and gray, while her mother drifted about, wan and red-eyed, avoiding Eleanor whenever possible. They wore their daughter's shame as if it were their own, telling no one, fearful of being judged.

One day Eleanor's father took her aside. "I've been praying long and hard on this, Ellie, and I think God has an answer for us." As though her pregnancy were as much his dilemma as hers. "Do you remember Joe Styles?" She nodded, vaguely recalling him from Sunday services, a square-set man with a weather-beaten face who sang the hymns in a deep baritone that carried above everyone else's voices. "Well, I spoke to him about you," her father went on, a grim set to his jaw, as if determined to get through this before he could weaken and change his mind. "I told him about your, uh, circumstances, and he thinks he can help. He's a good man, Eleanor. You could do a lot worse."

It had dawned on her then what her father was getting at: He expected her to marry this Joe Styles, a man she only knew to say hello to. Eleanor would have been mortified, if she hadn't been so numb. Instead, she only sat there in silence, listening to her father go on about Joe's attributes: He didn't smoke or drink, and that he owned his own fishing boat and a house to boot. She had such a sense of disconnect, she even found herself agreeing to meet with the man. A quick and painless death would have been equally welcome, but that wasn't an option.

The meeting took place the very next day, in the rectory parlor, with her parents no doubt hovering on the other side of the closed door. If Joe Styles had said one wrong thing, it never would have gone beyond that. If, for instance, he had told her he was willing to overlook the fact that she was pregnant with another man's child, in essence spoiled goods. Instead, Joe said only that he would be honored to have her as his wife, and that his home would be hers if she wanted it.

"It's not much. But it's solid and there's an extra room, for when the baby comes," he said of the house his father had built with his own hands. "As for that, you should know I'd treat it no different than if it was my own."

Seeing Joe perched on her mother's Hunzinger chair, surrounded by the porcelain figurines Verna collected, the old expression, bull in a china shop, came to mind. Joe wasn't so much a big man as one who gave the impression of brute strength, with those great meat hooks of hands and thick, veined neck that thrust from his shirt collar like that of a straining ox. Even the suit he was wearing was all wrong, shiny in spots, the jacket too tight, as if it had been purchased years before the daily effort of hauling in his catch had added twenty or thirty pounds of extra muscle to his frame.

Even so, Eleanor, recalling her father's words, had thought, *I could do worse*. Joe was a man of simple means and education, and not much to look at, but he was kind-hearted, and what more could she ask? It wasn't as if she were in a position to be choosy. The fact that she didn't love him and couldn't imagine ever feeling for him what she had for Lowell, didn't greatly concern her. This was a decision based not on want but on need.

"And if I were to agree to this, what would you be getting out of it?" she asked bluntly.

His face reddened at the implication, and he seemed at a momentary loss for words as he stared down at his thickly callused hands, curled loosely on his knees: a man clearly unaccustomed to expressing such intimate thoughts. "I'd want only what's freely given," he said at last, shyly bringing his head up to meet her gaze. "If you don't see fit to share my bed, I'll respect that." Looking into his eyes, she saw that he was sincere.

"I can't make any promises," she told him. "Why don't we see how it goes?"

"Does that mean . . . ?" Something flared in his eyes making her wonder if he'd had ideas about her long before her father had approved him.

"Yes, I'll marry you." She rose to her feet and extended her hand—as if it were a business deal they were concluding. Pride prevented her from showing any gratitude. She couldn't bear having him think that he was doing her any favors. "Would the Sunday after next be convenient?"

Over the years she had come to love Joe, in her own way. He was a good husband, better than she deserved, and a considerate, if uninspired, lover. More than that, he was utterly devoted both to her and to Lucy, who couldn't have been any dearer to his heart if she'd been his own flesh and blood. And as far as Lucy was concerned, the sun rose and set by her papa. After Joe shipped out, Lucy had moped about for days. Since then, she'd written to him religiously, at least once a week, often tucking into the envelope some remembrance of home—a pressed flower or a bird feather, a pretty picture cut out of a magazine. While Eleanor's letters were filled with the minutiae of daily life—the chimney she'd had to have patched and the rain that was wreaking havoc with her garden, the new pastor who'd taken over when her father retired—Lucy wrote about how heartbroken she'd been when her best friend moved away and the boy in school she secretly had a crush on. Each letter ended with her telling him she was counting the days until he came home and that she prayed every night for God and President Roosevelt to look over him.

On the morning of William McGinty's serendipitous visit, Eleanor woke her daughter after he had gone, singing out, "Rise and shine, sleepyhead, breakfast is getting cold."

Lucy sat up in bed, rubbing her eyes. She lifted her head to sniff the air, smelling bacon, which was odd. Usually they only had bacon on Sundays. "Do we have company?" she asked.

Eleanor grew warm, thinking of William and the surprising turn of events brought about by Yoshi's ill-timed appearance. "Now what makes you think that?" she replied briskly.

"I thought I heard voices." Lucy yawned, stretching her arms over her head. In her flowered nightgown she looked small and defenseless, her bare feet scratched from running shoeless about the yard. Eleanor saw that her silky auburn hair was clumped in back where a rat's nest had formed.

She used her fingers to work out the knots, ignoring Lucy's attempts to squirm out from under her. "A man was asking about puppies," she said.

Lucy grew still at once. "Is he going to buy one?" she asked hopefully. Already, at nine, she was aware of how thinly stretched their finances were. She turned her face up to Eleanor, small and heart-shaped, with Eleanor's green eyes and Lowell's olive complexion.

"We'll see. I told him to come back when Belle has her litter," Eleanor replied. "Now come on, get dressed. We have lots to do today." She shooed her daughter out of bed, then before Lucy had gone two steps she impulsively pulled her close, hugging her tightly. "That's for being so good. And for keeping our secret." She drew back to look her daughter gravely in the eye. "You know what would happen if you ever told?"

Lucy nodded, her expression solemn. "Yoshi would have to go away to a bad place, where they keep people locked up."

"That's right," Eleanor said.

"But why? He didn't do anything wrong." Lucy had been wrestling with this for some time, ever since Eleanor had explained about the internment camps to which Japanese Americans like Yoshi had been sent, in the wake of Pearl Harbor. To Lucy, it had been like finding out there was no Santa Claus, learning that the president she revered could do something so unjust.

"It's because of the war," Eleanor gently explained once more, stroking her daughter's head. "People are afraid of anyone who looks like the enemy. They think if they lock up all the Japanese we'll be safe. But they're wrong. The reason men like your papa are fighting this war is so the world will be free of just that sort of thing."

Lucy nodded slowly, her eyes welling with tears. "I wish Papa could come home."

"I know, baby. Me, too," said Eleanor.

But at the moment she wasn't thinking about Joe. Her thoughts were with the tall stranger who'd appeared on her doorstep earlier that morning. William McGinty. The compassion he'd shown went deeper than mere chivalry. Maybe he felt a need to prove his worth. Whatever the reason, fate had thrown them together, and after these long months of struggling to hold it together, with money tight and the ever-present worry of her secret getting out, it was a relief knowing she had someone to share the burden.

—

William McGinty was no stranger to hardship himself. During the Great Depression his parents had lost everything they owned. His father's prosperous dry goods business went under and the bank foreclosed on their two-story brick house in Omaha. With little more than the clothes on their backs, the family had had no choice but to go to live with his mother's sister and her husband, in McCredie Springs, Oregon, where the population numbered in the hundreds and moonshine was the main source of income. They were good, hardworking people, his aunt Lillian a nurse in a doctor's office and his uncle Ripley, Uncle Rip for short, the owner of a small plumbing supply business, but they weren't much better off financially. Uncle Rip's business was barely staying afloat and Aunt Lillian's salary only covered the rent on their two-bedroom house. William's mother and father and three sisters had all slept together in one room, while William and his brother shared the sofa-bed in the living room.

The two boys had always been close, but the tight quarters, coupled with the fact that their parents were so preoccupied with finding work that William and Stu were left to their own devices for the most part, made them inseparable. William, at nearly fourteen, had taken it upon himself to instruct his eleven-year-old brother in the art of manly pursuits, such as throwing a curve ball and shooting at tin cans with his BB gun.

It wasn't long before William graduated to Uncle Rip's old squirrel rifle. When his uncle took him hunting, William turned out to be as good at hitting small animals as tin cans. The difference was that he took no pleasure in the kill; it was only to put food on the table. And with so many hungry mouths to feed he couldn't afford to be what his uncle referred to, usually accompanied by a well-aimed wad of spit, as "soft."

One day when William was showing off to his brother, shooting at Coke bottles lined up along the fence, a shot went astray, catching Stu in the arm, near his shoulder. Stu crumpled to the ground, blood bubbling up from the wound and quickly soaking his shirtsleeve. For a terrible moment William thought he was dead.

In a panic, he sank to his knees before his brother, ripping off his own shirt and pressing it to the wound. "Oh, God, Stu. Please. Say something."

Stu's eyelids fluttered open and his mouth twisted in a pained smile. "Nice shot," he'd managed.

By the time William had half dragged, half carried Stu back to the house, his brother had lost consciousness again. The doctor Aunt Lillian worked for was summoned and, after an examination showed it was only a flesh wound, the bullet was removed. Everyone breathed a sigh of relief when the doctor pronounced that Stu would survive, none the worse for the wear.

Two days later an infection set in. This was before penicillin was readily available, especially in remote areas such as theirs. All they could do was apply poultices and hope for the best. But Stu only got sicker, developing a raging fever, his arm swelling to the size of an Easter ham. Throughout the ordeal, William, certain that it was all his fault, seldom left his brother's side, praying for the Lord to take him instead, should it come to that.

But either God hadn't heard his prayers or He'd had other plans for William. On the fourth morning of Stu's delirium, William woke from the doze he'd fallen into, as he'd sat slumped in the chair at his brother's bedside, to find that Stu was dead. His parents and sisters, aunt and uncle, were all gathered round, his mother weeping inconsolably, lost in her grief, while his sisters clutched to her with their faces buried in her skirt.

But William refused to believe it. *"No!"* He'd reared up and grabbed his brother's lifeless body, shaking Stu as he did on mornings when his brother pretended to still be asleep. "Stu!" he'd cried, half out of his mind. "Come on, this isn't funny. You're scaring everybody. Quit it now. I'm serious. If you don't get up off this bed right now, I'm going to . . . to . . . "

"That's enough, son." A heavy hand had fallen on his shoulder, and William had twisted his head up to find his father gazing down at him, a bleak, unforgiving look on his face that remained with William to this day, burned into his memory. His father hadn't spoken a word of blame, not then or in the days that followed, yet there was no question in William's mind as to whose fault it was. Even if his parents could have forgiven him, he knew he could never forgive himself.

He'd vowed then and there never again to pick up a gun, and all these years he'd kept that vow. It hadn't been a sacrifice until just recently, but with the war on, he had mixed feelings, memories of Stu mingling uneasily with his guilt at not being able to fight for his country.

And it wasn't just his guilt he had to contend with. Martha had lost her beloved younger brother at Pearl Harbor, and now her patriotic fervor knew no bounds. It wasn't easy for her, with every other man in uniform, to have her husband enjoying the relative comforts of the home front. She fought against those feelings, he knew, conscious of the fact that he wasn't to blame, but deep down she was ashamed of him. As a result he found it equally hard to be around her, and these days was quick to seize upon any excuse to get out of the house, like this morning when he'd volunteered to drive Danny to the meeting place for his Scout campout this weekend.

Now, as William guided his Packard over the rutted dirt road leading to the cove, he wondered how Martha would feel about his aiding in the concealment of a Japanese boy who in her eyes might well be an enemy

agent. He didn't regret his impulse—how could he? It was the only decent thing to do—but there was no getting around the fact that it wasn't
just himself he was putting at risk.

She deserves to know. But somehow he couldn't imagine telling Martha
about Eleanor Styles and the strange scene at her house. Martha wouldn't
understand why he hadn't immediately reported it to the authorities.
And if he couldn't confide in his own wife, what did that say about their
marriage?

Not that Martha wasn't a good wife in other ways. She was lively and
intelligent, and seldom refused him in bed. Only lately he could tell her
heart wasn't in it. She was so involved in the war effort, selling bonds and
organizing drives, it occupied her thoughts to the exclusion of all else,
except Danny, as if with each fresh display of patriotism she was com-
pensating for the very visible presence of her husband in wartime. In this
new, khaki-colored world, the only uniform William wore was his paint-
spattered shirts, and his only contribution to the war effort so far the
posters he'd done for the State Department, advertising war bonds.

For several minutes after he'd pulled into his yard and shut off the engine, he remained in his car, gazing out at the cove below. The tide had
gone out, leaving a glistening gray flat marked with pylons where Deets
had staked out his oyster beds. They'd lain fallow for some months now, a
reminder that his neighbor, like so many others, was off fighting overseas.
Other than that, in this peaceful spot, the war might have been a distant
rumor. Farther out at sea, a fishing boat was pulling in its net, gulls
swooping overhead, diving for scraps. If the weather held, he thought,
he'd set up his easel outdoors. In winter, when the sun's path was low, their
house lay almost perpetually in the shadow of the neighboring hills, but
this time of year, on nice days, the morning sun poured over the landscape, allowing him to capture its richly varied hues.

He got out of the car and started toward the house. He could see
Martha through the front window, polishing the breakfront where the
good china was kept. Her pale yellow hair was pinned up in back, the
curls on her forehead bobbing with each vigorous circular swipe of her

arm. She was frowning, as she often did when intent on some task, as if no amount of elbow grease would amount to an end result that would meet with her satisfaction.

But something else was on her mind at the moment, he could see as soon as he walked in. "Sorry I'm late," he said. She smelled of lemon oil and the perfume she wore, something flowery that made him think of the sachets she tucked into drawers. "I stopped to ask about a puppy."

She seemed too preoccupied to comment, though earlier they'd argued about whether or not Danny was old enough for the responsibility of owning a dog. "Have you seen the paper?" she asked, straightening, using the back of her wrist to push a wisp of hair from her forehead.

"No, why?" he asked.

She snatched up that morning's edition of the Bell Harbor *Sentinel*, which must have been delivered while he was out, and brandished it at him. "General Wainwright surrendered!"

"God help us." He stared morosely at the headlines announcing the fall of Corregidor.

"Do you know what this *means?*"

"It means that thousands more of our boys are now prisoners of war," William said, with a sinking heart, as he scanned the fine print.

"Well, yes, of course," she said, with an impatient sweep of her hand. "But it also means the Japs could *win* this thing. There'll be no stopping them now. We're barely hanging on in Midway as it is. Honestly, anyone would think MacArthur was asleep at the wheel!"

"I'm sure he's doing all he can."

She glared at him, as though he and MacArthur were in cahoots somehow, before conceding with a sigh, "I suppose you're right. It's just that I feel so helpless sometimes." She looked anything but. She was fully made up, wearing a dress that showed off her neat curves. No housecoat and slippers for Martha McGinty. If she were all alone in the house, she would be as perfectly turned out as if expecting company. He had to admire her for it. At the same time, he found himself thinking of Eleanor Styles, the silken brush of her slippered feet as they'd moved over the worn linoleum in her kitchen and the way her sleep-scrambled hair that was the color of autumn leaves had caught the sunlight slanting in through the window.

"You're doing your part," he reminded her.

"What good does it do to peddle war bonds and organize scrap metal drives when the whole world is going up in flames?" she demanded, her pretty face flushed with indignation. "I swear, if I were a man . . ." She caught herself before she could complete the sentence. "Never mind, you must be hungry. You've been gone for *hours*. Let me fix you some breakfast."

"I've eaten, thanks," he told her.

"I thought you were only dropping Danny off," she said, frowning in puzzlement.

William wrestled once more with his conscience, wondering if he dared trust her with Eleanor's, and now his, secret. Once upon a time they'd talked about everything.

But all he said was, "I told you, I stopped to ask about a dog. You know the house down the road from the old Pritchard place, the one with the sign out front? The woman invited me in for coffee and ended up feeding me. She sent me home with these." He held up the sack of eggs. "Anyway, she said she'd let us know in a couple of weeks."

"Know what?" Martha asked distractedly, bent once more to her polishing.

"About the puppy." A note of impatience crept into his voice. "I told her we were hoping to have it in time for Danny's birthday."

Martha shook her head, her lips pursed. "I swear, Will, you and that boy will be the death of me one day. As if I don't have enough to do as it is without a puppy to clean up after. No, don't give me that look. You know perfectly well whose shoulders it will fall on."

"I'll make sure Danny knows it's his responsibility," William said.

"All right. I'll think about it," she said, in the tone that meant she'd already made up her mind.

"He's a good boy. He doesn't ask for much." William remained firm. Usually he let her have her way, it was easier than getting into a fight, but this time he wasn't going to give in.

She relented with a sigh. "I suppose I don't have a choice, do I? It's two against one."

"The beauty of democracy." He smiled, giving her apron strings a playful tug.

Her scowl melted, and in that instant he caught a hint of the woman he'd married, following a whirlwind courtship in Paris, where at the time he'd been taking classes at the Sorbonne and she was the *au pair* for the children of a wealthy Parisian couple.

He was heading off to his studio out back when she called after him, "I'm going into town in a little while to pick up those pamphlets for the blood drive. Do you need anything?"

He paused, frowning in thought, then shook his head.

What he needed couldn't be found in any store. He didn't even have a name for it, this new restlessness of his. Like when he was a boy and he'd known it was time to leave home. Except he had no desire to leave this place. As he was stepping out the back door, he paused to look around. The snug cottage, with its exposed timbers and wainscoted walls, its stained-glass transom that cast a mosaic of light over the freshly waxed floorboards, was smaller than Martha would've liked, but on winter nights with the wind howling in off the bay and rain lashing at the windows, there was no cozier place.

It wasn't until he was letting himself into his studio that he realized the moment had passed for him to confide in Martha about the Japanese boy holed up at the Styles place.

CHAPTER SIX

PRESENT DAY

"I made your favorite—pork roast and scalloped potatoes," Lucy said as she led the way into the kitchen. "We've got to fatten you up. You're much too thin." She paused, turning to Alice with a look of consternation. "Are you getting enough to eat?"

"You mean, can I afford a decent meal?" Alice replied. She'd arrived on Sunday ahead of the others, so she and her mother were alone for the moment; they could speak frankly. "Don't worry, Mom. I'm not destitute yet." She still had almost ten thousand dollars of her grandmother's money left, though even with her watching every cent it wouldn't last long at this rate.

"Just remember, Rome wasn't built in a day." Lucy reached for Alice's hand and gave it a little squeeze. Ever the optimist. She would have given pep talks to a prisoner on death row.

"Don't worry," Alice assured her. "I'm not giving up. I can't afford to."

"Well, the important thing is, you're home. That's all that really matters." Lucy ran a thumb under one moist eye, saying with an apologetic laugh. "I'm sorry. I promised myself I wasn't going to do this. It's just that it's so good to have you back. I just wish your father . . ." She let the sentence trail off, her look of bright optimism momentarily fading. In the living room that had been done over in Alice's absence, with lots of ruffled chintz and pickled pine, devoid now of any masculine touches, she looked small and lost.

"I know, Mom. I miss him, too." Alice blinked back tears of her own. "It seems so strange not having him here." She looked around, as if half expecting to see her father.

"Don't you start, too!" Lucy scolded, shaking a finger at her. "This is supposed to be a celebration. Goodness, I can't remember the last time we all sat down around the dinner table." Though of course she knew how long it had been: exactly nine years. "Now why don't you finish setting the table while I check on the roast. Your sister should be here any minute."

She didn't mention Jeremy. When Lucy had called to invite him, he'd said he'd try to make it but that he didn't think he could; he had a test to study for. Alice hadn't given up hope, though. Maybe he would decide to come at the last minute. She set an extra place at the table just in case.

When she was done setting the table, she went into the kitchen to see what else she could do to help. She found her mother on her knees, wrestling a casserole dish from the jumble of pots and pans in one of the lower cupboards.

"Need a hand with that?" Alice asked, smiling at the picture her mother made.

"No . . . I've got it . . . it's just that it's wedged in with all this other—" With a clatter of pots, Lucy straightened, rocking back on her heels, the casserole dish triumphantly in hand.

Lucy set her to work dicing onions for the ratatouille she was making to go with the pork roast and potatoes. Alice, watching her move about the kitchen, was relieved to see her mother looking so well. The last time Lucy had visited her at Pine River, she'd been little more than a bundle of bones loosely wrapped in skin. She couldn't even be bothered with her hair, which she'd worn short, in a wash and wear cut that made her look less like a perennial schoolgirl than a very old elf. But last year's

hip replacement had made it easier for her to get around. She'd also regained most of the weight she'd lost after Alice's father died. Now, with
her face filled out and her hair in a shining silver bell, she was her old
self again.

"I've taken up water aerobics. Doctor's orders," Lucy informed her,
when Alice commented on her appearance. She paused to shake her head
in wonderment. "A year ago if you'd told me that three afternoons a
week I'd be paddling around in a pool with a bunch of old ladies, I'd
have laughed at the idea. But I should have done this years ago. It's done
me a world of good." She scooped up the onions and dumped them into
the oil sizzling in the frying pan, adding cut up peppers and eggplant.
She handed Alice a spatula, saying, "You stir that while I finish making
the gravy."

"Smells good," Alice said, when her mother pulled the roast, crackling,
from the oven. "Do you know, this is the first meal I've looked forward
to since I got back. At Pine River, the closest thing we had to gourmet
was creamed chicken on toast."

Lucy didn't respond, except to shoot her a pained look.

Alice, reminded of the scene at Denise's, felt her back go up. "What?
I'm supposed to pretend I was away on a long trip? Mom, I did time. I
ate my meals off plastic trays and worked in the prison laundry." She
held up hands that were still chapped and raw. "I had to ask permission
for every little thing, to get my hair cut, to have a reading lamp in my
cell, even for the luxury of being able to step outside for some fresh air."
After days of having doors slammed in her face, every one a reminder of
where she'd been, she wasn't in the mood to play this game of pretending
that chapter in her life was closed. Prison was a fact of her existence; it
had changed her in ways that were unalterable. Her family was going to
have to accept that if they wanted her back in the fold.

"Well, dear, that's all behind you now. Why dwell on it?" Lucy spoke
with forced cheer, becoming suddenly animated, bustling to and fro, rattling pans and running the tap, exactly as Denise had done when ducking
the subject. Alice suppressed a sigh. Some things never changed. Whatever

had happened to make her mother so fearful of any unpleasantness—the privations she'd suffered as a child during the war or the trauma of her beloved Papa coming home a changed man—it was as irreversible as the experiences that had shaped Alice.

Alice remembered a time when she'd been that way, too. Wasn't that what had led to her nervous breakdown? She'd kept up a brave front after David's death, until finally the effort had caused her to come apart and scatter like so many Pick-Up sticks. But prison had cured her of faking it. There, if you lived in a dream world or put on airs, the other inmates would beat it out of you, literally in some cases. Honesty, even when raw and hurtful, had been the only means for survival.

Suddenly she found herself missing her friend Calpernia. Calpernia King had a nose for bullshit as finely tuned as a Geiger counter, and would regularly bust Alice's chops when she tried to paint a pretty picture or give someone the benefit of the doubt. Like the time Alice had defended her cell mate, Sonia, after Sonia was accused of stealing. "You can talk all you like, don't mean shit. You just blowing smoke out yo' ass," Calpernia had sniffed, her corn-rowed head thrown back, her hands planted on her ample hips. A week later, Alice had found a book and pen she'd been missing under Sonia's mattress.

Lucy glanced at the clock. "I don't know what's keeping your sister." She lowered her voice to add confidentially, "Between you and me, I think she's stretched too thin. This Spring Hill business has her in a such a tizzy, she doesn't know whether she's coming or going. With all those rallies and whatnot, I'm surprised she has any time at all for her family."

"What about Gary? Where does he stand in all this?" Alice asked. She'd gotten the feeling he was only paying lip service to the cause in the interests of family harmony. Also, that all was not as it seemed when it came to her brother-in-law.

"Between a rock and a hard place, that's where," Lucy said, casting her eldest daughter a dark look. "He has certain responsibilities. It's not just his wife he has to please." A reminder that Gary, as deputy chief of police, wasn't exactly a free agent.

Meanwhile, the debate over Spring Hill raged on. The environmental group Denise was active in had filed a lawsuit, temporarily blocking the planned development, in what was shaping up to be a bloody battle. At the center of it all stood the mayor. Owen White had been the one to champion the development early on and put pressure on the planning commission, claiming it would create new jobs and pump much-needed money into the local economy. But there were those, like Denise, who weren't seduced by his promise to set aside a portion of the land for a wildlife preserve. What kind of wilderness would it be, she'd wanted to know, with condos and tennis courts a stone's throw away?

Alice's thoughts turned to Jeremy and the day they'd hiked up the ridge at Moran State Park. She hadn't seen him since then. He hadn't returned any of her calls, and when she'd spoken to Randy about it, her ex-husband had cautioned her not to expect too much right off the bat. It hurt knowing Jeremy was so close yet so far from reach, but she told herself this couldn't go on forever. Eventually something would have to give.

Meanwhile, she would continue on. Just as her grandmother had before her. Nana had been a survivor, too, taking care of her sick husband while single-handedly raising a child and putting food on the table. If it hadn't been for her resourcefulness, the property would have been sold off years before land on the island became so valuable. Alice's only regret was that Nana hadn't seen any of that money in her lifetime. It was only after her death, when the house was sold, that its value was realized.

"By the way, you know who I ran into the other day? Colin McGinty," Alice remarked, as she sprinkled herbs over the ratatouille now simmering on the stove. She warmed at the memory of their chance meeting at the library, recalling how at ease she'd felt in his company. She turned to her mother. "You knew his grandfather, didn't you?"

"A long time ago," Lucy answered, stirring flour into the pan drippings. "When I was a little girl, he used to come by the house to visit Mama. They were quite friendly at one time, as I recall."

Friendly enough for him to have painted her portrait, thought Alice. "I'm surprised Nana never mentioned him. Did they have a falling out at some point?"

"Oh, I don't think it was anything like that. It was just . . . well, you know it was the war and, after Papa came home, she had her hands full." Lucy paused in the midst of her stirring, her expression softening. "Poor Papa. I wish you could have known him before. He was the most wonderful man. Always smiling, and never too busy to make time for me and Mama."

"I could see that," Alice said, gently laying a hand on her mother's arm. The grandfather she'd known had been out of it most of the time, but he'd had his good days when glimmers of the old Joe would surface.

Nana had been devoted to him, too, but Alice had sensed that her grandmother had a hidden side to her heart. Could she have been in love with William? It was easy to imagine how it might have happened, the handsome artist and the young wife with her husband overseas. Theirs wouldn't have been the only such wartime romance. But if Lucy knew anything about an affair, she wasn't letting on. Either that, or she refused to believe her parents' marriage had been anything but storybook. Knowing her mother, Alice thought it was probably the latter. Lucy would deny the *Titanic* was going down as it was sinking.

Lucy shook her head slowly, staring sightlessly ahead. "Hard to believe they're all dead now. The years go by so quickly."

"Speaking of which, you know the portrait Mister McGinty did of Nana? Well, it seems he left it to Colin," Alice informed her.

Lucy brought her gaze back to Alice. "Is that so? I'd heard something to that effect, but you never know what to believe, with all the talk that's been going around."

"Anyway, I told Colin I'd never seen the actual painting, and he said I was welcome to stop by anytime I liked." On the spur of the moment, she suggested, "Why don't you come with me?"

Lucy appeared hesitant, and before she could reply Denise blew in, with Gary and the kids, apologizing for being late. Still no sign of Jeremy, though. When it became clear that he wasn't going to show, Alice quietly removed the extra place from the table, trying not to feel too disappointed.

Dinner was more relaxed than the other night at Denise's. Now that Alice's niece and nephew had gotten used to her, Taylor didn't stare at her as if she had two heads, and Ryan no longer acted as if she were company for whom he had to put on a polite show. Tonight, he might have been any teenager, teasing his sister and cracking jokes at the table. Alice, for the first time since she'd gotten back, felt like she was a member of the family once more.

Gary was the one false note. He was his usual jovial self, but it seemed forced somehow, as if he were only going through the motions. Alice sensed that he was uneasy around her, and she wished there was a way of reassuring him that she wasn't going to do anything to embarrass him. She had no intention of violating her parole and, if any of the townsfolk gave her a hard time, she wouldn't pick a fight. She didn't want any trouble; she only wanted to get on with her life.

"I heard you applied for the position at Svenigan's," he remarked at one point. Alice must have looked surprised that he knew, for he explained, "Ina mentioned it to me the other day when I stopped in for a bite to eat."

"Unfortunately, I didn't get the job." Alice kept her voice light, not wanting to spoil the meal with a lot of negative talk. Anyway, the opening had been for a waitress, and she was hoping to get closer to the kitchen, where she might actually get to do some cooking.

"Too bad. They could have used you," Gary went on, in that falsely hearty tone, as he helped himself to another slice of the roast. "In fact, I told Ina if she doesn't find someone soon, she's going to have to start giving customer discounts for the wait time."

Alice put her fork down, eyeing him across the table. "She told me the position had been filled."

Silence fell. Gary looked embarrassed. Even Denise was quiet for a change, the kids taking her cue and ceasing their chatter as well. There was only the clink of forks as Taylor and Ryan became suddenly fixated on what was on their plates.

"Would anyone like more potatoes?" piped Lucy brightly, at last.

For once, Alice was grateful for her mother's ability to act as if everything were normal in the face of even the most awkward situations. She smiled and held out her plate, though she'd lost her appetite. "Thanks," she said. "Everything's delicious, Mom. You really outdid yourself this time."

They were cleaning up in the kitchen afterward when Denise took Alice aside, saying, "I'm sorry about what happened—with Svenigan's, I mean. Gary didn't mean anything by what he said."

"I know he didn't," Alice replied lightly. "Anyway, it's no big deal."

"It *is* a big deal." Denise's cheeks reddened. She looked as if she were about to cry . . . or tear someone a new one. "They should have hired you. It's unfair. It might even be illegal." Her expression darkened. "In fact, I have half a mind to tell Ina Svenigan where she can put her marionberry pie."

"It's all right," Alice said, more firmly this time. "I can take care of myself."

"I know you can. It's just . . . people can be so petty sometimes. I hate to see you go on being punished for something that happened so long ago," she said.

"Relax, okay? I'm not one of your charity cases." Alice had meant it jokingly, but it came out sounding hard.

Denise drew back, hurt. "I wasn't implying . . . "

Alice laid a hand on her arm. "I know you weren't."

A corner of her sister's mouth turned up in a rueful smile. "Okay. I'll back off. But you have to promise to let me know if you need anything. Even us tree huggers need a warm body to rescue once in a while."

"I promise. But no hovering, okay?" Alice handed her a dish towel. "I'll wash. You dry."

Two weeks into her job search Alice was more discouraged than ever. She couldn't even get hired to do temp work. It all boiled down to one

thing: she was unemployable. A convicted felon who also had a reputation for being mentally unstable.

It had been another long and frustrating day when she dragged herself
to the eatery near her motel where she often took her meals, one rainy
day in November, a hole-in-the-wall seafood shack that specialized in
fish-and-chips, appropriately named Fisherman's Catch. She'd gotten to
know the owners, Captain and Baby, who were a couple of real charac-
ters. Baby, so nicknamed because of her tiny stature—she couldn't have
been but five feet tall—was perpetually bellowing out orders to her huge,
shambling ox of a husband, a retired merchant marine turned short-
order cook, in a voice loud enough to bring the whole fifth division running. Yet for all her hollering, he was devoted to Baby, and she to him.
"Ain't she something?" he'd say with a chuckle, gazing in worshipful ado-
ration at his red-headed scrap of a wife, as she bustled about, issuing orders, like the world's smallest commando.

With her customers, Baby liked to take charge as well and she saw to it
that they got what they needed, even if it wasn't what they'd ordered: a
kind word when someone was down, a piece of advice for those in need
of counsel, a kick in the ass when called for. What Alice liked most
about coming here was that Baby and Captain treated her no differently
than they would anyone else. They had to know her history—who on
this island didn't?—but from the way they acted it was obvious they
couldn't have cared less.

"What'll it be, hon, same as usual?" Baby rasped today.

"Soup of the day and the toasted cheese sandwich," Alice said, like
always.

Baby's response never varied either. "Sure you wouldn't like a piece of
pie to go with that? On the house."

Alice summoned a smile as she handed back the menu. "Thanks, not
today. Any more freebies and I'll be putting you out of business."

"That wouldn't be hard to do." Baby leaned in to confide, "Between
you and me, we're not exactly getting rich off this place. Fact is, we're
barely staying afloat. Some retirement, huh? Me and the Captain, we had

it all planned out. Sell when the time was right and move someplace warm, where it don't rain eight frigging months out of the year." She cast a doleful glance out the window, where the rain was pouring down in sheets, her brown nugget of a face crinkled in irony. "So much for that pipe dream."

"You'd really sell this place?" Alice was surprised. Baby and Captain seemed as much a fixture as the cloudy marine-varnished tables and fishing net that drooped from the ceiling, studded with dusty sand dollars and starfish so ancient they looked as if they'd turn to dust if you so much as touched them. "In a heartbeat," Baby replied without hesitation. "If some poor sucker was fool enough to make us an offer, we'd be out of here so fast you wouldn't see us going."

"I'd buy it, if I had the money," Alice said, indulging in a little wishful thinking.

She'd always fantasized about opening a restaurant. Randy used to joke that she was a frustrated chef, with all the dinner parties she'd thrown. Even when she wasn't entertaining, she'd loved experimenting in the kitchen, dabbling in herbs and spices and condiments the way a painter would with his palette, creating new recipes and coming up with fresh takes on old standbys.

The years at Pine River had been especially hard in that respect, because she'd missed all those flavors, missed having her senses come alive at the scent of a roast chicken pulled crackling from the oven or a simmering pot of fish chowder filled with meaty chunks of wild salmon and halibut. Prison food all looked and tasted the same: dull, pasty, gray. The first thing she'd done upon her release was to head straight for the nearest market, where she'd bought a hunk of aged Cheddar and a bag of sweet, juicy, Washington apples.

Baby's bright blue eyes narrowed speculatively. "You would, would you? Well, in that case you're as crazy as they say. No offense," she said, holding up a hand to silence the protest forming on Alice's lips. "You and I both know there's plenty of folks in this town got nothing better to do than wag their tongues. I don't pay them no mind. But ain't no getting around the fact that even if you had the cash, you'd need the customers. And, hon, you're about as popular as Typhoid Mary right now."

"Well, there's no point in discussing it." Alice felt embarrassed to have even brought it up. "It was just wishful thinking."

"Tell me about it. That's how me and the captain ended up in this leaky boat." Baby gave a rueful grin, showing a row of teeth that looked too big for her mouth, and too perfect, to be anything but dentures. "Now look at us. Too old and broke to swim for shore."

"But you love it!" Alice protested.

"I'll tell you something," Baby said, with a sigh. "You leave work every night smelling of fry oil, the bloom kind of wears off after awhile. Sure, I love it, but I hate it, too. And damn if my feet ain't begging me to quit. They're like a couple of old mules tired of pulling."

"Why *don't* you just sell it then?"

"Simple. No takers." The old woman gave a sanguine shrug. "Last time we put it on the market, half the folks who looked at it passed on account of its being too close to the highway for them to tear it down and build one of those fancy new McMansions in its place. The other half were smart enough to know what it took us ten years to figure out: You can't make money on a restaurant this far out of town when the tourist season's only four months out of the year."

"People will make a special trip, if it's worth their while," Alice reasoned.

Baby shot a look toward the kitchen, where Captain was pulling a batch of sizzling fries from the Fry-o-later. "Don't get me wrong, I love the old coot, but he ain't exactly Paul Prudhomme."

"I didn't mean . . ." Alice started to say.

"I know you didn't, hon." Baby gave her a motherly pat on the shoulder. "But let's be honest. You're not here for the food. You come 'cause it's cheap and there's lots of it. That, and ain't nobody gonna give you a hard time, not as long as I have anything to say about it."

Alice smiled. "I'll take that over oysters Rockefeller any day."

Baby eyed her thoughtfully for a moment. "Look, if you're serious about this, maybe there *is* a way." With a quick survey of the room first to make sure no one needed a refill or change for their bill, she sat down opposite Alice. It was between lunch and dinner hours, so the place was pretty empty, just an old man sipping coffee at the counter and a couple at one of the other tables getting ready to leave. "Course, I'd have to take it up with the Captain, but suppose, just for the sake of argument, that you were to make us an offer. Say, whatever you could afford right now, and so much a month once things get rolling."

"I don't know. I hadn't really thought it through," said Alice, her pulse quickening nonetheless. *This is crazy*, she thought. *Why are we even discussing it?* Even so, she found herself asking, "What sort of money are we talking about?"

"Just enough to tide me and the Captain over. We have our eye on a condo in one of those Sun City retirement villages. With our social security and a little extra thrown in, we ought to be able to swing it. There's just one thing . . ." Baby leaned in, her eyes narrowing. "How good a cook are you?"

Alice smiled. About that at least she had no doubts. "It's been a while, but I don't think I've lost my touch."

Baby nodded, seemingly satisfied. "Then I take back what I said before. If the food's great, they won't care who's in the kitchen, even if it's Typhoid Mary."

"You're serious about this?" Alice eyed her in disbelief.

"Serious as a heart attack."

"I couldn't offer you much as a down payment. Four or five thousand at the most." Even that would be stretching it.

Baby frowned. "That's less than I was counting on. But we might be able to work something out."

Suddenly it hit Alice: This could really happen. And was it really so crazy? With all she'd been through, it seemed fitting in a way, as bizarre as the circumstances that had brought her to this point. As she and Baby talked, a plan began to take shape. They settled on five thousand down, with the rest of the money to be paid in monthly installments once revenue was coming in. All of it subject to Captain's approval, of course, which they both knew was just a formality. Baby wore the pants in the family; Captain merely did as he was told.

The more they discussed it, the less crazy it began to seem. Alice calculated that she'd have just enough left over to upgrade the place a bit and purchase supplies. Money would be tight, but she might, just might, be able to swing it. And at least she wouldn't have to worry about finding a place to live. The restaurant came with a small one-bedroom apartment upstairs, which currently Baby and Captain shared with their three cats. There was just one catch . . .

"I'll need to apply for permits and there are people who could make it tough for me," she said, thinking of Owen. She wasn't being paranoid in imagining that he was behind a number of the doors that had been slammed in her face. At one place where she'd applied for an office job and been turned away, she'd learned later on that the building was owned by none other than Owen White. And at another, a souvenir shop on Harbor Street, a sympathetic young clerk had murmured to her as she was leaving, *A word of advice: Watch your back.*

Baby knew at once who Alice was referring to, and she sniffed in contempt. "You mean Mister Big Shot?" Clearly she had her own thoughts about the mayor. "I wouldn't let him worry you. You look like a woman who can take care of herself."

Hearing her own words to Denise coming out of Baby's mouth, Alice smiled. Even so, she knew she'd be making herself vulnerable. And even if she managed to get the permits and pass all the inspections, there were other ways of putting a restaurant out of business. One bad review or rumored report of food poisoning, and she might as well pack it in. At the thought, she felt some of the wind go out of her sails. But what was the alternative? If she were to walk away from this, she might as well admit defeat altogether.

No, she thought, something in her rising up in rebellion. *If prison didn't kill me, this won't.* Those first few days at Pine River, she'd been certain she wouldn't make it through the week. But she had. And the week after that, and all the ones that followed. She'd endured the numbing sameness of each day that began with the rude alarm clock of their automated cell doors clanging open and shut, the thousand and one indignities, the indifference and sometimes cruelty of the COs, the human tide of flotsam and jetsam that washed in and out over the years, and, hardest of all, being separated from her family. And nine years later she'd emerged with her sanity and her dignity intact. A survivor. If she could survive that, she could survive anything.

It all came together with stunning swiftness. Their lawyer drew up the papers and before the ink was dry, Baby and Captain were on their way to the airport, headed for Arizona. It wasn't until the dust settled and reality set in that Alice realized what a daunting task she faced. The kitchen, in keeping with the décor, hadn't been updated since the Nixon administration. The ancient Garland stove needed work as did the old Hobart mixer, and on the captain's last day, as if it too had decided to throw in the towel, the temperature control on the Fry-o-later had given out, nearly causing the grease to catch fire. As for the overall structure itself, according to the engineer's report, the plumbing was touch and go, the roof leaked in spots, and there were areas of dry rot.

How was she going to pay for all this? And even if by some miracle she managed to whip the place into shape, there was still no guarantee she'd be able to make a go of it. She'd have to generate business somehow. And how could she do that when she couldn't even afford to hire help?

That particular prayer was answered in the form she least expected. Several days into her new career as restaurateur she was in the kitchen scraping an archeological dig's worth of grease off the stovetop grill when the phone rang. A familiar voice greeted her at the other end.

"Hey, girlfriend."

"Calpernia!" Alice broke into a grin. She hadn't spoken to her friend since she'd left Pine River. "How did you find me?"

"Your sister."

Alice recalled now giving her Denise's number. She remembered too that Calpernia was supposed to have met with the parole board and was eager to find out how it had gone—a little apprehensive as well, knowing her friend's propensity for shooting off her mouth. "God, it's good to hear your voice. In fact, I was going to call you. You beat me to it."

"You'll never guess where I am."

"I give up. Where are you?"

"Bus station. They must've decided I wasn't a threat to society no more, cause, girl, you is talking to a free woman." Calpernia gave her signature laugh, low and rich and just a tad dangerous, like a cool ride on a hot day in a stolen car.

"Oh, Cal. That's great news. I'm so happy for you." Alice had been keeping her fingers crossed. "So what now?"

"I'm on my way to my daughter's. My baby, Shaniqua, she got her own place now, down in L.A. Still can't believe she all grown up and all, with a family of her own."

"You must be excited to see her." Alice recalled when Calpernia's daughter, eighteen at the time, had been pregnant. Shaniqua had visited regularly up until then, but after the baby came the visits had tapered off. Calpernia had yet to meet her nine-month-old grandson.

"Girl, you don't know." Her friend heaved a sigh, one that held years worth of pent-up longing. But, of course, Alice did know. She'd felt the same way herself, about Jeremy. Now, weeks later, what had she accomplished other than to drive him even further away? "But I ain't staying," Calpernia went on. "Week or two, and they'll be ready to throw me out. Shaniqua say the place so small you can hear the neighbors fart."

"Where will you go after that?"

"Hell if I know. But I'll work something out. How bout you? How you doing, girl?"

"Okay, I guess." Alice spoke in a measured tone, not wanting to burden Calpernia with her worries. "It's good to be back, but it's tougher than I thought it would be."

"Those white folks giving you a hard time?" It was an old joke between them.

Alice smiled. "Let's just say it's been interesting."

"What's happening with your boy?" Calpernia asked more gently.

"Not much." Alice gave her a quick rundown, feeling the old guilt wash in. Jeremy was right about one thing. Whatever her reasons, the fact was she hadn't been there for him all those years.

Calpernia listened without comment, then said, "He'll come around. He just hurtin,' is all."

"I hope you're right." Shaking herself loose from those thoughts, Alice said in a more upbeat tone, "Sorry, I don't mean to sound so gloomy. It's just that I'm a little overwhelmed right now. Did my sister happen to mention that I bought a restaurant?"

Calpernia let out a gasp. "No way. For real?"

"I'm afraid so. There's just one problem. Well, two actually. I'm up to my eyeballs in debt and I don't have the faintest idea what I'm doing." A crazy idea popped into her head and before she knew it the words were out. "Hey, how would you like to go into business with me?"

Calpernia laughed so long and hard, Alice thought she must be attracting attention at the other end: a two-hundred-pound black woman who looked mean enough to wrestle you to the ground and steal your purse while she was at it, busting her gut at some bus station pay phone. Finally, she stopped laughing and blew out a breath. "Damn. You one crazy white girl, you know that?"

"I'm serious," said Alice, realizing as she spoke that she meant it.

"Yeah, and how you gonna pay me? You said yourself, you broke."

"All right, I can't pay you much. But as soon as the money starts coming in, I can give you a share of the take."

"I ain't too good at arithmetic, but even I knows what zero out of zero come to."

"Look at it this way, we have nowhere to go but up."

There was a long silence at the other end. Just as Alice was beginning to think they'd been disconnected, Calpernia cut loose with another one of her hot-wired laughs. "Oh, hell. What do I got to lose?"

For a moment Alice wasn't sure she'd heard right. "You mean you'll do it?"

"I didn't say that." Calpernia was at once her old prickly, imperious self. "It ain't like I got no prospects of my own. Only one reason to do this that I can think of, and that's to save yo' skinny white ass. You don't know squat 'bout running no restaurant."

"Neither do you," Alice pointed out.

"That ain't the point. I been around. I know shit."

Alice laughed. "Well, I won't argue that."

"Long as you know you ain't my boss," Calpernia grumbled.

"Agreed."

"All right then. Now that we got that straight, when do I start?"

They talked for a few more minutes, making tentative plans, until Calpernia's bus pulled into the station. As she hung up, Alice recalled her first introduction to the force of nature known as Calpernia King. It was in her first week at Pine River and Calpernia had approached her in the yard, tailed by her posse, a huge, hulking presence, as black as the asphalt over which her broad shadow was cast. Her head a swirling mass of braided hair extensions, the tiny beads woven into them rattling like dice as she'd leaned into Alice's face, the whites of her eyes amid all that blackness seeming to jump out at Alice.

"Yo, white girl," she'd drawled. "What you in for, holding up a Mister Softee truck?" She'd eyed Alice with a disdain reserved for someone so far beneath her, it was a wonder she was even speaking to her. One of the women in her posse, a skinny black girl with bad teeth and tracks on her arms, had snorted in derision, as if trying to curry favor, and Calpernia had swung around to glare at her, demanding, "What you laughing at, bitch?"

Alice had said nothing; she'd just walked away.

That had set the tone for the next few months. Calpernia in her face, Alice doing her best to ignore it whenever she could. Until one day, after they'd been working alongside each other in the laundry for several weeks, somebody had said something that had struck Alice as funny and she'd started to laugh. She'd laughed herself silly, doubled over, tears

streaming down her cheeks, until the CO on duty that day, a tough old
lesbian named Rusty, had given her a look that meant she'd better get
down to business or else. The trouble was, Alice couldn't seem to stop.
Rusty had been on her way over, wearing a menacing look that spelled
trouble, when all at once Calpernia had walloped Alice on the back, then
grabbed her arm and squeezed it hard until the laughter died. She'd
called over to Rusty, "Don't you worry bout her. She a'ight now."

After that, according to the unspoken code of prison relations, she
and Calpernia were friends. As they got to know each other, Alice
learned that the 'tude, as it was referred to among the black inmates, was
merely a front and Calpernia's reputation largely the product of her own
invention, a means to ensure respect and a minimum of harassment. If
she was in for attempted murder, it had only come after years of abuse at
her live-in boyfriend's hands, the final straw being when she'd found him
messing with her then fourteen-year-old daughter. She'd waited until he
was passed out drunk, then beaten him bloody with a tire iron, breaking
nearly every bone in his body and leaving him blind in one eye. The
boyfriend had pressed charges, denying all her allegations of abuse, and
she'd had the further bad luck of being tried by an eager beaver young
prosecutor looking to make his bones. Her court-appointed lawyer had
attempted to persuade him to go with the lesser charge of aggravated assault, but Calpernia had stubbornly refused. In the end, she'd gotten
eight to ten, same as Alice.

Now it occurred to Alice that not everyone would see Calpernia as
she'd come to: a person you could count on to always have your back,
who for all her rough edges had a kind of nobility to her. In this mostly
white, middle-class community, she would blend in about as well as a
pimped-out Cadillac in a parking lot full of SUVs. But if anyone could
handle it, Calpernia could. And at least Alice would have company if she
went down in flames.

Denise came over later in the week to help out. Together they spackled
the holes in the walls and ceiling where Alice had taken down the nautical prints and fishing net with its hundred-year-old catch, after which
they spent the day painting the kitchen and dining area. When they were

finally done, they stood back to admire their handiwork. "I think we've earned ourselves a cold beer, don't you?" said Denise, idly scratching at a spot of dried paint on her nose. "Man, I don't know when I've worked this hard."

Alice fetched a Coors from the fridge for Denise and a Diet Coke for herself. Denise commented when Alice returned, "I forgot. You can't drink." She grimaced in sympathy. But Alice found her sister's making mention of the fact that she was a parolee encouraging. It meant the stigma had worn off somewhat, in Denise's mind.

Denise pulled chairs out from under the plastic tarp covering them. They were sipping their drinks, gossiping about old times, Denise with her feet propped on the rungs of Alice's chair, when the bell over the door jingled and Gary walked in. "Hey, ladies." He stopped to look around, giving a low whistle. "Wow. That's some job you did. I don't know when I've seen this place look so good."

"Yeah, you can hardly smell the grease," Denise said. "I swear I used to break out just walking into this place. You could practically see the fat globules in the air."

"Old Cap'n, though, he made a mean fish-and-chips," Gary recalled fondly. He gave Alice a long, considering look. "You sure you know what you're doing? No disrespect, but you haven't exactly had much experience running a restaurant. It takes more than a fresh coat of paint."

Alice wondered if his concern was that of a caring brother-in-law . . . or if he was hoping she'd fail. Gary was a hard one to read. He smiled a lot and said all the right things, but his eyes didn't always back them up: they were the eyes of someone looking out at you through a Polarized window. And there was no doubt his life would be easier if she were to slink away in defeat, forced to look for work on the mainland, thus removing a source of embarrassment from his otherwise orderly existence.

"I guess I'll just have to figure it out as I go along," she said, with a shrug. "You want a beer?"

"I'll have to take a rain check on that. I'm still on duty." He was wearing his khaki uniform, gun in its holster on his hip and his two-way clipped to his shirtfront. He turned his attention to Denise. "By the way, Taylor wanted me to remind you she has that thing at Scout hall tonight."

"What thing?"

"Beats me. I figured you'd know."

"Omigod." Denise abruptly sat up, clapping a hand over her mouth. "I completely forgot. I was supposed to bake cupcakes." She sighed, wearing the guilty, harassed look that seemed the sole province of motherhood. "I suppose I could pick some up at the store." She spoke as though it would be a sacrilege somehow.

"Why don't I whip up a batch?" Alice volunteered. "It won't take long, and it's the least I can do after all your hard work."

"You're sure it's not too much trouble?" Denise eyed her with naked gratitude.

"No trouble at all," Alice assured her. "Anyway, it's time I took this baby for a test drive." She gestured toward the newly rebuilt Hobart. "If I can't manage cupcakes, I'm *really* in trouble."

"All right then. I'll leave you girls to it," said Gary, with a tip of his hat. "You need anything, let me know. I have a meeting in town, but I'd be happy to stop at the store afterward."

"What meeting is that?" Denise wanted to know.

Gary turned away, as if to inspect the paint job, but not before Alice had seen the furtive look that crossed his face. "Just routine stuff," he replied with what seemed studied nonchalance. "I shouldn't be too long."

"Thanks, but I think I have everything I need," Alice told him, wondering what he was keeping from his wife.

"Okay then, I'm off." He dropped a kiss on Denise's cheek and headed for the door, his leather holster creaking and his boots leaving tracks in the film of plaster dust that covered the floor.

Denise sat there, shaking her head. "I can't believe I forgot."

"You mean you're not Supermom?" Alice teased.

Denise refused to be jollied out of her conviction that she was the world's worst mother. "What's happening to me? I used to be so organized," she groaned.

Alice suggested gently, "Maybe you're taking on too much."

"It's not just that. It's this damned development." Denise abruptly stood up, pacing back and forth in agitation. "I get the feeling that no matter what we do, they're always one step ahead of us. That's how it works around here. It's all about who you know and which strings to pull. I can't prove it, but I just know they have the whole thing wired."

"So why fight it?" Alice asked.

Denise whirled around, her face flushed and errant wisps of hair sticking out from under the bandana knotted around over her head. "I'll tell you why. It's not just because it's the last truly wild place on the island. It's because to give in would be like giving up. Look at you. What happened with you was awful, sure, but at least you took a stand. You didn't just roll over and die."

"It would have been better if I had. Look at what it cost me," Alice turned toward the window. The sun had come out, sparkling on grass that was still wet from the rain that had fallen earlier in the day. It was little things like that, the things other people took for granted—a view out a window not covered in steel mesh, a slice of blue sky, a leaf trembling on a branch—that stood as reminders of how much that single, irretrievable act had cost her.

"I'm sorry. That came out wrong. I didn't mean—" Denise broke off, and Alice turned to find her wearing a woebegone look.

"I know you didn't mean anything by it." Alice got up and went over to put her arms around her sister. "And it's not wrong to fight for what you believe in. I'd be right there beside you if I didn't have my own battles." She drew back to look at Denise. "So where does it stand now?"

"The court ruling should come down any day."

"And if it doesn't go your way?"

"I can promise you this much, we won't take it lying down," vowed Denise, with fire in her eye. "We'll chain ourselves to the trees if we have to."

"That could get uncomfortable, especially this time of year. Unless you plan on wearing a slicker and thermal underwear," Alice said, hoping to lighten the mood a bit. Her sister's concern was warranted, but she tended toward the extreme. There was only one right way, as far as Denise was concerned: *her* way.

Denise got the message and, with a sigh, she plopped back into her chair. "Let's talk about something else, okay? This is only going to depress me."

"All right then," Alice said. "On a more mundane subject, which will it be? White or chocolate?"

Her sister stared at her blankly for a moment before it sank in that Alice was talking about the cupcakes. "White. That way I won't be tempted to eat as many." Denise had always had a weakness for chocolate. "Just remember to save some for Gary, for when he gets home. Poor guy." She shook her head. "It's not enough he's on patrol all day, he has to contend with all that stupid bureaucracy. You think teachers have it bad, try being a cop."

CHAPTER SEVEN

The mayor's office, situated on the second floor of the municipal building, had a view of the more gracious pre-war courthouse across the
street, where at the moment a storm was brewing. From where he sat, at
his desk facing the window, Owen White saw no immediate cause for
concern. The sidewalk in front of the courthouse, still damp from the
rain that had fallen earlier in the day, was clotted with more fallen leaves
than people. But already a small crowd of activists had gathered and
soon there would be swarms of them: tree huggers like Gary Elkin's wife,
all shaking their fists and railing against the court ruling of which Owen,
privy to certain inside information, already knew would go his way.
Small-minded people who lacked the vision to see past their own noses
and who sought to turn this island into some sort of time capsule. Why,
if they'd been running the show in his father's day, Owen thought, there
would *be* no Grays Island as they knew it. The quaint waterfront downtown that drew in flocks of tourists each summer would still be a mucky
tidal flat and the properties that fetched such handsome sums today a
useless sprawl of farms and orchards.

Thankfully cooler heads would prevail in this current debate as well.
With a few well-placed phone calls, the mayor had made certain of that.

The court would rule in favor of the Lighthouse Foundation, the charitable institution to which the late Elroy Cuthbert had bequeathed eleven hundred acres of pristine woodland, with views of the sound that stretched from Moran State Park to Mount Independence. No matter that Cuthbert had left the land to the foundation intending that it never be built on or that Cuthbert's daughter, Eunice, was contesting the proposed development. The language of the trust was such that nothing specifically prohibited the sale of the property, which Owen interpreted to mean that the old man had been of two minds. The Spring Hill development—a hundred and eighty residences, as well as a golf course and a man-made lake stocked with trout—would go forward as planned and the money Owen had discreetly invested in it would yield a hefty return.

He glanced at his watch now and saw that it was close to four. In exactly two minutes the deputy chief of police would come knocking on his door. Owen insisted on punctuality; he believed it to be a sign of respect, respect for oneself as well as the person whose valuable time you were taking up. And he had little use for slackers and fools. Gary Elkins was neither. His problem was merely one of unfortunate circumstance: He had the bad fortune to be related, if only by marriage, to the woman responsible for ruining Owen's life.

Oh, he knew he was viewed as a success story, someone who'd triumphed over adversity, but Owen wasn't thinking about that or the prestige he enjoyed as mayor. He glanced down at his atrophied legs with a small, crooked smile. It was the first thing people saw when they looked at him: the wheelchair. Thirty-five pounds of steel and polyurethane that in a perverse way had proved to be the making of him. Because of it, people saw him differently, as noble, saintly even. Which was why Owen seldom referred to the tragic incident that had left him partially paralyzed; there was no need to: He made a statement simply by entering a room. Both times he'd run for office, first as county commissioner then six years later as mayor, it was what had been chief on voters' minds, how admirable it was that he hadn't allowed his handicap to limit him in any way.

He'd proved himself in other ways as well. Chiefly, in emerging from the shadow of his father, long gone but far from forgotten in the minds

of the townspeople. A triumph, given that Lowell's mysterious disappearance had been the defining fact of Owen's existence from boyhood
on. He'd grown up hearing the stories whispered about his father, endured the cruel rhymes chanted by the other children in the schoolyard.

Lowell, Lowell, where's the money you stole?

For it was discovered after Lowell's disappearance that there were certain discrepancies in his books. Large sums of money were missing from
his corporate account, money slated for shareholders of the limited part-
nerships he controlled. Rumor had it that the money was tucked away in
a Swiss account, and that Lowell had gone off to start a new life in some
foreign country with some mistress—for wasn't it a known fact he was a
womanizer? Others put forth a more innocent explanation, that he'd
been out on his boat that night and fallen overboard (which would have
been hard to do with the yacht moored in its berth at the time). Whatever the explanation, he was gone, leaving his family to a lifetime of uncertain status: his mother a widow for all intents and purposes without a
grave to lay flowers on, his children not knowing whether to revere their
father or revile him.

It hadn't helped that Owen was a sensitive, sickly child. His mother,
without her husband to focus on, had fussed over her only son, her obvious favoritism putting a wedge between him and his sister Caroline. It
wasn't until Owen went off to college that he was finally able to carve
out an identity separate from his parents. Eventually he returned to take
over the family business. He married and became active with his church
and various charitable institutions. Under his careful management, the
business became more profitable than ever. If it hadn't been for Fate casting Alice Kessler into his path, like a bad throw of the dice, he might
have gone on that way indefinitely, quietly living out his life, doing only
good works.

No one, not even his wife, had been aware of the extent of his drinking. He'd never embarrassed her in public and his conduct at work was
never once called into question. And if, during his rare blackouts, he'd
come to his senses on more than one occasion to find himself behind the
wheel of his car, luckily no one had been the wiser.

Until the night he'd run over David Kessler. Drunk as a lord and taking a turn too fast in his Mercedes, he'd been unaware of the little boy
riding his bike along the shoulder of the road until he felt the sickening
thud and heard the horrid crunch of metal beneath his wheels.

After that, he'd quit cold turkey and hadn't picked up another drink
since. Time might even have softened his memory of that terrible event,
or at least allowed him some measure of peace, except for one thing: the
boy's mother. Each time he'd looked into Alice Kessler's face, those unforgiving eyes, it had been as if he were peering through a window into his
own soul. Even if he were to beg for her forgiveness, she wouldn't give it
to him. And when she'd run him down that day, she'd done more than
make a cripple of him, she'd sentenced him to a purgatory in which his
failings were compounded by every sympathetic look, every show of compassion he received, in the very pedestal he'd been placed on. Each time he
hoisted himself into his wheelchair a small part of him knew it was because of a little boy who was dead because of him.

And now, just when he'd begun to put the past behind him, Alice was
back to torment him again. And this time she wouldn't rest until she'd
finished what she'd started. Not that he was worried she'd do something
rash. All those years in prison, he didn't doubt she'd had ample time to
regret her actions, if only for the toll it had taken on her. No, it was her
mere presence that he feared; it was like a cancer eating away at him. Ever
since she'd come back he'd had trouble sleeping at night, and the nightmares had returned—terrible nightmares of screeching brakes and
wheeling headlights, of a small crumpled body lying in the middle of the
road, that had him lurching upright in bed, in a cold panic. And with the
nightmares had come the headaches that used to plague him; not the ordinary kind, easily remedied with a couple of aspirin, but ones like some
medieval torture device clamped to his skull, growing more excruciating
with each turn of the screw.

Owen knew that if he didn't find a way to get rid of her, permanently
this time, there would be no peace for him, ever. No escape from those
eyes that saw him as he really was, the mind that knew the truth and the
heart that wouldn't forgive.

Not that she would be so easily gotten rid of. Not as long as her son was on the island.

From a distance, Owen had watched the boy, Jeremy, grow to manhood, knowing it was only a matter of time before Alice returned to reclaim him. He knew that Jeremy was a good student but that he'd had fallen in with the wrong crowd at school, a thuggish bunch led by a sterling character named Kurt Rudnicki. While Jeremy was busy polishing his college resume, Rudnicki was working on his rap sheet; at sixteen he had already been busted twice for shoplifting and once for minor drug possession.

Owen didn't think Jeremy was in any real danger of following in his buddy's footsteps—he was too smart for that—but he knew that bad things tended to come from keeping bad company, so who knew what might happen?

Which was why he was keeping his eye on the boy. On the rest of the family, too. It was like a game of chess: You always had to think several moves ahead. All he had to do was get his pieces in alignment while eliminating hers one by one, until she had no choice but to call it quits.

A knock on the door roused him from his reverie. With a hint of annoyance he called, "Yes, what is it?"

The door eased open and Gary Elkins poked his head in. "Sir? Is this a bad time? I could come back later on, if you'd like."

"No, no. Come in, Gary. Sit down." Owen waved a hand toward the leather sofa in the seating area at one end of his large office and wheeled himself out from behind his desk. "I was so caught up, I hadn't realized what time it was," he said with a smile. "This business with the parking meters—it took an hour just to weed through the memos." And if the tree huggers thought putting in a few extra parking meters downtown was a call to arms, what would they do when they learned of the court ruling on Spring Hill? Owen felt a grim pleasure at the thought. "What can I get you? Coffee, tea?"

Gary shook his head, his polite smile vanishing almost as quickly as it appeared. "I'm good, thanks." Owen watched him lower himself onto the sofa, looking as uncomfortable as a child called into the principal's office. "I don't want to take up too much of your time."

"Nonsense. I'm never too busy for my deputy chief of police," Owen said. He propelled himself over to the sofa, the mag wheels of his Invacare Tracer EX2 cutting twin tracks in the dense pile of the carpet. "I don't mind telling you, it's a comfort knowing I can count on you, with all that's been going on." He gestured vaguely toward the window, through which drifted the chants of the crowd gathering on the street below. "We may not always see eye to eye, but we both know how to get the job done, even if it means ruffling a few feathers along the way."

He chuckled softly, catching a glimpse of himself in the mirrored cabinet against the wall just then: a pale, balding man dressed in chinos and a navy sports coat over a pale blue Izod shirt, his upper body disproportionately bulky against his atrophied lower half. Despite the confident look he wore the strain he'd been under was apparent, if only to him, in the deepening of the lines around his eyes and mouth and in the pallor underlying his tan, which gave him a faintly jaundiced look. Disturbed, he averted his eyes, focusing on Gary instead.

Gary shifted on the sofa, his eyes darting around the room as though he feared that if he looked directly at Owen's they would betray him. Finally, when it became clear to him that the mayor wasn't in any hurry to state his business, he cleared his throat and asked, "Was there something in particular you wanted to see me about?"

"As a matter of fact, there is." Owen waited a beat, his expression hardening before he got down to business. "I want to know everything there is to know about your sister-in-law. Keep close tabs and report back to me. She doesn't make a move without us knowing about it. Do I make myself clear?"

Gary's face, with its broad Nordic cheekbones and deep-set eyes, a rough draft of the more handsome one it might have been had it not been so crudely drawn, flushed a mottled crimson. "I've already told you everything I know." A surly note crept into his voice. "It's not like there's a law against opening a restaurant."

"No. But may I remind you that she's on parole. All it would take is one little slip." He leaned forward in his wheelchair, fixing Gary with his ineluctable gaze. "You're an officer of the law. It's your business to stay on top of such things. Do you have a problem with that?"

Gary flashed him a look of pure hatred, then quickly dropped his gaze, mumbling, "I'll see what I can do."

"I'm not asking you to *see* what you can do. I'm asking you to do it." Owen's tone hardened.

Gary brought his head up to look at Owen. His eyes glinted and the mottled red in his cheeks had deepened to the color of old bricks. "It's just . . . if my wife ever found out I was spying on her sister—" He broke off, swallowing hard.

"Spying? I think you've seen too many James Bond pictures." Owen's face relaxed into a smile, and he lifted his arms off the padded leather rests of his wheelchair to show he meant no harm. "Let's not make more of this than there is. All I'm asking, Gary, is for you to do your job. And to keep me informed, so that there are no . . . surprises. Under the circumstances, I don't think that's unreasonable, do you?"

Gary met his gaze with surprising defiance. "Sir, I have to tell you I'm not comfortable with this. I'm not saying I don't think you have a right to feel the way you do." His gaze involuntarily shifted downward, taking in the wheelchair. "But, hell, she's family. And she's paid her debt. All she wants is the chance to start over, make a new life for herself."

"Do you see me preventing her from doing that?" Owen spoke in a soft, unthreatening tone. "If I wanted to put her out of business, all it would take is a single phone call."

"I don't see what you need me for then," Gary said sulkily.

Owen looked at him as if he were a dim-witted student slow in getting it. "You're a team player, aren't you, Gary?"

"I'm not sure I follow you." Gary eyed him warily.

"I don't believe I need to remind you of a certain matter that would be very embarrassing to you and your family if it should get out." Owen paused to let the message sink in. "Your son's on the football team, isn't he? And your daughter's, what, in the fourth grade? This is a time for them to enjoy being kids. It'd be a shame to spoil it for them," he went on in the same unthreatening tone. "Now, don't get me wrong, Gary. I like you. I like what you're doing for the community, and I'd hate to lose a good man over something like this."

Gary's whole body went rigid. Owen felt a strange sympathy for him in that moment. It wasn't as if Gary had accepted a bribe to turn a blind eye to some sleaze ball dealing in meth or child porn. It had only been to look the other way should one of the customers get a little too friendly with one of the girls at the gentleman's club out on Route 6. But a bribe was a bribe, and Owen had it all on videotape. He and the owner of the Kittycat Club, a low life by the name of Buck Duggan, had an understanding: Buck tipped Owen off to any dirty cops, in exchange for which he was allowed to remain in business. Owen had found it helped having members of the law enforcement in his pocket. Gary didn't know it, but he wasn't the only one. He merely happened to be most useful at the moment.

Gary nodded slowly in understanding, his eyes fixed on Owen with a mixture of keen hatred and grudging respect. "I copy you on that, sir," he said, with just enough irony to make his point. He rose to his feet, holding himself stiffly at attention. "Anything else I can do for you while I'm at it?" *Shine your shoes, wash your car, cut off my balls and hand them to you on a silver platter*, said the expression on his face.

Owen regarded the big man in the khaki uniform as if he hadn't noticed Gary towering over him. "Thank you, that will be all," he said crisply. He gripped the handrims on his wheels, giving his chair a neat turn, and was heading back to his desk when the rising chants from outside made him pause. Slowly, he wheeled around to face Gary. "Oh, just a friendly bit of advice. I'd keep my wife on a shorter leash, if I were you. This Spring Hill business isn't over yet, and it looks as if things could get ugly. You wouldn't want to see her get hurt."

—

"Go for it, dog," Rud urged thickly, his eyelids at half mast as he peered at Jeremy through his tequila-and-beer-induced fog. "Wha'choo waitin' for, an invitation to the *prom?*" The girl sprawled on the mattress, clad

only in bra and panties, was in a similar state of inebriation. She looked up at them, giggling as if Rud had said something wildly amusing.

Jeremy hung back, unsure but not wanting to appear uncool. "Fuck you, man. Look at her, she's wasted."

"Don't mean she don't want it." The mattress was on the bedroom floor, its bedding consisting of a single dirty sheet that was presently crumpled at the girl's feet. Rud nudged her with the scuffed toe of his motorcycle boot. "You want it, don't'cha, babe?" She mumbled something unintelligible, and he returned his bleary-eyed gaze to Jeremy. "See? What'd I tell ya?"

Jeremy wanted to say the party was over as far as he was concerned, he was out of here, only he thought it might piss Rud off. He was never quite sure of his footing with Rud, who, like a capricious king, could be all smiles and high-fives one minute and making you feel like a piece of shit the next. Jeremy settled instead for a contemptuous snort, adopting the pose of someone who was above such sophomoric stunts.

The evening had started out fun. Chuckie Dimmick's older brother, Mike, had given them the keys to his apartment, and Rud and Chuckie had invited some people over to party. But the fun had stared to sour after Rud proposed a game of strip poker, the penalty a shooter for each item of clothing lost in the match. Rud and Chuckie and Kenny Lambert had merely gotten drunk while keeping most of their clothes on, while Rud's girlfriend, Crystal, had ended up passed out half naked on the living room floor, her friends having drifted off one by one. All except this one.

What was her name—Karen? Carolyn? Jeremy, who'd consumed his share of alcohol, stood swaying on his feet, bare-chested, wearing only his jeans, as he contemplated how best to extricate himself from this sticky situation. He gazed down at the girl, who peeked up at him kittenishly through the tawny hair tangled about her face. He felt a sudden tug of desire that left him sickened.

"What, you a faggot or something?" sneered Chuckie Dimmick, whom Jeremy had mentally dubbed Chuckie Dimwit, a real mouth-breather who wasn't capable of an original thought. Jeremy didn't know why Rud hung out with him—Rud was way smarter than that—unless it was because every king needed his sycophants. Chuckie was looking at Rud now, seeking his approval. "Yeah, I bet he likes it up the ass. Don'cha, Jizz?" He nudged Rud with his elbow and cackled drunkenly at his own joke.

"Shut the fuck up, moron," Rud snapped at him. Chuckie's pimpled face went slack with a hurt expression that was almost comical, exaggerated as it was by a combination of stupidity and alcohol. Rud turned his attention back to Jeremy, slinging an arm around his shoulder and leaning in to mutter, "Dude, you don't want people thinkin' you some kinda pussy. That wouldn't be cool, would it? Now do your uncle Rud proud. I'm countin' on you." He drew back to wink slyly at Jeremy, as if they were in on some private joke.

"Fuck you," growled Jeremy, only he was grinning as he said it, so as not to confirm his own growing suspicion that he was, indeed, a pussy.

Rud leaned in close once more, advising in a low and noticeably less warm voice, "Yo, don't be trippin' on me, man. You makin' me look bad here, being as I'm the one who set you up and all."

"You guys are so full of shit," Jeremy said with a laugh, not wanting to jeopardize his already tenuous standing with them. He shook his head in mock disgust, and tried to push his way past Rud and Chuckie. Before he knew it, Rud had him by the arm and was shoving him onto the mattress, accompanied by hoots of laughter from Chuckie and Kenny. By the time Jeremy managed to scramble to his feet, the other boys were tumbling out into the hallway.

The door slammed shut and the room was plunged into darkness. Jeremy could hear his friends' muffled guffaws and the sound of a heavy piece of furniture being dragged across the floor on the other side. He staggered over to the door. Finding it wedged shut, he banged on it with his fist. "Come on, guys! Open up! This isn't funny!"

Behind him the girl—Carolyn? Carrie Ann?—said, with a drunken laugh, "What, you scared of the dark? Big boy like you?"

Jeremy's hand, which had been hovering over the light switch, dropped to his side. "I didn't say that."

"Come over here," she called. After a moment's hesitation, Jeremy crossed the room and sat down on the mattress, pulling his knees to his chest. "Sorry, what's your name again? I'm a little fucked up at the moment, in case you hadn't noticed." She gave a soft giggle that turned into a hiccough.

"Jeremy," he said.

She squinted at him with one eye shut. "Jeremy. That's cute. You like girls, Jeremy?"

"Yeah, I like girls," he shot back defensively. Now that his eyes had adjusted to the dark, he could see that she wasn't half bad-looking.

"So you're not gay?"

"Don't listen to them. They're full of shit." Jeremy jerked a thumb in the direction of the door, behind which the cackles and guffaws were fading as his friends moved into the next room. "Look, this wasn't exactly my idea," he said coldly, "so if I'm not in the mood to party, you'll have to excuse me."

"Whatever." She let out a soft burp and flopped onto her back, peering up at him through a web of tangled hair. "You know what? You remind me of someone. That guy in the movie, I can't think of his name. You know the one about the geeky kid who gets the girl in the end? I think Jeff Bridges was in it. He plays the dad."

"I don't think I know that one," said Jeremy, with as much sarcasm as he could muster.

"Too bad. It rocked." She skimmed a bare foot along his blue-jeaned thigh, and he instantly felt himself go hard, which only made him more pissed. He pushed her foot away.

"Don't do that."

"What?" She resumed her rubbing.

"What you're doing." He scooted over a few inches.

"What's the matter? You don't like me?" She put on a mock offended face.

"Sure, I do. It's just . . ." Suddenly Jeremy couldn't think why he was being this way. Maybe Rud was right; maybe there *was* something the matter with him. He wasn't gay, or anything; that much he knew. The throbbing in his groin testified to that. But there had to be something seriously fucked up with a guy who just sat there like lump while a nearly naked girl played footsie with him, his dick about to pop the zipper on his jeans.

"What?" she prompted.

She ran her nails down his arm, nails polished a metallic blue that glittered in the moonlight slanting in through the blinds, making him break out in goose bumps. This time, when he didn't pull away, she looped her arms around his neck and drew him down beside her. The next he knew they were kissing. She tasted of stale beer and cigarettes, but for some reason that only excited him further. He opened his mouth and let his tongue play over hers.

He wondered if she could tell that he was a virgin. Was it possible to know a thing like that just from kissing someone? Would it make any difference to her if she did? Concerns that, sober, would have left him paralyzed with anxiety, but that in his present drunken and aroused state seemed as harmless as the IM chatter popping up on his computer screen at home.

They kissed a while longer before Jeremy was sufficiently emboldened to work a finger past the elastic band of her panties. Timidly at first, stopping when he felt the electric brush of her pubic hair against his fingertips. But she didn't push his hand away, so he kept on going.

She was wet. Oh God. He felt as if he could come just from touching her down there.

She unsnapped her bra and wriggled out of her panties. He brought his hand up, and he could smell her on him and it was like he was tripping on some drug, like the time he took Ecstasy, his blood fizzing in his veins and his skin so sensitive to the touch it was as if the whole world was being absorbed through his pores, the thoughts that had been troubling him all week—thoughts of his mother—tucked off in some remote region of his brain, where they drifted like smoke from a distant fire.

He cupped her breast, running his thumb over the nipple, which stiffened at once, sending a new jolt of pleasure through him. He'd done that. Him. It would have been the most perfect moment in his thus far pathetic life if just then she hadn't murmured thickly, "Jimmy. Oh, yeah, baby. Do it."

Jimmy? Who the fuck was Jimmy? Had she meant to say Jeremy? He froze for an instant, the part of him that was whispering that this might not be such a good idea nearly getting the better of the other, fired-up Jeremy who had only one thing on his mind. *Fuck it,* he thought. She wanted it, she'd said so herself. If it wasn't him, she'd be doing one of the other guys. And did he want to die a virgin? Not just a virgin, but a *pussy,* who'd messed up the one chance he'd had to do something with his dick other than jerk off.

With the speed of someone scrambling for the last seat on a life boat he shed his jeans, kicking them off with such force they hit the floor and kept right on going, skating with a soft slithering sound over the floor-boards before pooling against the wall. Naked, he stretched out along-side her, the room spinning, as if the mattress were a raft slowly rotating along the eddies of a stream. They kissed some more, and then her hand was on his dick, fingers curled about the shaft moving in slow, delicious strokes . . . *oh God, oh Christ . . . if she doesn't stop I'll come. . .*

But he didn't want her to stop. He wanted this feeling to go on forever.

Once again, more feebly now, the voice of reason asserted itself. *She's drunk. She doesn't know what she's doing. She thinks you're some guy named Jimmy. Better quit before this gets out of hand.*

But it was just static in his head, and he tuned it out. Who cared if she thought he was someone else? If she was too wasted to know the differ-ence, that was her problem. And if he didn't happen to have a condom on him it was probably all right. She hadn't said anything about it, which meant she'd most likely done whatever it was girls did to take care of such matters. She clearly wasn't inexperienced.

As he entered her, she cried out. *Yeah, like that, don't stop.* It was all the en-couragement he needed. Then he was coming, in a blinding rush. He rolled away moments later to find her passed out cold. The dizzying high he'd been on gave way to shame. Carrie Ann, her name was Carrie Ann, he remembered it now. She was lying on her back with her eyes closed and her jaw slack, her legs splayed limply apart, snoring lightly. He kissed her gently on the lips, and she stirred, muttering something in her sleep.

"Carrie Ann?" he whispered. But she didn't rouse; she was dead to the world. And what would he have said, anyway, that he was sorry? For what? For fucking her when he knew it was wrong, or for not being this Jimmy guy? No, it was better this way. With any luck, by morning she wouldn't remember a thing. It would be like it never happened.

—

When he was called into the principal's office the following day, one look at Mr. Givens's face told him that he hadn't been summoned to discuss helping another kid who may have been struggling in math, the usual reason Mr. Givens wanted to see him. The expression on the principal's face was grim. As he sank into the chair opposite Mr. Givens's desk, Jeremy sensed he was in trouble, the kind of trouble that had last night's activities written all over it. A cold wave of panic went through him, and he felt his hangover drain away like so much dirty water from a stopped-up rain gutter, leaving him clear-headed, every circuit in his brain buzzing.

"I just got off the phone with Missus Flagler," said Mr. Givens. Jeremy must have looked blank, for he added, more pointedly, "Carrie Ann's mother."

Jeremy's spine stiffened, and he nodded slowly in mute acknowledgment that he did indeed know Carrie Ann.

"She's extremely upset," the principal went on, his normally jolly face—with its polished-looking pink cheeks and clipped white beard that made him look like a modern-day Santa Claus—flat and expressionless. "It seems Carrie Ann ran into some trouble last night. Would you know anything about that, son?" He stared hard at Jeremy across the cluttered surface of his desk.

Jeremy rearranged his features in what he hoped was an innocent expression. "Uh, well, yeah we were at a party last night. Me and her and some other people. Okay, we had a little too much to drink, but . . ." He shrugged, as if to say, *you know how it is*. But even as he spoke, images from last night flashed through his head: Carrie Ann passed out drunk on the mattress, her thighs sticky with his come; then later, he and Rud and Chuckie carrying her outside while Kenny, the only one sober enough to drive, brought the car around. Shame welled up in him when he thought about how they'd dumped her in front of her house, like so much garbage.

"I'm afraid it's not as simple as that."

"She's all right, isn't she?" A new fear crept in. Jeremy had heard about people dying of alcohol poisoning. Suppose something like that had happened to Carrie Ann?

"She's fine," said the principal, in a tone that conveyed that, while she wasn't in any mortal danger, something was seriously wrong nonetheless. "But the police have been called in, so if there's anything you need to get off your chest, I think now's the time."

"The police?" Jeremy's voice went up an octave.

"She claims she was raped."

After several moments of silence, in which every noise seemed amplified—the distant shrilling of the third period bell, the humming of the fax machine and tapping of a keyboard in the outer office—Mr. Givens prompted him once more. "Well, do you have anything to say for yourself?"

Jeremy shook his head, which wobbled as if too heavy for his neck. "No, sir."

The principal's eyes narrowed. He seemed to be trying to assess whether Jeremy was holding back or if it was the shock making him so uncommunicative. He must have decided that Jeremy was innocent, at least until proven guilty, for he said, not unkindly, "In any case, I don't think you should say anything to the police, not until we've spoken with your dad. I have a call in to him. I've left several messages, in fact. Do you know where I might be able reach him?"

Jeremy searched his mind, which was running in crazed circles, trying to think where his dad might be. Randy always kept his cell phone on, so

Jeremy could reach him in case of an emergency, but parts of his territory were in areas that had spotty service.

Some impulse made him reach into the back pocket of his jeans and
pull out a folded piece of binder paper with a phone number written on
it. He'd been carrying it around for weeks, with no thought of ever need-
ing it. Not until now.

He handed it to Mr. Givens. "Try my mom."

CHAPTER EIGHT

It took Colin several days just to weed through the junk in the Henleys' shed. With only a vague idea of what to do with the equipment now piled in his grandfather's old studio, he located, with the help of the Internet, a small-scale oyster farmer down on the Kitsap Peninsula, by the name of Len Jarvis. Colin was on a plane the next day, and hours later he was standing ankle deep, in rubber boots, in the shallow water off Hood Canal, listening as Len Jarvis took him through the process of stake and line oyster culturing.

Len dipped a hand horned with calluses into the water and pulled up a half shell to which clung a dozen or more baby oysters no bigger than the nail on his pinkie. "Now that there's your mother shell," he said, explaining how the discarded shells of shucked oysters were mixed with oyster larvae. Once the larvae had adhered and were sufficiently grown, the mother shells with their "babies" attached were fixed to lengths of rope with a stringing machine, like so many bulbs on strands of Christmas tree lights. The lines were then strung out in evenly spaced rows along the tidal flat, fixed at either end with lengths of PVC pipe embedded in the silt. It took several years for an oyster to fully mature, so it wasn't for those seeking quick results, Len warned.

"You have your predators, too," he went on. There was a tiny snail called an oyster drill, and something known as Denman Island disease. Starfish could be a problem, too. There were also the herons, seagulls, and otters that patrolled these waters in search of food. "We don't mind 'em taking their fair share, but they can be greedy little bastards, if you let 'em." He squinted off into the distance at the lines strung out in rows, held by barnacle-crusted stakes at either end. "Course the *real* culprits are our own kind."

Colin gave a solemn nod.

"Back in my father's day, the pulp mills had killed off most of the shell-fish around here," Len said. "We've come a long way in bringing 'em back, but with pollution it's an ongoing battle." He turned to Colin. "You planning on doing this as a hobby, or are you looking to go into business?"

"I'm not in it for the money," Colin said.

"Good. Because you won't get rich." He regarded Colin for a moment, sizing him up. "Funny sort of work for a man like you. I'd have pegged you more as a city boy. Just out of curiosity, what got you interested?"

Colin told him about Mr. Deets, and the summers he'd spent on Grays Island, smiling to himself as he reflected on happier times.

They spoke a bit longer, Len refreshing Colin's memory as to the different varieties of oysters cultivated in these parts: the Pacific, which could grow to the size of a man's fist; the Olympia, which was the only native to these shores; the small, sweet Kumumoto, which had been brought over from Japan. As they walked back toward shore, Len dipped a hand into the water once more, this time extracting a fully grown specimen. Using the shucking knife he pulled from his back pocket, he pried it open, severing the abductor muscle and running the knife along the crevice between the two halves of the shell, all in one expert motion. He offered it to Colin, who tipped it into his mouth, briefly savoring the salty-sweet taste of it on his tongue before it slid down his throat. If the best memories of his childhood could be distilled into an essence, it would be this, he thought.

Two hours later, after a tour of the hatchery, during which Len introduced him to the astounding fact that a single oyster could produce up to five million eggs, Colin was on a plane headed home. He didn't know if he'd be as productive, but he felt the glimmerings of excitement, a sense of what the future might hold, a feeling he hadn't had in very long time.

In the days that followed he set about fashioning the rudiments of an operation. With the table saw he'd salvaged from the Henleys' shed, he cut PVC pipe into even two-foot lengths, into which he drilled holes with which to secure the ropes. The work was repetitive and time-consuming, but it didn't bother him. It eased his mind and kept his hands occupied. And at night, for the first time in years, he had no trouble falling asleep.

He wasn't without company, either. The dog, Shep, seemed to have more or less taken up residence at his place. He'd sit on his haunches, at a dignified distance, following Colin's every move. Occasionally Colin would find himself talking to the dog, explaining what he was doing or simply shooting the breeze. There was a queer kind of formality to the proceedings, Colin hard at work, with the Border collie standing in silent attendance, like a butler in his morning coat.

After a long day at his workbench or down on the cove pounding in stakes when the tide was out, Colin would return to the bungalow, which he still thought as his grandfather's, and light a fire to take off the chill. Often, as he did so, he would find himself gazing at the portrait over the mantel. It haunted him. Something about the expression on Eleanor Styles's face was both playful and melancholic, as if she'd known the contentment she was feeling in that moment wouldn't last.

His thoughts would turn then to Alice Kessler. Something about her had stayed with him as well. Maybe it was that he felt a kinship with her. She too was struggling to build a new life amid the rubble of her old one. He'd heard from his grandfather's caretaker, Orin, whom Colin had kept on to do odd jobs on an as-needed basis, about the café she'd bought and was in the process of renovating. He admired her courage in taking on such a risky enterprise; not only was she refusing to be beaten down, she was flying in the face of her detractors.

He was disappointed that he had yet to hear from her, but supposed he would eventually. The portrait would still be here, whenever she had the time to stop by. For much to the regret of the dealers who'd called with offers, he'd decided to keep it. If his grandfather had wanted it in some stranger's possession, he would have sold it years before.

One day in late November, Colin happened to glance out the window and noticed an old green Toyota coming up the drive. He watched as it pulled to a stop and a slender brown-haired woman climbed out, a woman he recognized at once as Alice Kessler. As he hurried off to meet her, he felt his pulse quicken.

"Alice. What a nice surprise," he greeted her.

"I'm sorry, I should have called first." Her eyes dropped to his jeans and work shirt, streaked with dirt and PVC dust. "Is this a bad time?"

"Not at all. I was just about to take a break," he fibbed. "Why don't we go inside. I'll make some tea."

Her gaze fell on the Border collie, who sat looking up at her, his head cocked and ears pricked. "Hello, boy. Don't I know you from somewhere?" She bent down, holding out a hand. Shep took a tentative sniff, his plumed tail sweeping slowly from side to side. She straightened, observing to Colin, "Looks as if you've found yourself a pet."

"More like he's found me." Colin smiled down at Shep. "He's a very discerning fellow. He doesn't give his affections easily. I'm still not sure if I've made the final cut."

"Well, at least you have each other for company. It must get lonely out here." Her gaze took in the wind-scoured bluff and cove sparkling below, and to the east the high brow of the ridge, with its line of trees like bristles on a comb.

"It does at times," he conceded.

She looked better than when he'd last seen her. Healthier. The jeans that had hung on her before were filled out nicely in all the right places and the hollows in her cheeks not so pronounced. But her eyes hadn't lost their look of melancholy. And he sensed a certain tension in her as well, as if this were more than a social call.

In the kitchen, he put the kettle on to boil. He'd given up coffee; it reminded him too much of AA meetings, the ever-present smell of it in the air and seeing those new in sobriety, like him, clinging to their Styrofoam cups as if to a lifeline.

"So, I hear you bought a restaurant," Colin remarked, as he put the kettle on to boil.

"Word travels fast." Alice smiled ruefully, removing a stack of newspapers from one of the chairs before taking a seat at the table. "Yes, I'm now the proud owner of a former fish-and-chips joint. It was pretty much on its last leg, but it's amazing what a few cans of paint and a liberal application of elbow grease can do. The grand opening is next week. Nothing fancy, just family and friends. I hope you can make it."

Colin warmed. "I wouldn't miss it for the world."

He turned to find her eyeing him curiously. "What about you? From the looks of it, you've been doing more than catching up on your reading."

"As it so happens, I'm thinking of going into business myself." More than thinking, but he didn't want to commit himself to anything just yet.

"Would it have anything to do with oyster farming?"

He broke into a grin. "Don't tell me you're a mind-reader on top of everything else?"

"No. Just observant." She gestured toward the brochures he'd left sitting out on the table, picking up a pamphlet entitled *Small Scale Oyster Farming in the Pacific Northwest.* "I'll say one thing, if you were looking for a change, this is about as extreme as it gets."

"That it is." Extreme as a dive into an icy-cold lake—just the wake-up call he needed. "Maybe that's why I like the idea."

"Does this mean you're giving up on lawyering?" He caught a flicker of consternation in her eyes, and wondered why it should matter to her one way or the other.

He shrugged. "Looks that way. For now, at least."

She lapsed into silence, and he caught that preoccupied look on her face again. Then she roused herself and put on a smile, saying, "Well, good luck with it. I guess we're sort of in the same boat. I just hope the gamble pays off for both of us. If the road to hell is paved with good intentions, I'm sure that's true of failed enterprises."

"Look at the bright side," he said. "You'll have at least one customer you can count on. If your cooking is any better than mine, which is a pretty sure bet, you'll be seeing a lot more of me."

She smiled then, a slow-breaking smile that lit up her whole face. All at once he felt absurdly happy to have her here. It was the first time since Nadine's death that he'd felt that way about another woman. With Alice, he knew he didn't have to fake being okay. He could just be himself, wounds, warts, and all.

"What a lovely place," she said, as he led the way into the living room carrying the tea tray. "I can see why you and your grandfather were so close." He shot her an inquiring look, and she explained, "You can tell a lot about a person from their house, and it's obvious what kind of person he was. Very unpretentious, I'd say. Someone who didn't put style over comfort and who probably didn't give a hoot what anyone thought. The kind of man," her eyes, dancing with bemusement, dropped to the tray Colin was lowering onto the coffee table, "who'd serve tea in chipped mugs and sugar out of a box."

Colin smiled somewhat sheepishly. "I'm sorry it's not fancier, but it's the best I can do on such short notice. As for my grandfather, that's him in a nutshell."

While he poured the tea, she moved in to get a closer look at the portrait. For the longest while she didn't speak. She appeared dumbstruck.

He stepped up alongside her. "Nothing prepares you for it, does it?" The reproductions he'd seen were a classic case of something being lost in the translation. "Do you think it looks like her?"

Alice studied it, frowning. "In a way, yes. But she looks . . . more at ease than I remember her. My grandmother was always running around doing six things at once. She didn't have a lot of time to sit and relax." She sounded sad, for some reason.

"As for whether or not she meant something to your grandfather, I asked my mother about it," she went on. "Unfortunately, she couldn't tell me much. Either she doesn't know, or she didn't want to tarnish Nana's memory. I have a feeling they might have been lovers, though, and seeing this . . ." she gestured toward the portrait, "I'm almost sure of it." She turned to face Colin. "I know this going to sound strange, but I can't say I disapprove. She deserved to be happy, even if it was with someone other than my grandfather. Not that she didn't love Grandpa Joe, but it wasn't a marriage in the typical sense. He wasn't . . . all there."

"I guess we'll never know the real story," Colin said.

"No, but thank you for this. I'm glad I finally got to see it," she said, her gaze returning to the painting. "I would have come sooner, but—" She broke off, turning to him with a contrite look. "Look, I have a confession to make. I had an ulterior motive in coming here." She retreated, sinking down on the sofa. "It's my son. He's in trouble."

"What kind of trouble?" Colin asked, thinking it was the kind of trouble that needed a male perspective, or maybe someone to counsel the boy. Her next words took him completely by surprise.

"He needs a lawyer."

"I see." Colin blinked in surprise, and sat down.

"He didn't do anything wrong," she rushed to qualify. "He's being falsely accused."

"Of what?"

Some of the color went out of her cheeks. "Rape."

"That's pretty serious."

"If you knew Jeremy, you'd know he isn't remotely capable of doing such a thing. It's all a big mistake. Or . . ." Her expression darkened. "He's being set up."

"Where is he now?" Colin asked.

"At home, with his dad. They booked him down at the station, but his uncle—my sister's husband—arranged it so he could get out on bail before the arraignment."

"His uncle's a lawyer?"

"A cop, actually. Deputy chief of police." She paused. "Which is where you come in. We need a good criminal attorney, and the lawyers around here . . ." She spread her hands in a helpless gesture. "Let's just say they haven't had a lot of experience with this kind of thing."

Colin, feeling something akin to panic at the thought of climbing back into the saddle, hastened to set her straight. "I wish I could help, but the thing is, I'm not practicing anymore. Of course, I'll do whatever I can, to help you find someone else to represent him, if you'd like."

Her face fell, but she quickly rallied, saying, "I don't want just anyone. I need someone I can trust."

But Colin was already shaking his head. No, he'd left all that behind. The mere thought of entering a courtroom . . . "I understand, and believe me, if it were anything else—"

She didn't let him finish. "When you said you weren't practicing, does that mean you can't or you won't?"

"I'm still licensed, if that's what you mean. But that's not the point. I haven't been inside a courtroom since . . ." *I lost my job for being drunk twenty-four seven.* He sat back. "Well, you know the story. Trust me, I'm not just saying this for my own sake. Your son deserves better than someone on as shaky legs as he."

Alice went on eyeing him with a directness he found unnerving. "Tell me something," she said, her eyes piercing through his defenses. "Were you good at it?"

"Yes, I was good at it," he replied wearily. So good, in fact, that his boss had continued to cut him slack long after he would have fired anyone else.

"That's all I need to know."

"It's not as simple as that," he started to say, but she cut him off again.

"Look, I realize it's a lot to ask. We barely know one another. But this is my *son.* If anything happens to him—" She broke off with a small, choked sound. He could see that she was struggling not to give in to tears. "I already lost one son," she said, when she'd regained some of her composure. "I can't lose another one."

Colin wavered, torn between the strong desire to come to her rescue and the equally strong desire to rescue himself. At last, he came to a decision. Letting out a breath he hadn't realized he'd been holding, he told her, "All right. I'll see what I can do."

She looked so relieved that for a moment he thought she was going to burst into tears. "Thank you. You don't know what this means to me."

Colin, feeling as if he were digging himself in deeper with each passing minute, said only, "You can thank me when I've actually accomplished something."

"So what happens now?"

"If we're lucky, the judge will let him off with probation. He's young and he's had a clean record up until now. That counts for a lot." Colin paused, asking, "He *hasn't* been in trouble before, has he?"

"No, of course not. At least, not as far as I know," she added, more hesitantly. Color rose in her cheeks. It had to pain her that she'd been so out of the loop. Then her expression hardened. "But one thing I *do* know: He didn't rape anyone."

Colin felt obligated to caution her, "That may be the case, but if he pleads not guilty, it'll mean a trial, and believe me you don't want that." His standard rap in situations like these, though in his role as assistant D.A. it had been self-serving, since his job had been to put criminals away, even if it meant having them cop to a lesser plea. "Don't look so worried," he said, more gently. "If what you're saying is true, the case could be dismissed due to lack of evidence. We'll know more after I've spoken with the D.A. I'll also need to have a word with Jeremy."

She perked up. "We could drive over there now."

Colin pondered it a moment, a grayness settling over him like the thick fog that had engulfed him in the months after Nadine's death. Was he only giving her false hope? And putting himself at risk of drinking again? It wasn't too late to back out, he told himself. He hadn't committed to anything yet.

At last, he rose heavily to his feet. "Let me get my coat."

—

She was quiet on the drive to her ex-husband's. Colin didn't doubt the situation would be complicated by some residual tension there. She hadn't spoken a word against her ex, but he sensed there was some history. How could there not be? In any event, it was bound to make a bad situation that much worse, which made Colin wonder again if he was doing the right thing.

But then he'd look at Alice, and think about all she'd been through, what she was still going through, and his reservations would fade. She needed him, and it had been a long time since Colin had felt needed.

After a series of winding roads they finally pulled up in front of a split-level ranch house on a street lined with other, similar looking houses. He was getting out of the car when she placed a hand on his arm. "I'm not asking you to go easy on him, but he's had a pretty rough time of it," she said, in a voice soft with appeal. "Just . . . keep that in mind, okay?"

"And if he's not telling me everything I need to know?" said Colin, testing her to see if she was capable of dealing with the fact that her son might not be as innocent as she believed.

"Then you'll do what you have to," she said. Her face was pale but her tone firm. She clearly wanted the truth, at whatever cost.

Jeremy Kessler was nothing like the punks Colin was used to dealing with. The boy who rose from the living room sofa to offer him a limp handshake was slightly built, with curly dark hair and his mother's watchful gray-green eyes. He looked younger than his age and utterly defenseless. The kind of kid who'd probably been picked on in school. He didn't strike Colin as sexually experienced, much less someone who would force unwanted attentions on a girl. On the other hand, Colin knew that looks could be deceiving. One of the most difficult cases he'd ever tried had been a baby-faced fourteen-year-old from the Bronx, who with several fellow gang members had robbed a bodega at gunpoint, pistol-whipping the owner to within an inch of his life. At his sentencing, the boy had cried for his mommy.

Jeremy's father—tall, fair-haired, with the look of an aging high school athlete—stepped forward to introduce himself. "Hi, I'm Randy. Thanks for coming on such short notice." He had a salesman's ready smile and firm handshake, but beneath Randy's manufactured grin, Colin sensed the man was just as worried as his ex-wife.

"No problem," Colin said. He cast a quick glance at Alice, who wore a carefully neutral expression, before he turned his attention to the boy. In a mild, conversational tone, he observed, "I understand you're in a bit of trouble, Jeremy." Jeremy gave an almost imperceptible nod, and Colin went on, "First time?"

"Yeah," Jeremy replied, in a voice that was barely above a squeak.

"How about school-related? Detention, suspension, that kind of thing."

"I'm not sure what you're getting at," interjected Randy, the bonhomie of a moment ago giving way to an impatient scowl. "But let's be clear on one thing: *He's* the injured party here."

Colin turned to Randy, saying, "I can't help him unless I know all the facts."

"The only thing you need to know is that he's being railroaded." Randy rushed once more to his son's defense.

Colin ignored him to address Jeremy. "Is there someplace we can talk in private?"

Jeremy looked to his dad for approval, but before Randy could weigh in, Alice spoke up. "Jeremy, why don't you take Mister McGinty to your room?" Jeremy shot her a veiled look, but he didn't offer any protest.

Colin still wasn't sure he would take the case; some of it depended on how cooperative Jeremy was going to be. So it was with surprise and no small degree of concern that he found himself slipping easily into that role, the gears meshing as smoothly as if the machinery hadn't stood idle for the past five years.

———

When Colin and Jeremy left the room, Alice cautiously lowered herself into the wing-backed chair by the fireplace. The living room that had been eclectically furnished and cluttered with toys when she'd lived here had been done over in her long absence. It was now an almost exact replica of her former mother-in-law's, down to the ginger jar lamps and framed Audubon prints on the walls. Which suggested that the only woman currently in Randy's life was Mrs. Kessler senior. Alice wondered why he hadn't remarried. Randy was still a handsome man. He could have almost any woman he wanted. But it wasn't any of her business, so there was no point in speculating.

Randy sank down on the sofa that still bore the faint imprint of their son's lanky frame. "This feels a little like déjà vu, doesn't it?" she said to break the ice.

Ignoring the reference to her own past legal woes, Randy asked point blank, "What do you know about this guy, other than the fact that he was some hot shot prosecutor back in New York?"

"I know that he's good. And that there's no one else on the island even remotely qualified." Alice didn't need to remind him that most of the crime around here was on the level of petty theft and DUIs. Warren Brockman, who'd represented Alice during her trial, had primarily handled civil cases before that.

Randy sighed, dropping his head to push his hands through his hair, which was longer than he used to wear it and styled in a way that flattered his square, defense line back's face. He looked as if he'd been up all night, which he probably had. "Point taken. Sorry, I didn't mean to go off on the guy like that. It's just that . . . hell, Alice, I don't have to tell you, of all people, how this could end up. I don't want to see the same thing happen to Jeremy."

"I don't want that either," she said quietly.

"Look, I don't mean to open old wounds. It's just that I've been worried sick." Randy eyed her morosely across the expanse of thick-pile carpet that no doubt had been selected by his mother, a shade of Arctic blue that Alice would never in a million years have chosen. At last, he let out an audible breath. "Would you like a drink? I could use one myself."

"Thanks, no," she said.

He rose and went into the next room, returning a few minutes later with a tumbler containing his usual whiskey and soda. He sank back down on the sofa, where he sipped his drink in silence, absorbed in his thoughts, separated from her by more than the four or five feet of space that stood between them. After a minute or so, he roused himself to ask, "So, how have you been? Things going okay?"

"As well as can be expected," she said, with a shrug.

"There's a rumor going around that you're opening a restaurant."

She smiled. "I've heard the same rumor myself."

"So is it true?"

"The grand opening is a week from tomorrow. I hope you and Jeremy can make it."

Randy looked surprised but pleased to be invited. "I'll try, if I'm not on the road."

"Jeremy tells me you were promoted. Congratulations."

Randy gave a snort. "Yeah, for what it's worth. All it means is more territory to cover. If I didn't need the money, I'd be cutting back on my hours instead. This thing with Jeremy . . . I can't help thinking that if I'd been around more . . ." He shook his head, a distraught look on his face.

"You can't blame yourself," Alice said. She knew all about blame. Hadn't she blamed herself, for everything from David's death to the fact that Jeremy wanted nothing to do with her?

"Who else should I blame?" he threw back at her.

"Maybe no one's to blame. Things don't always happen for a reason."

There was a pause before Randy said softly, "You mean David." They exchanged a look more expressive than any words. "I still think about him. A lot."

"Me, too." Her throat tightened.

"I should have been there that night. If it weren't for these crazy hours . . ." His hands balled into fists, and she could see a muscle working in his jaw.

Alice felt something give way in her chest, an anger against Randy she hadn't realized she'd been holding on to. The years had taken their toll on him as well. He appeared humbled in a way that was obvious only to someone who knew him as well as she did. In her long absence, he'd clearly had a lot of time to think. She wondered now if he regretted more than not being there the night David was killed. "It's funny," she said. "I always thought you blamed *me*. I was there. I should have kept a closer eye on him." *Why hadn't they talked about this before? It might have changed everything.*

"Listen to us. Ten years, and it's like it happened yesterday," Randy observed with a dry little croak of a laugh. He contemplated this for a moment, sipping his drink as he stared sightlessly ahead. When he brought his gaze back to her, she saw that his eyes were bloodshot. "Maybe I did hold you responsible in a way, but it wasn't because of that. I didn't understand why you couldn't let go. Why you wouldn't stop hounding the guy."

Our son's killer, you mean, she silently amended. Alice sat back, the flicker of a connection she'd felt with him fading. "I guess there are some things we'll never agree on. Why don't we just leave it at that?"

Just then, the door to Jeremy's room cracked open. Jeremy stepped out into the hallway looking shaken. Colin emerged behind him wearing a flat, unreadable expression. Alice felt herself go cold. What had they talked about in there? Had Jeremy told him things he wasn't comfortable sharing with her or Randy?

Randy put his drink down on the coffee table and jumped to his feet, closing the distance between him and Jeremy in several long strides. "You all right, son?" he asked, putting an arm around Jeremy's shoulders.

Jeremy nodded, but Alice could see how pale and shaken he was. She wondered if this was indeed history repeating itself.

CHAPTER NINE

NOVEMBER 1942

In the summer of that year the Allied forces under the command of General MacArthur began waging an all-out assault on Guadalcanal. The letters Eleanor had been receiving from her husband started coming less frequently. Each night, she and her daughter would gather around the old Philco, straining toward its amber glow as toward a feeble flame by which to warm themselves, listening to the latest broadcasts out of Washington. When the news wasn't good, they would trudge off to bed burdened by the weight of their fears. Eleanor knew that even the victories weren't without casualties, and she and Lucy lived in dread of a telegraph from the War Department.

Lucy had stopped asking when her papa was coming home; several of the children in her school had lost fathers to the war and she knew there was a chance she might also lose hers. Eleanor worried, too. The difference was that, while Joe remained Lucy's chief preoccupation, Eleanor's thoughts had been straying to other things. Whenever she was reminded of the reason for that distraction, a slow heat would unfurl up her neck to flood her cheeks, and at night, as she knelt beside her bed, she would pray all the more fervently for her husband's safe return.

The man responsible for this new and unwelcome tide of emotion was William McGinty. In the months since they'd met he'd been coming by the house once or twice a week, sometimes more often. He never showed up empty-handed. Usually it was basic supplies he brought, food and items of clothing he thought Yoshi might need. But always there would be at least one luxury item tucked in with the staples: a small sack of coffee or sugar, a pound of butter, a bar of soap. If he wasn't in a hurry to get back, he would stay and chat.

Eleanor had come to treasure those stolen hours, hoard them like the rationed sugar he brought. Conversations with friends and neighbors usually centered around the war, but William talked about things that took her mind off such weighty concerns, stories about his student travels abroad and all the fascinating people he'd met along the way. He brought her a Europe untouched by war, one of ancient canals and labyrinthian streets so narrow they could barely accommodate a car and a bicycle at the same time; outdoor markets where you could buy any kind of foodstuff or household item imaginable; rural villages where humble thatched-roof cottages stood side by side with soaring cathedrals.

In her mind, she could see the moon reflected in the waters of the Seine off the Pont du Change, the pigeons that flocked Venice's San Marco Plaza, and the special way the light fell over the rooftops of Florence, a phenomenon known as *chiaroscuro*, she was informed. She learned about the artist named Gaudi and his famous palace in Spain, ugly and beautiful at the same time, from which the word gaudy had come; and the wonders of the Louvre where William had studied the techniques of the Old Masters. There were fondly recollected meals, in which she could almost taste the wine, made by vintners who'd been doing it exactly as had their ancestors for hundreds of years, and the bread baked in great, crusty loaves in wood-fired ovens. It was if he'd handed her the keys to a hidden door, though which she could escape, for brief intervals, to a better world.

One day in early November they were sitting at the kitchen table, chatting while they sipped coffee and nibbled on freshly baked gingerbread, Eleanor telling him about a wedding she'd attended the weekend before, when William asked with his usual forthrightness, "What about you and Joe? How did you two meet?"

Eleanor's eyes darted to the doorway, through which she could see Lucy, seated cross-legged on the living room floor with Yoshi, who was teaching her how to tie a sailor's knot. She lived in dread of Lucy's finding out that Joe wasn't her real father, so it was a subject she normally sidestepped. Now she turned her gaze to the window, gazing out at the rain pouring down, wondering how best to reply.

She looked back at William to find him eyeing her intently. She searched his face for some hint that he'd gotten wind of the old rumors that must have circulated around the time Lucy was born, but his blue eyes were clear and guileless. "We met at church," she told him, settling on a partial truth.

"So was it love at first sight?"

Eleanor felt warmth steal into her cheeks. "I don't know about that. I thought he was nice. And apparently he liked me well enough. Beyond that, we didn't really know each other all that well when we got married. I suppose you could call it a whirlwind courtship."

"And if you had it to do all over again?"

"Goodness, what a question!" She dropped her gaze, feeling self-conscious all of a sudden. "Why, yes, of course. Why do you ask?" Time and again she'd asked herself the same question, and it always came back to the same thing: Lucy. For Lucy's sake, yes, she would do it over again.

"I'm sorry, I don't mean to pry. It's just that the war has got me thinking. Every day we're reminded of how fragile life is, how it can be snuffed out at any moment. You can't help wondering if you're making the most of it, if you wouldn't be happier doing something else . . . or with someone else."

He bent to run his hand absently over the thick ruff of the dog curled at his feet. He never went anywhere without Laird, named after William's Scottish forbears and every inch the aristocrat, with his sleek lines and perfectly shaped head, his thick glossy coat black as midnight, except for his paws snow-white and the patches of white around his eyes and on his chest. For it seemed the now-grown puppy intended for his son preferred

William's company. Laird lifted his head to give William a questioning look, and when it was clear nothing was required of him, he settled back down with a contented sigh.

"Would *you* do it differently?" she asked, wondering once more about his wife. He rarely mentioned her except in passing, but from what little Eleanor had been able to glean, their marriage clearly wasn't what it ought to be.

"Honestly? No." His reply brought a jab to her midsection that caught her unawares, a blow she hadn't thought to protect herself against. One that was softened by his next words. "I wouldn't have my son if I hadn't married Martha."

"So no regrets?"

He shrugged. "We all have regrets. It's human nature, I suppose."

Eleanor ventured hesitantly, "Your wife. Does she know about these visits of yours?"

William fell silent, peering out at the rain-soaked yard. Beyond it lay the field that bordered on her property, where the grass that had stood high in summer was broken and stubbly and the blackberry vines reddish-brown with autumn's rust. The far end of the field was marked by a nearly impenetrable wall of green, Douglas firs and hemlocks mostly, through which she could make out only faintly the path that wound its way up Spring Hill, where she enjoyed hiking in the warm weather months. When he spoke at last, his voice was quiet, troubled almost. "No, she doesn't know. I couldn't think of a way of telling her without putting you and Yoshi at risk."

"I suppose it's for the best," Eleanor said dubiously. "It's just . . . I can't help wondering what she would make of your spending so much time in the company of a lady whose husband is overseas." It was the closest she had come to voicing what she'd long suspected: That these visits were spurred by more than mere generosity on his part.

She saw in his eyes the answer she'd been seeking, and felt all at once giddy with the knowledge, like at her friend's daughter's wedding, when the champagne she'd drunk had gone to her head. When he spoke,

though, his voice was flat. "Martha's pretty preoccupied with the war efforts. I doubt she even notices when I'm not around," he said. "Besides,
she's used to my wandering off in search of things to paint." He paused
to sip his coffee. "Speaking of which, I have a favor to ask."

"Anything," she replied without hesitation. "Whatever it is, I'm sure it
won't come close to repaying you for all you've done."

His expression turned shy. "I'd like to paint your portrait."

It wasn't at all what she'd been expecting, and she said the first thing
that popped into her head. "Why ever would you want to do that?" She
self-consciously brought a hand to her cheek, toying with a curly tendril
that had slipped out from under the scarf she'd tied around her head that
morning when she could do nothing with her hair.

"You'll have to take that up with my muse," he said, with a laugh.

"Your muse?"

"She decides what I'm going to paint. She can be bossy about it, too. I
have very little say in the matter."

"I see." Eleanor got into the spirit of it. "And this muse of yours has
decided you should paint me?"

"Apparently so."

"I suppose I should be flattered. On the other hand, it could just as
easily be a rock or a tree. Or the ocean on a stormy day," she added, with
a glance out the window, at the patch of slate-colored ocean off in the
distance, pressed under the heel of an ominous sky.

"True, but the ocean never sits still for long, and I'm hoping you will,
for this."

"What exactly is involved?" A little flutter of unease worked its way
up from the pit of her stomach.

"I'll do a few preliminary sketches first, but all in all it shouldn't take
more than three or four sittings."

"It would have to be mornings, when Lucy's at school." She spoke
slowly, hesitant to commit herself. It wasn't that her daughter required her
full-time attention these days. When Lucy was around, she spent almost
as much time with Yoshi as with her. Right now, for instance, she'd aban-

doned her knot-tying to follow him outside. Eleanor watched through
the window as they sloshed across the muddy yard on their way to the
kennel, Lucy in her slicker and boots and Yoshi with his head ducked low
and the collar of his jacket pulled up around his ears. No, it wasn't so
much the shirking of her parental duties that concerned Eleanor as her
reluctance to have Lucy witness the spectacle of her mother posing for a
portrait, like some society lady or . . . or indolent mistress. She blushed,
too, at the thought of all those hours alone with William, him studying
every nuance of her face and form. Would he be able to read in her face
the feelings she did her best to hide? Would her eyes tell him what her
heart could not?

And what would people think, if they knew? Something like this,
however innocent, could resurrect the old rumors about her hasty wedding and the baby that some had speculated wasn't Joe's. Those who
had whispered about her before would find her current behavior even
more shocking, she a married woman with her husband off fighting
overseas.

And Joe, what would *he* think?

"Would tomorrow be convenient?" William's voice broke into her
thoughts.

"Tomorrow?" She turned toward him, her fears subsiding at the sight
of his open, smiling face. "Tomorrow will be just fine."

Minutes later he was pushing back his chair, saying, "I should be off. I
promised Danny I'd take him to see the new Cary Cooper picture. Have
you seen it yet?"

She shook her head. "I don't get to the pictures much." In fact, she
hadn't seen a movie since the war broke out.

A wistful look flitted across his face, as if he were thinking about all
the places he'd like to take her. Then he turned to go, Laird at his heels,
only lightly touching her shoulder in passing. At the door, he paused to
ask, "You're sure you're all right with this? I wouldn't want to impose."

"It's not that." She hesitated before going on, fearful that he would
think she was making too much of this. It wasn't as if he'd asked her to

pose nude, for heaven's sake. "It's just . . . Are you sure it's wise? People might get the wrong idea. Not just Martha."

"Ah. I see." He nodded slowly, wearing a thoughtful look. "Well, in that case, it'll be our little secret." He broke into a grin, and she thought, *Isn't that just like a man? Problem solved, case closed.* Even so, she gave into a small smile of her own.

"We seem to be in the habit of keeping secrets," she observed dryly.

"Loose lips sink ships." He quoted the slogan on the poster displayed in every other shop window in town, along with the more lurid one depicting a caricature of the enemy, with exaggerated slant eyes and a protruding front teeth, that read simply *Jap Beast.*

What ships were in danger of being sunk here? she wondered.

Outside the dogs began to bark with the high yipping noises they made when let out to romp in the yard. All of last season's pups had found homes and the only dogs remaining were the two males, Panda and Cab (named after Cab Calloway), and her three bitches, Suki, Niobe, and Jasmine. Laird was Jasmine's son, the only male in that litter, and now his ears pricked at the sounds in the yard and he whined softly at the door, glancing up at William in mute appeal. William's eyes, though, were on Eleanor as he turned the knob, the hint of wistfulness she'd caught earlier now nakedly apparent. A look passed between them, in which Eleanor saw mirrored in his face all of her inchoate yearning.

Then he was out the door, and she was left trembling on the threshold of something she dared not name, wanting it and fearing it at the same time.

William was well aware of the risk involved, but whatever trepidation he might feel had nothing to do with the threat to his or Eleanor's reputations. It was his own heart he feared. In painting her portrait he would be expressing with his brush what he couldn't in words. And what if, once unleashed, those feelings could no longer be contained? Would Eleanor be scandalized? Would she put a stop to any further visits? He would rather go on this way, in a perpetual state of longing, than risk being cut off from her.

For there was no denying it any longer: William was in love.

It was a feeling he hadn't known in such a long time, it was a revelation for him. Everywhere he looked colors seemed brighter and even the bleakest landscapes were washed in light. He felt more kindly disposed toward the world in general, even those people he didn't particularly like. Alone in his studio, he'd catch himself staring idly at the half-finished canvas propped on his easel, a seascape commissioned by a retired boat builder in Oregon, seeing only Eleanor's face. He would imagine how he'd paint her, what pigments would best bring out the red and gold highlights in her hair and capture the luminous quality of her skin.

He sensed that she shared those feelings, and thought it would have been easy to seduce her. The notion didn't strike him as morally reprehensible, not in any general sense. While living in Europe he'd abandoned the hidebound morals inculcated in him as a child. But it wasn't just the quick pleasures of the bed he desired. He wanted more than that; he wanted a life with Eleanor. And how was it possible? He had his family to think of; hers, too. The thought of Eleanor's husband off fighting for his country, while he, William, fulfilled his lust in their marital bed, left him feeling slightly queasy. It would eat at Eleanor most of all, he knew. He'd have to stand by helplessly and watch the woman he loved be consumed by guilt, knowing he was the cause of it.

Martha deserved better, too. He had loved her once, and if that love had grown fractured with time, she was still his wife, the mother of his son. He owed it to her, and to Danny, not to let his small lie grow into an even bigger one.

And yet . . .

He dreamed of Eleanor with his eyes open. He imagined what it would be like to lie next to her in bed, her bare flesh gliding over his, his face buried in her hair that was twelve different shades of brown and red, her soft mouth parting at the touch of his lips. He saw her face framed by the white of her pillow, her green eyes beckoning to him. He saw the smooth plane of her belly and her long legs opening to him, taking him in.

If he couldn't make love to her, painting her portrait would be the next best thing. For the first time in months he itched to pick up his brushes and palette. Already he was plotting how best to capture her on canvas. He wanted to depict her as he saw her: a woman gloriously in her prime who mistakenly believed the best years of her life were behind her.

—

"Don't look at me. I'm a wreck," she said, with a breathless laugh as she let him through the door. "Are you sure about this? You'll be wasting a perfectly good canvas." She was wearing a faded housecoat, her hair haphazardly pinned up, the dogs roiling at her feet. Yet to him, she had never looked more beautiful. She bent to grab hold of a dog collar, scolding, "Now, look, you, it's back to the kennel if you don't behave yourself." The offending creature instantly sank onto its haunches, looking up at her shame-faced until she stroked its head and let it loose.

She straightened, tucking a stray tendril of hair behind one ear, her face flushed with exertion. "I'm a little behind schedule," she apologized. "Lucy was late getting off to school. And the dogs—" she pointed toward Niobe, now romping on the braided rug in front of the fireplace with Laird "—must have known you were coming. The only way I could get them to stop barking was to let them into the house."

He smiled. In one hand, he carried the battered wooden case containing his paints and brushes and in the other his folded easel and a blank canvas wrapped in brown paper. "The more, the merrier," he said. "They can keep Laird company while I paint."

"Wait here while I change. I won't be a minute." She spun on her heel, disappearing down the hall. Only then did he notice she was barefoot. Minutes later, in less time than it would have taken Martha to change hats, she was back, wearing a red print dress belted at the waist, her hair arranged in loose curls on top of her head. Dangling from one hand was a pair of high-heeled pumps.

"No, leave them off," ordered William, when she bent to put them on. "I'd like you barefoot." He hadn't planned to paint her that way. But seeing her all dressed up in her Sunday best without her shoes, he realized it captured her, the two sides of Eleanor that were often at war with each other: the part that wanted to be respectable and the part that wanted to run wild, like a child through high grass on a summer day.

She shot him a quizzical look, tossing the pumps aside. "If you insist. But I won't look very elegant."

"You're perfect just as you are." It was a moment before he could tear his eyes away.

"I'm afraid my last pair of stockings has a hole in it," she said, glancing down at her legs in dismay, which, like her feet, were bare. "They're so hard to come by these days, I might as well wish for the Eiffel Tower. So where do you want me?" Her eyes darted around the neat, if somewhat shabby room, with its threadbare furnishings and woodwork polished to a shine.

Naked in bed, came his silent, unbidden reply. But all he said was, "Why don't we try the sofa. You'll be more comfortable and the light's good." He waited until she'd positioned herself on worn, plush cushions, her legs tucked under her, her toes peeking from the folds of her skirt. "There, like that. Don't move an inch." He got out his pad and a stick of charcoal and began sketching her. Midway through his third failed attempt at capturing her on paper, he paused, frowning. "You look tense. If you're uncomfortable, we could try another position."

"It's not that," she said. "I was just wondering what you plan on doing with the portrait once it's finished. I mean, if it's going to be on display . . . "

"I haven't given it much thought," he answered truthfully. "I may decide to keep it."

Her eyes widened in consternation. "Won't your wife . . . I mean, she'd have to wonder . . . "

"She might," he agreed, "if I were to show it to her, which I have no intention of doing."

Silence rose up to fill the room, eddying with all the implications of his words. William saw the troubled look on Eleanor's face, and for a panicked moment he thought she might decide to call the whole thing off.

But the silence held and the moment passed.

"What do you look for in a subject?" she asked, after a bit.

He paused to consider it, absently scratching his chin. "I'm not sure I can explain it. It's different with each one. Like, for instance . . . Have you seen the portrait I did of Mister Humphrey that's hanging in his store?" Wizened old Humphrey, who had to be at least ninety years old, owned the stationery shop downtown where William bought a lot of his supplies. "What made me decide to paint him were his hands. They're all twisted and knobby, but beautiful in their own way, like tree roots pushing up out of the ground."

"And what do you see in me?" Her green eyes looked directly into his, and a silent communication passed between them. William felt the tiny hairs on the back of his arms and neck stand up.

"I see a lady in waiting."

She arched a brow. "Because of Joe, you mean?"

"Well, no, not exactly." He searched for the right words. "It's just . . . there's so much out there you haven't seen. A whole world. And here you are . . . " *Trapped with a man you don't love.* "Living out in the middle of nowhere." He held up a hand before she could voice the protest forming on her lips. "I don't mean that you're not here out of your own free will, but I'll bet you can count on one hand the number of times you've been off the island."

He could see from the way her face was reddening that he'd hit a nerve, but she only laughed and said, "You're wrong. I'd need both hands." She held them up, fingers splayed apart, the tiny diamond in her wedding ring winking in the pale light filtering through the window. "Still, it doesn't mean I'm not adventurous. Just poor."

"I'm sorry, I didn't mean to offend you," he was quick to reply. "All I'm saying is that you're different from most of the people around here. You have a curiosity about the world. I never would have suggested to Mister Humphrey, for instance, that he ought to get out more. He's perfectly happy right where he is."

She stiffened a bit. "And I'm not?"

"I'm not the one to answer that," he said gently.

"I have a child to think of. I can't just waltz off whenever I feel like it." Frowning, she said, "Anyway, how did we get on this subject? I thought you wanted to paint me, not dissect me."

"Point taken," he said with a smile, bending once more to his work.

When William was finally satisfied with what he'd drawn, he set up his easel and unpacked his paints, unrolling the felt cloth smelling of linseed oil in which his brushes were wrapped. Before long he was so absorbed in his work he scarcely noticed the minutes slipping by. It wasn't until Eleanor stirred and stretched that he glanced at his watch and saw that more than an hour had passed. He called a break, and Eleanor went into the kitchen to fetch them something to drink. William, alone in the room with nothing to occupy him, became aware of the sounds drifting in from outside: the rusty caw of a crow; a hammer banging in the yard; the more distant drone of an airplane.

Not bad, he thought, contemplating the progress he'd made so far. He'd captured something in her expression, a combination of youthfulness and womanly experience. And her eyes . . . they seemed to be gazing out at those far flung places she dreamed of visiting one day. He decided he would title it simply *Woman in Red*. The image would speak for itself.

Over the next few days they fell into a routine, William coming over every morning after Lucy had been packed off to school. Now, when he dreamed, it was of Eleanor in the red dress. Barefoot. And after a while what was in his mind's eye became blurred with what he saw in reality, like watercolors running together, lending a vibrancy to her image that he couldn't have created on his own. He became obsessed with the portrait, working in a kind of fever, as if guided by some unseen force.

The irony wasn't lost on him, either. What was perhaps his best work might never see the light of day. Yet surprisingly the thought didn't trouble him. He wasn't doing this for money or fame; he was doing it out of love.

It was well into the morning of the fourth day that he realized the bulk of his work was done. The details he could take care of back in his studio. He felt a strange sense of loss as he put down his brush and said, "Want to come have a look?"

He hadn't allowed her to see it before this, not wanting to grow self-conscious. Now she peered over his shoulder, asking with a kind of wonder, "Is that really how you see me?"

He tilted his head to look up at her. "You don't think it looks like you?"

"I didn't say that. It's just . . . it reminds me of someone I used to know."

"Who?"

"Me, when I was young." A wistful smile played at her lips, as she stood there studying the canvas, her hand resting absently on his shoulder.

Something made him reach up and touch her face. "You're still young."

Color rode up on her cheekbones and her eyes shone with what might have been tears. Slowly, she shook her head, saying, "It's been a long time since I felt that way."

Something made him ask, "There was someone before Joe, wasn't there?"

She nodded, her gaze fixed on a point just past his ear. "I thought I loved him at the time. Now I realize it was just infatuation. I didn't know any better, you see. The proverbial minister's daughter." She gave an ironic laugh. "And he . . . well, he turned out to be the proverbial rake." She paused before continuing on. "If it had been just a broken heart, it would have been all right. Broken hearts mend. But there was a . . . complication."

At once, he guessed what she was getting at. "You were pregnant."

"Yes," she said in a small voice.

Eleanor did something then that took him completely by surprise. She slowly sank to her knees and placed her head in his lap, almost as though in supplication. For a moment William scarcely dared to breathe, as if with some shy woodland creature he feared he would startle into bolting. A hush fell over the room, in which the ticking of the clock over the mantel seemed unnaturally loud. One by one, he removed the pins from her hair, freeing it to tumble down her neck and shoulders. It slipped through his fingers like heavy silk, parting to reveal the soft indentation at the nape of her neck, with its little tuft fine as a baby's. He might have been making love to her for how alive he felt, how keenly in the moment.

Her voice floated up from the cradle of his lap. "You asked me once why I married Joe. I wish I could say it was because I loved him, because I do now . . . in my own way. He's a good man. He married me when no one else would have. And Lucy . . . she's his heart. The way he dotes on her, you'd never know she wasn't his." Eleanor lifted her head to look up at him, her eyes searching his for any hint of the judgment she'd so liberally heaped on herself. "Promise you won't tell anyone. You're the only one who knows besides Joe and my parents. I haven't even told Lucy. She worships Joe. If she found out . . ." Eleanor grew pale at the thought.

"I promise." William smoothed back the hair that lay in a delicate web over her cheek, holding her chin cupped as he looked into her eyes. "There's just one thing I want you to promise me in return."

"What?" she asked, with obvious trepidation.

"That you'll stop thinking of yourself as a scarlet woman. You did nothing wrong. As for me, I could never think less of you, no matter what."

"Thank you." The look of gratitude she wore was almost more than he could bear. He was only saying what any decent human being would. Why should that make him a saint?

The moment stretched on, moving from mere silence into a realm where nothing else seemed to exist. They were on a plane far removed from this shabby little room, poised as still as the image on the canvas before them, a tableaux in real life: William with his hand cradling her chin as Eleanor kneeled before him, seeming to rise like some beautiful flower from the silken puddle of her dress spilling across the floor at his feet.

Then in some distant part of his brain William became aware of the sound of a car approaching along the drive. Eleanor quickly rose to her feet, patting her hair and smoothing her skirt as she hurried over to the window to peer out at the shiny, dark Buick pulling to a stop in front of the house.

plague. He couldn't afford to. Small comfort, but at this point she'd take what she could get.

The night of the party Jeremy came in, accompanied by his dad, a half hour or so after everyone else had arrived. He approached her cautiously, submitting limply to a hug.

"Sorry we're late," Randy apologized. "I didn't get in until just a little while ago."

"You're here now, that's all that matters." She gave her ex-husband a peck on the cheek. His hair was still damp from the shower and he smelled of Brut, the scent of which evoked memories of when they used to date in high school.

"Nice turnout," he said, glancing about the crowded room.

"Amazing, isn't it? It seems I still have a few friends left." Alice spoke lightly, but she'd been deeply touched by the show of support, proof that not everyone was against her. In fact, over the past weeks, friends and acquaintances from the past had been quietly making their allegiance known. Like Patsy Rowland, who'd been on the cheerleading squad with her in high school. It was Patsy who'd donated the tables and chairs for the restaurant, from the hotel she and her husband used to own.

"More than a few, I'd say." Randy seemed genuinely pleased for her. "From the looks of it, you shouldn't have too much trouble drumming up business," he said. "I like what you've done with the place, too. Very cozy."

Alice, seeing it through his eyes, was struck with new appreciation for all she'd accomplished, in a relatively short amount of time with very little money. The old walls that had been gray with grime were painted now in soft peach and apple-green hues, and the windows hung with the gingham curtains her mother had stitched. An antique butter churn stood by the front door, alongside a crate of apples from Denise's trees. The old pine floorboards had been stripped and refinished and she'd had wainscoting put in. Above it were shelves that displayed homemade preserves and pickles, along with various items scavenged from the flea market: souvenir plates, an old pewter coffee service, a splatter-ware pitcher and matching bowl, vintage bottles and tins from companies long defunct.

A man in uniform wearing a somber look got out, and she clapped a hand over her mouth, letting out a muffled cry. "No," she pleaded in a voice barely above a whisper. "No, please."

She froze at the knock on the door, and William could see that she was trembling. She appeared to age a dozen years in the time it took her to trudge across the living room and down the hall.

From where William stood, just out of the line of sight of the man poised in the doorway, he could see only a burly khaki shoulder and the crisp brim of a military cap. He heard a deep voice intone with regret, "Missus Styles? I'm afraid I have some bad news . . ."

CHAPTER TEN

When Alice was little her favorite thing in the world had been helpin
her grandmother in the kitchen: Nana, cupping her hand over Alice
smaller one, guiding it as she cut floury circles of dough with the biscu
cutter, or teaching Alice the proper way to frost a cake, applying a th
layer first to catch the crumbs. So it seemed appropriate that Alice chri
ten her newly refurbished restaurant the Pantry, in honor of her gran
mother's, which had been so well-stocked the family used to joke that sl
could have survived off it the rest of her days without another trip to tl
store. Besides, none of it would have been possible without Nan
money. Her grandmother, she thought, would have been pleased to see
so well spent.

The only cloud over the occasion of the grand opening was tl
thought of what lay ahead for Jeremy. At the arraignment, the jud
hadn't cut him any slack. Despite Colin's efforts to have the case 1
manded to juvenile court, Jeremy was to be tried as an adult, on the fi
count of rape. It was almost more than Alice could contemplate mu
less cope with, but she was doing her best. And if there was a silver li
ing to the cloud, it was that her son no longer avoided her like t

"Thanks. I wish I could take all the credit, but I couldn't have done it without Denise's help," she said.

He smiled. "I remember when you two used to sit out in the hot sun all day selling lemonade."

A reminder of just how long they'd known each other.

She laughed and shook her head. "God, I can't believe you remember that far back."

"I remember a lot of things." He held her gaze a beat longer than necessary, giving Alice a funny feeling in the pit of her stomach.

Eager to get off this subject, she grabbed his elbow, saying, "Come on, let's get you something to eat." She showed him to the buffet table, where Jeremy was already helping himself to a plate of food.

"It doesn't seem to have affected his appetite, at least," Randy murmured. He and Alice exchanged a smile, that of parents enjoying a small reprieve from their shared worry over their son. If she'd harbored any bitterness toward her ex-husband, it was gone. Randy had been a rock throughout this latest ordeal, calling often to strategize about Jeremy's case, his solid presence the other day in court keeping her on an even keel. She didn't know how she'd have managed without him.

Jeremy, on the other hand, seemed to coping well enough. He'd lost that pale, shell-shocked look, she noted, watching him with his cousin Ryan, the two of them chatting as they shoveled food into their mouths. She couldn't tell whether or not he was having fun, but at least he wasn't hiding in a corner.

A short while later, as she was wandering over to the buffet table to have a word with Patsy Rowland, she ran into Jeremy, on his way back for seconds. For a moment he just stood there, looking ill at ease, holding his plate awkwardly in one hand. Finally, summoning his manners, he said, "Food's good. Especially that crab thing, with the mushrooms."

"Thanks. I'm glad you like it."

"You do all the cooking?"

"Your grandma did some." Alice had made the curried chicken salad and mushroom-crab strata, the garlic roasted string beans and creamed

escarole; Lucy had supplied her signature Coca-Cola ham and candied
sweet potatoes. She leaned in to confide, "Though between you and me
I'm not quite sure how I'm going to manage when I'm on my own." She'd
hired the daughter of one of Denise's teacher friends to wait tables and a
kid from down the road to wash dishes, but other than that it looked as
if she'd be flying solo, at least until Calpernia arrived. "If you know of
anyone who's looking for something part-time, I could use an extra hand
in the kitchen. The pay isn't much, but meals are included."

"I might know of someone," he said.

"Great. Tell whoever it is to give me a call."

"Actually, I was thinking I could use the extra hours myself." He was
regarding her in a way that made her think of Colin McGinty's skittish
dog: shy and hopeful at the same time.

Alice was so astonished, it was a moment before she could respond.
"What about Mister Barbour?"

Jeremy shrugged, and looked away. "He cut back on my hours. The
season's kind of winding down, so he doesn't need me as much anymore."

"Well, in that case, of course I'd love to have you work for me." She
tried to keep the enthusiasm from her voice, not wanting to overwhelm
him. "How soon can you start?"

"I have this thing tomorrow after school, but I'm free the rest of the
week."

"How about Tuesday then?" He nodded, and she said with more feeling, "Thanks, Jeremy. This will be a real help."

"Yeah, well, I just thought . . ." Color bloomed in his pale cheeks. "You
know, since you're helping out with Mister McGinty and all, that I should
do my part. I'll even work for free, if you don't have the money to pay me."

Alice's throat grew tight. "If anyone deserves to be thanked, it's him."
Colin had refused any payment, saying he would agree to handle the case
only on a strictly *pro bono* basis. "As for your working for free, I wouldn't
dream of it." She placed a hand lightly on his arm. "You don't owe me a
thing."

She scanned the crowd in search of Colin and spotted him talking to
Gary. He'd donned a sports coat and tie for the occasion, which made

him stand out amid the other, more dressed-down guests. But he would have stood out regardless. There was something about him that drew the eye, an intensity that showed, not in the restless energy of someone like Denise, but in the quiet assuredness he brought to everything he did.

She'd seen it the other day in the courtroom, when he'd stood up to address the bench. "Your Honor, my client is a sixteen-year-old boy, with no history of juvenile delinquency or school misconduct," he'd argued, after the judge had refused his request to have the case remanded to juvenile court. "He's an ordinary teenager engaging in age-appropriate activities. He went to a party, he met a girl, they engaged in consensual sex. I see no reason this should even go to trial, much less that he be tried as an adult."

The district attorney, a wiry man with brushy, graying hair who couldn't sit for long without twitching in his seat like someone with a bad case of hemorrhoids, had sprung to his feet to interject sarcastically, "Where you come, Mister McGinty, a rape charge might be commonplace, but around here we take such things pretty seriously." Earlier, Alice had seen him dart a nervous look at one of his colleagues when the judge had granted Colin permission to practice in this jurisdiction on a *pro hac vice* basis. Clearly, he hadn't been expecting a heavyweight from out of state to be handling Jeremy's case.

Ignoring him, Colin had steadfastly kept his eyes on the bench. "Your Honor, with all due respect, no one is disputing the seriousness of the charge, but we would like to make sure this young man is not being made an example of beyond what justice is called for."

The prosecutor had jumped in once more. "If this young man is old enough to engage in sexual activities, consensual or otherwise, he's old enough to be tried as an adult!"

"Mister Cantwell has a point," Judge Voakes had weighed in.

Finally, Colin had turned to the prosecutor, observing coolly, "I take it Mister Cantwell never engaged in sexual activity himself as a teenager." The prosecutor's rabbity face reddened, as Colin continued, "As for the rest of us, if it were a crime, we'd all be on trial."

A ripple of laughter had gone through the courtroom, and Alice had thought, *Score one for Colin.* She'd believed in him, in the face of his own doubts, and her faith had been validated. He clearly hadn't lost his touch. For the first time since the start of the ordeal she'd felt hopeful.

"So you guys are like, what, friends or something?" Jeremy was asking now.

Her cheeks warmed. What Jeremy wanted to know was if there was something going on between her and Colin. She chose her words carefully. "I haven't known him very long, but, yes, I'd say we're friends."

"So you like him?" Jeremy wasn't letting her off the hook so easily.

"The main thing is, do *you* like him?" She was quick to turn the tables.

"Yeah. He's cool."

"That's all that matters then," she said. "But he can only help you if you're willing. Just remember, he's on your side. We all are."

Jeremy looked down at his feet. When he raised his head at last, that strained look was back and he had trouble meeting her gaze. "Look, I wasn't being completely honest with you before . . . about Mister Barbour. The truth is, I was fired."

"Fired?" she echoed, in disbelief. "Why?"

"Because of what happened."

"With the girl, you mean." It wasn't a question.

Carrie Ann Flagler. Alice couldn't even bring herself to speak the name aloud. In court, she'd tried to catch the girl's eye, to force her to look over at them and see what her lie was costing them, but they might have been invisible as far as Carrie Ann was concerned. She'd sat flanked by her parents, a thin, nervous-looking woman and her bulldog of a husband, who at one point had shot Alice an evil look, as if the fault could be traced back to her. Carrie Ann herself had struck Alice as plain and unremarkable, a moon-faced girl with close-set eyes and brown, professionally streaked hair, who'd docilely answered the questions posed to her in a barely audible voice, every now and then flicking glances at her father, as if to be sure her responses met with his approval.

"He didn't say that was the reason," Jeremy replied with disgust, "but I know it was. I heard it from one of the other guys."

"I guess Mister Barbour has never heard of innocent until proven guilty," she said, indignant.

"It's no big deal," Jeremy said, with a shrug. "I probably would've quit anyway. He was always riding me about something."

They were interrupted just then by Denise, swooping down on Jeremy as if she hadn't seen him in ages. "Hey, you! Where have you been keeping yourself? You forget about your old aunt, or what?" She grabbed hold of him and gave him a squeeze, rocking him from side to side for a moment before releasing him. Her sister had had too much to drink, Alice noted. Not that Denise wasn't entitled. She was a one-woman mule team, always looking after everyone else while putting herself last. It was nice to see her cut loose for a change. "How have you been? I mean, really." She dropped her voice, looking deeply into Jeremy's eyes as she stood there swaying slightly on her feet. "You're not going to let this get in the way of your studies, are you? This other thing," she went on, dismissing the court case with an airy wave, "will get sorted out in no time. But college . . . sweetie, that's your future."

"Yeah, I know, I'm the Great White Hope of Grays Island," Jeremy replied, in a voice thick with irony. "Can't let anything screw that up."

But the irony must have been lost on Denise; either that, or she was choosing to ignore it. "That's my boy." She patted him on the cheek. "It'll all work out. You'll see. In the meantime, we're rooting for you, kiddo. You know that, don't you?"

"Yeah, I do. Thanks, Aunt Denise." He looked eyed her affectionately.

Seeing the bond between them, Alice felt a quick, hard thrust of envy. At the same time, she knew that if it hadn't been for Denise all those years, Jeremy would have been the worse for it.

Jeremy wandered off, and Denise leaned in to Alice. "Am I imagining it," she whispered urgently, with a gust of boozy breath, "or is Susie Quinn hitting on my husband?"

Alice glanced over to where Gary was having what looked to be a perfectly innocent conversation with an old school chum. She peered at them nonetheless, as if to assess the situation, saying in a theatrically hushed voice, "I couldn't say for sure, but they *do* look awfully cozy." When Denise got like this, the only way to handle it was with humor. Usually her sister ended up laughing at herself. But this time she seemed determined to milk it for all it was worth.

"I always knew Susie was a slut," she said, as if her suspicions had been confirmed. "Ramona Saucedo told me that, in high school, she slept with half the football team."

"Not half. A third maybe," Alice acknowledged. Never mind that Susie was now a happily married mother of two.

"Well, she'd better keep her hands to herself," Denise growled, sotto voce. "If I ever found out Gary was cheating on me, he'd be one sorry son of a gun, by the time I got through with him. Divorce would be the least of it."

Alice knew that Denise didn't really believe that Gary would ever be unfaithful to her; Alice was less certain. He had been acting so secretive lately. Suppose he *was* having an affair?

They were interrupted just then by their mother, on her way to the kitchen carrying a stack of dirty plates—never mind Alice's having told her to leave the clean-up for Eduardo to take care of in the morning. "You girls, always whispering about something," Lucy clucked, shaking her head in mock exasperation. "What are you two plotting now?"

Alice and Denise exchanged a look, and Denise answered with a giggle, "Nothing you want to know about." Lucy, without meaning to, had succeeded where Alice had failed in reducing Denise's fears to the stuff of meaningless girl talk.

"Having a good time, Mom?" Alice asked, turning to her mother. She couldn't recall when she'd last seen her look this elegant. Lucy was wearing a stylish print dress and low-heeled pumps, her silver hair clipped back on one side with a marquisette barrette. She'd even had her nails done.

"Oh, yes. It's a wonderful party!" Lucy's eyes shone and her color was high, no doubt due to the half-drunk glass of champagne in her hand. It didn't take much to get her tipsy. "And whatever anyone says, I just know the restaurant will be a huge success."

"Just what *have* people been saying?" Alice wanted to know.

Lucy looked uncertain, as if wishing she'd kept her mouth shut. "Oh, honey, it's nothing. Just a few mean-spirited busybodies who think you don't deserve to get ahead." She spoke airily, in an attempt to make light of it. "But if they imagine some silly boycott is going to put you out of business—" She broke off, color flooding her cheeks.

"Boycott?" Alice stared at her in shock.

Her mother's brow creased in consternation. "I'm sorry, dear, I shouldn't have mentioned it. Please don't let it worry you. It's just a handful of cranks with nothing better to do than stir up trouble. I'm sure it'll all blow over in no time."

"Did you know anything about this?" Alice swung about to face Denise.

From the sheepish expression her sister wore, it was clear that she'd known all along. Even now, she attempted to minimize it, saying, "Mom's right. You shouldn't pay any attention to those idiots. Anyway, they're the ones who'll suffer, not you. Think of all the great meals they'll be missing out on."

Alice didn't doubt that it would blow over, but the mere thought that there were people plotting behind her back had drained all the fun out of the evening. She didn't want to spoil it for her mother and sister, though, so she only said, "You're right. To hell with them. Here, Mom, why don't let you let me take those? I was just on my way into the kitchen." She relieved her mother of the plates and headed off, feeling a sudden, urgent need to be alone.

She bumped into Colin along the way. "Need a hand?" he asked. "Or maybe someone to vent to?" he added in a lowered voice, taking in the grim set of her jaw.

"You're supposed to be enjoying yourself, not listening to a tale of woes," she told him.

"Okay, I confess, I have an ulterior motive. You see, parties aren't really my thing. If you put me to work, you'd be doing me a favor. Cook, bottle-washer, lawyer, advisor, whatever . . . I'm at your service." He gave a little bow, flashing her a lopsided grin.

Alice didn't know quite how to respond. Lately, she'd found herself growing increasingly dependent on him, and that bothered her. Still, it would be rude to reject his offer outright.

"All right, you can keep me company. But that's all. You're not allowed to lift a finger." She continued on her way, Colin falling into step beside her. "So have you always hated parties, or is this a recent thing?" she quizzed him, as she pushed her way through the swinging doors into the kitchen.

"I used to love them. But that was in the days when parties were just an excuse to drink. I don't remember what went on at half of them. Now that I'm sober, it's a little like being thirteen again, trying to get up the nerve to ask the pretty girl to dance." He flashed her a smile that made her blush, and disregarding her command took the dishes from her, scraping them and stacking them in the sink.

"I know what you mean," she said. "I tend to get a little maxed out on socializing. A function of prison life. You get so little privacy, you end up craving it after a while." He showed no sign of discomfort at the direction the conversation had taken, and now she abruptly turned to face him. "You know, I just figured out what it is I like about you."

"What's that?" he asked.

"I don't have to tiptoe around you," she said. "Most people act as if my having done time is a disease that might be catching. My own family, for instance. They look pained if I so much as mention it."

He shrugged. "It can be a pretty sensitive subject."

"But you're not like that."

"I come at it from a different perspective. Besides," he went on, "We're not related."

"Meaning?"

"Maybe your family feels they let you down."

"That's crazy. Why should they think that?"

He shrugged. "No reason. But that doesn't always stop people from feeling guilty."

"There was nothing anyone could have done," Alice insisted.

"I'm not sure I buy that, at least not where your lawyer was concerned."

"What do you know about it?" she asked, eyeing him suspiciously. The years at Pine River had left her deeply wary of people nosing around behind her back. Usually when they did, it wasn't because they were planning a surprise party for you.

"I looked it up," he told her. "They have all the old newspapers on microfiche down at the library. I also got hold of the transcripts from your trial, over at county records."

"Why go to all that trouble? I could have told you what you wanted to know."

"I thought it might help with Jeremy's case. And from what I could see, he's not the only one who got a bum rap. If you don't mind my saying so, your lawyer didn't do such a good job defending you."

"What makes you say that?" she asked, though privately she'd come to the same conclusion.

"For one thing, he should have moved for a change of venue."

"Maybe, but unless you know of a way to turn back the clock, what good does it do to second-guess him now?" she asked in frustration.

He shrugged, leaning back against the counter. "My point is that lawyers make mistakes. Even good ones."

"What are you saying?"

"It's not too late to find another lawyer for Jeremy."

"I don't want another lawyer." Alice had seen him in action; she knew what he was capable of. "What I *want* is for son's name to be cleared. Tell me honestly, what are his chances?"

He eyed her thoughtfully for a moment, as if gauging how much information she could handle. "I spoke with the D.A. on Friday, and he's not prepared to offer any kind of plea deal. From our conversation, it was pretty clear that he thinks he can win this one."

"Based on what evidence?" She wrapped her arms around her middle, shivering in the warmth of the kitchen.

"The rape kit, for one thing. So far the test results are inconclusive, which doesn't exactly put Jeremy in the clear. But they're still waiting on the results of the DNA sample, which could add another wrinkle."

Alice seized upon that. "You mean Jeremy might not have been the only one who was with Carrie Ann that night?"

"There's always that possibility. And the eyewitnesses all testified that the three other boys had been drinking heavily." Colin spoke guardedly, as if not wanting to get her hopes up.

"And if it turns out she *was* with one of those other boys?"

"It wouldn't let Jeremy off the hook, but it would shoot some pretty big holes in the prosecution's case. They'd have to show probable cause, and that's a lot harder to do when there's more than one suspect." Nonetheless, Colin was quick to warn, "I don't want you to pin too much on this, though. Chances are it'll turn out to be a dead end."

Alice felt her spirits, briefly buoyed, sag once more.

Slowly she let out a breath, looking around her. The kitchen that had been so chaotic earlier in the day was quiet. There was only the low hum of the refrigerator and the muted din of voices from the next room. Suddenly she was sure she had bitten off more than she could chew. The hulking old Garland, the scarred butcher block counters, the Hobart mixer under its plastic shroud, all seemed to mock her in some way, as if daring her to make a go of this possibly doomed enterprise. And how would she be able to save Jeremy if she couldn't save herself?

She felt Colin's touch against her arm, and she turned her head to find him eyeing her as if he knew exactly what was going through her mind, because in a sense weren't they in the same boat, both struggling to stay afloat? "I just wanted you to know what's at stake here," he told her. "You should think it through carefully before we move ahead. I might be good at what I do—or at least I was at one time—but I've only been sober a little over seven months. And as we say in the program, however long it took you to screw up your life, that's how long it'll take, and then some, to get it straightened out."

"We all have our baggage," she said.

"I'm not trying to compare it to what you went through . . ." He paused, as if searching for the right words, before continuing, "I'm not sure if anyone who hasn't been through it themselves could possibly know what that's like. But there are other kinds of prisons, and the kind people like me end up in, believe me, they can be just as hard to get out of." His gaze turned inward, and she saw the pain on his face, coupled with some deep yearning.

"But you got out," she said gently.

"For now, yes. But most days I feel like I'm barely hanging on." He pointed toward the shelf over the counter, which held an array of bottles, various oils as well as the wine she used in cooking. "That bottle of Bordeaux there. I'll bet you wouldn't even have noticed it, if it you didn't know it was there. Me? It was the first thing I saw when I walked in. Not so long ago I'd have headed straight for it and, after I'd drunk every drop, gone in search of the wine cellar. And the next day I'd have woken with a wicked hangover and done the same thing all over again. So you see? I'm not exactly the Rock of Gibraltar."

She shook her head. "I don't expect you to be. That's not why I asked you to take Jeremy's case. I did it because you know what it's like to be knocked off your feet. And you picked yourself up and moved on. I see that as a strength, not a weakness."

His eyes searched her face, and she felt some powerful current pass between them. Mutual attraction . . . even lust . . . wouldn't have explained it. It was more than that. She had the sense that they were the only two people in the world, a man and a woman who were barely hanging on and who saw in each other a kind of life-line. Colin seemed to feel it too. He reached up, lightly brushing her cheek with the backs of his knuckles as if to remind her, or perhaps himself, that they were still in the land of the living. She shivered, feeling tiny sparks ignite under her skin where he'd grazed it. "Well, here we are. We survived, didn't we?" he said, wearing an expression that was both sad and ironic. "I guess that's something in itself."

She took a step back, as from a high place from which she might tumble. "So are we okay? You're not bailing out on me?"

He shrugged once more. "I'm game, if you are. Now all we have to do is get Jeremy on board."

She eyed him in confusion, feeling a small pulse of alarm. "What makes you think he isn't?"

"For one thing, he's not entirely convinced that he's innocent."

"What do you mean? Of course, he's innocent!" she said, taken aback. Had Jeremy told him something in confidence that she and Randy weren't privy to?

"I think the line is blurred in his mind," Colin went on to explain. "He doesn't seem to understand that taking advantage of a girl when they'd both had too much to drink doesn't necessarily make him a rapist. Just a teenager who exercised some bad judgment."

"Should I talk to him?" she asked.

"No, why don't you let me handle it. I think I'm making some headway."

"There's something else, isn't there?" she said, taking note of the troubled look on his face. "What is it? What's wrong?"

"I'm not sure," he said, his frown deepening. "But I'm getting a funny feeling about all this. I haven't been around long enough to know all the politics at play here, but I agreed with Randy—I think Jeremy's being railroaded."

Alice felt the blood leave her face. Colin was merely confirming her own suspicions. "You're not imagining it. In fact, I'm pretty sure that's what's going on." She shared her concerns about Owen White. "I would have said something to you sooner, but I didn't want you to think I was being paranoid."

Colin nodded thoughtfully. "I'll nose around a bit, see what I can find out. You think your brother-in-law might be able to give us some insight?"

"Gary?" She hadn't thought of it before, but now it occurred to her that if anyone was privy to what went on behind the scenes, it was him. As deputy chief of police, he knew where all the bodies were buried, so to speak. "I'll talk to him," she said. "He can keep an ear to the ground, if nothing else." Another thought occurred to her, and she frowned, saying, "There's just one problem. Say we get wind of something fishy. How are we going to prove it? It's not like we'd have evidence."

"You never know when a piece of information will come in handy. Even something that might not have seemed relevant at first," Colin said, with the same air of authority he'd shown in the courtroom. "One way or another, we'll get to the bottom of it. And if what we suspect is true, we'll find a way to nail the bastard."

Alice was far less certain. "Sometimes I think Randy's right—I should have left well enough alone," she said, thinking about her own situation. "If I hadn't known the truth about David's death, if I hadn't witnessed it with my own eyes, I probably would have believed Owen's lies, and we'd all have been better off in the end."

"It's different this time."

"Why is that?"

"You have me." He gave her a crooked smile, as if to say, *For whatever it's worth.*

Alice didn't know how to respond. It was almost more than she could take in, that this man who until a short while ago had been a complete stranger, linked to her only through some remote connection involving their grandparents, would be sticking his neck out for her. In prison, when someone did something for you, there was almost always a price tag attached. Even Randy, who'd vowed to stick with her through good times and bad, had let her down. If her own husband, David's father, couldn't stay the course why should she believe that Colin would?

And yet . . . somehow she did. It wasn't so much a matter of friendship as of fellowship. In helping her, maybe he was helping himself in some way. Either way, his words were like balm, calming her fears and soothing some ache deep within her. It had been a long since she'd allowed herself to grow close to another human being, with the exception of Calpernia. And here was this man offering the one thing she wanted most: the chance to save her younger son that she'd been denied with her firstborn.

"I don't know how I can ever repay you," she said.

"You don't have to." He was standing directly underneath the overhead light fixture, its harsh glow throwing his face into stark relief. His eyes glinted darkly from shadowed sockets and his jaw line and cheekbones were as sharply defined as if honed by a blade.

Their eyes met and held, and for a moment she could have sworn he was about to kiss her. She could feel it almost as surely as the pulse throbbing at the base of her throat. She had a sudden wild urge to twine her arms around him, to kiss him all over and taste the salt of his skin on her lips. Tension gathered as the moment stretched out, and a fiery bolt shot down through her belly, spreading through her lower regions: a heat so intense it bordered on discomfort. She hadn't slept with a man in nine years—or a woman for that matter, despite the commonly held belief about prison life—and however starved she was, the thought was terrifying. And from the look on Colin's face it was obvious he was equally fearful.

Alice was the first to speak, "Well, I hope you'll at least allow me treat you to some free meals," she said with a shaky laugh. "While I'm open, that is, which might not be for long. I hear there's talk of a boycott. It seems the scarlet *A* stands for Alice, in my case."

Colin didn't look too concerned. "I don't see you letting the local witch hunters stop you, not after all you've overcome so far."

"They don't worry me as much as Owen does." Having expressed her fears aloud, they seemed more real than ever. And now the scope of what she faced unfurled before her, frightening in its dimension. "He could shut this place down in a heartbeat. I have a feeling the only reason he hasn't so far is because he has something bigger in mind. Something that'll take me down along with Jeremy."

—

Alice was cleaning up after the last guest had gone when the front door swung open and a familiar voice called out, "Damn, girl, don't tell me the party's over? And here I done got all dressed up for nothing."

Alice looked up to find Calpernia King filling the doorway like a total eclipse of the sun. Suitcase in hand, decked out in tight white jeans and a white rabbit chubby over a hot pink jersey top with the word *Diva* spelled out in shiny metal rivets across the mighty prow of her chest. When they used to talk about the first thing they'd do when they got out, Calpernia's plan had been to head straight for the nearest beauty salon, which was just what she'd done, judging by her three-inch nails painted in a mosaic of iridescent colors and the multitude of braided hair extensions coiled atop her head like some elaborate tribal headdress. Now she spread her arms wide to take in the flying missile of Alice hurtling toward her.

Alice hugged her long and hard before pulling back with a grin. "God, it's great to see you. Why didn't you tell me you were coming?" She'd sent an invitation but hadn't heard back.

"Thought I'd surprise you. I'd a got here sooner but the damn car broke down. And ain't like you got ferries running every hour." Calpernia broke into a wide smile that showed the gap between her front teeth and instantly transformed her from bad-ass street to soul sister.

"You should have at least phoned," Alice chided. "I would've picked you up at the ferry landing.

"And spoil the surprise? Girl, you know me better than that."

Alice did indeed. At Pine River, Calpernia King had more or less ruled the roost, defining her own order as she saw fit. In the yard and gen pop she'd always had a little knot of other inmates around her, like a large tree providing shade, or, in her case, protection from rival inmates. Calpernia had a natural air of superiority about her that said *don't mess with me if you know what's good for you* and, for the most part, no one had, including the COs—to the best of Alice's knowledge there had never been a clash between Calpernia and another inmate that resulted in bodily harm.

"Well, you're here now, so as far as I'm concerned the party's just begun," Alice said, finding a couple of clean glasses and popping the tab on a can of leftover Mountain Dew she'd pulled from the cooler. It might not be champagne, but it was cold and bubbly and would do the trick. She lifted her glass in a toast. "Here's to our release. May we live long and prosper."

"I don't know 'bout that," said Calpernia, tipping back her glass, "but I sure do plan on getting me some peace and quiet. I ain't hardly slept a wink since I got out. Shaniqua's place, I might as well been back inside, with the baby and all that ruckus next door."

"Speaking of which, I found you a place," Alice informed her. Calpernia would have been welcome to stay with her, but the terms of their parole prohibited them from living together. "It's not much, just a one-room studio over a garage, but it's free."

At once, Calpernia's back went up. "I ain't no charity case. I can pay my own way."

"You will, just not out of your pocket." Alice explained the circumstances. The house was for sale, and the owner, a friend of her mom's, had agreed to let Calpernia stay on as caretaker until it was sold. All she had to do was water the plants and keep an eye on the place.

Some of the fire went out of Calpernia's eyes. "Okay. Long as I don't owe nobody nothing," she allowed grudgingly.

Alice chuckled, feeling a surge of wicked pleasure. "One thing's for sure. This island won't know what hit it."

"Yeah. This ol' milk bucket 'bout to catch itself a fly," said Calpernia in her most exaggerated Southern drawl. "They see me coming, they gon' run for cover." She threw her head back in a rich, deep laugh that rippled through her in waves, like heat off sun-baked asphalt.

"Most people around here are happy to leave you alone as long as you mind your own business," Alice assured her. "It's just a handful who go out of their way to make things difficult." She thought once more of Owen White. "Normally I'd tell them to take a flying you know what, but I can't afford to right now. I need all the customers I can get." She recalled what her mother had let slip, and felt the small stitch of anxiety in her belly tighten.

"Girl, you got this place looking so fine, if the cooking's half as good, y'all have folks lining up at the door." Alice would have hugged her again if Calpernia hadn't been strutting around, surveying the room. She paused to finger an embroidered tea towel, eyeing it as she would an artifact from a lost civilization. "Just take me some time for me to get used to all this white bread shit, is all. I feel like I'm in one of those shows on Nick at Night. *Fresh Prince of Bel-Air* or the one about the old guy moves his family uptown."

"*The Jeffersons*," Alice supplied, smiling at the image of Calpernia in the role of George Jefferson.

Calpernia swung around to face her, hands on hips. "See. That's what I'm talking about. You know shit like that." But she was grinning, so Alice knew not to take her seriously.

"Sit," Alice ordered, pulling out a chair. "I'll get you something to eat."

"Good. 'Cause I ain't eaten all day." Calpernia plunked down in the chair without further ado. "I'm so hungry ol' Lorena's cooking would taste good," she said, referring to the head cook at Pine River, a three-hundred-pound former school dietician with the humorless countenance of a Sumo wrestler, who'd managed to make everything taste like wet cardboard.

In the kitchen, Alice put together a plate of leftovers and made hot cocoa for them both—the kind with real milk, which still seemed an impossible luxury after having been in a place where everything came out of packet. Being reunited with Calpernia was reminding her of all she had to be grateful for: her family and friends, and the fresh start she'd been given. Colin came to mind as well, the thought warming her as she stood in the kitchen stirring the cocoa, recalling the scene that had taken place earlier in the evening in that very spot.

By the time Calpernia had cleaned her plate and they'd finished their cocoa, Alice's eyelids were drooping. She'd been up since four-thirty that morning and the next day's wake-up call would be the same. "Better get used to it," she told Calpernia, as they were turning in. "We're open for lunch and dinner, which means by noon you've already put in a full day."

Calpernia eyed Alice incredulously, as if she thought she'd arrived in the nick of time to keep her from burning up upon reentry. "And you was figuring on doing it all yourself?"

"Just the cooking. I hired a girl to wait tables, and someone to wash dishes. My son offered to help out, too." Calpernia paused on the staircase, giving her a probing look. "So you and him is a'ight?"

"Let's just say I've been making progress." Alice let them into the small apartment at the top of the stairs, which still held remnants of its former occupants, such as the spectacularly ugly floral drapes and Windex-blue shag carpet stained with cat pee. "At least we're communicating," she said, bending to pull the cushions from the fold-out sofa. "It's a start. Though it's partly because he can't afford to shut me out of his life right now. You see, he's in a bit of trouble . . . "

"Girl trouble?" Calpernia guessed, no doubt thinking of her daughter's getting knocked up.

"In a way." Alice told her about the false charges against Jeremy, and they exchanged a look that could be shared only by those with firsthand knowledge of where something like that could lead. "Pretty ironic, isn't it? I can't seem to escape the past, no matter where I turn." She shook herself free from those thoughts, and straightened, turning to smile at Calpernia. "Which is why I'm glad you're here. You're the only one who knows exactly what I'm going through."

"Mmmmhmmm. Yeah. Ain't that right," said Calpernia, in the singsong call and response of the Baptist church, whose rhythms were almost as familiar to Alice after nine years.

"It's funny when you think about it," she mused aloud. "Way back when, who'd have thought that one day we'd be in business together? I can remember when I'd have been dead meat if I'd so much as asked you for the time of day."

Calpernia let loose with another of her deep, throaty laughs. "Never thought I'd be sleeping on some white chick's sofa, neither," she said, shaking her head. "But, girl, you a'ight, you know that?"

As Alice went to fetch sheets and blankets, the worries that had been crowding her head all day drifted away. For the moment, it was enough to know that she wasn't alone. Whatever lay ahead, Calpernia King would have her back, just as she had at Pine River.

***

When the Pantry opened for business the following day, Alice was satisfied that she'd done everything she could to ensure its success. She'd placed a sign along the main road leading to the turnoff for Fisherman's Lane. She'd taken out an ad in the *Courier* and gotten her niece and nephew to pass out flyers around town. The rest was in God's hands.

And it seemed God was smiling on her for a change, because at lunch and dinner nearly every table was filled, friends and family for the most part, some of the same loyal souls who'd attended last night's party. Alice didn't let it worry her too much when business slowed to a trickle in the days to come. She recalled her mother's cautioning that Rome wasn't built in a day, and thought to herself that Rome wouldn't be fed in a day, either. But by the end of the week she was close to despair. It wasn't just the out of the way location, she knew. Nor was it the food—the word of mouth reviews, even from those without a vested interest in boosting her confidence, had been mainly positive. Which meant the boycott she'd gotten wind of from her mother was more than just a handful of Owen White loyalists out for blood, as Lucy had naively chosen to believe. Either that, or people believed the rumors about Alice and were steering clear of her because they thought she was crazy. Hadn't she already shown what she was capable of? Who knew that she wouldn't poison them?

The only customer she could count on, rain or shine, was Colin McGinty. She found herself looking forward to the familiar sound of his voice greeting Katie out front, and to the moment when he would stick his head into the kitchen to compliment her and Calpernia on the meal. If she refused to let him pay, he always left a generous tip, sometimes more than the cost of the meal.

The new routine seemed to be having a positive effect on him, too, for the faint air of melancholy that had clung to him had dissipated. His step was lighter these days, his tone more buoyant. She could almost forget at times that he was her son's lawyer, that they were bound by something other than friendship and an appreciation for good food. Until one day he made a special appointment to see her during off hours. It was during the lull between lunch and dinner, when the restaurant closed. Alice took off her chef's whites and poured them each a glass of Perrier.

"This is about Jeremy, isn't it?" she said, as they sat down at one of the tables in back.

He nodded, his expression growing somber. "I would've phoned, but I figured you'd want to hear it in person." He paused, before continuing. "The D.A.'s office just faxed over the results of the DNA test on the semen. Apparently Jeremy was the only one Carrie Ann Flagler was with that night."

Alice had known that the chances were slim of a less damning result, but she'd continued to hope nonetheless. Now she could see that there was no easy way out, not unless the girl decided to come clean. Still, she postulated, "Unless one of the other boys used a condom."

"Possible, but hard to prove. All three boys deny having sex with her."

She drew in a breath, trying to steady her nerves. "So, okay, Jeremy was the only one. That doesn't make him a rapist."

"No, of course not, but it's not just his word against hers. Of course, we'll get our own experts to run tests, but in the meantime . . ." Colin's voice trailed off, his expression telling her all she needed to know.

Alice, holding her hands clasped in her lap to keep them from trembling, asked, "So what are we looking at?"

"Mostly likely, it'll go to trial.

"When?"

"I can probably buy us another six months. We still have the evidentiary hearing, and there are pre-trial motions I can file. Meanwhile, drum up as many witnesses as you can who'll testify to Jeremy's good character."

"What about *her* character? There must be people who could testify that she's not exactly the Virgin Mary."

"I'm sure that's true, but it won't do us any good. The D.A. will file a motion *in limini* to block any testimony on her sexual history. At least, that's what I would do in his place."

It hit Alice then, with the full force of a blow. "So there's a real possibility Jeremy could go to prison?"

"There's always that chance, yes." His eyes met hers and she saw the compassion in his face, mixed with a hard dose of reality—he knew better than to pull punches with her. But Alice needed no reminding of what was at stake. *It's happening all over again,* she thought, *only this time with Jeremy.* Colin's voice seemed to come from very far away as he went on, "But I'm still optimistic. And don't forget, a lot can happen between now and then." He dropped his voice. "What did you find out from your brother-in-law?"

"Nothing so far," she told him. When she'd floated the idea of foul play, Gary had looked at her as if she were insane. But it wasn't so much what he'd said as what he *hadn't* said. Gary hadn't asked what she was basing her suspicions on. There had been something evasive about his manner, too. He'd seemed jumpy and he'd had trouble meeting her gaze. Had he been hiding something, or was it just that she'd placed him in an awkward position?

Colin echoed her thoughts, asking, "Do you think he knows something?"

"I can't be certain, but I got the impression he wasn't being a hundred percent straight with me." She chose her words carefully, not wanting to portray her brother-in-law unfairly.

"Maybe your sister can get it out of him."

Alice frowned, reluctant to drag Denise into this. "I wouldn't want her to think I was accusing him of withholding information."

"I'm sorry," Colin said, putting his hand over hers. "I know this puts you in an awkward position."

"I'm sorry, too," she said. "But when it comes to my son, I'll do whatever I have to." Even if it meant putting her beloved sister on the spot.

Colin drained his glass, then pushed his chair back and rose to his feet. "I should get going. I have a biologist from Western Washington coming out to the house. He's supposed to be one of the country's foremost experts on bivalves."

"How's that going?" she asked, walking him to the door.

"So far so good, but I'm still a long way from being fully operational. It keeps me occupied, though, and that's sort of the point." His eyes were clear as he spoke, his expression that of someone looking to the future, not mired in the past. Clearly this fledgling enterprise of his, however unlikely an undertaking for a big city lawyer, was just what the doctor had ordered. "For such a simple creature, oysters can be pretty complicated. You'd be surprised how many things can go wrong."

"I never thought running a restaurant would be this hard, either," she said "If it gets any slower, we won't even have to bother opening up."

"I hope it doesn't come to that. I sure would miss your cooking."

"You and about five other people," she said, with an ironic laugh.

He made a sympathetic face. "I wish I knew what to tell you. You seem to be doing everything right."

"The trouble is, it's not enough. We need some sort of gimmick to get people in the door."

Calpernia, busy setting the tables for dinner, must have overhead, for she appeared before them just then. Dressed in a flowing skirt and scoop-necked jersey top that swagged like bunting from her breasts, her hair coiled atop her head in elaborate whorls and sporting earrings the size of chandeliers, she might have been the deposed queen of some newly democratized African nation. "Long as it don't involve no black folks putting on costumes," she muttered seditiously, folding her arms over her chest.

"The thought hadn't occurred to me. But if you have any other bright ideas, I'd love to hear them," Alice remarked dryly.

Calpernia pondered it a moment, frowning in thought. Then all at once she erupted into motion, smacking her forehead with the heel of her hand. "Damn! Don't know why I didn't think of it before. My old grandpa down in Mississippi would've come up with it in about two seconds flat and he never made it past the second grade."

Then she told them her idea.

CHAPTER ELEVEN

Jeremy was enjoying a newfound popularity. Other boys who'd barely acknowledged him in the past were giving him knowing leers or thumbs-up signs when they passed him in the halls. And the other day Jimmy DeLorenzi, a jock who'd only spoken to him once before, to ask if he could borrow Jeremy's notes for a class he'd missed, had taken him aside during study hall to murmur, with a brotherly clap on the back, "Hang in there, buddy. Everyone knows Carrie Ann's a slut. We got your back, okay?" Even the girls were nicer to him. He was no longer a nameless, faceless neuter. In their eyes, he carried about him now a hint of danger, a suggestion of non-parental approved activities. With one regrettable drunken episode, he'd gone from invisible man to cool dude, while Carrie Ann Flagler was shunned, a social pariah.

Jeremy should have been happy about it, but he was miserable. He knew he should hate Carrie Ann for what she'd done, but more and more, it had come to seem as if they were in this together, like in movies where two people are trapped in a collapsed mine shaft or clinging to a life raft in the wake of a shipwreck. Maybe in her mind she wasn't lying; maybe she truly believed what she'd told the police. Things had a way of getting distorted when you were drunk—who knew that better than him? And she'd been so wasted that night. They both were. If Jeremy's memory of that seminal event weren't so clear—however crappy it ended up, you didn't forget your first time—he might have wondered if it had, in fact, happened just the way she'd said.

Most of the time, when he didn't have to meet with his lawyer or appear in court, he didn't think about it. Whole hours would go by, and then out of the blue it would hit him: He'd been accused of rape. Him. Jeremy Kessler. Who'd never so much as grazed a girl's breasts before this. It was so surreal, he could almost believe it was happening to someone else.

One blustery day in early December he was hurrying along the corridor at school, trying to make it to his science class before the final bell, when something he spotted out of the corner of his eye brought him to a sudden halt. Carrie Ann. She was crying, scrubbing furiously with a wad of wet paper towels at graffiti that had been scrawled on her locker with what looked to have been a Magic Marker: the single, crudely drawn word SLUT. He watched her for a moment, feeling vaguely responsible somehow, though anywhere but in this upended universe, where all normal rules were suspended, her humiliation would have been cause for celebration.

She didn't appear to notice him, she was so caught up in her frenzied scrubbing. He was about to sidle past when she whipped around suddenly. *"What are you looking at?"* she hissed, her face screwed into an angry red knot.

Heat flared in his cheeks. "N-nothing," he stammered. He'd been warned by his parents and Mr. McGinty to steer clear of her. Until now, that hadn't been a problem. She wasn't in any of his classes. But Jeremy should have known he'd run into her eventually. He should have been prepared.

"It's all your fault. *This whole thing.*" She flung her arm out in a gesture that seemed to take in, not just the defaced locker, but the whole school. She was quivering, her voice choked with tears. "You've been shit-talking me. Telling everyone I made the whole thing up. Haven't you? Go on, admit it." She advanced on him, the wad of paper towels in her hand, now reduced to a blackened clump, thrust at him accusingly.

"I haven't said a word to anyone, I swear," Jeremy blurted in knee-jerk defense. At the same time he was thinking, *This is all wrong. Shouldn't I be the one accusing her?*

"Yeah, right," she said in a sarcastic tone. "I saw you talking to Jimmy. Now suddenly you're his best friend? He didn't even fucking know you *existed* before this." She swiped angrily with the back of her wrist at the tears running down her slapped-red cheeks. It came back to him now, Carrie Ann calling out Jimmy's name while they were having sex. He recalled, too, that she and Jimmy DeLorenzi used to be a couple, before Jimmy dumped her for supposedly cheating on him. "In fact, I'll bet you put him up to this," she gestured toward her locker

"Why would I want to do that?" Jeremy spoke with such surprised innocence that Carrie Ann halted in her tracks, her angry expression switching to one of narrow-eyed disbelief.

"You're kidding me, right?"

"I don't think you're a slut," he said, his face growing even hotter at the hazy memory of them tangled together naked on the mattress in Mike Dimmock's apartment.

"You hate me, though." She spoke as though it were a fact.

He shrugged. "Yeah, I probably should."

Her eyes widened. "You mean you don't?"

He thought for a moment, probing the recesses of his mind the way he might have probed an infected tooth with the tip of his tongue. Finally, in a tone of near-wonderment, as if he were having difficulty believing it himself, he replied, "No. I guess I don't."

"Wow." She stared at him incredulously.

Now that they were actually having a conversation, if that's what this was, Jeremy felt emboldened to continue. "Look. I'm sure I *would* be pissed if I thought you were doing this just to mess with me. But I'm guessing you really believe that stuff you told the police. Why else put yourself through all this?"

He expected her to erupt in anger again. After all, wasn't he all but accusing her of making the whole thing up? But Carrie Ann just stared at him with a thoughtful, assessing look, as if she were seeing him for the first time. When at last she spoke, her voice was surprisingly calm. "I'm not supposed to be talking to you, you know. My parents would kill me if they knew."

"Yeah. Mine, too." A corner of his mouth hooked up in a tentative smile. He didn't see Carrie Ann as his tormenter, but more as a kid who'd been playing with matches and who'd accidentally started a fire, one that had quickly spread out of control. "Want some help with that?" He indicated her locker, where the first two of the letters scrawled on the front had been rubbed into a indecipherable gray smear, leaving only the U and the T.

She frowned. "What if someone sees you? It'd look pretty weird, wouldn't it?"

He glanced around. "Yeah, well, there's no one to see."

Jeremy fetched more paper towels from the boys' bathroom and helped her scrub off the rest of the graffiti, neither of them speaking another word. They were just finishing up when the third period bell rang. That was when the full realization hit him: He'd blown off Biology to help a girl who could send him to jail.

Reflecting on it as he hurried off to his next class, he thought that as bizarre as it might have seemed to others, it had felt like the right thing to do. There was no reason his parents or Mr. McGinty had to know. They wouldn't understand. Jeremy wasn't sure he understood it, either. All he knew was that after weeks of feeling like shit, he felt a little better about himself. Not so much better as *different*, more in charge.

He imagined how it had gone down with Carrie Ann: her parents confronting her that night when she'd stumbled into house, and Carrie Ann blurting out some tearful, drunken version of what had happened. And once adults got involved, things had a way of snowballing. Look at his own parents. A month ago they hadn't even been speaking and now they were on the phone with each other practically every other day. Jeremy

didn't know how he felt about that. Part of him was glad that his parents
were getting along, but another part of him was fearful. He and his dad
had been managing just fine without his mom all these years. Wasn't it
better for things to stay as they were than to risk getting hurt again if
down the line she decided to take off?

Luckily, his fourth period class was gym, for Jeremy doubted he'd have
been able to concentrate right now on anything more mentally taxing
that kicking a ball around the soccer field. He was so preoccupied with
the thoughts tumbling in his head—Carrie Ann, his mom, the Bio class
he'd blown—that he didn't see Rud until he'd practically bumped into
him.

"Yo, dude. Just the man I wanted to see." Rud greeted him as if they
were the best of friends, as if he and his buddies hadn't left Jeremy
swinging in the wind. "Me and Chuckie are heading over to Mike's after
school, to check out the bro's new hog. Wanna come along?"

Jeremy ducked his head, mumbling, "I don't know. I've got some stuff
to do." He felt confused by this sudden onslaught of attention. Lately,
Rud had been seeking him out more and more, where before Jeremy
would have been invited along only if he happened to be standing there
when they were all piling into the car. Either Rud felt guilty for not
sticking up for him or Jeremy, in his new notoriety, had suddenly become
worthy of his friendship.

"Dude. This is a brand-new Harley we're talking about. A *Harley*,
man." An unlit cigarette dangled from the corner of his mouth, and now,
as Rud leaned in, Jeremy caught a whiff of stale smoke and a trace of
some flowery scent that had to be his girlfriend's perfume. "Now let's
you and me take that sucker for a spin and you can forget about all this
other crap. Do you good, dude."

Jeremy kept his eyes averted. He knew that if he were to look into
Rud's face and see the warm affection with which Rud was no doubt regarding him, he'd be sucked in. For what few outside Rud's inner circle
would have guessed was that, for all his bad rep, Rud could be extremely
charming when he chose to be. And if it was just an illusion, it was a

seductive one. In that moment Jeremy wanted nothing more than to bask in that warmth, to believe that Rud really gave a shit about him. It seemed like the hardest thing he'd ever had to do to say, "I'm sorry. I wish I could. You . . . you guys have fun without me."

"Whoa. Dude. You're the one missing out, not me."

Rud took a step back, his eyes dismissing Jeremy with a cool glance that let him know he'd committed a major social blunder in even suggesting that his going or not going would in any way affect Rud's ability to have a good time. Jeremy was at once filled with an almost crushing regret. Only the thought of how much he'd hate himself for doing so kept him from belatedly accepting Rud's invitation, if it was even still open. As he trudged off to gym, any sense of empowerment he'd felt in helping Carrie Ann dissipated, leaving him feeling lonely and depressed.

He ran into his cousin a few minutes later in the locker room.

"Hey, Germ. What's up?" said Ryan with a grin, greeting him by his childhood nickname.

His cousin was just out of the shower, naked except for the towel wrapped around his waist, his hair standing up in wet spikes. Under any other circumstances, when faced with his cousin's blatant physical superiority, Jeremy would have indulged in the usual comparisons. He'd have keyed in on the cut of Ryan's biceps, his six-pack abs, the mat of hair on his chest (Jeremy's sported only a few feeble outcroppings), not to mention the sheer confidence with which Ryan strode naked through a locker room filled with other boys making similar comparisons. But right now he was so preoccupied, he scarcely noticed.

"Nothing much," he lied. "What's up with you?"

"We just got slaughtered. Four and oh, and Resnick fumbles a pass in the final quarter. Shit, we'd have had it, if it weren't for that," Ryan reported cheerfully enough, even as he shook his head in disgust. If it had been a playoff instead of a practice game, it would have rolled off him just the same. Nothing much got in the way of Ryan's naturally optimistic approach to life, a trait Jeremy used to envy but which right now irritated him.

Growing up, they had been close, more like brothers than cousins. Then, the summer between the eighth and ninth grades, Ryan had morphed overnight into the man-sized individual standing before him now, while Jeremy, still a skinny, scab-kneed kid, was left to fumble his way through adolescence. He'd still been playing with action figures when Ryan became interested in girls—an interest that was returned in spades. Every other girl in school, it seemed, had a crush on Ryan. Not only that, he succeeded at everything he set out to do, whether it was sports or trying out for the lead in a school play. In short, Ryan was everything Jeremy wasn't.

"That sucks," he said now, in a lackluster tone.

His cousin gave him a funny look. "You okay?"

Jeremy shrugged, saying sarcastically, "Sure. Why wouldn't I be? I just blew off Mr. G's class, and I'm sure he'll expect a damn good explanation, which unfortunately I don't seem to have. Not to mention I may get my ass thrown into jail for something I didn't do."

Ryan nodded slowly, as if in appreciation of the gravity of the situation, but his innate good cheer remained intact. "I wouldn't sweat it too much, if I were you. My dad says the worst that could happen is you'll get probation, maybe community service."

Jeremy felt a flash of anger toward his cousin. What did Ryan know? His whole life, he'd had everything handed to him on a silver platter. "On the other hand, I could end up doing time," he said. "Like mother like son, right?"

"Cool it, Germ. You're starting to creep me out." Ryan was still smiling, but a small crease had appeared between his brows. "Anyway, what happened with your mom . . . that was different."

"Yeah, I suppose rape must seem pretty tame next to attempted manslaughter. Especially since I'm not into knives or duct tape."

Without warning, his cousin grabbed him by the arm and steered him over to a deserted row of lockers, where he shoved Jeremy onto the bench. "You shouldn't talk that way, not in public," he warned in a low voice. "*I* know you're only joking, but some of these other guys . . ." He cast a glance over his shoulder. "You don't want to get in even worse trouble."

Suddenly the events of the past few weeks descended on Jeremy in an avalanche. "Since when do you give a shit?" he shot back. He knew it was unfair to take it out on Ryan, but at the moment he was too pissed off to care.

"I'm your cousin, dumb ass. Of course I give a shit." Ryan seemed more surprised than offended that his loyalty was in question.

"Really? I hadn't noticed."

Even as he heaped scorn on his cousin, part of Jeremy wanted nothing more than for it to be like it was when he and Ryan used to ride around on their skateboards and hang out after school in Mr. Kim's store leafing through comic books and sneaking peeks at *Playboy* when Mr. Kim wasn't looking. But he knew that wasn't possible. They'd both gone their separate ways. If this were a race, Ryan would be up near the finish line and Jeremy lagging far behind.

Now Ryan was giving him a pitying look. Somehow that was what hurt Jeremy most of all. He was so insignificant, he couldn't even get a rise out of his cousin. "Maybe you would, if you didn't spend all your time hanging out with that loser Rudnicki," Ryan said, not unkindly.

Jeremy felt the sting of truth in his words, which only made him feel compelled to defend Rud. "You don't know him the way I do."

"I don't have to," Ryan replied, in a tone that meant Rud's reputation spoke for itself.

"Yeah, well, what's it to you? I don't see *you* breaking a leg to hang out with me."

"If you didn't have your head so far up your ass you can't see straight, you'd know why that is." Jeremy caught a flash of anger in his cousin's eyes. "*You're* the one who's always making excuses whenever I invite you anywhere."

With the last shreds of his dignity pulled around him like a tattered cloak, Jeremy informed his cousin, "Thanks, but I don't need your sympathy." The only reason Ryan had asked him along all those times, he was convinced, was out of a sense of familial duty.

Ryan smacked the flat of his hand against an open locker door, slamming it shut with a loud clang that echoed off the concrete floors and walls, causing Jeremy to start. "Jesus, you're a piece of work, you know that? Did it ever occur to you I might *like* hanging out with you? Or are you so busy feeling sorry for yourself you haven't noticed what a selfish prick you've become?" Jeremy opened his mouth to object, but his cousin was just getting warmed up. "Do you even care what's going on with me? That my mom's turned into a raving lunatic? Christ, she's talking about chaining herself to a tree! You'd think it was our own house that was going to be bulldozed, the way she's acting. Would it have killed you to stop by and talk to her? To see if maybe there was something you could do to help? She's been good to you, man. We *all* have."

Jeremy rose to his feet. "Thanks for the lecture. I don't feel so bad now about missing Mister G's class." He spoke with cool disdain.

"Are you even listening? Have you heard one thing I've said?" Ryan was visibly upset, his eyes flashing and his normally smiling mouth set in an angry line. Jeremy felt a small surge of triumph. He'd managed to get a rise out of his cousin. That was something.

He was about to walk away when his gaze dropped to Ryan's bare torso. With all the superiority he could muster, he said, in a voice very much like Rud's, "Dude. You should put some clothes on before you catch cold."

It wasn't until his anger ebbed that Jeremy was able to admit to himself that there was a grain of truth to what Ryan had said. More than a grain, in fact. How long had it been since he'd had dinner at their house or even stopped by to say hello? Aunt Denise was always inviting him over, but he'd given her nothing but excuses. Lately, he'd felt as if she and his mom were in cahoots somehow, both trying to get him to do stuff he didn't want to do, feel things he'd just as soon remained buried. Though hadn't he brought a lot of that on himself by volunteering to work for his mother?

He hadn't planned on it. It had just sort of . . . come up. And now, as he stood bent over in front of his locker, tying the laces on his gym shoes, a voice whispered in his head, *No one was twisting your arm.* Whatever his initial motives, though, he'd found that he *liked* working at the restaurant, even if it was just bussing tables. It was a point of pride, too, his wanting to prove to her that he was as worthy of her love as David, that the wrong son wasn't buried in the Episcopal churchyard where David had been laid to rest. Maybe then she wouldn't be so quick to leave, if it should come to that; maybe she'd even ask him to go with her. He wouldn't, of course. But it would be nice to be asked.

Something else occurred to him then, something that sent a chill shimmying down his spine: If anyone was going to be leaving, it would most likely be him, when they carted him off to jail.

———

Jeremy forgot his bad mood when he arrived at the restaurant later that afternoon to find most of the tables filled. The funereal atmosphere of the past few weeks had given way to a bustle of activity. Katie, sweeping past him in her waitress uniform, a forties-style gingham pinafore that his grandmother had sewn out of the leftover fabric from the curtains, seemed frazzled, her cheeks flushed and runaway strands trailing from her ponytail. Jeremy found his mother in the kitchen moving at the same warp speed.

"Amazing, isn't it?" she said over the machine-gun sound of her chopping. "It's been this way all day."

"Did something happen that I don't know about?" he asked, bending to pick up a piece of celery that had flown from the flashing tip of her knife onto the floor. He'd missed two days of work, due to a dentist's appointment and an overdue paper for English that he'd had to scramble to finish.

"We can thank Calpernia," Alice said. "Remember her uncle, from Memphis?"

Jeremy nodded. "The pit master." It was all his mother and Calpernia had been talking about for the past week or so.

"Well, he's here. And he's got the barbecue up and running."

"I thought I smelled smoke." Jeremy helped himself to a cube of bread she'd cut up for croutons.

"Well, apparently you're not the only one. It's been drawing in customers all day. It's like a miracle. Only who knew the burning bush would
turn out to be Uncle Monroe's hickory chips?" She gave a breathless
laugh, reporting, "We can hardly keep up with the orders. So much for
haute cuisine. I guess *boeuf bourginon* can't compete with down home ribs."

"Be careful what you wish for, right?" said Jeremy, with a grin.

"No kidding. I never thought I'd be running a rib joint, but, hey, whatever works." Alice paused in the midst of her chopping to shake her head in
wonderment, wearing a small, ironic smile. After a moment, she brought
her gaze back to Jeremy. "If you're looking for something to do, you can
start on those dishes," she said, pointing with her knife at the mountain of
dirty plates in the sink. "Of all the days for Eduardo to call in sick!"

Jeremy reached for the apron on a peg inside the storage closet. He
didn't mind being put to work, even a job as menial as loading the dishwasher. It warded off the black thoughts that flocked in his head like
crows whenever he had too much idle time on his hands. Besides, his
mom depended on him. It wasn't like with his old boss, Mr. Barbour,
who could fire you one day and replace you the next as easily as changing
a gasket on his car engine. His mother was just squeaking by, and even
with the increased business it would be a while before she could afford to
hire extra help.

He was scraping the last of the plates when Ryan's words floated back
into his consciousness. Now he felt the slow burn of them in his belly.
Had he been a selfish prick with his mother, as well? Seeing her through
the eyes of a hurt, lonesome little boy instead of those of a nearly grown
man? Punishing her for something that wasn't her fault?

Normally he would have scoffed at the idea, but the unsettling en-
counter with Carrie Ann and bruising he'd gotten from his cousin had
shaken him up, made him reassess things. Not that he was ready to throw
himself into his mother's arms and tell her all was forgiven. Just that it
might not hurt to cut her a little slack.

Jeremy finished loading the dishwasher, then carried out the trash. He
found Calpernia in the back yard conferring with an old guy, with hair

like steel wool and skin the color and texture of beef jerky, the two hovering like a pair of conspirators over some backwoods contraption fashioned out of an oil drum fitted with what looked to be spare parts from the junkyard. Smoke curled from under its hood and from the length of stovepipe sticking up on top, like a mad scientist's experiment, the air around it shimmering with the heat it was throwing off.

"Jeremy honey, this here's Uncle Monroe," Calpernia introduced them. "I know he look like a dried up old thing can't lift a crate of marshmallows, but he as hardworking as any mule and ain't no ribs you ever tasted like his."

"Mouth on her like the *wrong* end of a mule, but she ain't half bad either." Uncle Monroe grumbled, turning to beam affectionately at his niece. He had to be close to eighty, skinny as the barbecue fork in his hand and missing one of his front teeth. He turned his attention back to Jeremy. "So what you think, son, ain't she somepin?"

For a moment Jeremy thought he was referring to Calpernia, then he noticed the old man gazing proudly at his contraption. "It's something, all right," he agreed. He just wasn't sure what. Yet from the enticing smells wafting his way, it was obviously doing the trick.

"'Course you got to have the touch," said the old man, lifting the lid to give the ribs sizzling on the grate a poke with his fork. "Ain't somepin you can learn overnight."

Calpernia turned to Jeremy. "He just holding out on me, is all. Don't want nobody knowing the recipe for his secret sauce. He say it's pro-*pri*-etary. Old fool don't even know what that word mean," she added with a throaty chuckle.

Uncle Monroe put on a mock injured look. "Do so. Looked it up in the dictionary."

Jeremy listened to their banter a few minutes longer. But if Calpernia's attempts to pry the recipe out of her uncle had been unsuccessful so far, Jeremy would bet a week's pay she'd get it out of him eventually. She wasn't the type to take no for an answer.

At first he hadn't known what to make of her. There weren't many black people on the island, and none like Calpernia King. In fact, she was unlike anyone he'd ever met: tough, streetwise, with a mouth that made Rud's seem tame. Nor did she seem all that interested in Jeremy's opinion of her, good or bad. But after initially being put off, he'd found himself intrigued. He even admired her in a way. She was unafraid and unapologetic. She refused to be defined by the bad hand life had dealt her.

The only thing that still seemed odd was the bond between Calpernia and his mom. In his fuzzy memories of childhood, the mother he had known would never have been friends with someone like Calpernia. She'd have been polite if they'd happened to meet, but that was as about far as it would have gone. Not because she was prejudiced, but because they had nothing in common—their skin color was the least of their differences. Whatever had happened to her in prison, he thought, it had made his mother a more interesting person.

Jeremy sampled the forkful of brisket Uncle Monroe had speared, which tasted even more delicious than it smelled. "Wow. That's amazing. You sure it's legal?"

Calpernia chuckled. "Better be, or I'm in trouble."

Jeremy lingered a few minutes more before saying reluctantly, "Well, I guess I'd better get back to work. My mom has her hands full in there. I've never seen it this busy."

"Son, you ain't seen nothing yet. We just getting warmed up," said Uncle Monroe.

Calpernia chimed in, adopting her uncle's Southern drawl, "Yeah, soon as this ol' fool teach me all his tricks, I be showin' y'all a thing or two." She chuckled, wagging her head, as if at some private joke.

Jeremy noticed the change in atmosphere as soon as he stepped back inside. A hush had fallen over the restaurant, and in the kitchen, with its counter that opened onto the dining area, his mother stood as motionless as a statue, gazing out at the packed tables.

"It's him," she said in a strange, flat voice.

"Who?" Jeremy felt his heart start to thump.

She turned to him, and he saw the fear on her face, the defiance too. "Mister White ."

Jeremy looked out into the dining area, where the mayor was seated at a table by the window. He looked perfectly at ease, as if he were any patron perusing the menu, trying to decide between a hot or cold appetizer. He was so inconspicuous Jeremy might not have singled him out if it hadn't been for the wheelchair. That, and the sight of his mother, her face drained of all color, as she looked upon the man who had cost her everything she held dear.

CHAPTER TWELVE

APRIL 1943

Eleanor Styles was holding up remarkably well, they all said. Though some privately speculated that the reason no one had seen her shed a tear might have more to do with her strange, proud ways than deep shock brought on by her husband's death. For while she'd joined the ranks of war widows, she kept mainly to herself. She was rarely seen about town and if she worshiped on Sundays it wasn't in any church. When someone did run into her by accident, turning down an aisle in Kingston Grocery or waiting in line at Caldwell's Pharmacy, it was like glimpsing an apparition—a ghostly figure dressed in black, regal somehow in her mourning, often clutching the hand of her equally subdued daughter.

There was something about Eleanor that didn't invite conversation. Most of the islanders had known her since she was a little girl, but only a handful felt they had more than a nodding acquaintance with her. From early childhood on, the minister's youngest daughter had been set apart, by her beauty and by the rumors that later swirled around her: that she was fast, that she kept company with older men, namely one Lowell White. Even her marriage to Joe Styles had raised eyebrows. Why him and not one of the dozens of more suitable men her age who'd have walked over hot coals to be with her? More than a few had their suspicions about the timing of the union, given the arrival of Joe and Eleanor's daughter seven and a half months later, but Lucy had been a scrawny infant, weighing less than six pounds at birth, so she could indeed have been premature, as was claimed. And certainly no one could find fault with Mrs. Styles' conduct, which was beyond reproach.

Even her widowhood seemed more poignant somehow than that of others who'd suffered similar losses. Mourning had only heightened her pale beauty and made her more arresting in her quiet dignity. Those wives with husbands home from the war or on leave were secretly glad that Eleanor kept to herself, that she didn't partake in any of the social activities that might have thrown her into contact with them. For however bravely those men might have conducted themselves in battle, few would have been a match for Eleanor Styles. Without even meaning to, she could slay a man with a single glance.

One of those men approached her as she was collecting her mail at the post office one unseasonably warm morning in April, with the red-flowering currant in bloom and the gray whales making their annual pilgrimage to mate in the waters offshore. "Missus Styles," spoke a familiar voice in her ear. She turned to find herself face to face with her former lover. She'd spotted him in passing through the years, but they hadn't exchanged a word in nearly a decade. It was a shock now to see him standing before her, lean and louche as ever in a fedora and gray pinstripe suit too fine to have been purchased on the island. He smiled, the creases around his eyes and mouth deepening, as if with some private amusement. "Well, isn't this a nice surprise. It's been a long time, hasn't it?"

She froze for an instant, but quickly regained her composure, conscious of the postmistress's eye on her. No news by post or wire ever traveled faster than that carried by Edna Polhouse's tongue. "Yes, Mister White, it has. A very long time," she replied in a formal tone. "What brings you out this way?" Normally it would have been his secretary sending a package or collecting the mail, just as Eleanor had done on his behalf any number of times.

"Express delivery," he replied, producing a wrapped parcel from under his arm. "Wouldn't you know, everyone in my office is out sick with the flu. So here I am, left to fend for myself."

"Well, I'm sure you'll manage."

"And you? How are you getting along these days?" His jaunty smile gave way to an expression of sympathy. "Terrible about your husband. I read about it in the paper. Guadalcanal, wasn't it? "

She gave a stiff little nod of acknowledgment.

"I didn't know him well," Lowell went on, "but he did some work for me once. He seemed like a good man."

"He was." Eleanor cringed at the patent insincerity of his words. But she felt the hot fingers of her grief tighten their grip around her heart nonetheless, a grief magnified by the guilt she felt. For, as unreasonable as it was, she couldn't shake the suspicion that her love for William had somehow been the cause of her husband's death.

"Well, if there's ever anything I can do. Anything at all . . ." Lowell's eyes seemed to convey something more than sympathy.

Haven't you done enough? Her polite expression remained frozen in place, Eleanor wishing only for this unpleasant exchange to be over. What if Lucy had been with her? How awkward it would have been! And suppose someone had noticed the resemblance between father and daughter? Seeing them side by side, it would have been hard to miss. Eleanor grew cold at the thought.

"Thank you, but I'm managing just fine," she said. A lie really, but how was he to know?

She stepped past him to drop her mail into the slot: some overdue bills she'd finally been able to pay with the money from Joe's death benefit, and a letter to Joe's sister in Oregon, pleading the excuse of being under the weather to prevent her from visiting. Ever since word had come of her brother's death, Imogene had been insisting that she come, seeming to think Eleanor would benefit from the company of someone with whom she could share her grief, but Eleanor wished only to be left alone.

She was walking across the parking lot, headed for her car, when Lowell called after her, "Eleanor!"

She halted in her tracks. *He's going to say something about Lucy*, she thought. Her heart began to pound and wings of panic beat in her breast. It was a struggle to retain her cool demeanor, but somehow she managed it, pretending she didn't notice the purposeful way he was now planting himself in her path or the intensity of his gaze, which seemed intrusive somehow.

"Yes, what is it?" she replied somewhat impatiently.

"I just wanted you to know I truly am sorry. About your husband. About . . . the girl, too." In that moment, he almost seemed sincere.

Eleanor, though, was unmoved. She eyed him coldly. "She has a name. Lucy."

"Christ. You think I don't know? She's my daughter!" Lowell snatched off his hat, pushing a hand through his hair. The only other time she'd seen him this agitated was when she'd told him she was expecting. "You can't imagine what it's been like for me. So many times I've wanted to . . . to make it up to you somehow. But there was Joe. And if Dorothy ever found out, she . . . well, I'd rather she didn't."

Dorothy. His wife. The suitable match he'd made after he'd finished sowing his wild oats. Eleanor had read about it in the paper when the engagement was announced. Dorothy Jasper, daughter of Texas oil baron Henry Jasper and a graduate of Vanderbilt University, where she'd belonged to the Phi Delta Kappa sorority. Years later, upon Henry's death, the entire estate had gone to Dorothy, his only child, thus more than doubling Lowell's already vast wealth. But there was one thing he'd never lay claim to, and that was Lucy. Not as long as Eleanor had breath in her.

"How *is* your wife?" she inquired pointedly.

"Very well, thank you," he answered distractedly. "But, say, that's not why I—"

She plowed on resolutely. "And your children?" She'd seen them around town, a girl with her father's dark good looks, and a boy who was the image of his wan milk-skinned mother.

"Let's leave my family out of this, shall we." The faux warmth went out of his expression, and now he cast a furtive glance about the parking

lot, as if suddenly becoming aware of being out in the open where anyone might have seen them. Luckily, no one was about. The only signs of
activity were the bees bobbling amid the honeysuckle vines along the
fence and the sparrows pecking at the blossoms that had drifted down
from the maple tree overhead and were sprinkled in a fine gold carpet
over the pavement. "Listen, Eleanor, I know this is awkward for you. It is
for me, too," he said, adopting a more conciliatory tone. "Is there somewhere we can talk in private?"

"I don't see that we have anything to talk about," she replied.

"Look, I'm only trying to help. I know things have been rough for you
lately."

"I don't need your help." She started to move past him, but he grabbed
hold of her arm. She recognized the wild, unfocused look he wore, and
she felt a flicker of panic. It was the same way he'd looked at her before
kissing her for the first time.

His face was the same now as then, a bit more lined perhaps, yet it no
longer held any appeal. There seemed something almost feminine in the
Brillantined perfection of his dark, wavy hair, brushed now with gray. And
in the harsh light of day, the pouches under his eyes that had once made
him look excitingly decadent by candlelight merely made him look old.

"Don't be stupid, Eleanor. It's not going to be easy for you with Joe
gone. I know. I checked your bank records." Her mouth fell open in
shock, but he was unapologetic. "You don't have to look at me like that.
It's not as if I was spying on you. Believe me, my only interest is in your
and Lucy's welfare."

She quivered with indignation. "How dare you. "

"My point is," he went on, as if she hadn't spoken, "whether you like
it or not, you're going to need money. And that, my dear, is the one thing
I have plenty of."

"I don't want your charity!" she hissed.

"Call it a back payment on what I owe you then."

"Knowing you, you'd expect something in return."

He drew his head back to fix her with an injured look. "Do you really
think as little of me as that? I'm not the terrible person you paint me to

be. Honestly. The way things ended with us . . . I handled it badly, I'll admit. And don't think I haven't had my regrets."

Regrets? What did he know about regrets? "I stopped caring about all that a long time ago," she informed him coldly. "Really, there's no reason to trouble yourself on my account." She wanted no part of Lowell White, neither his money nor his belated regrets.

"We have a child. Isn't that enough of a reason?"

Blood surged up into her head, swelling against her temples, making them throb, but she managed to remain outwardly calm. "Lucy doesn't know anything about you. And I'd prefer to keep it that way." The thought of Lowell's getting anywhere near Lucy made her suddenly glad that Joe wasn't alive, for that would have killed him more surely than any bullet.

"She doesn't have to know," he said, wearing a cozily conspiratorial look that made her skin crawl.

Eleanor felt like screaming, *Enough!* She'd had her fill of secrets. First with Lowell, then with William. And, like toadstools flourishing in the dark, they had poisoned all that she'd held dear. In the case of William McGinty, by allowing feelings to grow where they shouldn't, which had very nearly led to an indiscretion. She shuddered now to think what might have happened, with Joe's body scarcely cold, if Captain Lewis from the home guard hadn't showed up at her door when he did.

She hadn't seen William since, nor did she intend to. The fact that it was torture to be apart from him only added to her resolve. She'd told him to stop coming to the house, and when he disregarded her wishes, she refused to let him in. Lately, he'd taken to leaving boxes of supplies on her doorstep. Eventually she would have to put a stop to that, too, but so far she hadn't had the heart.

Now she had Lowell to contend with.

"I see no point in continuing this conversation," she told him. "You've offered your help and I've told you I don't need it. Now if you'll excuse me, I have errands to run."

She attempted to move past him, but Lowell only tightened his grip on her arm. In the hard press of his lips against his teeth and cold depths of his eyes she saw his true nature: a man unaccustomed to being thwarted. "All right, we'll postpone the discussion. But you can't put me off forever, Eleanor. Don't forget, she's my daughter, too."

Eleanor reared back to fix him with a fierce look. "You don't want your wife to know that," she said in a low, warning voice. "It might not go over so well with her."

He laughed, as he once had at her provincial ways that he'd claimed to find so endearing. "You think I believe you'd say anything to my wife? Think what it would do to your reputation, my dear. You'd go from sainted widow to fallen angel overnight."

"I don't give a fig for my reputation."

"That much I believe," he said, eyeing her thoughtfully. "In fact, that's what I've always found so attractive about you. You're not like the rest of them, are you? Not under the skin. You only pretend to be because it makes life easier. But I know what you're really like." He languidly traced a finger along her cheek, sending a shiver of loathing through her. He seemed to be enjoying her discomfort. "There's something you seem to have forgotten, though. If this gets around, Lucy will know, too. Are you prepared to take that risk?"

Eleanor felt all the fight go out of her. He knew her all right. He knew she'd do anything to shield her daughter from the truth. Lucy was having a hard enough time as it was dealing with Joe's death. This would devastate her.

"All right," she said, in a weary voice of defeat. "Pick me up outside your office tomorrow, before work. We'll go for a drive. We can talk then."

"No, someone might spot us. It's better if I come to your house."

She felt herself stiffen. "I'd rather you didn't."

"What, you don't trust me, Ellie? You think I'll try to seduce you?" He smiled, as if at her naiveté. "I suppose I should be flattered that you still think of me that way."

She hadn't considered that. She was thinking only of the danger to Yoshi. But what was the alternative? If she offered any further protests Lowell might grow suspicious and do some nosing around on his own.

And at least in the privacy of her own home, surrounded by mementos of her life with Joe, a life that had been solid and good, she wouldn't feel so unclean.

Yoshi would just have to make himself scarce. There was an old, abandoned cabin along the trail up Spring Hill where she occasionally stopped to rest on long hikes. The boy would be safe there for the duration, well-hidden from view.

It was with trepidation nonetheless that she gave Lowell directions to her house. "Woodbury Lane, the last house on the left. You can't miss it."

His smile stretched into a grin that left her chilled, even as she stood in the warm spring sunshine with birds chirping in the trees overhead. "I know the way," he said.

—

The following morning Eleanor could scarcely concentrate on her chores, she was so wound up. She'd spent a restless night, thoughts of Lowell scampering through her head like the mice she could hear rustling in the walls as she'd tossed and turned in bed. Yet somehow she managed to get Lucy dressed and fed and off to school. She was in the midst of packing Yoshi off to the cabin, with explicit instructions that he was to stay put until she came to fetch him later on, when the boy hung his head, saying in his broken English, "I go, not come back. Better for you that way."

Eleanor's voice was firm as she told him, "No, Yoshi. You have a home with us, as long as you need it. And I promise it won't always be this way. This war can't go on forever. And when it's over, things will go back to the way they were before."

"Not same as before. Mister Joe not come back." Yoshi lifted his head to eye her mournfully. He'd loved Joe like a father and was taking his death hard.

"No, Mister Joe won't be coming back," she echoed sadly, her gaze drifting past him.

As she stood there, staring out the window, momentarily lost in thought, she was struck by the irony of it. Given how she felt about William, one might have thought a part of her would feel secretly liberated by her husband's death. Yet she missed Joe, more than she would have thought possible. She missed his kindness and his ready laugh, the unfailing courtesy with which he'd always treated her. Joe hadn't been a demonstrative man, but he'd always made sure she knew he loved her. Little things, like rising in the dark of winter mornings to get the fire started so the house would be warm when she and Lucy got up and driving into town to fill the car with gas whenever he knew she'd need to use it. What made it worse for her was that his body had yet to be recovered. According to Captain Lewis, he'd gone down with the *Hornet* when it was sunk.

She looked back at Yoshi. "Here. I packed you a lunch." She handed him the picnic basket she'd filled with enough provisions to last several days, including the little Japanese rice balls stuffed with bits of cooked fish and vegetables he'd taught her to make. "You might get bored, but at least you won't go hungry."

"I read book." He proudly held up the early reader, one of Lucy's old ones, with which Eleanor had been teaching him English.

She smiled at him. "I think you're ready for something a little more challenging than *Dick and Jane.*" Yoshi might not have had the advantages of a privileged upbringing, but he had a quick mind and he loved to learn; in no time he'd mastered the alphabet and worked his way through Lucy's primary and secondary readers. Now Eleanor plucked a tattered book off the bookshelf, one of Joe's old *Hardy Boys* mysteries, and tucked it into the basket, saying, "This ought to keep you busy for a while. Now scoot." She shooed him out the door, remaining on the stoop a while longer watching him trudge across the spring-blown yard: a slight figure in an old canvas jacket of Joe's that hung on him like a sail at half mast, his shoulders bowed and his fine black hair falling over his forehead. When the war was over she'd miss having him around, she knew.

Yoshi darted a glance over his shoulder as he was nearing the gate that opened onto the field, and she saw the worried look on his face. He knew only that she was expecting a visitor, but it must have been obvious to him from how keyed up she'd been all morning that it wasn't just a social call. He might even have thought Lowell's impending visit posed some sort of threat, and he would have been right about that.

For while it was true that Lowell had a vested interest in letting sleeping dogs lie, Lucy was his child nonetheless, and where blood ties were concerned people had been known to act in ways that flew in the face of reason. So the night before, in the midst of her tossing and turning, Eleanor had come to a decision: If all Lowell wanted was to salve his conscience, she would take his money and hopefully that would put the matter to rest. Every cent would go into a savings account for Lucy, though.

What was less easily resolved was the matter of William. As she went back inside to finish washing up from breakfast, she thought that perhaps the real threat didn't come from her former lover but from her own wayward heart. Where she ought to have been on guard was in allowing herself to care so deeply for William. The fact that they'd never so much as kissed did nothing to erase the guilt she felt. For in her heart, she knew she'd betrayed her husband a thousand times over, with a married man no less. And now that Joe was dead, gone too was the chance to atone. The most she could do was banish William from her sight, knowing that otherwise she might weaken.

It was a wonder she was still functioning, really. It wasn't just her husband she missed, but William, too, with an acuteness that bordered on desperation, as if he were some essential element she needed in order to survive, without which she was slowly withering away. The only thing that kept her going was knowing she had to be there for Lucy.

An hour later Eleanor had finished tidying up and was tackling the ironing when she heard a car pull into the drive. She unplugged the iron and peered out the window. Lowell was striding up the front path, holding an enormous bouquet of flowers. The sight was at once absurd and deeply unnerving, causing her to let out a small cry, muffled by the hand she clapped over her mouth. What on earth . . . ? Why, anyone would think he'd come courting!

"Thank you," she said stiffly, as he handed her the bouquet. She left him standing in the entry as she hurried off into the kitchen in search of a vase, taking advantage of the opportunity to collect herself.

When she returned he was seated in the easy chair by the fireplace. Joe's chair. The sight of Lowell's Brilliantined head resting against its high back, the spot left darkened by Joe's sweat—that of a working man who'd earned an honest wage, by his hands not his cunning—filled her with sudden rage. For a moment she was tempted to send him packing. But she reined in her emotions. The sooner they got this over with, the better.

From the pocket of her shirtwaist she produced a snapshot, which she handed to him. "Here. I thought you might like to have this." It was a photo of Lucy, taken the year she'd turned five, on a summer day when they'd all been out on Joe's boat. Eleanor had chosen it because Lucy, with her hair bleached several shades lighter by the sun and her face freckled from the outdoors, looked the least like Lowell than in any of the other photos. But Lowell only glanced at it before tucking it into his pocket, prompting her to remark, with barely contained contempt, "Don't you even want to know what she looks like?"

"I know what she looks like," he said.

Eleanor was taken aback, not only by his response but by the ease with which he'd spoken. It was as if he knew everything there was to know about Lucy. The unease she felt deepened, and for the first time she felt a flutter of real panic.

She lowered herself onto the sofa opposite him, smoothing her skirt over her knees. If he'd been an invited guest she would have offered him a cup of coffee or something to eat. But Lowell wasn't welcome, and she didn't care if he thought her rude. "Well. I suppose we should get this over with," she began, when it appeared he was in no hurry to leave. "I've given it some thought and, if you still insist, I'm prepared to take whatever it is you want to give me in terms of . . . of compensation. On one condition: This is in no way entitles you to anything as far as Lucy's concerned. You're to keep away from her." She fixed him with a hard, uncompromising stare. "Do I make myself clear?"

"Perfectly." A smile broke across his face. He seemed as relaxed as if he'd had it all planned out, right down to her response.

"You *do* understand, this isn't in exchange for visits . . . or anything of that nature," she emphasized.

He nodded, saying mildly, "I don't think that would be in either of our best interests."

"Well, then. I'm glad we can agree on that much, at least." Her fears should have eased, but for some reason she remained on guard. With Lowell's next words, she understood the real reason for this visit.

"You drive a hard bargain," he said, the smile lingering on his lips. "But that doesn't mean *we* can't see each other."

Eleanor was rendered speechless. It wasn't until Lowell rose from his chair and came over to where she sat, sinking down beside her on the sofa, that she found her voice. Jumping to her feet and pacing over to the fireplace, she said, "I think you'd better go."

Lowell stood up as if to leave, but instead of going to retrieve his hat and coat, he walked over to where she stood. "What's the matter, Eleanor? We're both adults, and it's not as though you'd be cheating on your husband." He cast a glance at the framed photo on the mantel, of Eleanor and Joe on their wedding day, Joe with his arm around her, appearing somewhat dazed, as if he still couldn't believe his good fortune, and Eleanor in her pale pink bridal suit, looking grimly determined to make a go of it. "Besides, we both know you wouldn't have married him if you hadn't been pregnant. With my child," he added, bringing his gaze back to her, his lips curled in a lazy, vulpine smile.

All at once Eleanor hated him, more than she had ever hated anyone in her life. "My husband was a good man. A good *father*," she said in a voice as cold as the ashes in the fireplace. "So I'll thank you not to drag him into whatever sordid little scheme you have in mind."

"Your loyalty is admirable, my dear," Lowell said, leaning with his elbow against the mantel, one ankle crossed insouciantly over the other, as perfectly at home in her house as if he owned it, "but I'm afraid your husband is no longer in a position to object."

Eleanor, seared by the callous insolence of his remark, lashed back. "He fought and died for his country! Which is more than I can say for you."

She could see that she'd hit a nerve—Lowell was at an age, late forties, when he was no longer eligible for the draft—for his smirk fell away. But he recovered quickly, giving a coarse laugh.

"Why go to war when there are so many pretty widows in need of comforting?"

He slid his arms around her waist, pulling her close. She was too stunned at first to resist, but she quickly recovered her wits and attempted to push him away, to no avail. He merely tightened his hold. She was only able to draw back far enough to take a swing at him, an open-handed blow that caught him clean across the jaw. He winced in pain, but it only seemed to inflame him further. He brought his mouth down against hers, not tenderly as in the past but with a roughness that was bruising.

Eleanor used all her might to wrench free. "If you don't leave this instant, I'm calling the police," she threatened with a bravado that might have been convincing if her voice hadn't been trembling. Lowell's response was to laugh. She glared at him. "You think I won't? Try me."

"Oh, I don't doubt you're capable of anything you set your mind to," he replied, in that lazy, mocking voice of his that was made all the more horrid by the knowledge that she'd once imagined herself in love with him. "But you don't really want the police in on this, do you? Think how it would look. The widow Styles entertaining her former lover when no one's home. People might get the wrong idea."

"You bastard!" she hissed, taking another swing.

He ducked, and she missed him. He straightened, forking back with his fingers the hair that had fallen over his forehead, which seemed as artfully placed as that of some movie villain: the heartless but irresistible rogue he no doubt fancied himself to be. His smile widened. "If I'm a bastard, there was a time it suited you just fine. I seem to recall, my dear, that before you joined the ranks of the respectable you couldn't get enough of this."

"Please. Just leave." It was more of a warning than a plea, for Eleanor felt certain that if he didn't something terrible would happen. Something irreversible.

"Gladly," he said. "But not until I've gotten what I came for."

With that, he fell on her.

Eleanor struggled against him, but it was useless. He quickly overpowered her. As she was dragged to the floor, her hip struck the end table by the sofa, and the lamp that stood on it came toppling down, its ceramic base shattering in an explosion of shards that dug into her like tiny sharp teeth when he threw her down on the rug. Then she forgot her pain, and there was only the terror, as Lowell straddled her, pushing her dress up over her thighs, tugging at her underpants. His breath came in hot little bursts against her face and neck, which made her feel dirtier somehow than what he was doing with his hands. She threw her head back and screamed but there was no one to hear. No one to prevent him from doing what no decent woman would have permitted, however foolishly she'd behaved in the past.

She didn't hear the car pulling up outside.

—

For William these past months had been a quiet agony. Eleanor had refused to see him and he hadn't been able to reach her by phone. He would have slipped a note under the door, but what if her little girl should be the one to find it? So in the end he'd said nothing, holding all his feelings inside, where they grew like a cancer, until he began to know the true meaning of heartsick. It wasn't just a figure of speech, it was a real sickness that left you weak and feverish. It robbed you of your appetite while at the same time eating at you until you could concentrate on little else. It left you lying awake, night after night, hating the wife sweetly slumbering beside you, whose only crime was in not being the one you loved. Whatever he'd felt for Eleanor before, it was magnified a thousand times over by his forced exile.

All he had left was the portrait.

These days, it was his sole occupation, William devoting himself to it at the expense of his other work, commissions that would have brought in money. With painstaking brushstrokes, he went over each fold of her dress, the light illuminating her face, the dozen different shades of her hair, making sure it was rendered perfectly. It haunted him even when he wasn't at his easel. At night, it was there behind his closed eyelids, a gallery with but one work, a show of a single artist's obsession.

When he wasn't holed up in his studio, he was out walking the lonely stretches of shoreline that bordered his property. He would walk for miles, with no destination in mind, the dog his only companion. Anyone who might have happened upon him during one of those peregrinations would have been struck by the sight of him: a tall blade of a man with his unruly black hair blowing in the wind, lurching along the path with the aid of a walking stick, his Border collie trotting at his side, William wearing a frown of concentration so fierce it made him appear slightly mad.

He knew he needed to get a grip. Martha had begun to remark on his odd behavior and frequent absences, and soon she'd wonder what he'd been doing holed up in the studio all those hours when he had nothing to show for it. But just as a man wracked with delirium must wait for the fever to break, so it was with him: He had no choice but to ride it out and hope this madness ended before any real damage was done.

The morning of Lowell's ill-fated visit to Eleanor's house, William had gone into town to pick up the gallon of turpentine he'd ordered from the hardware store. Martha had given him a list of items she needed as well, so afterward he headed over to the market. His mind was occupied, as usual, with thoughts of Eleanor. It had been several weeks since he'd been to her house, so he bought some things he thought she might need. If she wouldn't see him, then he could at least provide for her.

He understood the reason for his exile, that in her mind he'd somehow become tangled up in her husband's death, but that didn't make it any easier to bear. As he negotiated the winding roads to her house in his Packard he was thinking that if he'd been free to pursue her he'd have pounded on her door until she had no choice but to open it, torn it off its hinges if necessary. He wouldn't have allowed her to hide away, steeping in misguided guilt. But he *wasn't* a free man. He had a wife and son. And what right did he have to disrupt Eleanor's life any further when he had nothing to offer her but love?

He noticed the other car as soon as he pulled into the drive, a Cadillac convertible, midnight blue, with white-wall tires. Who did Eleanor know who would drive such a car? It must be someone on official business.

His first thought was that it had something to do with the bank loan she'd alluded to in one of their conversations. Even with Joe's military pay, she'd been having trouble keeping up with the payments. Was the bank coming to personally deliver the bad news of a foreclosure? He couldn't bear the thought of Eleanor and her daughter being forced out in the cold. Whatever he had to do, even if meant getting her to swallow that stubborn pride of hers and take money from him, he'd make sure that didn't happen.

He got out of his car and strode up the front path on legs that seemed to grow stronger with each step. He was barely limping by the time he reached the house. But there was no answer when he knocked on the front door. After a moment's hesitation he tried the knob, and the door swung open. He stepped inside and was about to call out her name when he heard a noise coming from the next room, a thump followed by a muffled sound that might have been a cry of distress.

William didn't stop to think; he acted on pure instinct, snatching the shotgun from atop the oak hall stand, where it was stowed. A woman all alone out in the country couldn't be too careful, Eleanor had reasoned, when he'd questioned its necessity. And he'd smiled at the time, thinking the threat of a wild animal or an intruder remote.

He wasn't smiling now.

As William catapulted into the living room, shotgun in hand, he encountered a scene that made his blood rise in a silent howl of outrage:

Eleanor, in a welter of disheveled clothes and hair, held pinned to the floor by a large, dark-haired man. She was struggling to free herself, but she was no match for her attacker—he had to have outweighed her by at least eighty pounds. He was holding her down with one knee while reaching under her skirt to tug at her underthings, blind to anything but his sick purpose.

William froze for an instant, scattered bits of memory swirling in his brain, memories of the last time he'd held a shotgun in his hand, so many moons ago the smoothness of the oiled stock against his palm, the heft of the barrel along his forearm, shouldn't have felt as familiar as it did. In a series of rapid stereoscopic images, he saw the blood flowing from the wound in his brother's arm, blooming on his shirtsleeve like some hideous crimson flower; Stu, pale as birch bark, the doctor hovering over him; and the look their father had given him later on, as Stu lay dead.

William lifted the gun and fired.

CHAPTER THIRTEEN

He might have been any middle-aged man sitting there at the table in the window enjoying his meal—Judd Cove oysters, pan-fried flounder with butter-sage sauce, and a side of green beans. No messy ribs for him; he was too fastidious for that, Alice thought, watching as he delicately forked a piece of fish and brought it to his mouth. From where she stood, there didn't appear to be anything remotely threatening about Owen White. He wasn't big or menacing. If anything he appeared defenseless, sitting there in his wheelchair, his disproportionately muscular arms offset by the pampered softness of his belly. Next to the male visitors of her fellow inmates at Pine River, with their tattoos and piercings, their missing teeth and faces like roadmaps of their histories, he seemed almost comically bland.

But she knew what he was capable of.

Even as he sat minding his own business, his presence was creating a stir. He was like a stone plunked into a well, sending out ripples that could be felt from one end of the restaurant to the other. The other diners kept surreptitiously glancing his way and heads were bent together in whispered conversation. Soon they would be burning up the phone lines and everyone on the island would know.

But what would they know? Alice wondered. It didn't appear the mayor was here to make trouble. All they would see was a man willing to let bygones be bygones. More than that, one who was showing a generosity of spirit, not to mention a certain degree of trust, in partaking of a meal she had prepared.

Alice had a moment's doubt herself. Had she blown things out of proportion? Seen a conspiracy where there was none? Then the moment passed, and she knew with a certainty that had little to do with logic or appearances, one that was bone deep, that Owen was up to something. She was almost certain that he was behind what was happening to Jeremy. Why else would the D.A. be adopting such a tough stance, treating a sixteen-year-old kid whose worst offense until now had been talking out of turn in class, as if he were a hardened criminal? But if Owen was applying pressure, she wasn't sure what he hoped to gain. Was it pure revenge, using Jeremy to attack her in her most vulnerable spot? Or was it part of another, even more insidious plan?

All at once she felt as powerless as she had in prison, her body heavy with the same kind of inertia that had dragged at her those first months, when all hope for a retrial had faded and she'd had to accept that there was no way out. *Was there any way out of this?* Or was she doomed to have history keep repeating itself?

She became conscious of Jeremy edging up alongside her. She turned to find him eyeing her anxiously, and she was swept with a sense of déjà vu, thinking of the last time he'd been at her side and Owen within striking distance. Jeremy had to be wondering what her next move would be.

She knew one thing: She was not going to cower in the kitchen like a cornered mouse. Rearranging her features in what she hoped was some semblance of calm, she said, "I should go see what he wants."

"Maybe he's not after anything. Maybe he just heard the food was good." Jeremy sounded dubious even so.

"Maybe," she said. "But what do you want to bet it'll be the health inspector next. Looking for rats."

"The only rat I see is the one sitting over there," Jeremy muttered, casting a dark look at the mayor. Alice hadn't shared her suspicions with him, but it was clear he had his own feelings about Owen White. He hadn't forgotten that it was Owen who'd been the cause of his brother's death and of his mother's being taken from him.

As she pushed her way through the swinging doors into the dining area, Alice knew she had to be strong. If she failed by showing weakness, she'd be failing Jeremy as well. And that would be worse than anything Owen could dish out. Bolstered by that thought, she made her way over to his table.

At Pine River, she'd become a master at disguising her emotions. Cons had a nose like a bloodhound when it came to smelling fear or weakness, and they didn't hesitate to use it to their advantage, so it had been a matter of self-preservation. And now, even with her blood running high and fear pushing up from her sternum like something trying to claw its way out, the face she presented Owen was one of cool professionalism.

"Mister White. I hope everything's to your satisfaction."

He looked up from the roll he was buttering, seeming not the least bit surprised to see her. Obviously, he'd been expecting her. He swallowed the food he was chewing, his thin lips rolling back from his teeth in a smile that from a distance might have appeared sincere but that didn't match the cold look in his eyes. The smile of a politician making false promises or that of a CEO getting ready to eviscerate an opponent. Or a man with a secret who would do almost anything to protect it.

"Perfectly," he said, without a trace of irony. "In fact, that was the tastiest meal I've had in quite some time." In the hush that had fallen over the room, his voice seemed to carry, loud enough for all those listening in to hear every word.

She acknowledged the compliment with a little nod. "Thank you. I'm glad you enjoyed it."

"I must congratulate you, too, on what you've done with this place. It shows a lot of imagination." He cast an admiring glance around before leaning in to add, in a lowered voice that for all its manufactured warmth seemed to hold a note of menace, "But we all know that's something you're blessed with in abundance."

He was playing on Alice's biggest fear: that maybe she *was* crazy. After all, she'd suffered a nervous breakdown and it had been *her* behind bars, not Owen. How could she not have questioned her sanity? Yet, seeing him now, there was no doubt in her mind. She hadn't imagined any of it. For if Owen had nothing to hide, why was he going to such elaborate lengths to convince everyone of that? Aware that she was being scrutinized, she maintained a neutral tone, even with her heart pounding and every nerve quivering. "Is there anything else I can get you? Coffee? Dessert? We have an excellent crème brûlée today."

"Tempting, but I'm afraid I'll have to pass." He patted his belly. "I have to watch every bite. It's so easy to put on weight when you can't get around on your own two feet."

He spoke without enmity, but Alice knew that she was being reminded of the fact that she was the reason for his limited mobility. With a single, seemingly innocent remark he had her cornered. If she showed no remorse, she would appear heartless. If she displayed anger at the way she was being manipulated, she'd look vindictive, possibly even unstable. "Why don't I have Katie box something up for you, in that case," she told him, wearing a smile that felt as if it had been carved into her face with a box cutter. "Our mascarpone cheesecake. Compliments of the house."

She signaled to Katie, who hurried over at once. From the anxious look on her face it was clear she was aware of what was going on. The exchange between Alice and Owen had taken place without a raised voice or even a harsh word, but it had been a showdown nonetheless, and all those listening in—Joe Miner, from Island Excavating; the harbormaster, Roman Delgado, and his wife, Jan; Danica and Kurt Fellows, who owned the Old Depot Inn—to name a few—had to be conscious of that.

It wasn't until Alice was back in the kitchen that something in her let go and she began to tremble uncontrollably. When she went to pick up her knife, Jeremy reached over and gently pried it from her grip. "I can do that," he said. He seemed to eye her with new respect.

"Watch your fingers. It's sharp," she cautioned, as he started in on the scallions she'd been in the midst of chopping when Owen arrived.

He glanced up at her, wearing a funny little half smile. "Relax, Mom. I know what I'm doing. Who do you think fixed dinner all those nights Dad was on the road?"

His tone had been lighthearted, but for Alice it was yet another painful reminder of the years she'd been away and the family meals she'd missed. Jeremy and Randy, from what she'd been able to gather, lived like a pair of bachelors, without any of the comforts of a real home. All because of an act that had taken place in mere seconds and which had caused a lifetime of untold grief.

"I should go see how Calpernia's doing," she announced, after a minute or so of circling the kitchen aimlessly, looking for something to do that wouldn't result in a finger getting chopped off or third-degree burns.

"Mom?" She paused, turning to face him, expecting him to make some comment about Owen, but he only asked, "Have you talked to Aunt Denise lately?"

"Just the other day. Why?"

"I don't know. Something Ryan said. Sounds like she's pretty wigged about all this Spring Hill stuff. "

"Oh, that." Alice sighed. "You know her, she takes everything to heart." Alice felt bad about it, too. Like Denise, she'd have loved nothing more than to see the island's last true wilderness turned into a nature preserve. It had sentimental value for her, too; she had fond memories of catching tadpoles in the creek and of her grandmother taking her and Denise on hikes. But she had bigger worries at the moment than the impending development of Spring Hill. "What else did Ryan have to say?"

"Nothing much." Jeremy resumed his chopping. He suddenly looked preoccupied, and she wondered if his cousin had told him something that he didn't feel comfortable sharing. Something having to do with the tension she'd noticed lately between Gary and Denise.

"I'll call her tonight. See how she's doing," Alice said.

Jeremy shrugged, his head bent to his task. "Yeah, I think I will, too."

Excavation of the twelve hundred acre parcel slated for development on Spring Hill had begun the week before. The handful of activists who'd chained themselves to trees had only succeeded in delaying the inevitable. They might have held out longer but for the weather, which had turned suddenly nasty. With temperatures plunging and icy rain pouring down, even the most hardcore among them were forced to concede defeat before the police could move in with their bolt cutters.

Denise would have been among them, if at the last minute Gary hadn't put his foot down, saying he drew the line at having to arrest his own wife. In the end, Denise had backed down, but it had been a black day in their house nonetheless when the bulldozers rolled in. Their roaring could be heard all the way down to the main road as they bullied their way up muddy tracks made even slicker by the rain, uprooting trees and unearthing boulders that had sat untouched since their equally catastrophic formation a millennium ago in some mass, primordial upheaval. It had rained so incessantly that long-time residents whispered it was the curse of the Orcas Indians who'd once inhabited the island and who, it was said, had ancestors buried up on Spring Hill.

When, in the second week of the excavation, the bulldozers unearthed a moldering bundle of bones that proved to be human remains, it seemed the old-timers had been right. It wasn't until they were examined by a forensic expert on the mainland that it was determined they dated back no more than fifty or sixty years, and were those of a middle-aged man, a little over six feet in height, who'd died of a gunshot wound.

The consensus was that the unknown victim had been some vagrant passing through or perhaps an itinerant farm hand. Who else could it have been? Anyone else would have been reported missing at the time, and records showed no missing person who fit that description.

All except one.

When dental records established the deceased's identity as none other than the long-missing Lowell White, the news rocked the island with a force not known since the last earthquake, back in '88. Lowell, it seemed, hadn't gone off to some South American country to live like a king with his mistress. He'd been murdered.

Excavation on Spring Hill was brought to a temporary halt and the case was turned over to the police. Owen White made a public statement that, though saddened to learn of his father's death, he was gratified that the truth had come out at last. Even if the case was never solved, he said, at least his father's tarnished reputation had been restored.

Alice, meanwhile, was enjoying a temporary reprieve—the court date for the hearing on Colin's latest motion had been postponed due to a recent spate of arrests, those of protestors who'd attempted to block the excavation of Spring Hill. Taking advantage of the lull, on a Monday when the restaurant was closed, she decided to pay a visit to Colin. Since business had picked up at the restaurant she'd been so busy they hadn't had much chance to talk, except when meeting to discuss Jeremy's case. Conscious of the fact that he wasn't charging her for all those hours, she'd baked him a pie to show her appreciation. It was the least she could do, she told herself. Though deep down she knew that it was really just an excuse to see him.

Since that night at the restaurant when she'd sensed something between them, something so powerful it had left her shaken, she'd kept herself at an emotional distance. The last thing she needed right now was to add a whole new set of complications to her life by getting romantically involved, she'd reasoned. But that hadn't kept her from thinking about him. Again and again she'd replayed that charged moment in her mind, imagining what it would have been like if he *had* kissed her. It had been so long since she'd known a man's lips on hers, a man's touch against her bare skin, she scarcely remembered what it was like—at the age of thirty-nine she was like a virgin all over again. And now it seemed that part of her, buried for so long she'd almost forgotten it existed, was rising up in revolt. It invaded her thoughts and dreams, and it was what had propelled her out the door and onto the road to Colin's house, despite her asserting that she had absolutely no intention of sleeping with him.

She was passing the turnoff to Denise's house when her thoughts turned briefly to her sister and Gary. Her brother-in-law seemed particularly on edge these days. Alice recalled his hostile reaction when she'd approached him the other day, in the lingering hope that he'd be able to provide some scrap of information that would validate her suspicions about Owen.

"I'd drop it, if I were you," Gary had advised, eyeing her coldly. They'd gone for a ride in his cruiser, so they could talk in private, and were parked along a remote stretch of road out near Mountain Lake.

"Why? Is it so far-fetched?" she'd pressed on nonetheless. "Come on, Gary, we both know the reason I ended up getting the maximum sentence. Ten years, Gary. *Ten years.* I'd still be serving time, if I hadn't gotten paroled. You think I'd have been left to rot if it'd been someone other than Owen? He knows people. He knows which levers to pull."

"You want to blame someone, blame yourself," Gary had snapped. In the sunlight glaring in through the cruiser's windshield, showing off every smear and bug splat, his eyes peered from hollowed sockets, the skin around them bruised-looking. "You brought all this on yourself. And it wasn't just you who had to suffer. Christ, when I think of all the nights your sister cried herself to sleep. And your poor mom, having to cope with that while your dad was dying. Not to mention Jeremy."

Stung, Alice had been momentarily silenced. "I know I caused a lot of pain," she'd said softly at last, "and I'm sorry for that, truly I am. But if you care about Jeremy, don't you owe it to him to find out if there's any truth to what I'm saying?"

But this new Gary who'd taken the place of her normally considerate brother-in-law had merely given a scornful laugh. "So having me chase some paranoid delusion is your idea of helping? Jesus, Alice, sometimes I think the kid was better off with you in prison."

Alice had been more taken aback by the transformation in Gary than by his cruel words. In the old days, he never would have spoken to her like that. He'd always acted as the family peacekeeper, the calm voice of reason when Denise was on one of her leftist rants or when an argument between the kids needed refereeing. As a cop, he had a reputation for settling domestic disputes without further inflaming already sore tempers, and for cutting motorists a break if they had a good reason for going over the speed limit.

Even Gary had seemed to recognize that he'd gone too far, for he'd continued on, in a gentler tone, "Okay, let's just say, for the sake of argument, there's some truth to what you're saying. You start poking around where you don't belong, you could piss off some powerful interests."

Alice had grown suddenly alert. "So there *is* something to it."

"I'm not saying that," he'd said.

"What *are* you saying then?"

"Nothing." His mouth had settled into a grim line, as he'd stared out the bug-spattered windshield, as if seeing something other than the strip of gravel on which they were parked.

She'd placed a hand on his arm. His muscles were so taut they were almost vibrating, like an aerial cable in a high wind. "If you know anything, anything at all, please, you have to tell me. I promise no one will ever know where I heard it from. Not even Denise."

"So now you want me keeping secrets from my own wife?" With a violent twist, he'd thrown her hand off his arm, as if it had been a biting insect. "Christ, Alice. You should listen to yourself. You want people to forget about the past, stop acting like some crazy person. And stop hanging out with ex-cons, like your friend Big Mama."

With that, he'd slammed the cruiser into gear, sending it slewing over the gravel before it hit the roadway at a speed best suited for when the bubble light was flashing. Alice had been more confused and worried than angry. Gary was clearly under a tremendous strain. But what was causing it? Did it have something to do with the way Denise had been acting lately? Or was it some work-related pressure?

When Alice arrived at Colin's house, there was a note pinned to the front door that read simply *Gone fishing*. She set off along the path that led down to the cove, using a hand to shield her eyes against the sunlight that seemed almost blinding after the spate of rainy days they'd had. The tide was out and the waters of the sound calm, glinting like so many capsized stars. Down below she could see Colin, in a hooded jacket and rubber boots, wading through the shallows, the lengths of PVC pipe he'd planted in evenly spaced rows stretching out before him like a field of newly sprouted cornstalks, while Shep watched from a safe, dry distance onshore. Colin spotted her and waved, sloshing his way toward her.

"Catch anything yet?" she asked, noting the plastic bucket he carried in one hand.

"Just starfish."

"I didn't know they were edible."

"I wasn't planning to make a meal out of them. In fact, they're the ones doing the eating." He explained that, to starfish and other predators, his fledgling oyster farm was nothing more than a giant snack bar. "I'm just thinning out the population to give my guys a fighting chance. Don't worry," he assured her. "They're not going to end up in some souvenir shop. I turn them loose in the bay." He pointed toward the larger body of water on the other side of the cove.

Colin's face was ruddy from working outdoors. He was looking more robust these days; not only that, more at peace with himself.

"Very considerate of you," she said, smiling. "It must help that they don't put up much of a fight. I mean, it's not exactly the battle of the *Old Man and the Sea* you're waging here."

"Oh, I don't know about that." He fished a starfish from the bucket and held it up, dripping, saying with a twinkle in his eye, "This guy looks pretty fierce. I wouldn't want to be at the receiving end of one of these suckers." He prodded an arm waving in sluggish protest before dropping the creature back into the bucket. "Now what do you say we take a ride over to the point and show these guys their new home?"

"I'm game, as long as it doesn't involve touching anything slimy."

"I promise to do all the dirty work," he said, as he started up the path, Shep at his heels. The Border collie appeared to have settled into his new role as Colin's surrogate pet, as though he'd come to regard Colin, if not as his true owner, then as an ally at least. Shep waited politely to be invited along before hopping into the Volvo and settling onto the backseat.

The entire trip took less than half an hour, and they were back at the house by lunchtime. "You're not in any rush, I hope," said Colin, as they were getting out of the car. "I thought I'd fix us something to eat to go with that pie you brought."

"Why not? It's my day off," she reminded him. There were a million things on her to-do list, but at the moment she couldn't think of any better way to spend the afternoon than with Colin.

"I'm not as good a cook as you, but I make a mean shrimp salad," he said, as he led the way through the back door, pulling off his boots in the mudroom and slipping into an old pair of Weejuns.

In the kitchen, he set about assembling various bags of greens and bottles of condiment. "Anything I can do to help?" she asked.

"No, you sit. Can't have you working on your day off." He waved her toward one of the chairs at the old dinette, where she sat watching in amusement as he muddled through the process of tearing up lettuce, chopping vegetables, and peeling the cooked shrimp.

"Delicious," she pronounced, upon taking her first bite. "And the fact that I didn't have to lift a finger makes it taste all the better."

"You did your part. You brought dessert. How did you know pumpkin pie was my favorite?"

"Actually, it's sweet potato," she corrected him.

"Well, whatever, it looks good. I'll have to order it next time I'm in the restaurant."

"It's not on the menu, actually. I only make it for family."

He smiled at her across the table, a smile that caused a slow heat to rise in her cheeks. "In that case, I feel doubly privileged."

After coffee and pie, they headed back outside. It was chilly, but after all the weeks of dreary weather, the sunshine that had broken through the clouds earlier in the day was like an unexpected gift. Bundled in their jackets, they sat in the wicker chairs on the porch with their heads tipped back to receive it, like some sort of blessing or absolution, while Shep lay stretched out asleep on the old, scuffed floorboards at Colin's feet.

Talk turned inevitably to Jeremy's case.

"Cantwell's been applying pressure to set a date for the trial," Colin said, informing her of the latest. "I don't know how much longer I can stall. I filed a motion seeking a continuance to interview more witnesses, but I'm not sure the judge is going to grant it."

"And if he doesn't?" Alice felt a ripple of anxiety.

"We'll just have to hope that we have a strong enough case as it is."

His faintly troubled look prompted her to ask, "What is it? Is there something you're not telling me?"

After a moment's hesitation, he said, "I just got the results back on the rape kit from our own expert, the pathologist I told you about, in Spokane. It's nothing bad," he hastened to assure her. "It's just that I was hoping the findings would be more conclusive."

"But if they're not conclusive, doesn't that mean the D.A.'s case isn't very strong either?" she asked.

"It depends on which expert the jury finds more credible."

"So this doctor in Spokane, what's he like?"

"Actually, it's a she. And she strikes me as highly credible. She's a lot like you, in fact. Strong and decisive."

Alice gave a self-conscious laugh. "That's funny. Most days, it seems like I don't even know which shoe goes on which foot."

"Well, then, I guess appearances can be deceiving." Colin smiled at her, tiny lines radiating from the corners of his eyes.

Alice pondered his words, as though fingering some small, shiny treasure she'd accidentally stumbled across. Was she really that person he saw when he looked at her? It was almost too much for her to contemplate, so she brought the discussion back to Jeremy's case, asking, "What are his chances of a fair trial?"

"Depends." Colin gazed out at the cove, frowning in thought.

"On what?"

"On whether or not our suspicions are correct about your friend, Owen." He turned to face her. "Have you been able to find out anything yet?"

Alice thought once more about her frustrating conversation with Gary, and shook her head. "Nothing so far, but I'm still working on it." She'd put off going to Denise, in the hope that her sister would have better luck appealing to Gary, but Alice could see that she had no other choice. She sighed, adding, "The thing is, unless we can come up with some pretty compelling proof, no one's going to believe Owen's behind it. Especially now, with all this public sympathy over his father."

"That certainly adds a new wrinkle," Colin agreed.

"Do you think they'll ever get to the bottom of it?" she asked, out of curiosity.

A murder that took place half a century ago? With no weapon, no eyewitnesses, no suspect even." Colin shook his head. "You'd have better luck solving Amelia Earhart's disappearance."

"I suppose you're right. Still, I can't help wondering if he's somewhere on the island. The killer, I mean. Someone you might pass on the street and not think twice about. Someone we might even know." Suppose, like her, he wasn't a common criminal, but someone who'd simply snapped under pressure. In a peculiar way, she found the idea comforting. It meant she wasn't the only one capable of doing the unthinkable.

"If he's even still alive, he'd be pretty old by now," Colin said. "We don't even know if it's a he. It could be a she."

She nodded thoughtfully. "Maybe some woman he was involved with. He could have promised to leave his wife for her and when she found out he was just stringing her along, she went crazy and shot him. You know, like Jean Harris and that diet doctor."

He turned to her with a smile. "So you think it was a crime of passion?"

"From what I've heard, he was quite the ladies' man."

"If that's true, then your theory makes sense."

They lapsed into silence, and for a long while there was just the sound of the wind in the trees, a sound like the whispering of a thousand secrets, and the distant cries of seagulls. After a while, Colin remarked, "This was my grandfather's favorite spot. He used to love sitting out here after a day at his easel, especially in good weather."

"It must have been lonely when you weren't around," she said, thinking of the long winter months holed up in this remote place.

Colin shrugged. "I suppose. He never talked about it. He wouldn't have wanted me to feel guilty for not visiting more."

"What about your dad? Did he visit?" Colin seldom talked about his family, and now she realized how little she knew about them.

"No. Never." From the hardness of Colin's tone, it was obvious there had been some deep animosity. "My grandmother saw to that. She poisoned my dad against him."

Alice made a sympathetic face. "Their divorce must have been bitter." She was thinking of hers and Randy's, a dissolution that had seemed more of a sad withering than anything else.

"Yeah, but the weird thing is I never really knew why they split up. It's not something my grandmother likes talking about. In fact, to this day she refuses to have his name spoken in her presence. And my grandfather . . . well, he was too much of a gentleman to say anything that might have made her look bad." "

"That must have been hard on your dad."

"It was." She could see the muscles tightening in Colin's jaw. "And after my grandmother moved to New York, William didn't have much chance to rectify the situation."

"Why was that?"

"For one thing, they lived at opposite ends of the continent. Travel wasn't so easy in those days. For my father it would have meant hours on an airplane, and he was just a little boy." Colin shook his head in regret. "By the time he came of age, it was too late, the damage was done."

"So how did you and William end up having a relationship?"

"That was my mom's doing. She thought it was a shame, us boys growing up not knowing their grandpa. She was the one who needled Dad into letting us visit. In the end, though, it was just me who went. My brother always had something going on. Little League, junior varsity, cross country. Then once Patrick discovered girls you couldn't have pried him loose with a crowbar, especially not after he started having sex, and believe me, he didn't waste any time in that department. His wife was pregnant when they eloped, the two of them barely out of high school."

"That must have gone over well with your parents," she commented dryly, thinking about the current situation with Jeremy.

"No kidding. I thought they were going to go through the roof." Colin shook his head, chuckling as though at some private joke. "You'd have thought the odds of that marriage working were next to none, right? But amazingly, Pat and Ginny are still together. They just celebrated their twentieth. Their oldest is in college and Mikey just graduated high school."

"Do you see much of them?"

"Not as much as I should. I was kind of out of commission there for a while. I even went a few years without seeing my grandfather, and by the time I was up to it, it was too late." A source of deep regret, she could see, from the sorrowful look that crossed his face.

"I didn't know your grandfather," she said gently, "but he sounds like the kind of person who'd have understood. The main thing is, you got sober. I'm sure he'd have been happy about that."

Colin regarded her for a moment, a small, considering smile on his lips. "You know a lot for a normie." At the puzzled look she shot him, he explained, "As in normal. It's AA speak for someone who's not an alcoholic."

She gave a wry laugh. "I'd hardly describe myself normal. In fact, I'd say I'm anything but."

"Maybe that's what I like about you."

"Oh? And I thought it was just my cooking."

His smile widened. "That, too."

Alice noticed that the shadows had lengthened; the patch of sunlight in which Shep lay had shrunk to the size of a dollar bill, which glowed atop the furry hump he made curled there on the porch. Reluctantly, she said, "I should be going. It's getting late."

Colin didn't attempt to persuade her to stay, which made her wonder if she'd already worn out her welcome. As she rose to go, she felt strangely let down. She hadn't expected anything to happen—in fact, it was the last thing she needed—but foolishly she'd thought it might. Whatever she was feeling, it was clearly one-sided. Probably when he looked at her, he saw only a woman who'd spent her youth behind bars and who was now past her prime.

She'd turned and was about to walk away when she felt his touch against her elbow.

"Alice."

Just that, her name, spoken so softly it might have been a whisper, and she knew. It hadn't been her imagination after all: He wanted her. The knowledge brought a rush of joy so intense she needed a moment to compose herself before she could turn to face him.

Colin appeared uncertain, as if engaged in some sort of internal struggle. Then a corner of his mouth tipped up in a smile that was both hopeful and guarded. "I was just wondering what you would think if I kissed you."

Alice was rendered speechless. None of the old flirtatious comebacks came to mind, the coy lines from back in the days when such repartee had come as naturally as breathing. In the end, she simply spoke the truth. "Actually, I'm not even sure I remember how. It's been a long time."

"For me, too." He shoved his hands deep into the pockets of his corduroy trousers, as if suddenly not knowing what to do with them.

All of the perfectly valid reasons with which she'd been attempting to convince herself that now wasn't the time to be embarking on an affair, building her case as thoroughly as Colin had Jeremy's, vanished from her mind. She took a deep breath. "Well, then, what do you say we give it a try."

He took her in his arms, tentatively at first. She closed her eyes as his lips brushed over hers. So far, so good. Then the kiss deepened and all at once she knew she was in trouble. She had the sensation of falling, as if she were tumbling over and over in mid-air. Yet, strangely, it didn't terrify her. Instead, she only found herself wanting more.

She wound her arms around his neck, pulling him close. How was it possible she'd gone so long without this? That she'd shut down to

such a degree that even the most basic human needs had come to seem
like impossible luxuries? Now the rush of being liberated was almost
overpowering.

She sensed that Colin, too, had been unprepared for the suddenness
with which they were swept up in . . . whatever this was. His hands that
hadn't known what to do with themselves were all at once taking charge,
moving over her, touching her in places she hadn't been touched in so
long his fingers might have been brushing over her bare skin, the sensations were so acute. He kissed her neck, her earlobes, the hollow at the
base of her throat, where a runaway pulse would have given her away if
her own hands and mouth hadn't already done so. The greedy kisses of a
man who, like her, had been wandering in the desert for too long.

There, amid the lengthening shadows, they each found what they'd
been looking for without realizing they'd been in search of it: a place to
lay their burdens down, a temporary respite from the ghosts that haunted
them. Love didn't necessarily enter into it. That could come later, she
knew. Right now all that mattered was that, for the moment at least, they
weren't alone.

"Shall we go inside?" Colin murmured when they finally drew apart.

"We'd better. Unless we want to give the neighbors something to *really*
talk about," she said, with a breathless little laugh. Never mind the nearest neighbor was half a mile away.

Indoors it was quiet. There was only the slow ticking of the regulator
clock on the mantel and a fly buzzing against a windowpane. Colin led
the way into the bedroom, a room so full of history that Alice felt it settle over her like the thick down comforter Colin used to cover her as she
stretched out on the old sleigh bed.

The last of the sunlight slanting in through the curtains had faded,
but Colin didn't bother to switch on the lamp. In the soft gray light of
dusk, he unbuttoned her shirt and eased off her jeans. With each new
item of clothing removed it was as if she were being released somehow,
from the chains that had held her bound for so long. For once, she wasn't
fretting about what the future would bring. She wasn't questioning his

motives or her own. She was too busy luxuriating in the feast of delicious sensations and in this new, giddy sense of freedom. She gave herself over to it, surrendering herself to his hands, as they moved over her naked body, and to his mouth that had kissed her so tenderly on the lips and was now exploring her with equal tenderness below.

She quickly grew acquainted with his body as well: the long, lean contours of his torso, the hair on his chest that tapered to a downy trail on his belly, his arms that had grown sinewy with muscle from all the outdoor work. Each crevice and plane and ridge was a fascinating new discovery. Colin was bigger than Randy, and adept in ways her husband hadn't been. In bed, he wasn't shy. Using his hand to guide hers, he showed her what pleased him and how she could let him please her.

Alice moaned as he pushed two fingers into her, rolling her hips up to bring them deeper into her. She felt as if she could come this way. And then she *was* coming, in waves so intense it was as though she were being turned inside out. When it was over, she fell back with a gasp. It was a moment before she could catch her breath and whisper, "Now you."

But Colin pulled away, murmuring, "Next time." He hadn't thought to buy condoms, he explained somewhat sheepishly. He hadn't exactly been planning to seduce her.

"You mean all you thought about was kissing me?" she teased.

"I didn't say that. But X-rated fantasies can't get you into trouble," he replied, nibbling on her ear.

He showed her then just how to pleasure him. An act she found more exciting, in its own way, than if they'd made love. Even then, it seemed they weren't done. He gently pushed her onto her back and gave her more of what he had earlier, only this time with his mouth. Afterward, Alice could barely move. She felt as though she'd been drugged.

At last she managed to roll onto her side, propping an elbow under her head. Colin was lying on his back, staring pensively up at the ceiling, wearing a satisfied smile, but already she sensed him beginning to withdraw.

Alice touched his shoulder. "You're not sorry, are you?"

He turned to look at her. "God, no. You?"

She should have felt reassured, yet there'd been something in the quickness of his response and the fleeting expression of guilt that had crossed his face that gave her pause. *He's thinking about his wife.* Even though she was dead and the woman lying next to him very much alive. More alive, in fact than Alice had felt in years.

She was quick to stow away her own emotions, not wanting to get hurt. "We're both adults and, as far as I know, unattached." She aimed for a light, *laissez faire* tone.

Alice waited for him to respond, but he'd gone back to staring up at the ceiling, still wearing that pensive look. His thoughts taking him places where she couldn't follow. At last, he shifted so that he was facing her and reached up to smooth back a stray lock of her hair, saying, "That was amazing. But I should warn you, they don't encourage this sort of thing in the program, not until you've been sober at least a year."

"It's not as if we planned it," she said.

"I know. I just wanted you to be aware of what you're getting into. I'm not exactly prime relationship material."

The pleasure Alice had felt abruptly faded. "This is hardly the time for me to be thinking about getting into a relationship," she said, in the same airy tone, "so you can put your mind at ease on that score, at least. As lovely as that was, I'm not looking for anything permanent." It was the truth, she told herself, so why did she feel like a liar saying it?

Colin's expression softened. "Alice—"

She cut him off, peering at her watch and saying, "Will you look at the time? Now I *really* have to be going."

"So soon?" he asked, but at the same time she could sense that a part of him was relieved, the part that wanted to be alone with his thoughts.

"I'd love to stay, but I have some things to do at home," she said briskly, bending to retrieve her clothes, which were scattered over the floor. They both got dressed, an awkward silence settling over them. They didn't speak again until she was on her way out the door.

"Drive safely," he said, kissing her lightly on the mouth.

Alice nearly laughed out loud. Drive safely? He should have cautioned her about losing her heart.

—

For a long time after Alice had left, Colin sat on the sofa, absently rubbing his jaw as he stared off into space, mulling over what had just happened. It wasn't that Nadine wouldn't have given her blessing, he knew. In fact, whenever they'd played that particular game of *what if . . .* she would always teasingly run through a list of friends whom she thought would make compatible replacement wives.

No, he thought, if anyone had a problem with his being with another woman, it was him. He'd been unprepared for the slew of emotions that Alice had unleashed in him. It was as if, having thought he was dredged dry, no more tears left to be shed, he'd discovered there was a whole new level of grieving to be done.

The only other woman he'd slept with since his wife's death had been a one-night stand, after too much to drink at an office Christmas party. But the following day, aside from the usual free-floating morning-after shame, there had been none of the complicated feelings he was experiencing now. Because the woman hadn't been a threat to Nadine's memory.

Alice, on the other hand, wasn't just some warm body to distract him from his grief. She meant something to him. What exactly he didn't know, but one thing was clear: He didn't want to see her get hurt.

His sponsor had warned him about this. *After the first six months you think you got it made in the shade. That's when you* really *gotta watch out,* Dave had said. Dave Coffey, a big, tough, former biker with scraggly gray hair in a ponytail and more tattoos than Colin had ever seen on any one person. But he'd known what he was talking about.

Colin had let his guard down, allowed himself to believe he was out of the woods, and there, just as Dave had predicted, was that old, familiar thirst, rising up in him, with all the intensity of those first weeks in sobriety. His hands trembled with it and his throat was parched. He felt the old St. Vitus's dance start up in him, too, as if any minute he was going to jump out of his skin.

Colin eyed the antique cherry cabinet where his grandfather had kept a small supply of liquor for the occasional visitor. Colin didn't know how much, if any of it, was left; he hadn't bothered to check. It would have been tempting fate and he'd already had one too many rendezvous with that particular siren. But now he found himself wondering if the key to the cabinet was in the same place he remembered it being.

He squeezed his eyes shut, running through all the reasons not to get up and unlock the cabinet. It would wipe out eight months of sobriety, putting him back to square one, and once he started down that road the life he'd been struggling to rebuild would be washed away, too, like so much flotsam with the tide. Too, he'd be letting down people who had come to depend on him, like Alice and Jeremy, as well as destroying any goodwill he'd managed to cultivate among the islanders whom he'd gotten to know and like.

For what seemed like an eternity Colin remained motionless, his eyes shut and his hands balled into fists. A light sweat had broken out on his forehead and he was trembling ever so slightly. An image of Nadine rose up behind his closed eyelids, her angelic face with its devilish smile, her eyes sparkling with the come-hither look she'd worn on that last morning. He held on to it as long as he could and, even after it had faded, it was with the greatest reluctance that at last he opened his eyes.

With a deep sigh of release, or perhaps regret, he rose from the sofa and crossed the room to where the cabinet stood.

CHAPTER FOURTEEN

It was late in the day and the air cidery with the smell of apples rotting on the ground in the orchards along Fox Valley Road. The season had long since peaked, even for the later varieties, like Winesap. Though only a few short weeks ago, it seemed, the boughs had still been heavy with golden and red Delicious, McIntosh, Cortland, and Pippin. As he drove slowly toward home in his cruiser, Gary Elkin thought back to the days when he used to help out with the harvest in his family's orchard, before the rise of gourmet outlets had created a demand for newer varieties, many of them imported, that sounded more like fancy drinks—Pink Lady, Jazz, Gala—had pretty much kicked the bottom out of the market for what they'd grown. Between that and the industrial agrigrowers, which had further driven prices down, mom and pop operations like theirs couldn't compete. When Gary was in the fifth grade his parents had been forced to sell the farm.

He would never forget the day he'd arrived home from school to find his mom and dad seated at the kitchen table wearing shell-shocked looks, like after the barn had burned down a few years back. Their eyes stared out of suntanned faces the color of the milky tea in mugs before them. *Sit down, Gary. We have something to tell you,* his mother had said, in the same grave tone she'd used when informing him of Grandpa Eddie's death. She told him they were moving to California, where his father had found a job as foreman with a big grower in Bakersfield. They would be leaving as soon as they'd packed up.

What about the horses, Popcorn and Winkie, and the goats and chickens? Gary had wanted to know, not quite understanding what this was all about.

They'll be fine, his father had assured him. *Their new owners will take good care of them.* He'd explained that they hadn't had any choice in the matter; if they'd tried to hold on to the farm, the bank would have foreclosed. His dad had looked close to tears himself as he'd patted Gary's hand, saying with a bravado that was unconvincing even to an eleven-year-old, *Don't worry, son. It'll be all right, you'll see. In fact, it'll be an adventure. A brand-new start for us all.*

Only it hadn't been a brand-new start. Rather, it had been the end of an era. The end of living in a community where everyone had greeted him by name and most of his friends were guys he'd known since kindergarten; the end of lazy summer days waking up to the smell of fresh-mown grass and the crowing of roosters, with nothing more pressing on his mind than whether he'd be having pancakes or eggs for breakfast; of his dad letting him practice driving the tractor down the rows of trees, and of helping his mom peel the apples that would go into the pies she was always baking for various charitable causes, so many that their house had carried the faint scent of cinnamon and apples and golden sugary crusts year round.

In Bakersfield, in place of their roomy old farmhouse, he and his parents and two younger brothers had been shoehorned into a small, one-story house on a street lined with similar houses. The winters were so mild, it had been hard to work up much enthusiasm for Christmas, and the summers hot enough to turn the sidewalk in front of their house into a griddle. The produce on display at the neighborhood Safeway had borne little resemblance to the fresh-picked fruits and vegetables he was accustomed to. And in the school Gary and his brothers had attended, his classes had been made up largely of children of the migrant workers employed by farms and orchards like the one his father was foreman of, Mexicans mostly, among whom he'd been the odd man out.

He'd vowed to himself that as soon as he was old enough to earn his own living he'd return to the island. And so he had, going into the police academy right out of high school, then putting in two years with the California Highway Patrol, and biding his time until there was an opening here. Soon after that he'd met Denise and they'd gotten married and started a family. It wasn't life on the farm, no, but it was a good life all the same.

Or it had been up until now.

Lately, Gary had been feeling as if the carefully woven fabric of his life were starting to unravel. Or maybe it was just *him* that was coming apart. The very system that had crushed his parents was now crushing him: the incestuous union of commerce and government that he thought of as Them. The irony was that until fairly recently he'd been one of Them. Each morning when he'd put on his freshly ironed uniform he'd felt proud to be serving his community. Sure, he bent the rules from time to time, but always for a good cause. Like the other day, in not giving the Shepherd boy a ticket for speeding when he'd been going well over the limit, knowing that Marge Shepherd was in the final stages of terminal cancer and her husband Paul working two jobs to make ends meet.

It had been just his luck that the only time he'd bent the rules for himself, he'd gotten caught. Now he was being blackmailed as a result. Whichever way you looked at it, he was in deep trouble. The kind that had him by the balls and was slowly squeezing him to death.

If his motivation had been pure greed, Gary might have felt he'd only gotten what he deserved. But he hadn't taken the money for himself. Ryan had so wanted to go on that summer trip to Paris with his French class, and Gary didn't have the heart to disappoint him. So when Buck Duggan, the owner of the Kittycat Club out on Route 6, had slipped him an envelope full of cash to turn a blind eye to the things that went on at the club that weren't strictly legal, he'd hesitated only briefly before accepting it, telling himself it was just the one time, that he wasn't the only cop on the take, that it wasn't wrong if it was for the right reasons. All the usual bullshit excuses, in other words. Then, a few months later, the transmission had gone out on Denise's ancient VW Rabbit, and Gary dipped into the well again—unaware that this time the entire transaction was being videotaped.

And now the mayor owned his ass.

In the beginning, Gary had naively thought that he'd eventually be let off the hook. But now he knew there was about as much likelihood of that as of peace in the Middle East any time soon. Instead, each time he did White's bidding, he only dug himself in deeper—not only in spying on his sister-in-law and keeping quiet about how his nephew was being railroaded, but in being forced to lie to his own wife. And that made him angry in a way that, with nowhere to go, was like acid leaking from a corroded battery. It had become a vicious cycle. Each time he lost his temper and lashed out at Denise or one of the kids, he'd hate himself even more, and that would only feed his anger.

Christ. If Denise only knew. If she'd had even the slightest inkling that he'd done his share of the dirty work in making sure nothing stood in the way of the Spring Hill development, by whispering in the right ears, by knowing which county commissioners to butter up and which ones needed a little extra persuasion in the form of a subtle threat. She might not divorce him—he didn't think she'd go that far—but life would never be the same. There were some things there was no coming back from and this was one.

Now all that was left for him to do was find a way to live with himself. If he could have talked to someone about it, it might have made it easier. But who was there to confide in? Not Denise. Not any of his fellow officers. And certainly not his parents, both retired now and living in Rancho Del Mar. It would have killed them to find out how far he'd strayed from the principles of honesty and integrity with which he had been raised. Principles that had been strictly enforced in their household. Like the time, when Gary was ten, that his dad had caught him pocketing a pack of chewing gum in Mr. Gowan's store. Gary had not only had to return the stolen merchandise, he'd had to spend the next two weekends helping out at the store. What would his father say if he were find out about *this*?

Ironically, the only one who would have understood was Alice. The day she'd come to him, asking for his help, it had been all Gary could do to keep from spilling his guts. But she was the last person he could confide in. If she knew what he'd been up to . . .

Lost in thought, he was surprised to find himself turning into his driveway. He could have sworn it had been only minutes since he'd pulled out of his parking space behind the stationhouse. It was the story of his life these days. One of the guys would comment on something that had happened that day, something he'd apparently witnessed, and he wouldn't have the vaguest idea what they were talking about. Or Denise would remind him of something he'd promised to do that he had absolutely no memory of.

He suspected it was mainly because he hadn't been getting much shut-eye lately. These days, he'd wake in the middle of the night, his heart going a million miles a minute and his mind spinning like a wheel in a rat's cage, and there would be no getting back to sleep.

Well, he would just have to be a man and suck it up. Wasn't that what his father had taught him to do? And it had always served Gary well in the past: in school with the kids who'd bullied him, while in training at the police academy and later on, as a rookie cop with the veterans who'd made a sport of yanking his chain. This was *his* problem, one that he alone had created, not his wife's or kids'; there was no reason for them to be dragged into it.

He pulled up in front of the house and got out of the cruiser, his boots crunching on the gravel as he approached along the front path. It was the only sound other than the distant barking of a dog and the thump of hooves coming from the barn—Taylor's mare feeling her oats. Through the window, he could see Denise setting the table for supper. She had the phone pressed to her ear as she laid out forks and spoons, all the while talking animatedly to whoever was at the other end. The sight of her smiling and laughing like her old self caused his spirits to lift. Denise had been down in the dumps since excavation on Spring Hill had begun, and his own black moods hadn't helped. They'd been arguing a lot lately and he couldn't recall the last time they'd made love.

But the minute he walked in, it was as if a switch had been flipped. The light in her eyes dimmed and her expression became guarded, as she said a hurried good-bye to whoever she'd been gabbing with on the phone. Clearly she was still pissed off about the fight they'd had earlier in the day. A dumb argument over Taylor's wanting to wear a skirt to school that had showed off nearly every inch of her prepubescent legs, never mind she'd been wearing tights. Gary had refused to let their daughter out of the house until she'd changed into something more modest, and Denise had accused him of overreacting.

"Dinner's almost ready," she informed him now in the cool tone he'd become accustomed to of late. "Ryan's at football practice, so he'll be a little late."

"How's it going with that?" Gary realized with a guilty start that it had been a while since he'd gone to any of his son's games.

"The coach made him starting quarterback."

Gary broke into a grin, briefly buoyed by pride in his son's achievement. "That's great! We'll have to do something to celebrate. Maybe go out for root beer floats after supper."

His wife paused in the midst of setting out napkins to roll her eyes. "Root beer floats? He's *sixteen*, Gary, not six. I think he's a little old for that."

"Same as Taylor, right?" The words were out before he realized he'd spoken.

Now Denise was squaring off, hands on hips, giving him that Look. "Are you going to start up with that again? I thought we'd settled it."

"Pardon me for thinking it's a big deal having our nine-year-old daughter walk around in public looking like a hooker," he said. *For Chrissakes, just let it go,* a voice pleaded in his head. But he couldn't stop. He was too revved up. "You know how many perverts there are out there just waiting to prey on little girls? The woods are full of them."

She gave a snort. "On Grays Island? Please."

"It happens. Remember the Gibbons kid?" he said. True, the guy hadn't exactly molested Joanie Gibbons, only flashed her, but even so . . .

"Gary, I know all about sexual predators," she said, in that excessively patient voice she used on kids who weren't paying attention in class. "But don't you think you're carrying this a little too far?"

He felt something shift in him, his anger turning ugly. Yet he seemed to have no more control over it than if it had been someone else's mouth the words were coming out of. "No, as a matter of fact I don't. What I think is that it's a good thing at least *one* of us cares what happens to our kids."

Denise's face went slack. She couldn't have looked more shocked than if he'd used his fist on her, something that in eighteen years of marriage he'd never even contemplated doing but which lately he'd been terrified might happen, if he didn't get a grip.

"I'm going to pretend I didn't hear that," she said.

Gary used a mental trick of his that had worked in the past, picturing himself pulling on the hand brake in one of those old-fashioned steam engines. But this time the brake was stuck and the runaway train continued to hurtle down the tracks. "Oh, so now I'm the bad guy? That's typical of you, Denise. You rag on the kids all day long. Do this, do that, don't forget to clean up your room," he mimicked in a whiney falsetto. "But I say one little thing to them and you're all over me like I'm some kind of dictator."

He could see that she was close to tears. "I never said—"

He smacked his fist down hard on the kitchen counter, causing her to jump. Some of the beer foamed up over the top of the can he was holding in his other hand, dripping onto the floor. "Don't contradict me! I'm still the man of this house, and what I say goes." Words that might have come straight out of his father's mouth and that shocked him as much as they surely had her.

"Gary, what on earth's gotten into you? Why are you acting this way?" Denise looked more worried than upset. Not just worried, scared. And for some reason that made him even angrier. Because he knew that *he* was responsible. He'd become a stranger to his own wife.

In a sudden fit of temper, he hurled the can at the wall. It landed with a hollow cracking sound, spewing a foamy geyser. For a long moment he just stood there staring at the beard of foam dripping down the light green wallpaper patterned with vines and miniature watering cans. Then, struck with horror at what he'd done, he sank to his knees with a groan, burying his face in his hands. He was scarcely aware of the puddle spreading across the floor and now soaking into the cuffs of his trousers; all he knew was that he was more scared than he'd ever been in his life: Another few inches and he'd have nailed Denise with that throw.

"Oh, Christ. I'm sorry. I didn't mean—" Dry sobs tore at his throat. Wrenched from him against his will, they were like the deep, hacking cough of a man choking to death. He was out of control and he knew it, but some part of him still insisted he could still get a grip if he just . . . if he just . . . rode this out a little while longer.

He felt Denise's hand on his shoulder and it was the last straw. He shook it off and lurched to his feet. He could barely see straight as he headed for the back door.

Through the roaring in his ears, he heard his wife cry out in alarm, "Gary! Where are you going?"

"I need some air." The words came out in a harsh rasp. "Don't wait up for me. I may be a while."

"What about supper?" She sounded panicked, and he knew it wasn't supper she was concerned about.

"You guys go ahead and eat without me."

He was letting himself out the door when he heard a small voice call after him, "Daddy?" He turned around to see Taylor poised there, in her leggings and Hello Kitty T-shirt, a worried look on her face.

The sight of her almost broke him, but he managed to pull it together just enough to say, "Everything's okay, sweetie. Daddy has to go out for a little while. I'll be back before you know it."

As soon as he stepped outside, Gary felt a strange calm descend on him. As he headed down the path, part of him marveled at the way his anger had magically dissipated, taking with it all of the tension that had been building over these past weeks. At the same time, the cop in him knew it wasn't unusual in situations like these. His years on the force he'd seen it all: bloody victims of accidents being carried off on stretchers, fretting aloud about some business meeting or lunch date they were going to miss; domestic disturbances where he'd arrive to find the wife casually making dinner or vacuuming the carpet, as though she hadn't just been beaten to a pulp; and once, memorably, a hit and run driver, who, when they'd finally tracked him down at his house, had calmly explained that he'd needed to get home and unload his groceries before the ice cream melted.

Psychiatrists had a name for it. It was called a fugue state. But right now all Gary knew or cared about was that it was a blessed relief from the tension that had been building in him for weeks. As he settled in behind the wheel of his cruiser and turned the key in the ignition, he might have been dreaming; one of those dreams where everything seems so clear you almost imagine you're awake. And like in dreams, he hadn't the vaguest idea of what was going to happen next; he was in the driver's seat only in the purest physical sense.

Twilight was approaching and long shadows lay over the road. He drove slowly, mindful of the deer that had a habit of wandering onto the road this time of day. When he reached the outskirts of town, he found himself taking the turnoff for Killibrew Harbor. The road curved along a horseshoe-shaped stretch of waterfront that had a quaint little marina, where the people who lived in the fancy homes nearby kept their boats moored.

Owen White lived in one of those homes, a great sprawling monument to excess dubbed The Birches. Gary had been there only once, a cocktail party that had been held out on the lawn, some political fundraiser. On that occasion he'd spent almost the entire time jawing with Bud Hogan, who ran the chamber of commerce, but at one point, after he'd gone in to take a leak, he'd had a chance to nose around a bit inside the house. He recalled the general layout. He knew its vulnerable spots. In his mind he could see the wheelchair ramp that angled up along one side of the house to a sliding glass door opened by electric eye. He could see the old, abandoned dog house, and the outdated security system that anyone with experience in law enforcement could have bypassed blindfolded.

As if this were a movie playing out toward its foregone conclusion, Gary saw himself turn onto the dirt road that serviced the private dock where at one time Owen's yacht had been moored. He switched off the cruiser's headlights, keeping a foot on the brake as he eased over the rutted surface in the near dark, watching for low-hanging branches. When he was within sight of the house, he shut off the engine and coasted the rest of the way.

He parked and got out, standing there for a moment, perfectly still with his head cocked, alert for sounds other than the chirring of nightjars and the hollow slap of waves against the dock. The Tudor-style mansion where Owen White lived with his wife of forty years sat on a low rise off to Gary's left, about a hundred yards or so from where he stood. As he set off in that direction, Gary's footsteps crunched pleasurably in the fallen leaves that littered the grass. He began to hum under his breath.

He was thinking about the time, when he was a kid, that he and his brothers had broken into an abandoned house down the block. They'd been hoping to discover something exciting, like a dead body or a dusty treasure, but all they'd found was a lot of broken glass and mice droppings. The excitement hadn't come until one of the neighbors, alerted by their flashlight beams, called the cops. Before they could make a getaway, they'd found themselves pinned against the outside of the house by a pair of headlights. Luckily, the officer, a big, burly Latino with a handlebar mustache who'd identified himself as Officer Ramirez, had gone easy on them. Even as he'd lectured them in a stern voice about trespassing, Gary could tell his heart wasn't in it. Afterward, he'd given them a ride home in his cruiser, agreeing not to say anything to their parents if they promised never to do anything like that again, a promise Gary had kept until now.

Now, thirty-some years later, here he was lurking about like a prowler. The part of his brain that was still functioning knew what he was doing was wrong, possibly even insane, and that if he were to get caught he'd lose more than his job. But the fugue-state Gary was paying no attention to that small, faraway voice; it might have been a mosquito buzzing in his ear.

He hoisted himself over the low stone wall that bordered the grounds, then he was strolling across the lawn. Dusk had faded into twilight and a white ghost of a moon sailed on a thin raft of clouds overhead. In one of the ground floor rooms a window was lit, throwing a soft yellow light over the grass and shrubs below. Gary caught sight of a shadowy figure moving behind the curtains and he froze, reaching for the .38 on his hip. But no floodlights came on, no alarm sounded, and after a moment he relaxed.

Minutes later he was making his way up the wheelchair ramp, with its automated glass door that slid open easily at his approach. Islanders didn't bother much with locks; he probably could have strolled right in through the front door if he'd wanted. A snippet from the conversation he'd had with Bud Hogan, at the party, floated into his mind now. *Crime? Why, I tell them it's almost unheard of around here. You're more likely to get mugged at Disneyland.*

Gary smiled at the thought as he stepped through the doorway into a room cluttered with knickknacks, most with a nautical theme. In his old life, Owen, like his father before him, had been an avid sailor. In a display case filled with trophies won in various regattas, was a large framed photo of him at the helm of his yacht. There were a number of family photos as well. Gary paused before one of Owen as a young boy, standing with his father on the wide porch of their house, as pale and skinny as Lowell was manly and robust. Sailing must have been the only bond between them.

His thoughts turned to the bones that had been dug up on Spring Hill. The old man's bones. At first, Gary had seen it only as a bad omen. They'd mucked around where they didn't belong and look where it had led. Now he found himself wondering what it must have been like for that little boy in the photo, growing up without his father, not knowing what had become of him.

But those were only idle musings. And now the governor that had taken charge of Gary's faculties was giving him a gentle nudge, reminding him that he had business to attend to. Gary tiptoed into the hall. He could hear the muttering of voices in the next room, but as he drew nearer he realized it was only the TV. When he reached the open doorway, he eased his gun from its holster, and positioned himself with his back to the wall, twisting his head around to case the room for any sign of danger, as he'd been taught to do in training exercises at the academy but had had little call to employ since. A stance that, under the circumstances, struck him as more than a bit absurd, as his eye fell on the room's sole occupant: a balding man, grown soft around the middle, seated in the wing chair in front of the TV, his wheelchair parked a few feet away.

Owen tore his gaze from the evening news as Gary walked in, an expression of surprise dawning on his face. Sitting there in navy sweats, a tartan throw covering his lap, he looked old and defenseless. He must have been aware of the picture he made, for as soon as he'd recovered, he demanded, in his most authoritative voice, "Elkins! What are you doing here? Who let you in?"

"Good evening, sir." Gary didn't bother to illuminate the mayor as to how he'd gained entrance. He merely tucked away the useful bit of information he'd been given: That Owen was alone in the house. Or wouldn't he have assumed that someone else—the maid, or maybe his wife—had let Gary in? He went on in the same queer, flat tone, "I'm sorry to bother you at home, but I'm afraid it couldn't wait. There's something we need to discuss."

Gary saw Owen's gaze drop to the gun in his hand, and now he saw fear flare in those pale, shrewd eyes. Glimpsing his own reflection in the darkened window, he could certainly understand why: In his disheveled, beerstained uniform, his eyes staring like a zombie's out of shadowed sockets, he was scarcely recognizable as the officer responsible for keeping the peace in this township. He almost had to admire Owen for the quickness with which he assessed the situation and attempted to defuse it.

"Well, in that case, don't just stand there," Owen said, his tone switching to that of a genial host. "Pour yourself a drink and sit down." He waved toward a burled-wood cabinet, atop which was arrayed a selection of liquor bottles and cut-glass decanters. "Please, help yourself."

Ignoring the offer, Gary calmly swiveled around and pulled the trigger on the gun, blasting a hole through the twenty-four-inch plasma TV. The sound and picture simultaneously died. "Beats remote control," he said, a maniacal giggle escaping his lips.

He heard a gasp and looked over to see that Owen had gone a pasty shade of gray. Owen licked his lips, asking in a noticeably less welcoming tone, "What . . . what is it you want?"

"What do I want? That's a very good question, sir." Gary appeared to ponder it a moment before replying with a touch more feeling, "For starters, you can stop fucking with me and my family."

The older man looked almost relieved. "Well, if that's all, consider it done. In fact, you should have come to me sooner. I'm not an unreasonable man, Gary, despite what you might think."

Gary laughed at the transparency of the lie. "I see. So all I had to do was ask nicely?"

"All right, you've made your point. Perhaps I *did* go a bit overboard," Owen hastened to concede. "But, where your sister-in-law's concerned, can you honestly blame me? She'd already tried to kill me once. How do I know she won't try something like that again?"

Gary wasn't buying it, though. "You know what I think? I think you were *hoping* she'd come back. I think you've been planning this for a long time. That's why you set me up, so you'd have someone to do your dirty work."

"Well, as far as that goes, you're free from any further obligation," Owen was quick to assure him. "In fact, you've served me and this community so well, I think a bonus is in order. Say, five thousand? Or, no, let's make it ten." Gary didn't react, which Owen must have misinterpreted to mean that he had some other compensation in mind, for he was quick to add, "Also, I can have the, ah, material in question delivered to you first thing in the morning." He tactfully refrained from referring openly to the incriminating videotape. "I'd give it to you now, but it's in a safe deposit box."

But it was much too late for that; Gary was too far gone. "You know, I think Alice had the right idea about you." He spoke in a queerly dispassionate voice. "The only problem was she didn't finish the job."

Calmly he raised the gun and pointed it at Owen.

Owen let out a little squeak. "Put . . . put that thing down. Please. Can't we discuss this like rational human beings? Really, Gary, there's no need for violence."

"What's there to discuss? As you can see, I'm the one holding all the cards." Gary advanced on Owen, a cheerless grin stretching across a face he wouldn't have recognized as his own just then. "How does it feel, now that the tables are turned? Not so great, huh? Well, here's the good news. You won't have to see the look on your wife's face when she finds out what an evil piece of shit you are. You'll be long gone by then. Just like your dad."

"Wait!" Owen shrilled, throwing up his hands. Hands that had once controlled Gary's every move and which now quivered pathetically. "Is it more money you want? I could call my bank, have them wire it into your account, if you don't trust me to write a check."

"Money? You think this is about *money?*" Gary gave a harsh laugh. He was feeling loosey-goosey, like when he'd had too much to drink, but he was perfectly lucid. He saw with sudden clarity that he'd been headed down this road all along, that all those weeks of agonizing had come from resisting what he'd known had to be done. Now that he'd given himself over to it, he felt strangely at peace. This wouldn't end well, but at least it would end. "You owe me more than that. I had to lie to my wife because of what you made me do. My own wife. She *cried* when those bulldozers moved in. She cried like a baby, and all I could do was stand there feeling sick to my stomach, knowing I'd had a part in it. And how do you think she'd feel if she knew that, on top of that, I was helping you drive her sister out of town?"

Owen lifted his chin in defiance. "That's putting it a bit too strongly, don't you think? All I asked you to do was keep an eye on Alice."

"That's not all, and you know it. You were out for revenge. An eye for an eye, right? Christ, don't you think she's suffered enough? And the kid, did you have to go after him , too?" Gary's voice rose.

"What happened to your nephew was entirely his own doing," the mayor protested.

"But you made sure they threw the book at him—an innocent kid."

"What makes you so sure he's innocent?"

"Because I *know* my nephew. He'd never do a thing like that, not in a million years."

"Given the right set of circumstances, people have been known to do a lot of things they might not have otherwise," Owen observed, giving him a pointed look that wasn't lost on Gary—wasn't he living proof of what a normally rational person was capable of when pushed too far? Now he saw that sweat had broken out on Owen's brow, making it gleam, and though the room was warm, he was shivering as if the temperature had plunged a good twenty degrees. As though from a distance, he heard the mayor go on, in a calm voice of persuasion that warbled only slightly, "Take you, for instance. I can see that I underestimated you, Gary. I failed to recognize your . . . your unique capabilities. In fact, Len's going to be retiring soon, and we could use someone with your leadership qualities to fill his shoes."

Gary shook his head in disgust. "Do you really think I'm stupid enough to think you'd make me chief of police? The minute I walked out the door you'd be on the phone with Len, and it wouldn't be to convince him to take an early retirement."

Owen slumped back in his chair, closing his eyes. He looked suddenly defeated. "All right, what do you want from me then? Anything, you name it. I'll do whatever you ask."

"What I want is this." Gary leveled the gun at his tormentor.

That was when he heard sirens in the distance. Apparently they weren't alone in the house after all—someone must have dialed 911. Gary felt a momentary pang of regret, thinking of his fellow officers, guys who'd have taken a bullet for him and vice versa, with whom he'd swapped shifts and joking insults through the years and unwound over beers after hours down at Frankie's, whose kids he'd watched grow up and whose wives called Denise when they needed advice. What would they think when they encountered *this?* But the concern quickly faded. He thought, *By the time they get here, it'll all be over.*

CHAPTER FIFTEEN

They buried the body at nightfall. First loading it onto a handcart and hauling it up the hill as far as they could go, until the trail became impassable. There, at the bottom of a deep ravine, where hikers and picnickers were unlikely to find it, they dug a mean grave, William and Yoshi plying the earth with their shovels while Eleanor stood watch at the top of the ravine, her eyes carefully averted from the tarpaulin-wrapped bundle at her feet.

Later, when all this was over, she would allow herself to think about it, she would let the bloody, fragmented images whirling in her brain to piece themselves into a gruesome whole. Right now, though, she needed to remain steady while they completed this unspeakable thing. Because no one must ever know. Lucy, most of all. If anything was keeping Eleanor sane, it was the knowledge that her daughter wouldn't be tainted by any of this. Earlier, Eleanor had phoned Sarah Donovan, the mother of Lucy's best friend, and asked if she could pick up the girls from school and keep Lucy overnight, explaining that something had come up rather suddenly, some urgent business she had to attend to.

Bloody business, Eleanor thought, biting down on her lower lip to contain the hysterical giggle forcing its way up her throat. Far off in the distance she could hear the dogs baying in their kennel, almost as they sensed something or had caught the scent of blood. Dogs were smart that way. Maybe that was why she preferred their company to most humans.' That, and because whatever your failings their devotion was unwavering. The way her husband's had been. And now Joe was dead. As dead as the *thing* (she couldn't bring herself to think of it as Lucy's father, the man she'd once believed herself to be in love with) lying at her feet.

The blood was what had brought it all home, as she'd rolled up the rug and scrubbed the floorboards on her hands and knees, wringing her cloth into a bucket of water gone red with the terrible fruits of her labor: Her husband hadn't merely ascended to some heavenly plane, he'd been shot to bits, or drowned, or, worse, left to a slow and agonizing death.

Now, staring down at the hole taking shape below, she began to tremble uncontrollably. She felt dizzy and realized she hadn't eaten since breakfast. The mere thought of food brought on a wave of nausea. Sick and shivering, she focused on the figures at the bottom of the ravine, bobbing in and out of the cone of light cast by the flashlight she was aiming their way, one tall and one slight, but at the moment more alike than they were different as they bent to their grim task.

The last bloody streaks of light had faded from the horizon by the time they were done, the ravine as deeply obscured from view as the town, on the other side of the sound, where the streetlights were dimmed and every shade pulled. Earlier in the evening, when Eleanor had gotten the blackout alert, three long and three short telephone rings, it had seemed like a signal from on high, some divine presence taking pity on her, for it meant that few would be out and about and the chances of their being discovered minimal. But now, as she helped the men drag the body down the steep, brushy slope, she felt only numb and exhausted.

She stumbled over a tree root and would have gone sliding the rest of the way down the slope if William hadn't caught hold of her just then.

He held her tightly for a moment, so tightly she could feel the pounding of his heart against her ribcage. "Just a little more to go," he whispered. "Can you manage?" She knew that it wasn't just the distance to
the bottom of the ravine he was referring to but the long and treacher-
ous road she'd have to negotiate in order to get back to some semblance
of normalcy.

She nodded, whispering back, "Yes, I think so."

She shone the flashlight on the men as they tipped the tarpaulin-
wrapped bundle into the hole they'd dug. For the rest of her days
Eleanor would carry that image in her head: of that crude grave hacked
out of the earth, dirt-clotted roots protruding from its rough-hewn
walls like skeletal fingers reaching out to reclaim their own, and Lowell's
body rolling into the pit with a dull thud, amid a scattering of loose dirt
and pebbles.

The men filled in the hole, tamping the dirt down as best they could,
the night alive with the scrape of shovels, the ring of metal against stone.
When the job was done they spread leaves over the grave to erase any evidence of their having been there.

The three were silent as they trudged back down the hill. Near dead
with exhaustion, Eleanor clung to Yoshi's arm to keep from stumbling, as
William led the way with the flashlight. She felt bad about Yoshi's being
dragged into this and she would have spared him if he hadn't insisted on
coming along. She was grateful to him at the same time, this boy whom
some might have called an enemy and who'd proved his worth in ways
that went beyond mere loyalty.

It was almost midnight by the time they reached the house. Eleanor
could hardly see straight, she was so tired, but there was one thing left
to do: They had to dispose of Lowell's car. William drove the Cadillac
to the ferry landing while Eleanor followed in her car. Luckily, they encountered no other traffic, due to the blackout. In any event, anyone
they should happen to have passed would have been hard-pressed to
make them out, in the all-encompassing darkness, with their headlights
dimmed.

At the ferry landing, William parked the Cadillac and got out. She watched as he walked to the end of the dock, limping more than usual, and hurled Lowell's key ring far out into the water—a glimmer of silver that was there and gone in an instant, like a falling star. Poor William, she thought. His only crime had been in coming to her rescue. Now he would spend the rest of his life looking over his shoulder. And what if he *were* to get caught? It wouldn't be just William who'd suffer; his wife and son would pay the price as well. He'd lose even his rightful place in history, remembered not for the brilliance of his work but as a murderer.

She would be held accountable, too, an accessory to the crime. And who would believe that Lowell had tried to rape her, with no one to corroborate it except William and the man who now lay buried in an unmarked grave up on Spring Hill?

She grew cold at the thought. This was all her fault. She'd been naïve to let Lowell come to the house, thinking that no real harm would befall her. Yet despite the horror of it all, she wasn't sorry he was dead.

William took the wheel on the ride home, Eleanor almost immediately falling into a deep sleep. She didn't wake until they reached the house, and even then William had trouble rousing her. He kept an arm around her waist as they made their way across the suddenly endless stretch of yard. As they were passing the barn, she saw that the window was dark—Yoshi must have gone to bed. She hoped she would be able to get some sleep as well. She would need to rest up for the sleepless nights to come.

As she stood on the doorstep fumbling with her keys, she wondered how she would get through this one—what was sure to be the longest night of her life. William must have read her mind, for he asked gently, "Would you like me to stay the night?"

Her eyes sought out his in the darkness. "What about your wife?"

"I'll tell her my car broke down." From the grim, exhausted look he wore, it was obvious he was past worrying about such a small lie, with the larger one of tonight eclipsing all else. "She won't suspect anything. She probably doesn't even know I'm gone."

Even so Eleanor hesitated. What wife, however self-absorbed, would believe such an excuse? Martha would wonder why he hadn't telephoned earlier, and what kind of car trouble it was that would keep him away all night. No, she thought, it was far too risky. And he'd risked so much already. Still, she lingered on the doorstep. "I couldn't ask that of you," she said. "Not after . . . after what . . ." She swallowed hard, unable to complete the sentence.

He nodded gravely. He seemed to have aged a dozen years over the course of the day, his face all planes and shadows, his eyes glinting amid hollowed sockets. "Let's talk about it inside," he said, taking her by the arm and gently propelling her through the doorway.

This time Eleanor didn't protest. She allowed herself to be led down the hall and into the kitchen, docile as a sleepy child, her step faltering only once as they passed the living room that would be forever be stained with the blood of her former lover, if only in her mind.

"I think we both need a drink," he said, retrieving the bottle of whiskey from the cupboard by the stove and pouring them each a glass.

"What I need even more is a shower," she told him. "I feel as if I haven't bathed in a week. Do you mind?"

"Take your time. I'm not going anywhere," he said.

As she was undressing in the bedroom, she could hear him dialing the phone out in the hall, followed by the low murmur of his voice. She stood alert, listening for any change in its tenor that would signal an angry wife at the other end, but there was none, and after a moment she relaxed.

In the bathroom, as she stood in the old-fashioned clawfoot tub that Joe had fitted with a shower nozzle, hot water coursing over her skin, Eleanor marveled at the simple pleasure of it and the ease with which she found herself slipping back into routine, even after what she'd been through today. She imagined it must have been like that for Joe, too, that amid the horrors of war there had been days aboard ship with nothing to do but swap stories and play cards, when the only thing on his mind hadn't been getting home in one piece but how he was going to play the hand he'd been dealt. Was it really possible to go on as though nothing had happened? She would have to. For Lucy's sake. For her own, as well.

After she'd toweled herself dry, she dressed in a worn pair of Levi's and an old flannel shirt that had belonged to Joe. By the time she rejoined William, he'd drunk at least a quarter of what had been left in the bottle, though he seemed none the worse for it. If anything, it was having a salutory effect. Some of the color had returned to his face and he appeared more relaxed. He smiled faintly as he poured her a drink and pushed it across the table to her.

"Here. Drink up. It'll help you sleep."

"I don't think anything could help me sleep," she told him, reaching for the glass nonetheless.

They sat in silence, Eleanor sipping her whiskey. The house's usual nighttime noises wrapped themselves around her, the creak of it settling on its foundation and grumbling of the furnace in the cellar, the hum of the icebox and ticking of the clock over the stove. It hardly seemed possible that an hour earlier they'd been digging a man's grave.

"What did your wife have to say?" Eleanor ventured after a bit.

"I think she was more upset at being woken up than anything else. Which doesn't mean I won't catch hell later on." He spoke lightly, but she could see that he was troubled.

"I don't want this to come between you and Martha," she said firmly.

"I'm afraid it's too late for that." He gave her a long look, and in his naked, bloodshot gaze, stripped of all pretense by the day's ordeal, she saw the true depths of his feelings for her.

And, yes, Eleanor was glad, may her soul be eternally damned to hell for it. She was glad, and at the same time frightened, not wanting to cause any more damage than that which had already been done. "You can still make it right," she said. "You don't know until you try."

"I'm done with trying."

"You say that now, but you'll feel differently in the morning," she insisted. "You can't be thinking clearly right now."

"My head's as clear as it will ever be," he said, in that strange, hollow voice that seemed to rise from the bottom of a well, those burning eyes of his fixed on her with unwavering intensity.

Eleanor turned her gaze to the darkened window, a shudder going through her as the image of Lowell's leering face loomed before her unseeing eyes. She emptied her glass, in a single medicinal gulp that burned its way down her throat.

"Unless you have another bottle stashed away, I'm afraid that's the last of it," William said.

"Just as well. Any more and I wouldn't be fit for polite company." The idea of her being fit for any company whatsoever, polite or otherwise, struck her as funny, and she began to giggle. Before long she was doubled over with hysterical laughter, gasping for breath.

William rose and took her by the hand, pulling her to her feet. "Come, let's get you to bed."

With a last hiccough, all the hilarity went out of Eleanor, leaving her limp and drained. William guided her down the hall and into the bedroom, Eleanor teetering like a frail old woman. She fell onto the bed, not even bothering to undress. He drew a blanket over her, dropping a chaste kiss onto her forehead, and he was about to tiptoe out of the room when she caught hold of his wrist. In the light from the hallway that fell across his lean, hawk-nosed face she could see the worry in his eyes. It was the look of a man who knows his life is about to change, not for the better.

"Don't go," she whispered.

He shook his head, saying gently. "You get some rest. I'll sleep on the sofa."

"No. Please. I don't want to be alone."

Wordlessly, he nodded, then sat down on the end of the bed to pry off his shoes. As he crawled under the blanket and stretched out beside her, the comfort of his presence warmed her like the shot of whiskey, the bulwark of his body nestled against hers, his arm curled protectively about her shoulders. He smelled of tonight's clandestine activities—sweat and dirt and piney resin from the branches with which they'd covered Lowell's grave—but for some reason it only made her love him more.

She snuggled up against him, saying in a groggy voice, "It's strange, isn't it? The two of us in bed together. All the times I've thought about it, I never imagined it would be like this."

"Me either," he murmured thickly in her ear.

"So you've thought about it, too?"

"More than you want to know."

"Is there something wrong with us, do you think, talking like this after we've just buried a man?"

"I think we threw out the rule book a long time ago," he said, his fingers brushing her cheek in the darkness. His voice was scratchy with exhaustion and his breath smelled of whiskey. "Now why don't we get some sleep. We can talk in the morning."

She started to say something else, but William was already fast asleep, snoring lightly. Moments later Eleanor drifted off, too.

She slept straight through until morning, waking to the sound of the dogs barking outside. Even then, she kept her eyes shut, suspended somewhere between the blissful ignorance of sleep and the dark thing hovering at the edge of consciousness. Then, all at once, the memory of yesterday's events came rushing up behind her closed eyelids. For a moment, in her half-awake state, she felt sure that she must have dreamed it, then she opened her eyes and saw William lying wide awake beside her, in his dirty, rumpled clothing, sporting a day's growth of beard, and she knew that it was all too real.

"It really happened, didn't it? For a moment I thought I'd dreamed it," she said. He gave a somber nod, and she fell back with a low moan. What had seemed possible in last night's befogged state struck her now, in the light of day, as utterly insane. They would never get away with this. What had made her think they could? "So what do we do now?"

"The usual things. Get up, get dressed, have breakfast. Unless you have a better idea."

"I don't suppose there's any point in turning ourselves in."

"None at all."

"They might still track us down, you know."

"If they do, I'm the one they'll arrest. You did nothing wrong."

"Who would believe that?"

William brought a hand to her face, running his thumb over her cheek. "Don't worry, they won't find out. The last thing Lowell would have done was leave word with anyone about where he was going, so no one even knows he was here," he reasoned, with more conviction than she guessed he felt.

Eleanor, desperate to grasp at any straw, told herself he was right. She had to believe that. It was the only thing to hold on to at the moment.

"Even if we don't go to jail, we could go to hell," she said. "Some would call it a sin, what we did." Her father's image rose in her mind, his pious face and his hands folded about his bible.

William held her gaze, her chin still cupped in his hand. "When I pulled that trigger, the only thing I was thinking was that if I didn't aim straight he'd hurt you. I can live with what I did, Eleanor, but *that* would have been unbearable."

She saw the love blazing from his eyes, and it was almost more than she could absorb in her current, fragile state. Her throat seized up on her, and when she spoke it was in a choked whisper. "Oh, William. When I think what might have happened if you hadn't come along . . . "

She buried her face against his chest. He kissed her tenderly on the top of the head, then when she raised herself up, not so tenderly on the mouth. The shock of his lips against hers went through her like a bolt of lightning, igniting something in her, something beyond all thought and reason and more powerful than any whispered endearments.

Later on, Eleanor would have no recollection of either of them getting undressed. Their coming together happened so naturally, it was as if they'd been born again in each other's arms. With the morning sunlight warming their bare limbs, they made love with an urgency that was like a living thing apart from them. She was consumed by it. Biting and bucking, crying out with an abandon that would have shocked her husband.

William became a different person as well. Gone was the quiet, considerate soul she'd grown to love, in his place a man barely able to contain himself. A beautiful wild creature who saw nothing wrong with what they were doing, who in fact celebrated it. They clung to each other as if otherwise they might be swept away, their sweat mingling, his hands covering every inch of her that wasn't already covered by his body, his fingernails, still embedded with dirt, digging into her flesh, making her arch with pleasure.

Even when it was over and Eleanor utterly spent, she was left wanting more. And after a few minutes, apparently, so was William. The next time, they took it slow, exploring every inch of each other's bodies, reveling in the minutest of touches, the least little flicker of a tongue, each brush of lips over bare skin. Soon enough it would be time for William to go, but for now they were in their own world, lost to the one beyond these walls.

Finally he could no longer put off the inevitable. He rose from the bed and Eleanor reluctantly followed suit. She fixed breakfast while he took a shower and put on the clothes she'd given him to wear, an old shirt and a pair of trousers that had belonged to Joe. The shirt was so big it flapped on him, as if on a clothesline, and the cuffs of the trousers barely covered his ankles, but William didn't seem to mind; they were clean at least.

They ate their breakfast in silence, but it wasn't a heavy silence like before, more the intimate one of lovers for whom there was no need for conversation. And what was there to say? Words wouldn't have changed a thing. Yesterday she'd watched a man die and this morning she'd made love to a married man. Not the sort of things that made for a happy ending.

William attempted to put a good face on it nonetheless. "It doesn't always have to be this way," he whispered in her ear, as he was leaving. They were standing in the doorway, cheek to cheek with their arms wrapped around each other, William taking slow, deep breaths, as if he couldn't get enough of her scent.

Eleanor drew back, her eyes filled with tears. "Don't. You'll only make it worse."

"I could ask for a divorce," he went on in that same reckless tone. "Martha doesn't need me. She hasn't for a long time."

"What about your son? He still needs you."

"Danny knows I love him. Nothing will ever change that." William's voice grew hesitant nonetheless.

"Yes, and that means you'd cut your arm off before you'd see him get hurt," she said, thinking of the lengths she would have gone to protect Lucy. "Now go home to your wife and son." She gave him a none too gentle shove before she could weaken and give in.

"Will I see you again?" he asked, his eyes searching her face.

Eleanor longed to tell him what he wanted to hear, but they would only be fooling themselves, she knew. "I'm not sure that would be a good idea," she told him.

"Maybe not, but who gives a damn."

"I do, and so will you, once you've had a chance to think it through."

He shook his head, pulling her to him, roughly almost. He was holding her so tightly she could scarcely breathe. "You really believe that? That I'll think better of it?" He gave a hoarse laugh. "God, I almost wish you were right. Life would be a damn sight easier. But don't you see? It's too late for that. I love you, Eleanor. I love you so much I can't bear the idea of us being apart. I want us to be together *always.*"

Eleanor wanted nothing more at that moment than to remain in his arms forever, damn the consequences, but she drew back to give him a sorrowful look. "We don't have that luxury. It's not just your family I'm thinking of. If we don't handle this just right . . ." She didn't have to remind him that they weren't out of the woods yet as far as Lowell was concerned. If a search party was launched and his body discovered, people might start to put two and two together. Any suspicious behavior on their part would be noted.

They didn't say good-bye when he left. That would have been too final. For while Eleanor despaired of ever seeing him again, a part of her clung to the fragile strand of hope he'd held out to her. If he let enough time pass before asking his wife for a divorce, so no one grew suspicious, maybe, just maybe it could work. A little voice, scratching in the back of her brain like a stuck phonograph needle, insisted, *Stranger things have happened.*

—

He arrived back at the house to find no one home. William, braced for an angry tirade from his wife, felt the speech he'd been rehearsing on the way over die on his lips as he walked from one deserted room to the next, calling out her name. Danny and the dog were nowhere in sight, either. There was no reason to think it odd—Martha could have dashed off on an errand, leaving Danny with their neighbor—but with the house's silence coming at him like a reproach, William knew in his heart that something was wrong.

Finally, he thought to check the garage, where he found Martha's jaunty little red Austin Healy right where it always was. Baffled, he stepped outside, frowning. It occurred to him then that Martha might have decided to go for a walk—unlikely in this weather, for it had started to rain, but where else could she have gone? He was crossing the yard on his way to the path that led down to the cove when he noticed that the door to his studio was ajar. He halted in his tracks, a dull alarm sounding at the back of his brain. He was almost certain he'd locked up when he'd gone out yesterday. But so much had happened since then, he hardly felt like the same the man who'd last walked out that door less than twenty-four hours before. His head spun with images from yesterday and his body was like something loosely strung together with wire. In the midst of it all, like a quiet eye at the center of a hurricane, was the thought of Eleanor.

He pushed open the door. At first all he saw were the canvases stacked against the wall and the one on the easel, over which a cloth was draped. Then he spotted her, huddled in the old mustard armchair that she'd long ago banished from the house, her feet tucked under her and her arms wrapped around her knees, like a child left abandoned and shivering on some stranger's doorstep. In the soft gray light that filtered through the rain-streaked skylight he could see that Martha had been crying.

His first thought was of his son. "Martha. What is it? Did something happen to Danny?" he asked, rushing over to her.

"He's fine. Though I'm surprised you care enough to ask." Her voice was cold as the rain trickling down outside. "In fact, I don't know why you even bothered to come home."

"So this is about last night." He felt a heaviness settle over him, mixed with an odd sense of relief at knowing there was no further need for pretense.

"I know what you've been up to." Martha's face twisted into something ugly. "Oh, I had my suspicions all along, but I kept telling myself that was for wives who'd let themselves go, who'd turned their husbands away in bed. Then after you phoned last night I went through your things. I found what I was looking for, all right. It's *her*, isn't it?" She jabbed a finger toward the canvas on the easel, and he saw now that the cloth that covered it was askew.

He didn't bother to deny it. "I'm sorry you had to find out that way," he said quietly.

"So you were planning to break it to me eventually? Yes, I suppose that would be the honorable thing to do," she said, looking at him with contempt. "You probably even fancy yourself in love with her, and you think *that* makes it all okay. The great artist and his muse." She swept an arm out in a scornful gesture. "Well, you won't be making a public laughing-stock of me, at least. I made sure of that."

He was gripped with a sudden sense of foreboding. He knelt before his wife, seizing her by the shoulders. It was all he could do not to shake her.

"Martha, what have you done?"

"What have *I* done?" she threw back at him, with a shrill little laugh. "I trusted you, that's what. I should have known better."

He knew there was no getting through to her right now, that she was in no mood for an explanation, but he made a clumsy attempt nonetheless. "I didn't go looking for it," he said. "It just . . . happened." He wanted to tell her about Yoshi, for her to know that his motives had been pure in the beginning, but that would only have made it worse.

"So now what? I suppose you want a divorce." She tossed her head, and he saw the challenge in her red-rimmed eyes. She wanted him to beg her to forgive him, to promise never to see Eleanor again.

But he couldn't do that, and the expression on his face must have told her everything she needed to know, for she began to weep.

"Martha . . . " He reached to console her, but she swatted his hand away.

"You're a coward, William. Not fit for duty, not even fit to be a husband. You couldn't even fight to save your own marriage."

What would she say, he wondered, were she to learn that last night he'd killed a man in cold blood? He smiled grimly to himself at the thought. Poor Martha. She really had no idea.

"I didn't see that there was anything left to fight for," he said wearily.

It was an honest response, not meant to be hurtful. In fact, it had surprised him to learn that Martha herself had thought there was something worth fighting for. Nevertheless, he could see at once that it was the wrong thing to have said.

His wife erupted off the chair, quivering like a drawn bow. "Are you insinuating that I drove you to it? How dare you! This is all *your* fault, William."

He sighed. "Honestly? I don't know anymore who's to blame." And right now he didn't care. His head throbbed and he wanted nothing more than to stretch out on the floor and close his eyes.

"Well, *I* know. And I'm not going to stick around and have you make an even bigger fool of me." She snatched up the sweater that she'd left neatly folded over an arm of the chair—even in despair, Martha didn't go about things sloppily—and tossed it over her shoulders. "I've already called Mother and Dad. They're perfectly happy to have us stay with them as long as we want."

We? William was at once on full alert. "You're not taking Danny with you." He was in no position to object, but all at once he knew with a sickening certainty that if he didn't put his foot down now, he could lose his son for good.

"Just try and stop me. I'll have my lawyer slap you with papers so fast your head will be swimming." Her eyes glittered with malice. William didn't think it was an idle threat. If Martha had gone off to battle in his place, the war would have ended by now, he thought.

"Where is he? Where's my son?" he asked, in a hard voice tinged with desperation.

Ignoring his plea, she said coldly, "I'll tell him you said good-bye." She stepped past him on her way out the door, pausing on the threshold to fire one last volley. "I'll spare him the sordid details, but make no mistake—Danny's going to know what kind of man his father is."

William stood there for a long moment after she'd gone, staring into space, listening to the rapid tap-tapping of Martha's heels as she hurried up the path to the house. None of it seemed real. Yesterday he'd shot and killed a man, and this morning he and Eleanor had made love. Now this. If a Japanese Zero were to have dropped a bomb on the island just then, it wouldn't have surprised him in the least.

Then he recalled his wife's words and raced over to the easel, snatching off the cloth. With a sinking heart, he saw how Martha had exacted her revenge.

The portrait of Eleanor was unrecognizable. It had been slashed with a sharp object until it was little more than shreds of canvas clinging to its frame. A low moan escaped him, and he slowly sank to his knees, feeling as if all the breath had been knocked out of him. She might as well have plunged a knife into his heart.

CHAPTER SIXTEEN

"You ain't be fooling me, girl. I know that look." Calpernia was giving her the eye, which meant not only was she on to you but you'd better not even *think* about trying to pull one over on her.

"I don't know what you're talking about," Alice said. She attempted to sidle past Calpernia on her way to check on the dough she'd left in the refrigerator to rise, but her friend shifted her bulk to block her path.

"The hell you don't." Calpernia was dressed in gray sweatpants and a warm-up jacket that looked as if it had come off an NFL linebacker, her braids gathered into a ponytail that bristled like a dried-flower arrangement. Alice had arrived home from Colin's to find her here. Calpernia preferred the restaurant, even when it was closed, to her studio apartment over Mrs. Meehan's garage, which she'd said reminded her of being in solitary. Suddenly, her fierce expression gave way to a grin. "Damn, girl, you done got yourself laid."

Alice threw her hands up in surrender. It would have done no good to deny it; Calpernia would have gotten it out of her one way or another. "Yes! All right! I slept with him."

"All I got to say is, it's about time." Calpernia just stood there, grinning.

But Alice was thinking about the look Colin had worn as they were saying good-bye. He'd been standing right in front of her, but he'd been somewhere else in his mind: If she was long overdue for this, then for Colin it might have come too soon. "Let's not make too big a deal out of it, okay?" she said. "It was fun, we both enjoyed it, end of story."

Calpernia watched, her arms folded over her chest, as Alice busied herself with the dough, dumping it onto the counter and carefully shaping it into loaves. Her friend had been cutting up onions when she'd walked in and now the sharp scent was making her eyes water.

"Want to know what *I* think?" Calpernia asked.

"Not particularly, but I'm sure you'll tell me anyway," Alice replied.

She glanced up to find Calpernia shaking her head, as if the diagnosis were grim. "Girl, you got it bad."

Alice, on edge, cried in exasperation, "What do you know? When was the last time *you* got laid?"

Calpernia tipped her head back in a haughty look, her eyes narrowing. "You think you the only one got it going on?"

Alice broke into a grin. "Why, Calpernia King. You've been holding out on me."

"A girl can't have some privacy 'round here?" Calpernia grumbled, pretending to be annoyed. "Bad enough you got me working myself half to death for shit pay make Mickey D's look good. I get me some on the side, ain't nobody's damn business but my own."

Alice, used to these sorts of rumblings, asked in amusement, "Who's the lucky guy?"

Calpernia deliberated a moment, then she heaved a mock sigh. "Know that big dude come 'round couple times a week? Always order the same thing, ribs and slaw, baked potato on the side?"

Alice could hardly contain her surprise. "Ralph Dwyer?" Ralph owned his own tire shop, Dwyer's Tires. He was a nice enough guy, polite, even a little shy. But, leaving aside the fact that he was white, he was old enough to be Calpernia's father. It took her a moment to recover before she could remark, "Well, they say there's a lid for every pot. If it fits, I guess that's all that counts."

Calpernia gave a snort of contempt. "This ain't no Tupperware party. I ain't said I was planning on marrying the dude. But if the man's fool enough to want what I got to offer, which Lord knows ain't much, I ain't turning it down neither." She gave Alice a hard look no doubt meant to convey that Alice would be equally foolish to reject what Colin had to offer. But what exactly was Colin offering her? Friendship, with maybe a little something on the side. Hadn't he made it perfectly clear he wasn't interested in a relationship? No, it had been a mistake to sleep with him, she thought. One she didn't regret, but a mistake all the same.

And it wasn't just Colin. The timing couldn't be worse for her, either. She was just getting back on her feet and had enough to do rebuilding existing relationships, like the one with her son. Also, she would be making herself vulnerable in a way that was frightening to her, more frightening than any of the stumbling blocks she'd met with so far. If that was love, Alice wanted no part of it.

She was contemplating that when the phone rang. It was Denise.

After a minute or so of chit-chat, her sister got to the real reason she'd phoned. "You haven't seen Gary, by any chance?" She affected a casual tone, but Alice could tell she was worried.

"Not since yesterday," she said. "Why? Is everything okay?" She kept her voice light so as not to add to Denise's worry.

Her sister was quick to reply, "Sure, fine. We just had a little tiff, is all. He took off about an hour ago, said he needed to cool off. I thought he might have stopped by your place."

"Do you need me to come over?" From the tension in her sister's voice, it was obvious it had been more than a little tiff.

"No, don't be silly. Everything's fine," Denise was quick to assure her. "I'm sure he'll be back any minute."

"Have you tried the station?"

"He got off duty a couple of hours ago."

"Still, it might be worth a call. Just to put your mind at ease." Alice knew what her sister was thinking: that he might have gotten into an accident. At least this way she'd be able to rule it out. If any 911 calls had come in over the past hour or so, the dispatcher would know about it.

Denise blew out a breath at the other end. "Yeah, you're right. If he's not there, I can always have the guys keep an eye out for him, if nothing else."

"Call me back as soon as you know anything," Alice told her.

"Will do."

Minutes later the phone rang again. This time all hell broke loose.

⎯⎯

Colin heard a noise and glanced over to see the dog settling onto his haunches in the doorway to the living room. Briefly, Colin wondered how he'd gotten into the house. Until now, Shep had refused to leave his post on the porch whenever he wasn't keeping Colin company down at the cove. But in Colin's present state of my mind, the thought barely registered before fading from consciousness.

He stared at the bottle of cognac in his hand. Remy-Martin. The seal on the cap was still intact and a fine layer of dust had gathered around the neck. *A shame to let it go to waste,* Colin thought. He twisted the cap, his senses coming alive with the crackle of the seal as it gave way, and poured a generous shot into the glass he'd found on one of the cabinet's upper shelves. At the familiar sharp scent he felt a pleasurable rush, as if the alcohol were already insinuating its way into his bloodstream. He was lifting the glass to his lips when he happened to glance once more at the dog.

Shep seemed to eye him with reproach.

"What are you looking at?" Colin asked. "You've never seen anyone tie one on before?"

Shep cocked his head and let out a low whine. Colin felt a prickle along the back of his neck, and in that instant he could almost imagine that it was his grandfather's spirit inhabiting the dog. And what would William make of the current situation? No doubt that his grandson was as much a disappointment to him as his son.

Colin's gaze was drawn to the portrait over the mantel. "You, too?" he asked of the woman looking down at him, with her Mona Lisa smile and melancholy eyes. In the soft lamplight, she appeared almost lifelike, and he had the eerie feeling that if he had brought his fingertips to that glow-ingly rendered flesh, it would be warm to the touch.

Ghosts. The world was full of them, and he'd best make peace with that fact or remain doomed to a lifetime of stumbling each time he tried to get past his. *Here's to you, my sweet,* he toasted silently, lifting his glass. His wife's spirit he felt most strongly of all. Yes, Nadine would have un-derstood about Alice. But she'd known him well enough to also know that it could never be. What could he offer Alice other than his legal ser-vices, when he scarcely knew what to do with himself?

The rim of the glass pressed to his lips was the sweetest of kisses, the sharp, fruity scent filling his nostrils more tantalizing than any perfume. He closed his eyes in a kind of swoon and was tipping the glass back when he abruptly froze. In a sudden flash, he saw what he was doing as clearly as if he'd been standing outside of himself, a neutral observer to the scene. *You can rationalize it all you want,* spoke the other, clear-eyed Colin, *but what it really boils down to is that you're just looking for an excuse to drink.*

With a trembling hand, Colin lowered the glass. Quickly, before he could think better of it, he dashed into the kitchen and poured its con-tents down the sink. Afterward, he stood bent over, gripping the edge of the counter, as weak as all the times he'd been sick to his stomach after too much to drink. He was filled with despair, not just because he'd come close to throwing away nearly nine months of sobriety, but because even now a part of him cursed the waste.

Disgusted with himself, he turned away and shuffled back into the liv-ing room, where he sank heavily onto the sofa. He knew he ought to phone his sponsor, but he couldn't seem to summon the energy even to pick up the phone. He was wondering how he was going to white-knuckle it until the next AA meeting when a low, doggy whine momen-tarily distracted him from his thoughts. He turned his head to find Shep standing before him, regarding him with worried eyes. He nudged Colin with his nose and, when that brought no response, he pawed at his arm. Colin absently stroked him between the ears, saying in a weary voice, "Yeah, I know. I miss my wife, too. But it's just you and me now. Misery loves company, right?"

The dog settled onto the carpet with a grunt of what might have been affirmation. Colin's thoughts turned to Alice and how much fun they'd had today, particularly in bed—that is, until his dark ruminations had spoiled the mood.

The phone rang, startling him. For a moment he thought it might be Alice and, as he went to answer it, his spirits picked up.

But it wasn't Alice; it was her son. Jeremy sounded in a panic. "I didn't know who else to call. My mom's not home and I couldn't get a hold of my dad. It's bad, Mister McGinty. Real bad . . . "

The boy's panic had a strangely calming effect on Colin. He found himself saying in a voice of cool-headed authority, "Slow down. Now tell me what this is all about?"

The words tumbled out in a breathless rush. "My uncle Gary . . . he . . . he . . . it's like he's gone crazy or something. He's holed up in there with his gun and he says he'll shoot if anyone tries to come near." He let out a groan. "Oh, God. It's like it's happening all over again. Like when my mom—" He broke off with a choked sound.

"All right, take a deep breath and start at the beginning." Colin spoke in a calm, reassuring voice.

Colin listened to Jeremy's garbled second-hand version of the story, which he'd apparently gotten from his cousin Ryan. Something about his uncle's going over to the mayor's house and the two of them getting into an argument—that was the theory, at least, no one knew for sure—during which Gary had pulled his gun on the mayor, who at the moment was being held hostage. What would have been routine stuff during Colin's tenure in the Manhattan D.A.'s office, one more act of desperation in a city full of people living on the razor's edge, but which struck him now, in the context of this sleepy backwater, as almost too bizarre to be believed.

"Where's your mom?" he asked.

"She and Aunt Denise are on their way over there now."

"If I come pick you up, can you take me there?"

"Sure. I know the way. Just please hurry."

The first thing Alice noticed, as they turned onto the private road to the mayor's estate, was the patrol car blocking further access, its radio squawking and the blue glare from its bubble light careening off the surrounding trees and shrubbery. An earnest-looking young officer climbed out. From the manner in which he approached, one hand held up like a stop sign and the other on his holster, it looked as if he'd seen one too many cop shows.

Denise rolled down her window and stuck her head out. "It's okay, Tony. It's just me."

His hands dropped to his sides and his face reddened. "Missus Elkins. Sorry, I didn't know it was you." Somewhat apologetically, he informed her, "I'm afraid I'm still going to have to ask you to turn around. The chief told me not to let anyone through."

"Well, as you can see, I'm not just anyone." Denise's voice was remarkably calm, Alice thought, given how upset she'd been on the way over. "Now, are you going to let us by, or do I have to phone the chief myself?"

Minutes later, after a hasty consultation with the chief on his two-way, he was pulling off to the side and waving them on.

After a quarter of a mile or so the road came to an end. Several more patrol cars were parked along the grassy verge that gave way to the more manicured grounds of the White estate. What looked to be half a dozen policeman were circulating about, and though there was clearly someone in charge—she recognized the chief of police, Len Chambers, a burly gray-haired man leaning against the open door of his patrol car, one foot propped on the running board, as he carried on a tense conversation over his cell phone—there seemed to be a general sense of confusion nonetheless. In the harsh noonday glare of the flood lights that had been set up along the perimeter, Alice could see the tense looks they wore as they conferred with one another in little huddles, the frosty plumes of their breath punctuating the air. It was obvious these guys had never before experienced anything like this, at least not on the island. Their gait seemed awkward and their movements stiff, as if even the Kevlar vests they wore over their uniforms had yet to be broken in.

Denise must have noticed it, too. She reached for Alice's hand, squeezing it tightly, the worry lines on her forehead deepening.

As soon as he'd gotten off the phone, Len jogged over to them. "That was Gary," he informed Denise, his square-jawed face set in stern lines. Len, paunchy with age and the mostly sedentary position he now enjoyed, made Alice think of a retired combat veteran, past his prime, pressed into service once more. "The good news is he sounded calm and coherent, so I don't think there's any immediate danger." He placed a hand on Denise's arm, saying in a gruffly reassuring tone, "Believe me, Denise, we're doing everything we can to make sure no one gets hurt."

"Let me talk to him," she said. It wasn't so much a request as an order. Len wordlessly handed her the phone. Denise punched the redial button and stood for a moment with the phone to her ear, then she let out a muttered curse. "Damn. I got cut off." The island's spotty cell phone service had never seemed more maddening. Not to be deterred, she thrust the phone back at Len, saying, "That's it. I'm going in."

The chief shook his head, his short gray hair bristling like the fur of some nocturnal creature caught in the floodlights' glare. "I know you're upset, Denise, but we can't have anyone panicking here." He spoke in a tone Denise herself might have used on a student who was being disruptive in class. "Now what I'm going to ask you to do here is to stay calm and let us handle this. We've got things under control."

"Len, that's my husband in there, so unless you plan on arresting me, I'm going in whether you like it or not." Denise's voice rose on a high, frantic note, her gaze sweeping the flood-lit perimeter as if she were already plotting her route.

The chief remained firm. "I'm afraid I can't let you do that, Denise. It's too risky. It's not just you and Gary—I have the mayor to think of, too."

"For God's sake, Len, I'm his *wife!*" Denise was near tears.

"All the more reason. Gary's in a highly emotional state right now. If you go in there, it might just push him over the edge." Len wore a look of profound sympathy. "I know you want to help, but trust me, this isn't the way."

Alice chose that moment to step forward. "Let me go instead."

The chief turned to look at her, as if just then becoming aware of her presence. Now his gaze clicked in: hard, cop's eyes. Len Chambers had been the arresting officer that long ago day when it had been her, not Gary, who'd been the cause of so much police activity. Clearly, Len hadn't forgotten it either.

Before he could object, Alice hurried on, "It makes sense. I . . . I know a little something about what he's going through right now. Maybe I can reason with him. It's worth a try." She knew it was reckless, possibly suicidal, but right now all she could think about was Denise. Her sister had always been there for her; now it was time for her to repay that debt.

"No." Denise gripped her arm. "Len's right. It's too risky."

Alice placed a hand over the fingers clenched about her arm. "Please. Let me do this."

They exchanged a long look, that of sisters for whom words weren't necessary, then Denise dropped her hand from Alice's arm and turned to Len with a questioning look. He appeared dubious, but clearly he'd run out of other options, for after pondering it a moment he said, "It could work. He knows you. More importantly, he knows your history."

Alice hugged Denise long and hard. Her sister smelled of the shampoo she bought at Costco in economy-size bottles and underneath the sour sweat of fear. "It'll be okay, I promise," she whispered. "I'll be back before you know it." As they drew apart, she saw a queer look cross Denise's face. "What?" she asked.

Denise gave a small, humorless smile. "That was the last thing Gary said before he left."

Alice was being fitted with a Kevlar vest by the lone female officer, a slender red-haired woman about her size, when she heard a familiar voice call out her name. "Alice!"

She swung around, surprised to see Colin. He was approaching on foot, Shep trotting at his side and Jeremy bringing up the rear. They must have parked out on the main road in order to slip past the roadblock. Alice felt something hot and quick leap in her chest. Colin had on the same flannel shirt and corduroys he'd been wearing when she'd last seen him—hours ago that felt more like days—only there was something different about him. Gone was the preoccupied look he'd worn then. He was looking straight at her as he walked toward her with a purposeful stride, his expression that of someone determined not to let her slip through his fingers a second time.

"You're not going in there alone," he told her. "I'm going with you." Alice opened her mouth to protest, but he cut her off before she could get a word in. "I happen to know a little something about hostage situations. And right now," his gaze dropped to the Kevlar vest, "it looks as if you could use someone to watch your back."

Alice was about to refuse—she couldn't let him risk his life—when she noticed the stricken look on Jeremy's face. He was staring at her, his face paler than usual, his eyes huge beneath the dark hair falling over his forehead: that of the little boy who'd watched his mommy being led away in handcuffs. "Mom," he said. Just that, a single plaintive note.

Alice hesitated, feeling her resolve weaken. She took Jeremy aside, saying in a low voice, "If you don't want me to go, I won't." If she got killed going in, she'd be abandoning him a second time. And as dearly as she loved her sister, her son came first.

Jeremy licked his lips, darting a look toward the house where his uncle was holding the mayor hostage. "Do you really think Uncle Gary would . . . would do something to hurt you?"

She could have soothed his fears, as she had when he was little in reassuring him that there were no monsters in the closet, but they'd been through too much for her to be less than honest with him now. "I'd like to believe he wouldn't, but right now I don't know what he's capable of," she said.

Jeremy thought for a moment, then seemed to come to a decision. "If you don't go, he might hurt himself." He glanced over at Denise, as if thinking about her being widowed and his cousins without their father. "It's all right," he said, giving Alice a brave smile that would have been more convincing if he hadn't looked so pale and shaken. "Do what you have to do. I know Mister McGinty won't let anything happen to you."

She nodded, not trusting herself to speak. She was about to walk away when, without warning, Jeremy launched himself at her, throwing his arms around her in a fierce hug that nearly knocked her off balance. In that moment she knew it was all worth it. If she died in there, it would be with the knowledge that her son still loved her.

Minutes later, she and Colin set out across the lawn, stepping from the hard white glare of the floodlit perimeter into the near black of the starlight night. It was a moment before Alice's eyes adjusted, then she was guided by the light of the full moon, which hung low in the sky, casting an almost diurnal glow and turning the grass over which they walked pale, as if with morning frost. They moved in silence, each lost in their own thoughts, the lovemaking of just hours before a memory from another lifetime. A short distance away, at the top of a grassy knoll, the house rose up out of the darkness, its lone illuminated window staring out at them like an unblinking eye. Its peaceful façade seemed to mock them somehow, as though the drama taking place inside were nothing more than a false rumor.

They'd nearly reached the house when Alice heard a high, agitated yip and turned to see the dog, whom Jeremy had been holding by the collar, break away and come streaking across the lawn toward them, a furry black and white projectile, the white blaze on its chest all that was visible as it was swallowed up by the surrounding darkness.

The automated door slid open at their approach, just as it had for Gary. Inside, they were greeted, not by gunfire, but by utter silence, which in its own way was more unnerving. As Alice and Colin made their way through the deserted trophy room and into the hallway beyond, accompanied by the dog, the quiet was broken only by the muffled tread of their footsteps and the low growl emanating from Shep. Alice glanced around, taking in the palatial surroundings. So this was how her son's killer had lived, while David had lain cold in his grave and she'd occupied a six-and-a-half-by-nine-foot cinderblock cell. She felt her blood rise and tasted bile at the back of her throat. But she quickly pushed the thought away. She couldn't afford to dwell on that now.

Colin must have sensed something, for he turned to her and whispered, "You okay?"

She nodded and they continued on. Light poured from an open doorway down the hall and, as they entered the room, the first thing Alice noticed was the blasted-out TV screen, broken glass littering the oriental carpet around it. When her gaze fell on her brother-in-law she almost didn't recognize him at first. Gary's eyes stared vacantly from hollowed sockets and the unhealthy pallor of his skin was that of cancer wards and plants robbed of sunlight. He was seated on the leather settee across from the mayor, holding his gun loosely on one knee and wearing the look of someone who'd stumbled into the situation quite by accident. Owen, slumped in his chair, merely looked drained.

She spoke softly. "Hello, Gary."

His head swiveled slowly toward her. He stared at her uncomprehendingly for a moment before a faint smile of recognition surfaced. "Alice. What are you doing here?"

"We came to see you. You remember Colin, don't you? Jeremy's lawyer?" She gestured toward Colin, who nodded at Gary, his expression carefully neutral.

"You think I need a lawyer?" Gary gave a scornful little bark of a laugh. "Not where I'm going. I'm afraid it's a little too late for that."

"It's not too late until you pull that trigger," Colin observed in a mild, conversational tone, gesturing toward the gun. "Take it from a guy who knows. Only in my case, the weapon of choice was a quart of booze a day."

"Well, in that case, by all means help yourself." Gary waved magnanimously toward the burled wood bar. "I'm afraid the party's already begun, but the more the merrier." His voice carried a note of almost manic glee. There was a strange kind of exhilaration, Alice knew, in releasing your hold on sanity and throwing yourself into the void. "You know our host, Mister White." He gestured toward the mayor, who, though clearly frightened, wore an oddly defiant look. "As a matter of fact, we were just talking about you, Alice. Mister White here seems to think your son could benefit from some jail time of his own."

Alice sucked in a breath. It was all she could do to keep her eyes averted from Owen, fearing that if she were to so much as look at him her already thinly stretched composure would desert her altogether. And Gary didn't need any further provocation right now. "You're not telling me anything I don't already know," she told him, struggling to keep her voice even.

"Yeah, but you don't know the half of it," Gary went on. "Nobody in that office takes a piss without his permission."

Colin stepped in, saying, "Why don't you let us handle it, Gary? There's no reason for you to get involved."

Gary gave a high, lunatic's cackle, and the dog, alert at Colin's side, let out another low growl. "Involved? Christ, I'm already in up to my eyeballs. He made me do things. Things I'm not proud of." Something glimmered in his blank-eyed expression, like a faulty bulb flickering to life, and the familiar face of her sister's husband briefly emerged. "I'm sorry, Alice. You deserved better." His voice cracked. "I never meant to hurt you. I was only trying to protect my family."

So Gary had been in this, too? Alice felt more than betrayed; she felt ashamed, thinking of all the times he'd stopped in at the restaurant when she'd naively believed it was to show support. How stupid she must have seemed, pleading for his help! It was all she could do to speak calmly to him now. "No one blames you, Gary." She kept her thoughts focused on Denise and how terrible it would be for her and the kids if this were to end in tragedy. "All we want is for you to come home."

Gary gave her a pitying look, as if she were the one who'd lost all touch with reality. "I can't. Don't you see? It wouldn't be the same. You, of all people, should know that."

Alice took a step closer to him. "I understand, Gary, believe me I do. But for me there really was no going back. You haven't crossed that line yet. You can still do the right thing."

Gary shook his head, tears coming to his eyes now. "Denise and the kids will be better off without me."

"That's not true. They'd be devastated." Alice's anger gave way to compassion. She knew the special brand of agony he was in; she knew what it could do to you. "Think about Ryan and Taylor growing up without their dad. And Denise . . . she'd never get over it. She loves you, Gary."

"She wouldn't, if she knew what I've done."

"You're wrong about that," Alice forged on. "There's nothing she wouldn't forgive you for. Yeah, she'll be pissed off and you might have a few uncomfortable days." Here, Gary cracked a small smile. "But you know her. She always comes around in the end."

"Like Randy did with you?" he said, with irony.

"It was different with us," she said. Or maybe it had just been different circumstances, their love for each other strained to the breaking point by David's death. "You and Denise . . ." She reached for the word that had best described them, before all this craziness. "You're solid. I used to envy that about you. The way you always worked as a team. One of you picking up the slack when the other was too busy or stressed out. Not like it was some big favor, but because that's just what you do when you love someone."

Some movement out of the corner of her eye made her glance over at Colin. But he was standing perfectly still, and she realized it was his gaze that had drawn her attention; it was concentrated on her with an intensity that was almost physical.

She thought about all he'd risked for her sake and knew it was time for her to take some risks of her own. She held out her hand to her brother-in-law. "Give me the gun, Gary. Please. You don't want to do this. Think of your family."

"They'll be better off," he insisted, shaking his head.

"No. They won't." She was thinking of David and how she would have done almost anything to have him back. She took another careful step forward. "Now give me the gun."

The moment stretched on, Gary staring at her without seeming to see her, as though looking inward. The only sounds were the low growl coming from Shep and the distant sounds of activity from outside. For Alice, it might have been taking place in slow motion. There was none of the stunning swiftness with which her own sanity had been hijacked on a day very similar to this one, a day when all the ones leading up to it had coalesced in a single flashpoint that had sent her spinning over the edge. It was as if time were standing still. There was only the silence and the sight of the tortured man before her, who had no idea what he'd be taking with him should he end his life.

"Please, Gary," she cajoled, her voice breaking.

But he went on shaking his head, those sightless eyes fixed on her like those of someone already dead, repeating, "I can't. You know what prison is like. I can't go there."

"You may not have to. I'll talk to them, explain it so they'll understand. What you need right now is a doctor. You're sick, Gary, but you can get better. Trust me. *I* did."

He focused in on her, as if seeing her for the first time. Not as the ex-con he'd been spying on or his wife's crazy sister, but the strong, decisive woman she was in Colin's eyes.

Then Gary's shoulders slumped, and when she reached down to pry the gun from his fingers, he didn't resist. Delayed shock hit her then and for a long moment she just stood there, the warm weight of the revolver against her palm the only thing anchoring her in reality. She watched, as if from a distance, as Colin moved in, accompanied by the dog, helping Gary to his feet and guiding him out the door, Gary shuffling along beside him like an old, old man. By the time she came to her senses, the room was empty except for her and Owen.

The awareness, when it came, was like someone stealing up on her from behind: *I could kill him.* She could claim it was an accident, that the gun had simply gone off in her hand. And why not? It couldn't be mere coincidence that she happened to be standing before him, holding a gun, with no one to bear witness. Perhaps she was even the instrument of some divine retribution.

"Go ahead. You'd be doing me a favor."

Alice started at the sound of Owen's voice, rousing from her thoughts as if from a dream. When she focused in on him, she saw that the spark of defiance was gone from his eyes; they were as bleak and empty as Gary's had been. The man who had once seemed so powerful looked small and shrunken to her now, a pale reflection of his former self, the faint rise and fall of his chest as he took in breaths the only thing marking his existence. She realized, to her amazement, that she was no longer afraid of him. She didn't even hate him—that would have been giving him too much. All she wanted was to be free of him.

Still, she found she was unable to walk away. David wouldn't let her. "I just want to know one thing. Why?"

He gave an almost imperceptible shrug. "You want reasons? I'm afraid I can't help you there, my dear. It was an accident, just like I told the police. The only detail I left out was inconsequential really. It wouldn't have brought your son back for it to have been made public. And, if it helps any, I haven't touched a drop since." He regarded her for a moment, then he sighed and said, "No, I don't suppose it does." He spread his hands in helpless gesture. "And there you were again after all those years, turning up like a bad penny on my doorstep. Just when I was beginning to think I could put it all behind me. So you see, you left me with no choice. I had to do whatever it took to get rid of you."

"Even if it meant sending an innocent boy to prison?"

"I wish your son no ill," he said. "He seems like a nice boy. A bit confused perhaps, but I suppose that's to be expected."

Something twisted in her chest. "Not surprising, considering he grew up without a mother."

Owen shrugged again. "As for that, I'd say I paid just as steep a price." He glanced down at his lifeless legs, canted at a funny angle that made them seem unconnected to the rest of him. But there was no self-pity in his voice and the look on his face was oddly dispassionate, as if this final outcome to the drama that had been playing out between them for years was to be expected, and in some ways would be a relief. "But you feel differently, I know, so go ahead, shoot me. You have nothing to lose. I'm sure your lawyer friend will find a way to get you off."

Nothing to lose? "You're wrong about that," she said. There was one thing left for her to lose; something that neither he nor the nine years she'd spent in prison had managed to take from her: her humanity. Carefully, she lowered the gun onto the end table next to the settee. She stared at it for a moment, the hard fact of it more real somehow than anything that had led up to this moment. Then without another word, she turned and walked away.

CHAPTER SEVENTEEN

JULY 1943

The war that had posed but a distant threat took a new and alarming turn when, in May, the same week as the pivotal battle at Midway, the Japanese invaded the Aleutians, off the coast of Alaska, seizing control of two of its islands. On Grays Island, this worrisome development brought the war even closer to home—it was practically in their backyard!— galvanizing them into new heights in their war relief efforts. Bond pledges reached a record high and as did yields for scrap metal, paper, and rubber drives. The home guard redoubled their efforts and a two-man watch system was instituted for the bunkers out at Pigeon Point, so there would be someone on the lookout round the clock for any signs of suspicious activity. This resulted in a few mishaps, nerves being as frayed as they were, such as when Arnie Sykes's trawler was mistaken one morning for a Japanese sub in the midst of a dense fog. Poor Arnie had the fright of his life when the fog lifted and he found himself surrounded by Navy coast guard cutters.

But the threat proved short-lived. Within weeks American troops regained control of the Aleutians. During that same period a much smaller drama was taking place on Grays Island. One of the dozens of uninhabited little atolls dotting its coastal waters, a scrubby knuckle of rock and pine, gained temporary prominence when the chamber of commerce successfully petitioned the governor of Washington State to have it renamed, due to its unfortunate moniker—Jap's Island. There was some debate over what the new name should be, and it wasn't until summer of that year that one was finally decided upon. Henceforth it would be called Victory Island, a tribute to all the men and women on Grays Island who'd loyally served their country.

One of the few on the island who didn't attend the official ceremony at the dock, which included speeches by the mayor and harbor master, was William McGinty. It had been some weeks since his wife had taken their son on what was billed as an extended trip to New York to visit her parents, and he'd grown tired of the endless inquiries about when they were coming home. Tired, too, of giving excuses that would seem all the more pitiful once the truth came out. For there was no longer any doubt in William's mind as to how this would end. In the few terse phone conversations he'd had with Martha, she'd made it clear that a reconciliation wasn't forthcoming, and William was past the point of trying to convince her otherwise.

He would have been able to make peace with that if not for Danny. William couldn't bear the thought of being such a distance from his son. For that reason alone he'd begged Martha to see reason, offering her the house, along with a generous share of his earnings, if she'd come back to the island. But she'd refused to even consider it. She and Danny would be staying on at her parents' indefinitely, she'd informed him, adding that, in the future, if he had anything to say to her, he could speak to her lawyer.

The only thing that kept William from utter despair was knowing that when all this was over he'd be free to marry Eleanor. In the meantime, they'd agreed not to see each other until the dust had settled. It wasn't just his impending divorce. The island was still buzzing with rumors about Lowell White's disappearance. Some speculated that he'd fallen overboard and drowned while out sailing, though that was unlikely given that his boat was found moored at the marina and his car parked at the ferry terminal. A likelier theory was that Lowell, a known womanizer, had run off with a mistress. A suspicion that was confirmed in their minds when the Seattle *Times* brought news of a thirty-year-old woman in Port Townsend who'd gone missing, accompanied by a photo of an attractive blonde.

In time the talk would die down, William knew, only to be replaced by a new flurry of gossip when his intentions toward Eleanor became known. He would no doubt be portrayed as a philandering cad and Eleanor as a merry widow. They would have to take it slowly so as not to fan the flames (he didn't give a whit about his own reputation, but they had their children to think of). But eventually that, too, would fade. What would take longer was their children's accepting the new reality. He didn't fool himself into thinking Lucy would be quick to embrace him, given how devoted she'd been to Joe, any more than Danny would Eleanor. But in the end, he believed, his and Eleanor's love would prevail. Until then, he'd just have to be patient.

Which was easier said than done, for he missed her more than he would have thought possible. He didn't even have her portrait to fill the empty hours. In fact, he hadn't picked up a brush in weeks. It was as if Martha, in destroying the one thing he'd cared about, had robbed him of his creativity as well. All he had left was Laird, though Martha would have taken him, too, if her mother hadn't been allergic to dogs. For William, the dog's presence was a comfort. Laird seemed to have an almost human understanding of the torment he was in and seldom let William out of his sight. No day ended without the dog curled at his feet, his furry black and white head resting on his master's feet.

Then one morning Eleanor phoned him out of the blue and asked if she could see him. It had been weeks since they'd last spoken and the sound of her voice acted on him like tonic, bringing a bracing rush of adrenaline and clearing his mind of its cobwebs. He would have driven over to her place right then, but she insisted on coming to his house instead.

William, spurred by the prospect of her visit, was tackling the weeds in the garden, which he'd neglected these past weeks, when she came rattling down the drive in Joe's old Ford pickup. From behind a clump of tall hollyhocks that partially screened him from view, he watched her step down from the cab. She wore a yellow checked dress faded from too many washings, her hair untidily pinned up atop her head, stray tendrils chasing the dappled sunlight that played over her cheeks and neck. She looked as beautiful as ever, yet from the shadows under her eyes, it was obvious the strain of these past weeks had taken their toll. Partly because of Lowell, he knew. Also, he suspected, because she harbored some guilt about Martha.

"Eleanor!" he called out her name.

She came to a halt on the path, her eyes darting about before she finally spotted him. William rose from his knees, brushing the dirt from his khaki trousers, while cursing his stupidity in not having changed into something less disreputable—he'd been so preoccupied he hadn't thought to do so.

He hurried over to meet her. "I wasn't spying on you," he said, with a grin, noting the faint look of reproach she wore. "Just enjoying the sight of you strolling up my path. You look right at home." He longed to take her in his arms, but something in her expression warned against it.

"And *you* look much too thin." Eleanor's fingertips brushed over his arm, a touch so light he barely felt it through the sleeve of his shirt. "How are you holding up? It must get pretty lonely out here."

She was smiling, but she looked troubled. A little sliver of worry nicked at the edges of his consciousness. Was it possible her feelings toward him changed? He dismissed the thought at once, telling himself it was just the workings of his fevered brain.

"It does at times," he confessed, "but I'm not exactly alone." He turned to look at Laird, lying in a patch of sunlight on the porch, his head resting atop his paws, snoozing, as was his habit, with his eyes half open so as to track William's movements. "You did well when you chose him for Danny. Only how did you know he would end up being my dog?"

She regarded Laird, hands on hips, her head cocked slightly. "I can't take credit for that. He did the choosing, not me," Laird picked his head up off his paws, as if he knew they were talking about him. "Some dogs are like that. They're bonded to only one person, and it's for life."

Her eyes met his, and William could see that she wasn't just talking about the dog. He felt a surge of relief. In her oblique way, she was telling him she loved him, that nothing had changed. "Shall we go inside?" he asked.

"Is it all right if we sit out on the porch? It's so nice out."

She settled into one of the wicker chairs on the porch, while William went to fetch them something to drink. When he returned she was sitting with her eyes closed and her head tipped back, savoring the sunshine. Summertime was when the rains that drizzled down throughout most of the year gave way to clear skies and dry, sunny weather, and today was no exception. The sky was a deep cobalt above the cathedral spires of the pines along the ridge and out beyond the cove the waters of the sound sparkled with pinpoints of reflected light. She opened her eyes at his approach, darting him a sheepish look, as if she'd been caught indulging in something she shouldn't.

"I hope it's not too sweet for you," he said, handing her a glass of lemonade and settling into the chair across from hers. "I made it myself, and I didn't know how much sugar to put in."

She took a sip, pronouncing, "It's perfect. Just the way I like it."

So polite. As if they hadn't made love. As if the man he'd killed for her sake weren't buried on the hill behind her house.

"How's Lucy?" He played along with the ruse, if that's what this was, that they were just a pair of old friends catching up after a long absence.

She smiled. "Getting taller by the day."

"And Yoshi?"

"As hard-working as ever. In fact, I'm already wondering how I'm going to manage without him once this war is over." She turned to William, wearing a look of polite interest that didn't quite disguise the troubled expression he'd noticed earlier. "And you? You must miss your family."

"I miss Danny," he said, not wanting there to be any confusion about where his sentiments lay.

She took another sip of her lemonade. "How's he taking it?"

"When we talk on the phone, he doesn't say much, so it's hard to tell. But it has to be tough on him, and Martha isn't making it any easier."

"She's hurt. She wants to punish you. Once she comes to her senses . . ." Eleanor trailed off at the perplexed look on William's face.

What was she getting at? he wondered, in a mild panic. Did she *want* him to reconcile with his wife? The only reason she would wish for that, he realized with a sinking heart, would be if her feelings toward him had changed. Suddenly he was afraid to find out what she'd come to tell him.

The telegram in Eleanor's pocket was like a hot coal burning through the fabric of her dress. It had arrived the day before yesterday, and since then she'd been in a state of turmoil, pacing about, unable to sit still for more than few minutes at a time, happy one moment and miserable the next. Just when she'd see her way clear, it would grow murky again and she'd be back to plowing little furrows in the rug with her restless feet. It wasn't until this morning, after yet another sleepless night, that she'd come to a decision. That was why she was here. To tell William.

Only he wasn't making it any easier. In a firm voice, he declared, "It's over with Martha and me." He eyed her across the small wicker table on which his glass of lemonade sat untouched. He appeared puzzled and more than a little worried, as if wondering what could have brought about this sudden change of heart on her part.

Eleanor sighed. She'd been afraid of this. "You don't know that for sure."

Comprehension dawned in his blue eyes. "This isn't about Martha, is it?" he said softly.

She dropped her eyes, answering, "No." In that moment, with his eyes burning into her, she found her resolve weakening. But she knew there was no other way. "This came the other day." With a deep sigh, she with-

drew from her pocket the flimsy yellow slip of paper, folded and re-
folded so many times it was coming apart at the creases. She held it out
to him. "They found Joe. He's alive."

William gaped at her. "But how . . . ?"

"He was in the hospital all this time, but it was a while before they
could identify him," she explained. "He'd lost his dog tags and most of
his memory it seems. The doctor I spoke with is hopeful it'll come back,
but no one knows for sure. He's well enough to be shipped home at least.
They're transferring him to the Naval hospital in San Diego. Lucy and I
are taking the train down. We leave first thing tomorrow morning."

"So that's it then." William spoke in a queer, flat voice.

She nodded, her throat tight.

She could see a battle being waged in his anguished face, between what
he knew was the moral thing to do and what he selfishly wished for. Finally his mouth shaped itself into some semblance of a smile. "I suppose
I should offer my congratulations, but right now I'm finding it difficult."

Eleanor's eyes flooded with tears. "This has nothing to do with you,
William. You have to know that. I'm . . . I'm grateful Joe's alive . . . but I
would give anything if it didn't mean—" She broke off, finding it suddenly difficult to speak.

Abruptly he jumped out of his chair and began pacing back and forth.
Laird brought his head up, ears pricked at the sight of his master in such
a state of agitation. Eleanor had never seen William this way either, not
even the night they'd buried Lowell. She watched him rake his fingers
through his hair, which had grown long in the weeks they'd been apart.
His eyes seemed to leap like flames from the bony planes of his face
when at last he swung around to face her. "Don't do it. Don't stay with a
man just because you pity him. From everything you've told me about
Joe, he wouldn't want that either."

Slowly she shook her head. "I couldn't do that to him. Not after what
he's been through."

But William was too crazed to listen to reason. "Haven't you sacrificed
enough? My God, Eleanor, you don't even love the man!"

"You're wrong about that. I *do* love him." She spoke with quiet finality. "Maybe not in the same way I love you, but enough to know I could never hurt him. Whenever I think I can't live without you, I wonder how I'd live with myself if I were to leave Joe, especially now when he needs me most." She seized hold of William's hands, tears spilling down her cheeks. She didn't bother to wipe them away. "Haven't we done enough harm? Look at you and Martha. And what about Lowell's family? How can we possibly destroy another man's life on top of all that? And my little girl? Lucy would never forgive me." This morning it had been something Lucy had said to her that had solidified her decision. *When Papa comes home I want to sleep in your room, so I'll always know where he is.*

But William only shook his head, unwilling or unable to accept what she was telling him. "No. I can't lose you. I *won't* lose you." He spoke through gritted teeth, his eyes hard and bright with tears that he refused to let fall. "You think something like this will ever come again? It's once in a lifetime. I had to wait almost forty years to find it and if I live another forty without you, I'll die a lonely old man. And you, Eleanor . . . every night you lie down next to Joe, you'll be thinking of me. Is that really what you want? Is that how you see this ending?"

She rose to her feet, reaching up to cup his dear face in her hands, feeling the warmth of his skin and the tensed muscles flickering underneath. "That's what makes this so hard. If it were any easier, it would be because I didn't love you so much."

Everything about him seemed to cave in at once, his shoulders sagging in defeat and his tall, bony frame swaying like a tree in a high wind. Eleanor felt unsteady, too, thinking that if she didn't go now, this very instant, she wouldn't have the strength later on.

William's anguished gaze met hers, stripped of all hope but showing the glimmerings of understanding. As he took her in his arms one last time, holding her tightly, she could feel the muffled beating of his heart through the soft fabric of his shirt, a heart that would stubbornly go on beating long after this was over. Life would go on, too. Maybe not as they wished it. But, in one form or another, it would go on all the same.

"Good-bye, William." She pressed her lips to his in the most fleeting of kisses. Moments later she was darting down the path, the honeysuckle that grew along the hedge assaulting her with its sweet scent as she raced past, blinded by her tears. She never looked back.

CHAPTER EIGHTEEN

The phone was ringing. Colin could hear it all the way back from the shed, where he was stowing away his equipment. He'd spent most of the morning repairing the damage done by the storm that had rolled in night before last, pounding in stakes that had come loose and digging out lines that were buried in silt. It was filthy, backbreaking work, with little reward, but the sight of the lines strung out in neat rows, the fledgling oysters clinging to them with the same tenacity he'd shown in his own efforts, was deeply gratifying to him in a way that he couldn't have put into words. Out on the flat with the tide retreating, his conscious mind seemed to recede as well. There was just the sun and the wind and the reedy calls of the seagulls circling overhead.

He was thinking of Alice, as he often did these days, as he walked toward the house to check the answering machine. He hadn't seen her since the night at Owen's, more than two weeks ago, and they'd only spoken on the phone a few times since, most recently when he'd called to let her know Jeremy's trial date had been set. They were both keeping their distance, backing away from the intimacy of that strange day, as if from a too hot fire. Colin ate most of his meals at home these days and Alice was so caught up in her work and in helping her sister cope with Gary's breakdown, she didn't seem to notice that he hadn't been to the restaurant in a while.

The moment of truth for Colin had come, oddly enough, when the hostage crisis was past, after he'd handed Gary over to the police. Looking around, he'd realized, to his horror, that Alice was still in the house. With Gary's gun . . . and the man she had every reason to want to kill. The scenario had spun itself out in his head, with all its frightening possibilities, and he'd been gripped with a terror greater than any he'd felt going in. Then, suddenly he'd caught sight of her, walking toward him across the lawn, a slender figure silhouetted in the moonlight. In the darkness, from that distance, she could have been anyone, and for a heart-stopping moment, in his nerve-shot state, he'd even imagined it was Nadine. Nadine emerging unharmed from the rubble of the Twin Towers, as he'd watched her do a thousand times in his dreams.

When Alice had finally stepped into view and he'd seen no evidence of the terrible things he'd been imagining, Colin had felt a rush of relief at knowing she was safe. And something else as well: the knowledge that he didn't have the strength to sustain another loss. The next time he wouldn't be able to pull himself out of the abyss.

When she'd phoned the next day to give him an update on her brother-in-law, Alice, perhaps picking up on his mood, had been guarded as well. The conversation, while friendly, had had the feel of a missed connection. No one listening in would have guessed they'd ever been intimate.

"Gary's lucky in one sense," she'd said. "If he hadn't been one of their own, he'd be in jail by now." Instead, Gary had been taken to a psychiatric hospital in Bellingham, she informed him.

"What do the doctors say?" Colin had asked.

"He should pull out of it. He's still pretty depressed, but they think the psychosis is only temporary."

"Which means he'll be declared fit to stand trial." Colin had found himself slipping on his lawyer's hat.

"I'm not sure it'll come to that. I can't imagine he'll get off with just a slap on the wrist, but Gary has a lot of influential friends. They'll bend over backward to cut him a break."

"Even if it means making an enemy of the mayor?"

"I don't think we'll have to worry about him anymore."

"What makes you say that?"

"Just a feeling," she said after a pause.

Colin had found himself wondering once more what had happened in those few minutes when she'd been left alone with Owen. But she hadn't volunteered any more information and he hadn't pressed her. "How's your sister holding up?" he'd inquired.

"Not so good. But she's keeping it together for the kids' sake. And I know she'll get through this. She's a survivor."

"It must run in the family," he'd said. And she'd laughed knowingly.

After they'd hung up, Colin had begun thinking about his own family. How long had it been since they'd had anything of real substance to say to each other. When he'd been in rehab, his parents and brother had dutifully attended family week, but in the end none of them had been willing to admit their own role in his dissolution. During the worst of his drinking, his mom would declare staunchly to anyone who even hinted that he had a problem that there was nothing wrong with her son that a new wife wouldn't fix, and Pop had always been quick to pour him another drink and point to Patrick, who could put away more beers on a Friday night than any man standing and who hadn't let it interfere with his life. It had taken a full flameout on Colin's part for them to finally accept that he was an alcoholic, and now that he was sober they referred to it only in the past tense, as if alcoholism were a curable disease, like meningitis.

He didn't blame them, though. God knew he hadn't made it any easier for them. Besides, they had their own troubles. His grandmother, for one. Marma, as she'd been nicknamed by Patrick at an early age when he couldn't pronounce her full name, Martha, was a bit of a terror. For years she'd had one or both of his parents running over to her house at least once a day, on some pretext or other. Things had improved some-what since she'd moved into an assisted living facility, but she hadn't abandoned her martyr role and no visit with her was complete without a litany of complaints.

Colin knew he owed her a call, and minutes later, when his mother's voice on the answering machine reminded him that it was Marma's birth-day tomorrow, her ninetieth, it only increased his guilt. He'd been so pre-occupied lately, he'd forgotten all about it. He phoned his mother back at once.

"I wish you could be here for it," she said, after the usual pleasantries, when talk turned to his grandmother's birthday. "It would mean so much to Marma. We're throwing her a little party. I'm making all her fa-vorite foods."

"I wish I could be there, too," Colin lied.

There was a sigh at the other end. "Who knows how many more birthdays she'll have?"

Colin laughed. "You're beginning to sound like Marma."

His mother gave a mock gasp. "Am I? Oh, God. It must be rubbing off."

"Don't worry about Marma. She's a tough old bird."

"I won't deny that." His mother chuckled knowingly. "But, really, Colin, it wouldn't hurt you to come for a visit. It's not just Marma. We *all* miss you."

"I know, Mom," he said, with a sigh. He missed them, too, in a way. At the same time, he found the mere thought of his childhood home in Queens, with its little patch of grass out back that only a fast-talking re-altor would call a yard, and its walls permeated with the smell of every meal that had been cooked in it for the past three decades, profoundly depressing.

They chatted a while longer, his mother giving him the latest status re-port on his dad's sciatica and telling him all about the house his brother and sister-in-law had bought in the Poconos. Colin provided a brief, gen-eralized update on his own activities, leaving out any mention of Alice. His mother lived in perpetual hope that he would remarry one day and he didn't want her to be disappointed when she learned that no wedding bells were in the offing.

After they'd hung up, he phoned his grandmother. For all her contrary ways, he admired the old gal. Forever blond and always dressed to the nines, in full make-up, she was the siren of Heritage Manor, where she reputedly had the men who were still sentient lusting after her. Last year for her birthday Colin had given her a subscription to *Glamour* magazine, and when she'd declared it to be her favorite present of all, he'd known she'd meant it.

"Did I wake you?" he asked, after she'd answered the phone in a groggy voice.

"In the middle of the day?" She snorted at the absurdity of such an idea. "Don't be silly. I was only resting my eyes."

"There's nothing wrong with taking a nap," he told her.

"Sure, if you're an old lady. I'm not old, I'm just getting on in years. There's a difference."

"You'll never be old, Marma," he agreed. "You're too busy keeping the rest of us on our toes."

She laughed heartily. Colin was the only one in the family who could get her to laugh like that. They didn't always agree, but the bond between them was tight. "Like you would know. I haven't heard from you in ages," she chided. "What are you doing out there that's so important you can't give your grandma a call now and then?"

"Not much," he admitted. "But that's sort of the point."

"How's the oystering business coming?"

"I'll let you know as soon as I have something to show for it," he said. "Right now, it's not much to look at."

"Never mind. Mister Deets would be proud. He was an old coot, but he knew his stuff. We had so many oysters they were coming out our ears. I used to make oyster stew every Sunday and feed what was left over to the dog. Imagine! How's the old place holding up?"

"I've had to do a few repairs, but all in all it's in surprisingly good shape."

"You don't get lonely rattling around in it?"

"At times, but I kind of like it. Seems a shame, though, that I'm the only one who gets to enjoy the view. It's pretty spectacular, especially on clear days."

"I remember it well." Her tone turned wistful.

On impulse, he said, "You should come out for a visit. Seriously, Marma. I'll even send you a ticket." He'd sold some of the antiques to finance the oyster farm and cover his living expenses: a pair of Tiffany lamps and the dining room sideboard, which had turned out to be a signed Stickley. He wasn't rich but he could afford the airfare.

There was a long pause in which he could hear the rustle of her breath, a sound that made him think of yellowing pages being turned in an old book, before she answered with regret, "Thank you, dear. It's sweet of you to offer, but I don't think I'd be up to it."

"Arthritis acting up again?"

"It's not that, and you can stop pretending you don't know perfectly well what the reason is," she said somewhat tartly.

"Actually, I *don't* know. We've never really talked about it." Normally he would have dropped the subject, but he wasn't backing away this time. Being in this house had made him wonder more and more about the circumstances of his grandparents' divorce. And now he could feel his grandfather's spirit chafing at the dishonesty and unspoken resentments that had been so corrosive to their family.

"I can't see what possible interest it would be to you. It's all ancient history," his grandmother said in a dismissive tone. "Anyway, if you'd wanted to know so badly, you should have asked your grandfather about it while he was alive."

"We never talked about it, either."

"I find that hard to believe." She spoke with a bitterness that was undiminished by the years. "I'm surprised he didn't fill your ear with tales about what a rotten wife I was."

Colin was amazed that his grandmother would think that. Clearly she hadn't known William as well as she thought. "Actually, he never had a bad word to say about you or anyone. All he ever told me was that you and he disagreed on how Dad should be raised."

Marma snorted in disdain. "He was upset because I took Daniel to live with my parents. But, honestly, what choice did I have?"

"You could have stayed on the island."

"What, and have everyone feeling sorry for me? Poor Missus McGinty, whose husband made a fool of her!"

"So it was another woman." Colin had guessed as much.

She hesitated before replying, as if realizing she'd already said too much. At last, she heaved a sigh that seemed to come down the long tunnel of years. "Yes. Her name was Eleanor."

"The woman in the portrait."

There was another long pause, and for a moment he wasn't sure she would reveal any more than that. But maybe it was the advent of another birthday, a reminder that she didn't have many more years left, or maybe that she'd simply decided the statute of limitations on his grandfather's crimes was up, for she replied, "It wasn't just an affair—I might have forgiven him that. He loved her."

"Did he tell you that?"

"He didn't have to. The portrait said it all."

"I always wondered about that, why he never sold it." Taking advantage of his grandmother's unexpected candor, he asked, "Why did you leave him? Was it because he refused to give her up?"

"Partly, though I probably could have persuaded him to—for Danny's sake, if not mine. But I had too much pride. And I loved him too much to stay, knowing how he felt," she said, in a strange, hollow voice. "Of course, I never told him that. He wouldn't have believed it, if I had. Our life had become . . ." Her voice trailed off. "After you've been married a while you get into a routine. And it was the war. I was doing my part along with everyone else. I suppose I wasn't paying as much attention to my husband as I should. And your grandfather . . . he did what men do. He looked elsewhere."

Colin found himself gazing up at the portrait that had stood at the center of his family's mystery and that even now carried a hint of intrigue. "So why didn't he marry Eleanor?"

"She was already married, for one thing. Her husband was off fighting in the war when they met. For a while everyone thought he was dead, but it turned out he'd only been missing in action." Colin listened raptly as the tale grew even stranger. "He was wounded pretty badly, from what I heard, and I suppose she couldn't bring herself to leave him."

"Once you found that out, you never considered going back?"

"No." Another deep sigh. "Even if I'd been able to forgive him, I doubt he would have forgiven me."

"Because of Dad?" Colin asked, knowing the bitterness it had caused when she'd taken their only child away.

"No, he'd have done almost anything to get Daniel back. It was the portrait." She seemed reluctant to continue.

"What about it?" Colin prompted, gazing at the portrait as he puzzled over her cryptic words.

After a moment Marma said, "That's how I found out about the affair. I came across the portrait in his studio, where he'd been working on it in secret. I knew the moment I laid eyes on it, of course." Her voice was soft with a kind of wonderment, as if she were surprised to find those memories, locked away all these years, still alive and intact. "No one but a man in love could have painted her like that. Almost as if she were glowing. I couldn't bear it, so I grabbed the first thing I could get my hands on—a pair of scissors. I wasn't thinking clearly at the time. I'm not even sure how it happened." She faltered a bit before going on. "By the time I was finished, there was nothing left of it."

Colin struggled to make sense of what his grandmother was telling him. "So the one he left me isn't the original?"

"He painted it again from memory. Every detail, exactly as it was. *Better* even." He heard the bitter pride in her voice. She might have scorned William in private, but she'd always seen the value in being Mrs. William McGinty. Why else keep his name? "When I saw it, I could hardly believe my eyes. I'd gone to a show of his works, at the Brooklyn Museum. More out of curiosity than anything. And there it was, up on the wall bold as you please. Like I'd only dreamed that I'd hacked it to pieces. Like . . . like I'd never existed. It wasn't until later on that I figured out what must have happened."

"That's quite a story." Stunned, Colin stood there shaking his head. He couldn't quite picture his grandparents as those younger people embroiled in all that drama. Briefly he thought about mentioning that he'd become friendly with Eleanor's granddaughter—more than friendly, in fact—but he decided against it. It would have been too much for Marma to handle.

"Well, now you know. I hope you're satisfied," she said.

"I'm sorry for dredging it all up," Colin apologized.

"Oh, I'll survive. I have so far. You don't get to be my age without your share of hard knocks. I might have had more than most, but I'm still here, aren't I?"

"That you are." William smiled. "Happy birthday, by the way. I'm sorry I didn't send you anything."

"Never mind. You've given me something far better than anything money can buy." From the note of affection in her voice, he knew that he was forgiven.

"What's that?" he asked.

"You didn't let the fact that I'm old and sick stop you from speaking your mind."

Colin chuckled. "Well, Marma, maybe it's because I don't think of you that way." More soberly, he added, "Anyway, I'm the one who should be thanking you. This explains a lot. Not just about Grandpa, but about our whole family."

"I'd rather you didn't mention to your father that we had this little chat," she said. "You know how he feels about your grandfather. It would only get him worked up."

What Colin knew was that if his father harbored ill will toward William, the seed had been planted there by Marma and nourished through the years until it could flower on its own. But there was no point in dredging up that, too. Besides, it wouldn't have done any good.

"I'll try to make it out next year for your birthday," he told her, as they were saying good-bye.

"If I live that long," she muttered.

"Marma, you'll outlive us all," he said, with a laugh, almost believing it at that moment.

The house seemed quieter than usual after he'd hung up. He sank down on the sofa, his gaze drawn once more to the portrait. His grandmother had told only one side of the story—the rest William and Eleanor had taken to their graves—but she'd provided a crucial detail. Her words came back to him now. *He painted it from memory. Every detail. Even better than before.* A revelation that had rocked Colin to the core, for it spoke of a love so powerful that nothing, not even time, could diminish it. A love that had enabled William to see Eleanor through the eyes of memory, as clearly as when he'd painted her in life. The kind of love that could only be when you know you're loved as deeply in return. Colin had seen it on his grandfather's face the one time he'd asked about the woman in the portrait: He'd been true to Eleanor till the end.

Colin could only imagine the exquisite hell of their living so close to one another yet so far apart. And yet both had stayed on the island. Maybe because to have moved away would have been even more unbearable. What would those two have made of the friendship, for lack of a better word, between the children of their offspring? That the happiness that had eluded them could have been his and Alice's for the taking? Might they even have had a hand in their being thrown together? Colin didn't believe in ghosts, except the ones of his own making, but at the same time he was having difficulty *not* believing that there was something more at work here than mere coincidence.

He thought now of Alice, warming at the memory of their lovemaking. This time it wasn't clouded by thoughts of Nadine. As if a fog had lifted, he saw Alice as clearly as the image in the portrait, to whom she bore such a striking resemblance, an image that shone now like a lighted window materializing out of the darkness at the end of a long journey, guiding the way as he searched for what was in his heart.

———

Denise sat on the edge of the bed, plucking absently at the balled-up Kleenex in her lap. "It's just so hard sometimes," she said, looking more dispirited than Alice had ever seen her. "Life doesn't just stop when something like this happens. Even when you're dying inside, you still have to get up and go to work every day. You have to put a smile on your face for the kids' sake, and so people won't be talking about you behind your back any more than they already are. Oh yes, I know there's been talk! They're saying our family is cursed." She turned swollen, bloodshot eyes to Alice. "What if it's true? What if we *are* cursed?"

"That's ridiculous, and you know it," Alice told her. "There's a perfectly good explanation for everything that's happened." Owen White had been at the root of it all.

She waited for that clenched feeling she always used to get whenever she thought of him, but it didn't come. It was as if, in confronting him, some burden had been lifted from her. He wasn't a monster, she'd realized, just a man so twisted inside he'd resorted to monstrous acts.

"That's a comforting thought," Denise said sarcastically.

Alice placed a hand over her sister's. "It's not the end of the world. It just feels that way right now."

Denise shook her head, refusing to be consoled. "It's like I don't know my own husband anymore. It's like visiting some sick relative I have to try to cheer up."

"I know you don't believe it right now, but you'll get through this, trust me."

"The question is *how*."

Alice got down to practical matters. "What does Gary's lawyer have to say?"

Denise brightened marginally. "Steve worked out a deal. Gary gets off with a suspended sentence, as long as he remains under a doctor's care. Brett Loggins," she said, referring to the assistant D.A., "is an old school friend of Gary's. They'd get together for a beer now and then." She paused, adding in a softer voice, "I suppose those days are over."

"You can't think that way. Some people will have a hard time understanding, sure. But when Gary gets home I think you'll be pleasantly surprised to find out just how many friends he has." Alice said, reminded of the old friends and acquaintances who'd supported her.

"Maybe, but that's only the half of it. What's he going to do for work? What about *us*?" Denise moaned.

"Have you two talked? I mean, *really* talked."

Denise shook her head. The Kleenex she'd been mangling had disintegrated, and now she stared down in misery at the tiny pieces scattered like snowflakes over her lap. "The doctor doesn't think it's a good idea to get into any of that stuff right now. He says Gary is still too fragile. But I know something's on his mind. I can sense it. What I can't figure out is why he's keeping it from me. We've always shared *everything*."

"Maybe he's afraid."

Denise's head jerked up, her eyes widening. "Afraid of what? Me? I'm his wife."

"It's the people you love the most that you least want to hurt," Alice said gently. She hadn't told her sister any of the things Gary had revealed to her that night. It would be better if she heard it from Gary. "Maybe he's only trying to protect you."

"Protect me from what? I already know the worst."

"Just let him know you'll love him, no matter what. Maybe that's all he needs to hear." She'd long since forgiven Gary herself, knowing the kind of pressure he'd been under.

Denise nodded slowly, her mouth turning up in a small half smile. "Just like the old days, huh? You giving me advice. Only back then I thought you had all the answers."

Alice gave a rueful laugh. "Not even close."

She was thinking of Colin, how wrong she'd been about him. That night, she'd felt the connection between them more strongly than ever. No man had ever gone out on a limb like that for her, not her husband, not even her father when he was alive. Moving side by side through the shadows, she'd felt closer to him than she ever had to another human being, almost as if they'd been one. She'd felt his strength flowing into her, giving her the courage to do what she'd needed to do. All her earlier fears and misgivings about him had faded away. *This must be what love is,* she'd thought, marveling for an instant, in spite of the trepidation she'd felt at the prospect of what lay ahead, that it had taken her this long to find out. Love was someone who knew instinctively what you needed and gave it without being asked or expecting anything in return.

But ever since then he seemed to have retreated back into his shell. Hurt, she'd kept her distance as well, wondering how she could have been so mistaken about him. No, clearly she didn't have all the answers. Who, after all, was she to give advice?

Denise rose heavily to her feet. "Well, I guess I should get started on supper. Though if it weren't for the kids I probably wouldn't bother. I don't seem to have much of an appetite these days—silver lining to every cloud, right?" She glanced down at her slacks, which drooped around her hips, she'd lost so much weight. She paused to ask Alice, as she was making her way to the door, "Should I set an extra place?"

"Thanks, no. I'm taking Jeremy out for pizza tonight." Just saying the words brought a little glow of satisfaction. Such an ordinary thing, yet for her it was anything but ordinary.

"Don't you have to work?"

"I'm taking the night off. Calpernia's holding the fort down, and that new guy we hired seems to be working out." Usually, Alice only took Mondays off, when the restaurant was closed, but business had been picking up lately—word was getting around and they'd had a nice write-up in the Seattle *Times*—so she could afford to take an extra day now and then. And she'd wanted to go out on a night when Jeremy didn't have school the next day, so he could enjoy their time together without worrying about his homework.

Denise hugged Alice as she was leaving. "Thanks. I don't know how I'd get through this if it weren't for you."

Alice thought again of all that Denise had done for her. Her sister had never stinted, not once. "Consider it payback."

—

"Okay if I tag along?"

Randy spoke casually, as if it had been a spur of the moment thing, but Alice could tell from the way his eyes cut away that he'd had it in mind it all along. Her heart sank. She'd been so looking forward to the time alone with her son. But, conscious of Jeremy watching them, waiting to see how she'd react, she tried not to let her disappointment show.

"Fine by me. If it's okay with you." She turned to give Jeremy a questioning look. He stood slouched in the doorway to the living room, a study in teenage insouciance, in his baggy cargo pants and Mariners sweatshirt at least three sizes too big, except for his eyes, which flicked back and forth between his parents, keenly attuned to their every nuance.

"Whatever." He shrugged, but she thought he looked pleased.

"All right then. Shall we?" She put on a smile that she hoped didn't look manufactured.

On the drive into town, the conversation was a bit strained. She couldn't remember the last time they'd all gone on a family outing. Her memories of the events that had taken place in the months after David's death all ran together in her mind like colors on a child's finger painting. Now, here they were together again. Alice felt sad, thinking of all the wasted years.

"I'm glad we could do this," said Randy, later on, as he was tucking into the last slice of pizza. Jeremy had run into a couple of friends from school—not the ones he usually hung out with, she'd been relieved to see—and after finishing his pizza he'd gone off with them to the video arcade in back. "I've been wanting to tell you how bad I feel that I wasn't around during that whole business with Gary. You shouldn't have had to go through that alone."

Her thoughts turned once more to Colin. "I wasn't exactly alone."

"Yeah, I know. Jeremy was pretty shook up," Randy said, clearly unaware of Colin's role in it. "How's Gary doing?"

"Better. He seems to be responding to his treatment."

"Poor guy." Randy shook his head in sympathy. "It has to be tough on Denise, too."

"It is, but she's hanging in there. Mainly, she's worried about how they're going to manage if he can't find another job."

"Maybe I can help with that."

"Really?" Alice perked up.

"I know a guy who manages a department store in one of those big shopping malls. They're always looking for security guards. I can probably get him to hire Gary."

"That would be great." It might not be ideal, but it was a job.

"I'll give the guy a call, see what he can do." Randy paused, frowning in thought as he chewed on a mouthful of pizza. "Of course, they'd have to relocate. How would they feel about moving off the island?"

"I'm sure they wouldn't be too happy about it, but they may not have a choice." It might even be preferable in a way. Life in a small community could get pretty uncomfortable when you were the subject of scrutiny, Alice knew from her own experience. Touched by the unexpected show of support from her ex-husband, she reached across the table and squeezed his hand. "Thanks, Randy. I really appreciate this."

He smiled at her with more warmth than usual. "No problem. Happy to do what I can." He pushed aside his half-eaten slice of pizza. "You know, Alice, we should do this more often."

She wasn't sure what he was getting at and didn't want to read too much into it, so she said lightly, "You're right, we should. I'm sure Jeremy would like that."

Randy gave her a meaningful look. "I wasn't just thinking of Jeremy."

"Oh." She felt heat rising in her cheeks. She dropped her voice, asking, "What exactly are you getting at, Randy?"

He took a deep breath and exhaled slowly. He appeared nervous for some reason. "Look, Alice, I've been thinking a lot lately. About us. I'll be honest with you. I'm not proud of the way I handled things in the past. But whatever you might think, I wasn't trying to punish you. I was only looking out for Jeremy, doing what I thought was best for him. For whatever it's worth, I was wrong. And I wouldn't blame you if you can't find it in your heart to forgive me. But if there's a chance, even a slight one, that we can put all this behind us and make a fresh start, don't you think we owe it to ourselves, and to Jeremy, to at least try?"

Alice was speechless. How could she have been so blind to the signals? There was a time she'd known Randy's every tic: that certain look he got in his eyes when he was being less than honest; the way the tips of ears reddened when he was feeling amorous; the heightened pitch of his voice when he was winding up to make a pitch, usually involving expensive things they couldn't afford—a Minolta camera, a trip to Hawaii, a new propane grill. And even when she'd known he was lying or when she didn't feel like making love or was annoyed at his spendthrift ways, it had been a reminder of how close they were. They'd been high school sweethearts. He was the first boy she'd kissed, when she was fourteen, under the bleachers after the homecoming game. The first boy she'd had sex with. In college there had been other guys and, she knew for a fact, other girls for Randy, but in the end they'd always come back to each other. Even if she hadn't gotten pregnant in her sophomore year, marrying Randy would have been a foregone conclusion.

Those old memories washed through her, but underlying them, like gritty sand, was the knowledge that Randy hadn't been there for her when it counted most. After David died, she had felt as if she'd lost her husband, too. But though he'd been wrong in keeping Jeremy from her, she knew he'd meant it when he'd said he had only done what he'd thought was best. She couldn't lose sight of the fact, either, that Randy had been there for Jeremy all those years when she couldn't be. He'd been a good dad, even if he'd made mistakes as a husband.

She found her voice at last. "I don't know what to say. I didn't see this coming."

He was gazing at her intently, his eyes bright with expectation, as if it were possible to get the answer he wanted through sheer force of will. "Will you at least think about it?"

"All right. I'll think about it." Maybe Randy was right. Maybe they owed it to themselves to try. It might be the best thing for all of them, not just Jeremy. But she wasn't ready to commit to anything just yet, so she cautioned, "Don't say anything to Jeremy just yet. I don't want him to get his hopes up."

"I won't say a thing." Randy smiled as if it were already a done deal, his eyes remaining locked on hers. She noticed, to her embarrassment, that the tips of his ears were pink. "I was thinking next time, it could be just the two of us. Someplace nice, with candles." He glanced up at the string of red lights in the shape of chili peppers strung along the exposed brick walls, and they shared an amused look. "I can always make up some excuse, tell Jeremy I'm going bowling with the guys or something."

"You don't bowl," she said, smiling.

"True, but I could always learn."

Alice thought about how long it had been since she'd been on a real date. Even if it was with her ex-husband, it would be nice to dress up, put on high heels for a change.

An image of Colin intruded once more. The tenderness with which he'd kissed her when they'd parted at his house, as if he'd known it was the last time. As if he'd already made his decision, a decision that, even though it pained her, Alice could respect. For didn't she feel the same pull of the past with Randy? Letting go was hard, even when all you had to hang on to was memories.

Jeremy reappeared at the table just then. His face was flushed and he looked more at ease than he had in a while. Alice smiled up at him. "Having a good time?"

He grinned in reply. "Kent and Tyson are heading over to Bucky's. There's supposedly a good band playing tonight. They want me to go with them. Is that okay?"

"As long as you promise not to stay out too late," Randy told him. "I want you home no later than midnight."

Jeremy looked a little surprised, as if it had been a while since he'd had a curfew, but he played along. And although it was clear to Alice that Randy was only exercising his authority in order to impress her with his parenting skills, she was touched by the effort.

"Mom?"

Alice became aware of Jeremy's eyes on her. She realized with a start that he was asking her permission as well—his way of letting her know that she was still his mother, no matter what. Her throat tightened, but she didn't want to embarrass him with a show of emotion, so she merely said, "Okay with me. Just remember, tomorrow's a work day."

Watching him bound off, like any teenager eager to get back to his friends, his impending trial seemed to her a distant threat.

CHAPTER NINETEEN

It hit him as soon as he walked through the door, a solid wall of sound, its pulsing beat seeming to surge up through the soles of his feet, filling him with excitement and a wild sense of possibility. Jeremy waited in line to get his hand stamped, but when he turned to his friends, Kent and Tyson were already moving off in the direction of the dance floor. Kent called something over his shoulder to Jeremy that he couldn't hear, then the two were swallowed up by the crowd. Jeremy started after them, but by the time he'd made his way through the crush of bodies, he'd lost them.

He hadn't known either of them that long. Kent Park was his lab partner in Bio, a quiet-seeming Korean kid who'd turned out to have an off-beat sense of humor—Jeremy had arrived at class one morning to find the frog they were supposed to dissect arranged in a prayerful pose, as if pleading to be spared. Through Kent, he'd gotten to know Kent's best friend, Tyson Fowler. They weren't the coolest kids in school, Kent a self-proclaimed tech geek and Tyson president of the chess club, but they weren't off the grid in terms of popularity, either; Jeremy's reputation wouldn't suffer from hanging out with them. Not that that was such a big deal to him any more; stuff like that had stopped seeming so important after he'd learned the hard way what it took to get noticed. And with Kent and Tyson he could be himself; he didn't have to put on an act to try to look cool.

Occasionally he still ran into Rud and his posse. They would always greet him with hooting calls and pump their raised fists at him, their idea of a friendly gesture, and he'd always wave in return. But on those occasions he didn't automatically fall in with them as he had in the past. Instead, he'd find himself noticing things he hadn't before, like the other day when he'd observed with a mild shock that Rud's hair was thinning, his pale pink scalp visible through the gelled spikes of his albino hair— *He'll be bald by the time he's thirty*, Jeremy had thought—and the time they'd walked past Bettina Stromberger and she'd screwed up her face and flapped a hand in front of her nose in their wake, at the stench from the smoker's pit that followed them everywhere they went.

Jeremy would marvel then that he had ever thought they were "dope," as Rud would have put it. His dad had been right about them. *You hang out with losers, you'll become one yourself*, Randy had cautioned. And by the time Jeremy was his dad's age, he sure as shit didn't want to be pushing a broom for a living or reading his name upside down off his shirt pocket. He had bigger plans for himself.

Then, inevitably, would come the sudden, sickening sensation in his gut, the realization that instead of going to college he could be spending the next few years behind bars. It was like his shadow, something he wasn't aware of most of the time but which followed him everywhere he went.

For a while he'd fooled himself into believing the whole thing would get buried in the shit storm over his uncle. But that wasn't proving to be the case. The same D.A. who'd come down so hard on Jeremy had been a soft touch with Gary. The matter had been handled quietly, and though his uncle wouldn't be returning to his job any time soon, he'd been spared a trial.

It helped that the mayor hadn't pressed charges. He'd been quoted in the newspaper as saying that, while Gary Elkins's actions had caused him and his wife a good deal of trauma—Mrs. White had been holed up in her room the whole time; it was she who'd called the cops—he understood that there had been no criminal intent; the former deputy chief of police had merely been reacting to the "mental stress" he'd been under.

Jeremy knew, from listening in on his mom's and Colin's conversations, that the old man had had something to do with his uncle's crackup and that he was in some way responsible for the D.A.'s coming down so hard on *him*. But they couldn't prove it, so nothing had changed as far as he was concerned.

While he was contemplating this, as he pushed through the crush at Bucky's he ran headlong into Carrie Ann Flagler. She was carrying a large plastic cup of what looked to be Coke—they only served non-alcoholic beverages on teen Fridays—and when he accidentally plowed into her, some of it splashed over onto her top. He froze for an instant, staring at her in horrified disbelief, before he managed to fumble out an apology.

"Shit! I'm sorry. I didn't see you."

Ignoring his apology, she began furiously dabbing at her top with the napkin in her other hand. In the dim light, he wondered for a second if she'd even recognized him. Then her head jerked up and she glared at him. "So, what, are you, like, *stalking* me or something?" she demanded, raising her voice to be heard above the loud pulsing of the music. Silvery flecks of light from the twirling mirror ball overhead funneled down like snowflakes, catching in her light brown hair and bouncing off the spangles sewn onto the scooped neck of her top, which showed a fair amount of cleavage. The spillover from the dance floor crowded in around them, gyrating couples bumping up against them, pushing them closer together, close enough for Jeremy to catch the scent of her perfume—something light and grassy that smelled like a meadow after a rainfall.

Jeremy shouted over the music, "Can I get you another one?" He pointed at her half-empty cup.

Unexpectedly, she shrugged in what he took to be an assent. They made their way through the crowd to the bar, where he bought them each a Coke. The situation was already so surreal that when she suggested they go outside, where it wasn't so noisy, it didn't seem all that strange.

Outside, she used a fresh napkin to dab once more at her top. "Shit, I think it's ruined. And this is only the first time I've worn it. What do you think, is it too late to exchange it?" She looked up at him, and he saw a small smile peeking from under her frown. "A joke," she said. "It was a joke."

He wondered if she also considered it funny to be falsely accusing someone of rape. "I get it," he said, in a surly voice.

Her smile abruptly fell away. They were standing on the concrete landing above the steps that led down to the parking lot. He could hear the music, muffled now, thumping on the other side of the door through which they'd just exited and smell the after-hours punch bowl odor of empty cups and rotting fruit that drifted up from the dumpster below. A breeze was blowing, lifting the hair off her face, lifting it and gently lowering it again. In the light from the quarter moon caught in the trees branches overhead, her eyes, ringed with mascara that had already begun to smudge, were bright as they fixed on him with the same look of faint bewilderment that Jeremy imagined he wore.

"This is weird, isn't it? If my dad could see us, he'd be calling the cops right now." A note of defiance crept into her voice, as if she were somehow thumbing her nose at her father, and Jeremy noticed that her words were slightly slurred. She'd been drinking. He knew that some of the kids who came to these things brought their own booze, which they either smuggled inside in flasks or drank outside in the parking lot. She wasn't drunk, though, like on the night they'd had sex. The mere thought of which made his dick stir.

What made him even angrier than what she'd done was that he could still be even remotely attracted to her. "Why, you scared I'm going to rape you?" he said sarcastically.

"I didn't say that." Now her defiance seemed directed at him.

"You didn't have to."

"It's not all my fault, you know."

"Oh, and just whose fault is it then?" Throwing aside every caution, from Mr. McGinty, from his mom and dad, he spoke his mind. "You fucking *lied*. You know what really happened, but that's not what you told the police."

A sullen look came over her face. "You're making it sound like it was on purpose. It wasn't like that."

He pounced. "So you admit you lied."

"That's not what I said. You're twisting my words."

Jeremy pressed on. "What I want to know is *why*. Why did you do it?"

Her eyes met his then, and he saw the confusion in them. "I don't know," she said, with a small shrug. "It just . . . kind of got away from me, I guess. Once my parents got the police involved, it turned into this whole big deal. Like, it wasn't really about *me* anymore, you know?"

"Not really," he said coldly.

"If it means anything, I'm sorry."

He felt a surge of hope. "So you'll tell them I didn't do it?"

She shook her head slowly, and tears welled in her eyes, making them shiny as newly minted nickels in the moonlight. "I can't. My dad would kill me. That's how this whole thing started. That night, when he caught me sneaking into the house, he went ballistic. It wasn't just that I'd been drinking. It was like he *knew* what had happened, like he could smell it on me. I was crying, my mom was crying, and somehow it all came out. I guess I must've made it sound like it was all you—shit, I had to tell him something, didn't I, or he'd have blamed *me*—and before I knew it, he was on the phone with the cops. What was I supposed to do?" Her eyes pleaded with him to understand.

But to Jeremy it wasn't at all complicated. "You could have told the truth."

"You don't know what my dad's like when he gets like that. He's scary. If I told him I'd made the whole thing up, I . . . I don't know what he'd do." She hugged herself, shivering, and Jeremy could see, from the look on her face, that it wasn't just from the cold.

Strangely, he wasn't unsympathetic. He used to think his family was more screwed up than anyone's, but lately he'd begun to realize that there were families worse off than his, like Carrie Ann's. He couldn't let that get in the way, though. She might be too scared to stand up to her father, but Jeremy was equally afraid of what would happen to him if she didn't. "There's got to be somebody you could talk to. A teacher, or maybe Mister Bradley," he urged her, thinking of their school guidance counselor, who really did listen and who didn't talk down to you. "If things are really that bad at home, there are people who can help."

It was the wrong thing to have said, he could see that at once. Her face closed off as suddenly as a door slamming shut. "You make it sound like he'd actually hurt me or something." Her tone turned belligerent. "Just because my dad has a temper, it doesn't mean he's some kind of psycho. Anyway," her eyes narrowed, "it's not like *you're* so innocent. How do I know it didn't happen the way I said? We were both pretty drunk that night."

"Because," he said, "If I *had* raped you, you wouldn't be talking to me right now."

Even Carrie Ann couldn't argue with that logic. She went on glaring at him, though, wearing the sullen expression that made her look closer to six than sixteen. In the parking lot below, he heard the sound of an engine roaring to life. As the car swung around, the glare of its headlights caught her full in the face. In that instant he saw in her eyes that she was torn, between what she knew was the right thing to do and her desire to protect herself and her family. He understood that desire. After his brother died, Jeremy had tried to protect his mother from the grief that he could see, even at such a young age, was tearing her to bits, and he'd failed. It was part of the reason he'd been so angry all those years. He'd been angry at himself as much as at her, for letting her down.

Then all at once Carrie Ann's face crumpled and tears began rolling down her cheeks. "I'm sorry," she said, in a low voice that was almost a whisper. "Please don't hate me."

He didn't know if she was sorry for what she'd done or if it was because she lacked the courage to make it right. But Jeremy recognized that
there was nothing more he could do, at least not tonight. Tomorrow,
when she'd sobered up, he'd try again. He touched her gently on the arm.
"Come on, let's go back inside. You must be freezing."

"I feel like dancing. Will you dance with me?" She blew her nose into
the crumpled napkin and a wobbly smile surfaced on her tear-streaked
face.

"You're not afraid of what people will say?" he asked.

"Fuck it," she said, and laughed.

Then they were plunging back in through the fire exit, into the pulsing heartbeat of the music and the heat of all those bodies crammed together, into the mingled smells of sweat, perfume, sticky spilled drinks,
and the burnt-toast stink of overheated amps, as if he and Carrie Ann
were being swept along by a rip tide, with only each other to hold on to.

CHAPTER TWENTY

Alice had been mulling over Randy's proposal for more than a week when her mother stopped by the restaurant one morning to drop off the last of the rosemary from her garden. Lucy stayed to chat while Alice cracked Dungeness crabs for the stuffed tomatoes that were today's appetizer special. It wasn't until she was getting up to leave that she happened to mention, "I don't know if you've heard—Nana's old place is up for sale."

Alice paused in the midst of her cracking, brushing bits of shell and crab meat from her fingers. "No, I hadn't heard," she said, looking quizzically at her mother. "I thought the people who bought it were planning to stay there until they retired."

Lucy shrugged, reaching for the blue quilted bag she carried with her everywhere she went. In it, along with the usual items, like wallet and checkbook and keychain, was a small arsenal of emergency supplies: breath mints and dental floss; ibuprofen and gum for when her ears plugged up on airplanes; a pocket-size Kleenex dispenser and little foil packets of pre-moistened wipes; a pen light, should she happen to get lost while driving after dark and need to consult a map (though there was little likelihood of that, on an island where she could've found her way around blindfolded); a small spiral-bound notebook with a pen clipped to it; a collapsible umbrella and a rain slicker that folded up into a pouch, in the event of a downpour. Her mother was too much of an optimist to live in fear of the sky falling, but should that ever come to pass she would be more than prepared.

"Herb Crenshaw? He'll never retire," she said, with a dismissive wave of her hand. "He can't afford to. I'm sure that's why they're selling. Don't repeat this to anyone," she dropped her voice and leaned in close, "but Darlene Overby, down at the savings and loan, let it slip that they're behind on their payments." Lucy prided herself on being the kind of person who minded her own business, and when passing on such tidbits of information she was fond of prefacing it with *Now you know I'm not one to gossip,* but very little happened on the island that she didn't know about.

"I wonder what they're asking for it," Alice mused aloud.

"The land alone has to be worth a fair bit. Prices have really gone up. I should probably think about selling myself. I could always get one of those nice little condos." Ever since Alice's dad died, Lucy had been talking about selling her house and moving into something smaller, but Alice knew it was just talk—when her mother moved, hopefully a long time from now, it would be to the burial plot next to her husband's. "Well, I've got to run. I have to get those jars of piccalilli over to Cora's. Did I tell you she's one of the judges this year?" Lucy hoisted her quilted bag onto her shoulder, waving goodbye to Calpernia, who was busy washing lettuce at the sink.

Alice recalled that today was the cutoff date for entries in the annual winter crafts fair, held ever year at Christmastime. Along with the crafts and edibles for sale, there was a booth displaying various baked goods and homemade preserves that had been submitted for judging. At last year's fair, her mother's pumpkin streusel tart had taken home the blue ribbon in the pie division.

"Then you can't miss," said Alice, with a smile. Cora Bradley was one of her mother's oldest friends.

Lucy pretended to be appalled that Alice would even suggest such a thing. Cora wouldn't let friendship sway her opinion, she declared staunchly. And while Alice thought that might be true, it was also true that, here on the island, it was all about who you knew.

Watching her mother fly out the door, clutching her coat with one hand and holding onto her quilted bag that held the cure for every one of life's ills with the other, Alice was thinking that the network of old ties and alliances by which business was conducted on the island had a dark side as well. One that Owen White had used to his advantage. He'd been like a spider sitting in the middle of his web, a web he himself was now snared in. For, just days ago, Gary had made a full confession. Not only owning up to the bribes he'd taken, but the mayor's role in it as well, how Owen had used the evidence that would have incriminated Gary to blackmail him into doing things that, if not exactly illegal, were highly unethical. In the firestorm that ensued, Owen had been forced to resign. Construction on the Spring Hill project had also ground to a halt, pending an investigation.

Unfortunately, none of this had altered Jeremy's case. Gary would testify on his behalf, of course, but he had little to offer that wasn't hearsay. Besides, in Gary's present condition, how credible a witness would he make? Now, with the trial date just weeks away, she'd given up hope of an eleventh hour save. They'd simply have to see this through to the end and pray that the jury would believe Jeremy's side of the story.

Alice's own attempts to do an end run had only made matters worse. The other day she'd driven out to the Flaglers,' thinking that if she could appeal to Mrs. Flagler, one mother to another, she might still be able to short circuit this whole thing. But Warren Flagler had arrived home as she was winding up to give her pitch, and had all but physically ejected her from the property. *You have a lot of nerve, lady!* he'd shouted, thrusting his angry bulldog's face into hers. *You and that kid of yours, you're two of a kind—a couple of bad apples. If I ever catch either of you anywhere near my family again, I'm calling the cops!*

But it wasn't all doom and gloom. At least now she knew Jeremy would be getting a fair trial. For one thing, the D.A., rather than currying favor with the mayor, would be distancing himself instead. For another, Judge Voakes had just this past week resigned, purportedly for health reasons (though Colin believed it was because he'd been in tight with the mayor and was looking to avoid being tarred by the same brush) and a new judge had been assigned to the case, whom Colin seemed to think would be more sympathetic.

Colin. As always, the thought of him brought a keen sense of regret. But maybe it was just as well that nothing had come of it. Maybe it was Randy who she was meant to be with. Could that be why he'd never remarried? Because deep down he'd been waiting for her all this time?

She was roused from her thoughts by Calpernia, who'd planted herself in front of Alice. Calpernia waved her arm in a shooing motion. "Go. Get. Baby, if you don't take a break, get yourself some R and R, you gonna trip on that long face of yours."

Alice shook her head and smiled, pretending to search for her claw cracker amid the pile of shells on the counter. Was she that transparent? With Colin, too, her feelings must be written all over her face. The realization made her cringe inside, feeling as vulnerable as she had in prison when her cellmate, Norma Fuentes, had gotten hold of her journal and read passages aloud.

When Calpernia showed no sign of backing off, Alice protested, "I can't just *leave.* What about all this?" She gestured to take in the crabs still to be cracked, the vegetables to be chopped, the chickens breasts to be butterflied. And that was just for starters.

"I ain't exactly sitting here on my butt." Calpernia planted her hands on her hips, wearing an obstinate look. The word no wasn't in her vocabulary. "And if that homie can't handle a little heat in the kitchen, he in the wrong profession," she said, referring to Terrel Louis, the short order cook who'd responded to the Help Wanted ad they'd placed and who, according to Calpernia, was the only other black person on the island. So far he was proving to be a good hire, but at the moment he was in town on an errand; he wouldn't be back for another hour at least. And Alice still had so much work to do . . .

"Really, I can't. I've taken so much time off already," she insisted, thinking of all the hours lost due to court appearances. It was amazing she was still in business.

"An hour or two won't kill you. Won't kill folks' appetite none, either. They be eating that food, same as always, if it was the devil himself who cooked it."

Seeing that her friend wasn't going to budge, Alice gave in at last. "All right. I'm going. But if we fall behind on orders, it's on you," she grumbled, slipping out of her not-so-white chef whites.

"Fine. Just tell me where you goin' off to, 'case we accidentally set the place on fire or something and need to reach you." Calpernia flashed her a wicked grin.

Alice had no idea where she was going, but on a whim, she said, "I may take a drive out to my grandmother's old place. I hear it's for sale."

She'd hadn't been back since it was sold, years ago, and as she headed out back to where her car was parked, she was reminded of all the happy times she'd spent there. Her nana hadn't been one to sit still—the only times Alice could remember her being off her feet was when she was knitting or sewing, and even then her hands had never stopped moving—but she'd never been too busy for her grandchildren.

Alice smiled, as she climbed into her car and turned the key in the ignition, thinking that if she knew how to cook, it was mainly due to her nana, who'd taught her to trust her instincts. She recalled her first attempt at making cornbread, when she was nine, with Nana supervising.

How much flour, Nana? she'd asked, poised on the step stool at the kitchen counter.

Oh, I always put in a couple of handfuls, Nana had said, standing at her elbow, wearing the flowered apron, faded from many washings, that had seemed as much a part of her as the hand reaching into the flour bin.

But my hand is smaller than yours, Alice had replied, frowning down at her stubby fingers.

That's why we have eyes and mouths. Nana had smiled and tapped the side of her head, where her crinkly hair that was the color of old pennies was growing gray. *You don't become a good cook by following recipes, Allie*—Nana was the only one who'd called her that—*any more than you can learn to ride a bike by reading a manual. It's about feel and taste, and having the courage to experiment.*

When the batter was ready, she'd had Alice dip a finger in to taste it. *Now tell me, quick, does it need more salt? Is that the right amount of sugar?*

Alice had told her it could use a bit more salt and Nana had beamed at her as if she'd solved a difficult math equation. *You see? You're a natural. Next time, you won't need my help.*

Thinking back on it now, Alice realized that it had been a lesson in more than cooking. Her nana had wanted her to have the courage to experience life in the same way. Maybe because her own had been one of compromises. Alice pondered that as she made her way in her car along the familiar winding road to Eleanor's house, a road lined with trees—Douglas firs, madronas, maples—that grew as thick as the memories crowding her head. Memories she'd drawn strength from while in prison, for that was what had been at the core of Eleanor's strength as well: she'd endured. Not only the war and the loss of her husband (for the man she'd seen off to battle wasn't the same man who'd returned) but the greatest loss of all, that of her true love.

Alice remembered the far-off look her nana would sometimes get. She'd be in the midst of some task, peeling potatoes or pulling weeds in the garden, when suddenly she would pause to gaze sightlessly out the window or to rock back on her heels on the loamy ground, staring off into the distance. The muscles in her face would loosen, and it would grow soft, girlish almost, with the same dreaming-awake look she'd worn in the portrait William McGinty had painted of her.

It was the portrait that had provided the final clue to the mystery. Now, piecing it together with what she'd learned, Alice finally understood: It was William for whom Eleanor had yearned.

There might still have been a chance for them late in life, but, sadly, when Grandpa Joe died of a stroke, in '86, Eleanor had followed shortly after. There had been a small tumor on her liver that her doctor had been keeping his eye on. While she'd been caring for her husband, it had remained inactive, neither growing nor shrinking, but as soon as she was no longer responsible for him it had begun to metastasize at an alarming rate. Almost as if, having willed it into submission, she could finally let

go of her grip. Within six months, she was gone, buried beside her husband in the small graveyard behind the church of which her father had
been pastor.

Alice wondered if it was the same graveyard in which William had been
lain to rest. It would be fitting somehow, that the lovers be reunited in
death. Though from what she knew about William, it would have been
more his nature to have been cremated, his ashes scattered over the ocean
or the wild, windswept cliffs he'd captured so vividly on canvas.

Half an hour later she was pulling into the drive at her nana's house. It
was overgrown in spots with the brambles and weeds her grandmother
had battled in her lifetime, now run riot, though the pot holes she remembered had been filled in. In the field off to her right, she saw a flash
of red amid the brown grass—a cardinal. She remembered that cardinals
didn't fly south for the winter, a fact she'd learned from her grandmother. The long walks they used to go on had been more than recre-
ational, Nana calling out the name of every plant and bird, animal and
insect; pointing out a bald eagle riding the thermals, or pulling a branch
out of a pond to show her the jelly-like sac clinging to it, dotted with
black specks that would become salamanders.

It's just nature. Nana would say with a laugh, when Alice wrinkled her
nose in disgust. *It's not always pretty, but it always has a purpose. And what could be
more beautiful than that?*

Her nana had taught her to listen for the frogs that heralded spring,
and to appreciate the music they made, chorusing in the ponds and
marshes; to spot the dark flash of brown bats diving after insects in the
twilight and the woolly bear caterpillars that clung to the undersides of
leaves, soon to morph into tiger moths. In winter, there had been lessons
in picking out various animal tracks from among the delicate tracery that
crisscrossed the snow.

The modest house at the end of the drive seemed almost an after-
thought, tucked behind a curly-barked madrona twisted with age, a tree
that had always reminded Alice of a wizened old man, his back bent under a heavy load. A new-model Plymouth was parked in the turnabout.

She pulled to a stop behind it and was climbing out of her car when a woman emerged from the house—petite with short blond hair, smartly dressed in a pantsuit and low-heeled pumps. The realtor, no doubt. With her was a middle-aged couple, prospective buyers presumably. She caught sight of Alice and paused to murmur something to her clients before walking briskly toward her.

"Hi! Are you here to look at the house?" she asked, when she'd caught up.

"Actually, no. This used to be my grandmother's place," Alice told her. "I heard it was for sale and I happened to be driving past . . . "

The woman brightened. "Oh! You must mean Missus Styles."

Alice nodded. "She was here a long time, over fifty years." Eleanor had seemed as much a fixture as that old madrona. So much so that when the house was sold after her death, the sense of loss Alice had felt had been almost as acute as when she'd watched her nana's coffin being lowered into the ground.

"Sylvia Brenner," the woman introduced herself, putting out a mani-cured hand. "Let me give you my card." She reached into the oversize leather bag slung over one shoulder.

Alice tucked it into her pocket, saying, "Do you mind if I take a look around?"

Some of the wattage went out of the realtor's smile and she glanced discreetly at her watch. Then her saleswoman's instincts kicked in, and Alice could almost hear her thinking, *You never know. It could lead to something.* "Not in the least," she said. "Why don't you have a look around inside while I show these folks the rest of the property. The front door's unlocked."

Moments later Alice was stepping through the door, assailed by the scents she associated with visits to her grandmother, that of old wood-work steeped in lemon oil, pine logs and smoke-blackened chimney bricks . . . and the dogs, of course. She didn't know if the current owners had pets, but that doggy smell, as musky and familiar as the old blanket by the stove that her nana's Border collies used to sleep on when they were allowed inside, was so distinct she half expected that any minute she'd be greeted by a wet nose and a wagging tail.

The house, too, was pretty much as she remembered it. The knotty pine walls in the living room and brass chandelier suspended by a dusty chain from the crossbeam; the river rock hearth where they used to pop popcorn over the open fire in a long-handled wire basket. As she wandered from room to room, she could see that the current owners had made some changes, such as replacing the old chiffarobes in the bedrooms with built-in closets and updating the thirties kitchen cabinets, but the essential spirit of the house was the same. It was in the kitchen that Alice felt her grandmother's presence most strongly. The curtains drawn over the open window might have been fluttering with the air stirred by Eleanor's ceaseless motion. Alice could almost see her pacing back and forth between the table and stove as she laid out supper, a path she'd traveled so many times her feet had worn away the linoleum in spots. She'd never appeared frazzled or in a hurry, but the sheer volume of what she had to accomplish in a day seemed staggering to Alice now, looking back on it through the eyes of an adult.

First thing each morning there had been Grandpa Joe to bathe and dress, a task he hadn't made any easier when he was having what Eleanor had called one of his "spells." If he'd had an accident in the night, which he became prone to in his later years, she would have to strip the mattress and put it out to air. All that before she'd even gotten breakfast on the table. The rest of the day, when she wasn't tending to her husband, was spent cleaning house, cooking and sewing, and gardening in summer. Sunday had been the one day of the week when she'd rested, after a fashion. Alice couldn't remember her ever going to church—that hadn't been Nana's style—but on afternoons when Grandpa Joe was napping she would go on long walks, taking Alice and Denise along if they happened to be staying over .

By that time, she'd long since boarded up the kennel, keeping only a few dogs as pets—Rufus and Checkers, and their mother, Jewel, a sweet old thing who'd been named after a rhinestone collar she'd been given as a puppy. Alice remembered when Jewel died, how Nana had wept as though her heart would break. Alice had been stunned to come across her stretched out on the bed in her room with her face buried in the pillow to muffle her sobs. She'd never before seen her grandmother cry. Come to think of it, Alice couldn't recall ever having seen her lying down in the middle of the day.

Nana had sat up, patting the space beside her, and Alice had climbed up onto the bed. "Are you sad about Jewel?" she had asked.

Nana had brushed at the tears on her cheeks with an age-speckled hand. "Yes, honey, I'm sad about Jewel."

She'd started to choke up again, and Alice had put her arms around her, beseeching, "Don't cry, Nana."

Nana had stroked her cheek, smiling through her tears. "It's good to cry, Allie. It helps you remember."

"How does it do that?"

She'd paused, as if searching for the right words. "When you mourn for someone you loved, it's like they're still a part of you. The only way you can really lose someone is if you forget them."

It all made sense to Alice now: She'd been talking about William. She shivered now, in the cool of the old house, which even in summer didn't retain heat. Poor Nana. How had she been able to bear it, knowing the man she loved was so close yet so far from reach? There must have been times she'd longed to run away from her responsibilities, run to William. Especially once Lucy was grown. But she'd stayed, and by the time she was free of those responsibilities, it had been too late.

Alice's reverie was broken by the sound of a car pulling into the drive. Another prospective buyer, no doubt. Minutes later the old strap hinges on the front door let out a squeal, and Alice looked up to see an elongated shadow fall over the scuffed floorboards of the entryway. It was followed an instant later by the figure of a tall, black-haired man, world weary but handsome in a tortured-hero kind of way, with eyes the blue of a banked fire and the kind of face you could never grow tired of looking at.

"Colin," she cried softly. She'd been so wrapped up in thoughts of William and Eleanor, it was almost as if she were seeing a ghost. "What are you doing here?"

"I could ask the same of you," he said.

"This was my grandmother's house," she told him. "I'd heard it was for sale, and I wanted to see it one last time." Her gaze traveled about the room. For some reason, she was finding it difficult to meet his gaze.

"It's charming," he said, looking around.

"You still haven't told me what you're doing here," she said. "Don't tell me you're in the market for another house."

He shook his head. "Calpernia told me where to find you."

"You could have called me at work and saved yourself the trip. What was so important you had to drive all this way?"

"I wanted to give you the news in person." Alice felt herself tense, but he was smiling, so she knew that it couldn't be bad. "I got a call from the D.A.'s office a little while ago. They've decided to drop the charges against Jeremy."

Alice was so stunned that for a moment all she could do was gape at him. "But how . . . ?"

"It seems Carrie Ann changed her story," he explained. "Without her testimony, there would be no a case. Also, I suspect it had become a political hot potato."

It finally sank in, and Alice let out a whoop, jumping up off the sofa and throwing her arms around Colin. She might have been dreaming, if not for the very real presence of Colin in her arms, as solid and comforting as this house. With an effort, she drew back to ask, "Have you told Jeremy?"

"Not yet. I wanted you to be the first to hear it." Colin was grinning.

"I think I need to sit down." The muscles in Alice's legs gave way, and she plopped back down on the sofa. Colin sat down beside her. "Does this sort of thing happen very often?" she asked.

"Actually, it's pretty rare," he told her. "Usually they'll go for a lesser charge in exchange for a reduced sentence, if the defendant agrees to plead guilty. Sometimes, if it's a bigger fish they're after, they'll give immunity. But I've only seen them drop the charges this late in the game twice in my whole career. All I can say is, Jeremy's one lucky kid."

"Do you think it was just luck?"

"Who knows? He said something about having run into Carrie Ann at Bucky's the other night. Maybe that had something to do with it."

"Funny, he didn't mention it to me."

"He probably didn't want to worry you. You know, in case she took out a restraining order or something."

"Am I that much of a worry wart?"

He smiled. "You're a mother. It's your job to worry."

She hadn't thought of it that way. *My job.* The realization drifted down through old, encrusted layers of guilt and self-recrimination. "Thank you for coming all this way to tell me," she said, her throat tight.

"My pleasure, but I'm afraid my motives were more personal than professional."

Alice saw from the look on his face that something had changed for him, that whatever he'd been struggling with before, it had lifted. She felt herself grow still, and she had a sense that things were about to change for her, too.

"I've been doing a lot of thinking," he went on. "Mostly about the ways I've screwed up, but about my grandfather too. How sad it must have been for him, losing the two people he'd loved most in the world. There was nothing he could have done about Eleanor, I suppose. But he tried hard with my dad. I think if he were here now he'd give me the same advice. He'd tell me not to give up on something this good before I'd even given it a chance."

She knew then that she hadn't imagined it: The connection between them was real. As real as the man sitting beside her now. "Your grandfather sounds like a smart man," she said.

"He was. Just unlucky in love."

"And you?"

Colin took her hand, lacing his fingers through hers. "I'm two down in the ninth inning, but the game isn't over yet."

"I didn't know you were a baseball fan," she observed, with a giddy little laugh.

"Growing up in my house, it would have been hard not to be. Though I think I was the only kid in Bayside who couldn't hit a fast ball to save his life." His expression turned serious. "Look, Alice, I know I'm a little late to the game on this one. I was so busy feeling sorry for myself, I couldn't see what was right in front of my nose. But I realized something the other day—that we don't always get a second chance in life. I don't want to lose you, too." In a more formal tone, he added, "I guess what I'm asking is, if you're willing to take a chance on a down and out lawyer with nothing to show for himself except a dog that doesn't belong to him and an oyster farm that so far hasn't made a dime."

"I happen to love oysters," she said. "I love dogs, too."

"Should I take that as yes?"

Her heart was so full that she had difficulty finding the words. Then together they rose, unbidden, as though it were scripted by an unseen hand. "Don't you know? You've already given me more than I could ever ask. All that matters to me is that you haven't given up, on yourself . . . on us. I can live with just about anything else, as long as I have that."

His face was that of a man who'd emerged from the shadows into sunlight, clear of any doubt. As he drew her into his arms in a slow kiss that seeped through her like water through porous rock, a memory stirred in her: how it had felt stepping out of the prison walls after her release, how she'd stood there a moment on the sidewalk with her eyes closed, feeling the sunlight on her skin and taking in deep breaths of air that had seemed newly invented just for her. Alice felt that way now, as though she'd been set free.

Sylvia, the realtor, chose that moment to poke her head through the doorway. "Oh!" she cried, looking startled and a little embarrassed to have found Alice kissing a strange man, as if it were their house and she the interloper. "I'm sorry. I came to lock up. Would you and your husband like to make an appointment to come back another time?"

Husband. Alice and Colin exchanged a smile at the misunderstanding. Not yet, she thought, and maybe not for a long, long while. If ever. But it had a nice ring to it.

EPILOGUE

ONE YEAR LATER

From the backseat of the cab, which was stalled in midtown traffic, Colin peered up at the Swarovski crystal snowflake suspended high above Fifty-Seventh Street, twinkling like the Star of Bethlehem. It filled him with holiday cheer, as did the street below, with its festive displays and fairy lights illuminating the trees and storefronts. Christmas in New York. He hadn't realized until now how much he'd missed the city, especially this time of year.

He turned to Alice. "You okay?" She'd been so quiet all evening, he worried that she might be finding this all too overwhelming.

She nodded and slipped a gloved hand into his. "I was just thinking that we have a lot riding on this."

He smiled, giving her hand a little squeeze. "First-time jitters. Don't worry, it'll pass."

He ought to know. He'd been to enough auctions with his parents through the years. William had been generous in sending them paintings from time to time, and whatever hadn't been sold to dealers was auctioned off. Colin felt a pang of regret now, at how those gifts had been cashed in, seemingly without a scrap of sentiment. But he supposed that had been William's intention, and the money had always been put to good use. It had tided them over during the period his dad had been out of work with a bad back and paid for Colin's college education.

Colin's own decision to auction off William's last remaining work had nothing to do with economic need, at least not his own—though he could have used the money. It had to do with Spring Hill. The big money interests behind its development, seeing that it would likely be tied up in court for the foreseeable future, had done the sensible thing in offering to sell it to the county, for the "rock bottom" sum of fifteen million. Local conservancy groups had done their part in raising some of the money, with corporate sponsors and a few wealthy benefactors kicking in, but that still left a shortfall of several million. The money realized from the sale of Eleanor's portrait, if it sold for anything close to the estimate, would cover a good portion of that.

That was where they were headed now, to Sotheby's. The auction, for works of important twentieth-century artists, would draw wealthy art patrons, museum curators and dealers from all over the world. *Woman in Red*, featured prominently in the catalogue, had already garnered a fair bit of interest, and hopes were high for a price that would break the record for previous sales of William McGinty's works.

It seemed fitting to Colin that the money go to such a worthy cause. It was what his grandfather would've wanted, for it would provide in death what had eluded William in life: It would bring him closer to Eleanor in a way, in helping preserve the land she'd loved. A bittersweet resolution that had Colin closing his eyes for a moment, reflecting upon all that had happened over the past year. When he opened them again, he found Alice looking at him in consternation.

"Country life must seem pretty quiet compared to this." Her tone was light, but he knew she was wondering how much of this trip was, for him, tied up in memories of Nadine. "Do you miss the bright lights?"

"Not a bit. For one thing, I don't know that I would've stayed sober here. Also, more importantly, I wouldn't have met you." He kissed her lightly on the lips, thinking she'd never looked more beautiful. Like the portrait whose image she resembled, she glowed in this setting, a rare gem in a vault of more ordinary ones.

"Good answer." Her face relaxed in a smile. "Though I wouldn't mind staying an extra day or two. I feel like we've barely made a dent."

"We have all day tomorrow," he reminded her. "If the weather's nice, I'll take you to the top of the Empire State Building. The view is pretty amazing. You can see all the way to New Jersey. Unless there's something else you'd rather do," he added, noting the uncertain look she wore.

She was silent for a moment before venturing, "I thought you might like to visit Ground Zero."

Now it was his turn to fall silent, the memories crowding in on him. At last, he shook his head, saying, "This may sound strange, but for me it's just a hole in the ground. Wherever Nadine is, it's not there." He was surprised by the ease with which he was able to talk about his wife. There had been a time, in the not so distant past, when the mere thought of her would have sent him reeling into darkness . . . typically the darkness of the nearest bar. She would always be a part of him, he knew, but what had changed was that he'd stopped believing his own life had ended that day. Alice was living proof of that. With her, he'd rediscovered the wonder, not only of loving again, but of being alive.

Marriage was still a way off, but he was working on that. First, he had to convince Alice to move in with him. So far she'd resisted, arguing that she needed to focus on Jeremy right now, but lately Colin had sensed he was wearing her down. They were talking about taking a trip to Italy next summer, all three of them. Jeremy was excited by the prospect. Jeremy also had his eye on the spare room Colin had subtly hinted could be his.

"Your dad ever get back to you about tonight?" she was asking him now.

Colin felt a familiar tightening inside, like he always did whenever the subject of his family arose. "Yeah, he's not coming." A bitter note crept into his voice. "His excuse is that Marma's sick and he wants to stay nearby in case she needs anything."

"What about your mom?"

Colin shook his head. "If she came without him, she'd never hear the end of it."

"Don't be too hard on them," Alice said gently. "They're not doing it to hurt you. It's just . . . they have a vested interest in keeping things the way they are. Anyway, I'm glad I got to meet them, at least."

Colin brightened, thinking about the afternoon they'd spent over at his parents' house. Alice had gotten along with everyone, forever endearing herself to his mother by lending a hand with supper and the cleanup afterward, and winning points with his dad and his brother by showing interest in their favorite subject: sports. Even Marma had been won over, though there had been a tense moment in the beginning, when he'd introduced them and his grandmother had just stood there, staring at Alice as if at a ghost. But she'd rallied, for his sake more than anything, Colin suspected, and before long the two had been chatting like old friends.

"Speaking of which," he said, "Dad wanted me to know they all think you're something special." Not that Colin had needed to be told. "But I'm warning you. Now the pressure will be on. Don't be surprised if your Christmas present from my mom is a subscription to *Bride* magazine."

"I think I can handle it," she said with a laugh, not committing herself one way or the other.

Colin suppressed a sigh. He'd just have to be patient. She would come around eventually. In the meantime, life was good. He was still sober: In three month's time, he'd be getting his two-year chip. And the oyster farm was coming along nicely; already he had orders for his first harvest.

Before long the taxi was letting them off at the corner of East Seventy-second and York, where Sotheby's was located, a modernist cube of a building with a sheer expanse of glass in front that, lit from within, lent it a theatrical glow. Chauffeured limos were double-parked along the curb, clouds of vapor rising from their tailpipes in the frosty air, with more pulling up every minute. Colin helped Alice negotiate the icy sidewalk in her high heels, which she was unaccustomed to wearing, as they made their way toward the entrance, picking their way around the clumps of dirty snow left over from the storm that had dumped six inches on the city the week before.

Inside, they found themselves caught up in the crush of people gathered near the coat check. As they waited in line, snatches of conversation rose in the heated air, along with the mingled scents of perfume. . . . *The Noguchi alone has to be worth. . . Not one of her better works, in my opinion. . . Did you catch the exhibit at the Whitney?* After they'd handed over their coats, they made their way into the lobby, where they were greeted by an attractive young woman in a slim-fitting skirt and cowl-necked sweater, who directed them to the gallery on the second floor.

Yesterday, one of the senior directors at Sotheby's, an elegant bow-tied gentleman by the name of Spencer Morton, had given them a guided tour of the works that were to be auctioned off. When they had reached the portrait of Eleanor, he'd paused, commenting in a hushed voice, "The photos don't do it justice. It's truly magnificent. I wouldn't be surprised if it goes to one of the museums. Several have already expressed interest."

"I wish Denise could see this," Alice had remarked to Colin, after Morton had been pulled away to attend to some other business. "She always said our grandmother deserved to hang in a museum, after all she'd been through. Though knowing Nana, she'd have hated that. She didn't like drawing attention to herself. And the worst thing for her was sitting idle."

"Your sister would know a thing or two about that." Colin had smiled, thinking about the fact that it was partly due to Denise's efforts that Spring Hill had been saved.

"She certainly has her hands full at the moment," Alice had said, with a sigh. "The last time we spoke she sounded like she didn't know if she was coming or going."

"It takes a while to settle into a new place." Not only that, a new job—she'd found a teaching position at the local elementary school—and a husband who was still getting back on his feet. "I'll bet it would cheer her up if you came for a visit. In fact, if you want, we could stop on the way back." They could rent a car at SeaTac and drive to Spokane, he told her.

"I keep offering, and she keeps putting me off." Alice had worn a look of sad resignation. "She'll have me come when she's ready, I suppose." She missed her sister, he knew, but she also respected Denise enough to allow her the space she seemed to need.

Now, as he and Alice made their way through the gallery in search of empty seats, Colin thought that it was a miracle any of them were still standing. But here they were, and from the sizeable turnout, it looked as if their fortunes were about to improve even more. Luckily, they found two seats near the front, where they wouldn't have to crane their necks to see over people's heads. As Colin settled back in his chair, it hit him that this was it, no turning back now. His grandfather's most prized possession—more than that, his paean to his lost love—would soon be in the hands of a complete stranger, someone who would know nothing of its history, of the tortuous route it had traveled to arrive at this point. Colin felt a twinge of regret, and at the same time he knew that it was for the best.

The bidding commenced with a minor work by Thomas Schiele followed by an Andy Warhol sketch. Both went for prices higher than their estimates, the Warhol to an anonymous bidder over the phone. The entire transaction had been conducted without so much as a hair being turned. The stylish older woman taking bids over the phone had only subtly lifted a finger with each new bid before finally, when the bidding reached its climax, confirming the buyer's intentions with an expressionless nod. She hadn't spoken a word, but every eye in the room had been fixed on her, as if on an actress doing a solo performance.

It was theatre, this business of auctioning off fine art, Colin thought. The auctioneer, a Brit from Central Casting, heralded each lot, as it was reverently placed on the spot-lit easel on the podium, in a voice like a drum roll. The hushed tension of the crowd, the hands going up holding their numbered paddles, as sums that would have dwarfed the average person's annual salary climbed ever higher into the stratosphere. Then the

final moment when the auctioneer's gavel came down and the tension
would go out of the room like an exhaled breath, replaced by a ripple of
excited commentary, a smattering of applause.

Woman in Red came up in the second hour. The auctioneer gave his
spiel, informing the audience of what they could see with their own eyes:
that it was William McGinty's masterwork. The fact that it had been in
private hands until now only added to its luster and to the air of mystery
surrounding it. Colin, seeing it anew through their eyes, noted how it
glowed in the spotlight, its colors as vibrant as when first painted, its
subtle flesh tones breathing life into its long dead subject. As much a
tribute to Eleanor as a work of art.

". . . Seventy-five thousand from the gentleman in the back. . . Do we
have eighty?. . . A hundred. . . ?" The ever escalating numbers rolled
smoothly off the auctioneer's tongue. He scarcely paused to take a breath
as they rapidly went from high five to six, then seven figures.

Colin wasn't aware of how tightly he'd been holding Alice's hand until
she winced at the pressure of his fingers. She leaned in to whisper,
"Who has that kind of money? Who *are* these people?"

One by one the bidders dropped out, until finally it was down to an
anonymous phone bidder and an older Asian man in back whose paddle
rose and fell as the numbers climbed to well over a million. Colin
twisted around in his seat, trying to make him out amid the shifting sea
of bodies—a round face, white hair combed straight back, a back as
erect as the cane he clutched in his other hand. Colin could feel the tension around them mounting as the quietly fought battle continued, its
intensity seeming to grow in inverse proportion to the languid hand
movements of the Asian man and that of the Sotheby's employee acting
on behalf of the phone bidder.

Colin was so tense himself he could scarcely draw a breath. Two million . . . three . . . three and a quarter. Finally, at just shy of three and a
half million, the Asian man, wearing an impassive face, raised his paddle
one last time. A hush fell over the room, all eyes now on the woman
manning the phone. She murmured something to the person at the other

end, and there was a pause during which Colin felt his heart buck up against his ribcage, then she shook her head to indicate that her bidder was withdrawing.

The auctioneer's gavel came down. Sold.

Alice looked as stunned as Colin. Before bidding commenced on the next lot, they quietly rose from their seats and made their way into the anteroom beyond, where they could talk in relative private.

"I can hardly believe it," she said. "My God, all that *money*. The guy must be seriously rich."

"Either that or he's representing someone who is," Colin speculated.

"I wonder what he plans on doing with it."

"Who knows? Lock it in a vault maybe." Colin certainly hoped that wouldn't be the case.

"Well, I just hope he appreciates the sacrifice, whoever he is."

They were heading for the stairs to the lower level when they noticed their mystery buyer waiting by the elevator. Up close, he looked even older, as he stood there leaning on his cane. And although the suit he wore was well-cut and his watch expensive, there was something humble about his appearance. He didn't look the sort to be throwing around millions.

His eyes lit up when they introduced themselves. "Ah, yes. I was hoping I would have an opportunity to meet you," he told Colin, speaking in perfectly enunciated English. "I am Mister Yamamoto. And you," he said, directing his smiling gaze toward Alice, "are the image of your grandmother."

"You knew her?" she replied, her eyes widening in surprise.

Mr. Yamamoto inclined his head in a reverent nod. "She was a great lady."

Alice shook her head in disbelief. "What an amazing coincidence." Then comprehension sank in, and she said, "It wasn't a coincidence, was it? That's why you're here."

Mr. Yamamoto inclined his head again. "You guessed correctly. And I will treasure your grandmother's portrait all the more because of our friendship." He turned to Colin. "I knew your grandfather as well. A good man. As kind as he was gifted."

"How did you come to know them, if you don't mind my asking?" Colin said.

Mr. Yamamoto smiled, a slow, remembering smile that transformed his wizened face into that of a much younger man. He said, "Please, if you are not in a hurry, come have a drink with me at my hotel. I will be flying back to Tokyo tomorrow, and there is much to tell."

Alice leaned forward impatiently. "Mister Yamamoto . . . "

"Yoshi, please," he corrected her. "Your grandmother always called me by my first name. She was like a mother to me, and now to my wife and children, whom I have taught to revere her memory."

"I don't understand. If you were so close, why is this the first I'm hearing of it?" Alice asked, looking perplexed.

The elevator pinged just then and its door slid open. With a smile, the old man took Alice by the elbow and gently but firmly steered her into the elevator, Colin stepping in behind them. "Come," he said. "Let us sit and discuss this at leisure. It's a long story."

I love hearing from readers. Any comments or questions, bring them on! You can email me at: eileeng@nyc.rr.com

Or check out my website at: www.eileengoudge.com.